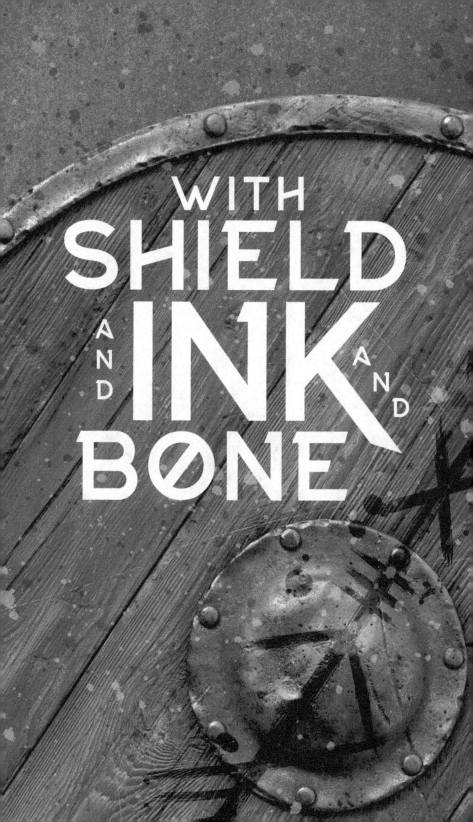

This is a work of fiction. All the characters and events portrayed in this novel are products of the author's imagination. The Vikings were known for their violence and this book spares none of those details.

Book Cover, Map and Interior Formatting
The Illustrated Author Design Services
Artist
@adamarart
Editor
Stacy Sanford, The Girl with the Red Pen

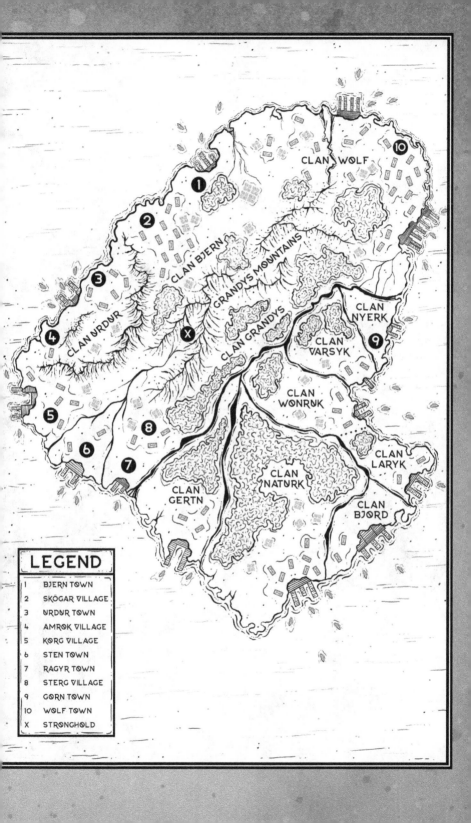

LEGEND

1. BJERN TOWN
2. SKÓGAR VILLAGE
3. URDUR TOWN
4. AMROK VILLAGE
5. KORG VILLAGE
6. STEN TOWN
7. RAGYR TOWN
8. STERG VILLAGE
9. GORN TOWN
10. WOLF TOWN
X. STRONGHOLD

ONE

The greatest mistake of Fenris Wolf's life was leaving me alive, even if only barely. Even if he expected me to give up. Even if he thought I was no warrior, that I was weak, and that I wouldn't beg to the gods or to any entity who would listen to save me and help me avenge what he had destroyed.

From pure hatred and spite, from the ashes left in the wake of his cruelty, and from the flesh and bones of my loved ones, my destiny was spun… and his fate, sealed.

The Urðr Clan, Amrok Village

TWO

On the eve of what should have been one of the most vital days in our lives, Hodor dreamt of our destruction.

My older brother looked pale and haggard as he stood bewildered in the beams of sunlight pouring in through the door. He shrugged on the same tunic he'd worn for the past few days despite the grime it bore and raked nervous fingers through his golden hair before hastily tying it back at his nape. He strode toward the basin where he gathered water in his palms, burying his face in it and harshly scrubbing his skin before gripping the edges of the carved ash bowl so tightly, his knuckles turned white. Hodor stared into the water for a long, long moment.

I wondered if he saw anything beyond his own reflection or if his dream kept spinning through his mind so that it was all he could see.

Sometimes, dreams were just remnants of things that had happened throughout the course of the day, things our minds tried to knit together to make sense of while we slept. Other times, they were warnings sent by the gods.

It was during moments like this that I longed for privacy, for me and for my brother. But the longhouse was built for our needs, not our wants.

I tugged a pale brown apron-dress over my head to cover my *serkr* underdress, slipped on my shoes, and quickly worked my hair into a long braid, keeping one eye on Hodor, who still acted shaken. He'd let go of the basin and stood in the doorway again, raking damp, nervous hands through his hair. His muscles were so taut, I thought one would snap.

Or perhaps *he* would.

From the other side of the house, Father combed his beard and barked at us to hurry and let the animals out of their pens and into the pasture to graze.

While Mother gathered the ingredients to make porridge, she yelled for the younger children to wake up. Though they lamented leaving their beds, they dragged themselves out of them and slogged to the table, their pale hair knotted and twisted in every direction. I smiled at them as Hodor waved me outside.

The near mountain was draped in fog, but only to the frost line, where the trees and air became thin.

"What happened in your dream?" I asked as we walked into the chill of the crisp, cold morning air gliding off the mountain and into the valley in which we lived. Winds in this place either came from the snow caps or the fjord, and they often collided and clashed like the blades of two enemies as fresh air met the salty brine of the sea.

Father trailed after us, his steps as heavy and loud as he.

Despite the fact that Father could hear him, he answered my question. "I dreamed I found Tor dead on the near mountain," he said, jutting his jaw toward the slope our feet had long cut paths upon. Tor was his beloved dog, his friend and companion.

Now that he'd mentioned him, I wondered where Tor was this morning. He wasn't in the fields or lying near the garden gate like he usually was, and Hodor hadn't let him outside when he woke. He hadn't come in to lay between us last evening, despite the chill.

Hodor's eyes scanned the landscape like mine did, but never snagged on Tor.

He was probably sniffing behind the other houses for scraps. Someone would wake, discover him, and run him off. He'd come home soon enough.

We walked to the pen of lambs and I held the wooden gate open as Hodor shepherded the flock out into the fields. He passed through when all were in the meadow and we made our way to the pen of goats.

Hodor paused at the gate, wrapping his fingers around the top plank. "When I came down, holding his limp body in my arms, I heard screaming. You were screaming, Liv. And you wouldn't stop." His haunted eyes met mine and goosebumps slid over my skin.

Father muttered something under his breath as he stopped to toss the pigs scraps from last night's dinner. Hodor stopped talking, flicking a glare at him.

I was glad Father didn't see it.

I held the heavy wooden gate open as Hodor held his arms out wide, clicking his tongue while driving the goats out. Once the two herds had joined in the pasture, some lapping at the shallow brook that slid down from the mountainside while others chewed the freshest tufts of grass that remained, I urged him for more details.

"There's more. I can tell. What else happened in your dream?"

I imagined Hodor's face when he discovered Tor dead. I imagined him running down the mountain paths with Tor in his arms, my screams echoing over the valley, over the fjord waters. The hairs on the back of my neck rose.

"A thick fog had settled over the fjord, and from the mist emerged a pack of wolves. The largest I'd ever seen."

My brows knitted. "They came out of the water?"

He shook his head. "They raced atop it, snarling and snapping. You scooped the girls up and yelled for Gunnar to run with you, then you screamed for Mother and Father. You shouted for me, but you were unable to find me. You didn't know where I was. I dropped Tor's body and ran, but no matter how hard I ran, I couldn't reach you."

"Enough!" Father roared from right behind us, startling us both. "We have much to do, and this nonsense is slowing us down," he said pointedly to my brother. "Dreams mean nothing."

Hodor's dream wasn't nothing. It had shaken my eldest brother, and Hodor wasn't easily rattled.

His temper and nostrils flared. "You want to know how the dream ended, Liv? We all died in the end. None of us survived. None," he snapped.

Father spun on his heel to face Hodor, but Hodor was ready.

He snarled at Father, said words I never imagined he'd dare say to him, and took off toward the mountain. For a stunned moment, Father seemed as shocked as I was. Then his temper flared and he started after him, but stopped himself, turning to me and pointing his finger in my face.

"Finish the chores," he snapped, turning away from me and stomping back toward the house. "There is much to be done and little time to do it."

Tomorrow morning, the Jarl would lead a great hunt into the mountains for wild game. But tonight, the whole village would gather for *Vetrnaetr*, Winternights, and we would slaughter the weakest animals in our herds and smoke the meat to put away for what promised to be a harsh, unforgiving winter. The third in a row. Just as the seer who came this way three years ago told our Jarl, our King.

There was a strangeness in the air, even though the morning drenched the land with bright sunlight that chased the shadows away. The spirits often crossed the divide between the living and the dead on this evening, but... not during the day.

Still, something seemed amiss. I just wasn't sure what. Perhaps Hodor's dream had rooted itself in my mind.

I tried my best to forget his words and the vision they'd painted, sorry I asked him to reveal more of it to me. Neither of us needed any distractions today. Tonight, Hodor would fight Father and I would fight Mother. We would have to be ferocious if we were to earn our shields.

If we didn't best them, we would be no better than our youngest siblings, considered little more than babes. And that wasn't enough, now that I could smell freedom as clearly as I could the dung on the ground, the scent of salt and change on the air.

Mother was a shield maiden and she wanted me to sail to new lands and fight with other warriors. To make my own name and place in this world, blade by blood-soaked blade. Father, on the other hand, wanted me to marry. He hoped to fetch a handsome prize for my hand.

My mother's vision for my future frightened me at the same time it thrilled me. I'd never left Amrok Village. I'd barely swum farther in the fjord than my toes could reach the bottom.

But Father's plans made my stomach turn. I didn't want to be given to someone for a herd of goats. Not even a wagon full of gold and riches would be enough for me to marry someone I didn't know and probably would hate.

Mother's laugh entangled with Father's from inside our home as the sun burned the thin frost from the grass and left the ground soft and loamy. I sat on an overturned bucket and slid another under the teats of our best milking goat and began to draw out the milk, slowly filling it. We were to provide loaves of bread and fresh butter for the celebration tonight.

A flock of blackbirds pecked across the grass beside me, keeping careful distance as I lost myself in thought and repetition, only startling back to the present when the birds took flight, weaving across the sky as if they were one and not hundreds.

The goat chewed on the tuft of hay I lay before her and stood still for me until my chore was complete. A brittle wind lifted hairs from my braid. I brushed them back, looking up at the sound of happy squeals and shouts.

My youngest brother and sisters chased each other along the fjord's rocky beach, brandishing wooden swords and stabbing and slashing at each other mercilessly. Gunnar somehow held his own against the girls, but Ingrid and Solvi fought him together, sisters to the end, always wanting to best the boy amongst them. Sometimes Hodor would join the fight just to even the odds, but it wasn't long until the girls pulled me into their sparring matches and the children shrank away as Hodor and I squared off.

I smiled at their carefree giggles and the sound of the blunt swords they thwacked and jabbed at one another. It was easy to fight without thought and not hold back when you knew no one would get hurt, that no blood would spill and no life would be severed by your blade. It was also easy not to hold back when you could see your enemy's blade and their intention to kill you in their eyes, when that blade sliced toward your throat.

My youngest sister's shrill squeal startled our goat. I ran my hand down her back to calm her again and fed her another tuft of hay by hand. She ground the hay with her row of teeth and settled, and I continued drawing milk from her.

I watched my younger siblings play over the coarse but soft, beige fur of her back, hoping they'd never see battle but knowing they would. Odin wouldn't spare them from it. Not when he coveted a good fight the way grown men coveted mead.

Father said that I'd fought well four years ago when our enemy snuck into our village in the middle of the night. Considering that I survived, I had to agree. But I hadn't come out unscathed. My skin wasn't flayed. My limbs hadn't been cleaved away. But the battle left a scar I desperately and constantly tried to hide, leaving shameful fear in its wake.

I was supposed to want my brother and sisters to charge into battle, to wield axe and sword and spear and shield alongside their peers. I was supposed to want them to die honorably. But I couldn't bring myself to wish anything but peace upon them. Perhaps that alone would bar me from Valhalla in the end.

Even so, I couldn't change my heart any more than I could change the stars.

Whenever I thought about the attack, all I could see was the glint of metal in the moonlight. All I could feel was the wavering of the muscles in my forearm as I held my play shield and hoped the woman attacking me didn't hack off my arm as she used her sword to cut through the thin wooden slats piece by piece. I remembered the sound of my teeth gritting, my heartbeat pounding a staccato rhythm in my ear, and the feeling of my tiny hand curling around the handle of the red-hot poker with which I ran her through.

I could still hear the sound of clashing steel and smell the sickening mixture of blood and sweat. I remembered the cries of men and the deafening silence that followed.

That was why Hodor's dream bothered me. Because it foretold of *another* attack, one none of us would survive.

You want to know how the dream ended, Liv? We all died in the end. None of us survived. None.

I finished milking two more nannies, trying to forget the morning but unable to do so.

Trying to focus on the fight I would have to win this evening... unable to do that, either.

9

When I finished, I brought the bucket of goat milk inside. Mother's eyes flicked from me to the two freshly made shields, unpainted and unadorned. Waiting for us to put our marks upon them once earned.

Father made them, cutting the wood and hammering the steel that held the boards together. It took him almost a week to make them both. Despite the fact that each day was shorter than the last and we still had much to do to prepare for the winter ahead, he took his time on them. The shields would not break. They wouldn't bend or yield. Father was much better with steel and wood than he was with his children.

Outside, Gunnar let out a battle cry and charged the tow-headed girls while throwing his play shield up to dodge blows the girls dealt in retaliation.

Fighting is in our blood, Father would say, ruffling my hair when I was their age. It was what made a warrior feel alive. It was the air we breathed. The pride that swelled our chests.

"They're excited about tonight. So excited, they started battling inside before the porridge was cooked through, which is why I shooed them outside. But it's ready now; call them in," Mother said, "and you come, too." She looked toward the near mountain, her eyes turning frosty. She knew Hodor was there, had probably heard the thing he said to Father, but I wasn't sure how she felt about the matter. She'd said worse to Father at one time or another. At others, she defended him fiercely. I wondered whose side she would settle on today.

I yelled for the children to come and eat, watching their battle continue as their tiny legs brought them closer to the house.

Father heard me yelling and nodded once from where he stood, staring up at the near mountain. He started this way with his head down. His shoulders sagged as if he wore a yoke around his neck, pulling a heavy cart up the knoll. The last two winters had aged him considerably. Not that he wasn't still strong. His steps just weren't easy like they once were. He lumbered now. But I wondered if time and age were the only things that weighed heavily upon him. If anything else bothered him, he would never admit it.

After the attack… Father found me first. He looked at the hacked-away shield on my arm and then the poker I'd thrown on the floor after tearing it from the woman's heart. At her lying dead on the floor.

The father who before that night had never once hugged me, dropped to his knees and held me to his chest, telling me I'd fought like a Valkyrie. That Frejya had blessed me with might and a stubborn will no one could pierce. Then he walked away to count his other children.

He considered himself blessed to have only lost one child.

But I saw no blessing in losing Oskar.

Mother stood beside Father as if she were carved of stone as we bid Oskar farewell.

Oskar was two years younger than me, only eleven when Father pushed his small boat into the fjord and tossed a torch inside with him. We watched as the flame slithered across the oil we'd soaked the wood with, as it spread and grew.

We watched him burn.

We watched him sink.

Father said that Odin came for him, that he watched the Alfather pluck Oskar's soul from his body and take it to Valhalla. He said that the heavens opened for just a second, and that what he saw was resplendent, what every warrior hoped to ascend to. That forever Oskar would dine with the Alfather and drink mead at his table, seated on the breast-plates of warriors in a hall whose golden roof was held up by spears, the finest furs draped over his shoulders.

I never saw Odin that day, but I heard my mother cry for the first time. I felt my fear, guilt, and sadness mix with Hodor's, spreading wider and wider across the fjord as if my feelings were ripples spreading over the water, reaching out to cradle Oskar one last time.

Ripples spread. They never stopped.

I looked at the fjord, to the spot where he slid beneath the cool surface, and still saw them.

Closing my eyes, I pushed the memory away.

Two heavy foot falls stopped short of me. Father stopped just outside the house and waved for me to join him outside. Mother plunked wooden bowls down in front of the children and began to fill them so they could fill their empty stomachs.

I walked to him, her sharp eyes watching as I left the room.

Father's dark eyes slid to mine. "Go to him. Calm him. I only make matters worse."

His tone was strange, like he was speaking to someone far away. He folded his thick arms over his chest and stared strangely at the near mountain, studying the bumps and ridges, perhaps looking for the white of Hodor's shirt.

"Are you worried at all about this omen, Father?" I rasped.

He tugged at his beard with his free hand. "A warrior has no worries. We have survived worse than ill dreams." His eyes darkened as if he, too, were stuck in the memories of that night.

Or maybe he'd lived through even worse than the night that stole our security and a piece of our family and hearts. I'd heard stories of his raids, of the riches he'd brought home for the Jarl. I'd heard how he cursed an entire army by sending a spear soaring atop their heads and claiming them all for Odin, and then how every man he cursed fell dead before them. Maybe he claimed Odin's favor because of his skill in battle. Maybe he truly saw him claim Oskar's spirit and take it into the sky.

"Liv…" Father searched for his words, which frightened me. He was usually free with them, oftentimes too free.

He pinched his lips together as if to save his words, standing tall as an ash tree and just as sturdy, wearing the sweater Mother and I had woven for him. We dyed it the same deep green hue of pine needles and Mother sewed a fine, red berry colored thread around the collar.

What could possibly be bothering him so badly? Was it that he would have to fight Hodor? Was he worried about losing, or would winning and besting his son be worse?

He turned to me. "A seeress has come into the village. She wishes to see you tonight."

My breath seized in my chest. "What for?"

His cool blue eyes locked onto mine. "I'm not sure, but… she called you by name." My breath caught in my chest. "Bring Hodor back home, then talk to your mother when you return. She'll tell you what you need to know about the seeress." Without another glance, Father left to separate the animals we would slaughter tonight.

Mother's eyes caught mine and then flicked toward the mountain. Toward Hodor. My mother was a shield maiden. She feared for nothing but the safety of her family.

But fear shone in her eyes as she stared, waiting for me to go after my brother.

14

THREE

Hodor's footprints were still fresh. I followed them up the trail that wound back and forth up the side of the mountain. The peaks of the jagged mountains were dusted in fresh snow and the winds at the top of the slopes roared, dragging snow in shimmering, sweeping arcs, just to let it fall to the earth again.

I found my brother near the frost line where the arctic air made me hug myself to staunch the shivering that began softly but now shook me in earnest. He crouched over something on the ground, his back to me, tensing when he heard my footsteps. "Hodor?"

His shoulders tensed before he threw a weary look over his shoulder. "It's happening."

My brows kissed. "What's happening?" I asked as I drew closer.

At his feet, stiff from death, lay Tor.

I stopped beside him, staring at the mangled body where a predator had gotten ahold of him. Though I didn't know what kind wouldn't have dragged him away to finish its meal later.

I ran damp hands over my dress.

"Liv," he croaked. "This is exactly what I saw in my dream."

"Exactly?" I asked to be sure.

He nodded. "The very same." A thread of fate had revealed itself to him, refusing to remain invisible, wanting to be seen. And the spinners, the norns... they foretold Tor's death, my family's, and mine as well.

"We should tell Father and Mother and warn the clansmen." My heart thundered as I backed away and started down the trail I'd just climbed. "What if it's happening now?"

"There's not a thick mist over the fjord like there was in my vision," he argued, gesturing toward the fjord where the sun sparkled over the water.

"What if the mist didn't matter? What if the wolves are all that mattered, Hodor?"

He scrubbed a hand over his face. "You're right. We need to go. Now."

We raced to our home.

Hodor was faster. He always had been. He ran, plunging his heavy feet into the soil, kicking mud onto my dress and face, but I didn't care.

When we made it back, Hodor ran into our house like a man possessed. I caught myself on the door frame and peered inside, letting my eyes adjust to the darkness. Mother turned to us, already reaching for the knife on her belt, easing her hand away when she saw it was only us.

Gunnar was busy cleaning the bowls and spoons from breakfast, while Ingrid and Solvi's aprons were covered in flour as they helped Mother knead thick knots of dough.

Mother wiped her flour-covered hands on a rag. "What is it, Hodor? You look like you've seen a spirit."

They were fine. Everything was. Father stomped up the trail behind me. "You found him," he said to me, giving Hodor a harsh glare. "Warriors don't abandon their work... or their families."

Hodor scrubbed a hand over his short beard and shot me a glance that said he was grateful the rest of his dream hadn't come true. He met our father's unflinching stare. "I didn't abandon anyone. I am here now, and I'll see that my work is done early."

Father huffed as if he didn't believe him.

"Where is Tor?" Solvi asked innocently, wiping a flour-covered hand over her brow, leaving white streaks in the wake of her fingers.

"Dead," Hodor answered coldly, still staring our father down. "Just as I dreamt. I found him in the place where I dreamt he'd be."

"Yet here we stand and breathe. It was only a dream," Father grunted, staring at Hodor in an open challenge. He stretched his arms out and turned a slow circle. "Where are the wolves you are so frightened of? Wolves that run atop water, you said. Isn't that right?"

Hodor pushed past me and stomped toward the fjord. He watched it for a long while, as if he expected the massive wolf pack he dreamed of to race across the water's surface at any moment. Only today, there was no mist. It was calm and bright. The sky was blue and you could see clearly across the water's surface to the horizon.

Eventually, he abandoned his thoughts, turned, and walked toward the animal pens. It was his duty to slaughter the animals Father had chosen.

I braided Hodor's freshly washed, still damp hair as he sat on a boulder, staring out at the water, crisp and calm. The sun burned in the western sky behind the mountains. Soon, the peaks' shadows would be cast over the land. The village gradually became noisy as our clansmen milled about, drinking ale and preparing for the night's feast and festivities.

Hodor had dressed in his best dark blue kyrtill and the brown trousers Mother had sewn for him. He'd grown taller during the summer and his other pant legs only stretched to the middle of his calves.

I was dressed almost to match, but wearing Mother's clothes. I had nothing but underdresses and apron dresses to go over them and couldn't fight well in those. They were too binding, and being constricted, even a little, could mean the difference between victory and defeat. Mother wore men's clothes when she raided, and she lent me a pair of dark grey trousers and a white tunic that was fitted at the waist.

A nervous feeling filled my stomach as I thought about sparring with Mother. I wondered if Hodor felt the same but was afraid to ask. "Was there more to your dream?"

"I told you everything about it this morning," he answered in a clipped tone, refusing to look at me as he stared broodily over the tranquil waters.

"Everything?"

He craned his head to the sky, clasping his hands behind it and letting out a long exhale. There was more, just as I thought.

"Tell me."

I thought that speaking it aloud might help him get it out of his mind, to share the burden instead of keeping it to himself like he was wont to do.

He resembled a younger version of Father with a short beard, long blond hair, and muscular build. He wasn't as tall as Father, but Hodor was just as sturdy and his reflexes were much quicker.

He folded his legs, perched his arms on his knees, and turned to stare at me. "You're the only one who cares."

I wasn't sure if he meant I was the only one who cared about the dream or about him, but both were true. Father and Mother cared carefully, the way some did when they'd experienced loss and couldn't allow their feelings to swell again to the point that another blow might crush them completely. Father would say he didn't want his son to die a coward's death. He would say that as long as he died bravely, he would be proud. That Odin, too, would be proud. He would say little else.

Somewhere deep inside, he does care, I thought. He wouldn't have sent me after Hodor if he didn't.

Mother was somewhat different. She couldn't stifle her love as easily. I remembered the fear in her eyes just this morning. She couldn't afford to let her worry escape the well she'd built to contain it. *Feed fear, and you will create a monster you'll never be able to contain*, she'd say.

Hodor's jaw muscle worked until he found his words. "It was so cold, I saw my breath plume before me. I looked out over the fjord, staring into it because it was shrouded in a thick mist. Almost… like it wasn't from this world. And from that mist poured a ferocious wolf pack, led by a snarling brown wolf. They cut through the fog like a warm knife through butter and came for us all. They were giants, shifting between wolf and man, ready for battle. They'd worked themselves into a frenzy, completely berserker by the time their boots hit the shore. No one stood a chance. I remember watching as one clamped down on the Iverson boy and shook him until his body went limp in its massive jaws." He held his hands out to show me how big the creatures were.

"It was strange, because although I was running from the mountain, it felt like I was here, on the shore as well, as if two of me were watching it unfold…" he said in a faraway voice, his eyes unfocused as they stared out at the water.

"You grabbed Ingrid and Solvi, one under each arm, and screamed for Gunnar to run. You made it to the house…" I waited, my heart in my throat. "When I made it to you, when I finally reached the house…" His voice was anguished when he said, "Solvi and Gunnar… they were lying on the ground in front of the house, dead. Father and Mother tried to fight the pack, but they were too weak." He lifted his head and locked eyes with me. "You got to them first. I'm not sure where you came from, but there was a shadow around you. You were terrifying and precise and brutal. You fought the brown wolf that led them here, courageous and beautiful, until his paw caught you unawares and swept your feet out from under you. He tore into your side and you bled out on the shore."

"How did *you* die?" I asked.

"Trying to protect you. Another wolf leapt onto me as I stabbed the wolf who bit you." He shook his head. "I sound like I've lost my mind, but it was like… It didn't feel like the stories of Ragnarök. The entire world wouldn't have ended from their attack. But it was devastating to me because everything in *my* world ended."

"Did you see what happened after you were killed?" I didn't know how, but I knew he'd seen it all.

"They just… left. Once everyone was dead, the pack of wolves raced back across the fjord and disappeared. I'm not sure how I knew that, because I was already dead. Maybe my spirit watched them."

I stepped in front of him and met Hodor's eyes. "I won't pretend to understand what happened with Tor, and I know how much you loved him. He'd been yours since we lost Oskar. But… I do know that wolves cannot run on water. I think the dream on the eve of Winternights was a bad omen, but you cannot let it shake you so thoroughly. Father is watching, and you'll have to face him tonight."

He nodded. "You're right. As usual." Hodor finally smiled. "And *you* will have to face Mother," he reminded.

"*And* a seeress. Father told me she asked for me by name."

Hodor's brows pinched.

I hated that she'd asked for me. Why couldn't she just visit the Jarl like all the others and bestow her wisdom upon him?

Hodor traded places with me and I sat on the boulder as he braided my hair back and out of my face. He and I had been close with Oskar, but after he died, the two of us became inseparable. There was a silent vow between us that both knew and never spoke. He and I would fight back to back if another attack occurred. Neither of us would let the other fall. We should have made such a plan before... and included our brother. Then he would be here with us. He would watch us battle tonight and have a nervous stomach as he waited for his chance to fight for his shield.

There was a huge age gap between me and Hodor and our three younger siblings. Mother gave birth to three dead sons between Oskar and Gunnar. She claimed to have been cursed during the attack and worried she'd never have another child to replace the one she lost. But she eventually conceived and then bore Gunnar, Ingrid, and Solvi. Three living children to erase the luck of the three born without breath.

Hodor and I were the only ones in our small village who were of age to fight for their shields. Most had grown up and moved on before us; many left the village for larger towns, or were too young, like our siblings.

"Good luck tonight," he said, finishing the final of three plaits.

"You too."

"At least Father's somewhat predictable. Mother... you never know what she's thinking or what she'll do next. She adapts moment by moment. She'll attack when you least expect it."

I blew out a breath. He was right. Father was straightforward. He just tried to cleave you in two. He was strong, but tired easily these days. Hodor just had to outlast his strong offensive.

Mother was a raging storm, and I was the only thing in her path this evening.

More than being worried that I wouldn't best her and earn my shield, I worried that I'd shame my parents. I'd sparred many times with her before and hadn't won once.

Hodor came close to beating Father a few times, especially when his back ached, but by now, Mother and Father were on their second or third cups of mead and feeling limber and more than ready to enter the sparring ring.

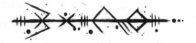

Father had shaved the sides of Gunnar's head and painted runes over the exposed skin. He was only six, but his small chest was puffed up. Father had tied a tiny shield onto his back and fastened his training sword to his hip with a piece of leather cord. "You look ready for battle." I nodded proudly.

"I am," he replied resolutely.

I raised my arm and he gave me a quick hug before straightening his clothes.

"Where are Ingrid and Solvi?"

"Mother is braiding Ingrid's hair. She wants you to tame Solvi's."

Ah, Solvi's pale, wild curls. The bane of Mother's existence.

Hodor walked to the pen holding the animals he would have to slaughter tonight, a length of rope coiled on his hip. He would lead them, one by one, to the celebration where he would end their lives quickly and collect the animal's blood for the seeress.

Hodor loved animals, even the weakest among our herds. But he knew his duty and would honor it well.

I walked inside our home and spotted Ingrid with her knees curled into her chest as Mother stood over her, working her hair into tight braids. Ingrid shot me a shy grin. She loved having her hair combed and toyed with.

Solvi leaped at me from the tabletop. I hadn't even noticed her climbing her way up onto it. I caught her and spun her around, then pretended to drop her into the hearth, catching her at the last minute. She squealed in delight. "Let's tame your hair, hmm?" I carried her across the room to her bed where she flopped down onto her knees and turned toward the wall. Her comb and leather ties were already laid out.

"Mother said the völva wants to speak to you," she whispered, her wide, blue eyes looking up at me.

"Seeress," I corrected. Some women, and men for that matter, were gifted by the norns who wove every living thing's past, present, and future. Seeresses could see and sense things we could not. They were sought after, respected, vital to a chieftain who wanted to plead to the spinners to allow his people to thrive.

A völva was something altogether different. The völva were witches, called by the norn Skuld. They were wed to their wands and their wands could spin the fates of humans. They were much more dangerous than a mere diviner. I'd heard they wore blood and read futures with the bones of animals. That they could kill with a look or raise the dead with a rune.

"She is right," Mother said from across the room, warning in her tone. "It is a völva who wishes to speak with you – *after* we spar."

A shiver scuttled up my spine like a millipede, each of its legs tickling my skin.

Her eyes locked with mine, hers flinty and filled with warning. "I cannot go with you to see her. She asked for you to come alone."

"I don't need you to come."

She gave a sliver of a smile. "I cannot go easy on you, either."

23

I gritted my teeth. I would never ask her to let me win. I'd rather return home ashamed. "I will *earn* my shield."

She nodded and assessed my clothing, clothes I'd borrowed from her. "You very much remind me of myself at your age, Liv."

It made her proud. I could see it in the easy way she turned back to her task, threading beads onto Ingrid's braids. In the way the corners of her mouth slightly turned upward.

Solvi's hair was soft as lamb's wool and just as difficult to deal with. I wet my hands in the basin across the room and raked the dampness through her curls, plaited them as fast as I could, and secured them with thin leather strips, tightly knotted. "I don't get beads like Ingrid?" she asked, her blue eyes shimmering with sadness.

I uncoiled one of the twin iron serpents from my own hair and wound it into hers. "There. Now we match."

She beamed a smile before running to retrieve her shield, Ingrid racing out of the room after her.

I looked over our home. After tonight, things would change. I wouldn't be forced out immediately, but when I claimed my shield, I would have to present myself to the Jarl, swear allegiance to him, and ask him to put me on a longship when the winter broke.

I would have to prepare to leave home.

I could almost feel the ship rock and sway beneath me.

FOUR

Hodor faced Father as the crowd of villagers formed a wide ring around them. My brother's feet were light as they began to circle one another. He needed that speed to keep Father moving.

Father wore his shield on his right arm and carried his sword in his left as he laughed at a friend's jibe.

The air was thick with laughter, music, sweat, and mead.

There were only half a dozen farms dotting the lands near the fjord, but many had travelled with the Jarl, who hosted the völva. I hadn't seen her yet. My eyes scanned the crowd, seeing both familiar and unfamiliar faces. She was likely one of them, though I expected a witch to stand apart from those who possessed no magic. If not in how she looked, in how she felt or how she drew crowds of her own.

Hodor banged his axe on his shield. *Thwack. Thwack. Thwack.* Over and over again. In his hardened eyes, I could see the rage that had been building for so long...

Father was more than a head taller than Hodor, but my brother was ready. Ready to move on and be done with this, to become a man. A warrior. And leave his childhood in the past.

Father was the first to strike, bringing his sword down hard upon Hodor's shield, but Hodor was quick of foot and spun to strike Father in the back, drawing blood but stopping short of hitting his kidney.

Father rained a series of powerful blows in response, gritting his teeth and roaring at Hodor for what he'd done. But Hodor deflected each, then kicked the back of Father's knee and sent him to the ground. Father wasn't fast enough and as he tried to rise, Hodor sliced his axe blade at his throat.

My breath hitched. Everyone's did.

If Hodor hadn't pulled back when he did, it would've been a death blow.

Hodor won, and he'd won breathtakingly fast.

He hadn't worn Father out; he took advantage of the weakness of his aging joints – as any enemy would've done.

I would not be so lucky. Mother was younger than Father, still very nimble and limber. Still fast. I rolled my shoulders and stretched my arms, back, and calves, smiling as the crowd went wild for my brother. Some of the men lifted him onto their shoulders and handed him horns filled with ale. He drank what he could, though most spilled down his tunic or onto the heads of those hoisting him. They celebrated him as Father rose, pride and humiliation shining in his eyes – a dangerous and volatile combination.

Mother clapped for her son from across the crowd, her eyes narrowing on me. It was our turn and she was going to show everyone that age had not taken her ferocity away. I could see it in the familiar glint, the dare she threw my way. *Humiliate me and I will end you, little girl.*

When I was no older than Solvi, she'd looked at Father, put the tip of her knife in his gut, and threatened to spill his insides. I wasn't sure what he'd done to make her so angry, but I knew she would do it if he said one more word to her.

He left the house that evening and didn't return for weeks.

She wasn't the least bit upset about his absence. If anything, she reveled in it. When he eventually came back, things were tense, but time softened the hurt between them, as it often did.

Mother grabbed the blank shield Father made me and waved me over. "Hold out your arm."

"I can do it myself," I argued.

She smiled. "I know, but this is symbolic. I give this to you… and you must take it from me – if you can." She ticked her head at Father and Hodor. "You watched your father tie on your brother's."

I held my arm out, knowing I'd test the comfort and tightness when she was finished.

She adjusted the leather bindings and cinched them, buckling them onto my forearm. "You will need someone to have your back if you plan to fight. You steady them. They steady you. And you rely on them to fight at your side and watch over you as you watch over them. In many cases, it's the only way you'll come out of a battle alive."

I nodded once, telling her I was listening to her advice as she slid her shield on, the soft leather fitted to her shape. Her wisdom was what Hodor and I had learned from tragedy, and what she'd learned from survival.

Her lips lifted on one side. "You will have no one to help you tonight, though."

"Neither will you," I quipped.

She gave a mirthless laugh. "Oh, I will enjoy this."

I grabbed the sword Father made for me. It was light-weight but strong. Neither too long nor too short. He'd woven dark leather over the handle, the grip settling comfortably along my finger's joints.

Mother preferred a lightweight axe with a long handle. Easier to reach an opponent from far away, but close up… the length of the handle could pose a problem. That was why Father bored a hole in the handle's end and had fitted a small spear inside. I'd have to watch out for both blades.

She nimbly twirled the axe, getting a feel for the weapon's familiar weight. We were dressed alike, stood at the same height, and our features mirrored one another's. She had years of fighting experience, had survived numerous raids and battles, and I was only now being tested.

She banged the head against the metal rimming her shield. Age hadn't settled on Mother's face the way it had Father's. The lines on her face were as superficial as the scar on her jawline. If anything, they merely added to her beauty.

More mead flowed past lips all around us. Father and Hodor finally made peace and settled among the clansmen, their eyes trained on us. Shouts and shrill whistles erupted into the night air along with popping embers from fires set along the beach as we circled one another.

Mother's eyes were calculating. Gone was the love that sometimes shone there.

In front of me, my mother was transformed. She was no longer the one who cared for my wounds and lay cold cloths on my feverish head, or the woman who taught me to weave and cook.

She was every inch a warrior. My mother was gone.

I wondered if she looked at me in the same way, if she saw a stranger where her daughter had just stood.

She waited for me to strike. She wanted to see what I was made of.

I was made of patience and knew she had little.

When she grew tired of dancing, she struck out. I shielded myself, striking fast toward her stomach. She caught my blade with her axe, anticipating the move, then crouched low as if she expected me to fight like Hodor, forgetting that we were nothing alike.

I brought my sword down hard on her shield. The metal hissed as it raked across the top metal rim. I dented it. I'd left a scar. One her eyes took sharp note of. Her jaw hardened. I could almost hear her teeth rake against each other.

She jabbed at me with the spear. I managed to bend at the last second to avoid a puncture, but she hooked it in my shirt and tore a hole at my side, then twirled the axe and arced it toward my head. My shield didn't buckle. It met axe blade and spear and protected me as it should.

Sweat beaded on her forehead, her impatience driving her into a rage. She rained blows upon me mercilessly, but I blocked them all. When she thought I'd rest and let her go on the offensive again, I struck.

I thrust my sword toward her, but she caught my blade with the head of her axe. Metal raked metal as we slid them apart.

She roared, running at me with quick steps.

She swung. I blocked, then chopped at her from the side. She sucked her stomach in and bent to avoid the blow, a vicious snarl ripping from her throat. Her cheeks puffed as she panted, adjusting her grip on her axe's handle.

I waited again to see what else she would throw at me.

She fought me backward with a series of sharp, blunt blows, then swiped her long axe toward my shins. I jumped and tucked my feet into my body, behind my shield. The crowd gasped, then cheered.

Whether she liked it or not, I was her equal.

I just needed to become *better*.

There was only one way to do that, and though she might hate me for it, it had to be done.

I kept her occupied with my sword, keeping her axe busy, and when she wasn't looking at my shield, used its metal edging to crack her hand. Her mouth gaped open in surprise.

Her grip relaxed – long enough for me to use my sword to disarm her. Her axe fell to the gritty soil.

She clamored to reach it.

I leapt toward her and placed my fur-lined boot atop her handle just as her fingers touched the wood, positioning the tip of my sword under her jaw. Her breath hitched as she panted, her eyes sliding from the axe she could touch but not retrieve, to me.

"This shield is mine," I panted.

The look she gave me was part hatred, part respect. I reveled in it. I reveled in the victory and the first taste of true freedom.

I removed the tip of my blade from her skin and slid it back into the loop at my waist, holding a hand out to her. The crowd hushed as she considered it, but then she laughed and took hold of my palm. "Well done," she finally said. "Liv Eriksson, *Shield Maiden*."

She made a fist with the hand I hit, but never admitted that it hurt. I hoped I didn't break her bones. I wasn't sure how hard I hit her, but it must've been intense for her to let go.

Father and Hodor approached, both putting the spar behind them. Father and Mother shared an exhausted laugh. "I can't believe both of them won," Father said. "I believe age is catching up to us."

Gunnar and Ingrid chattered between me and Hodor while Solvi climbed Father's back and sat atop his shoulders. They were discussing what to eat first, their noses pointed toward the tables piled with food just beyond the still-boisterous crowd of clansmen.

"I never dreamed anyone would best you, Hella," a loud voice boomed from behind us.

I turned to see who'd spoken. I didn't recognize the man, but the way he looked at my mother while stroking his fat-soaked beard set my teeth on edge.

Mother's smile fell away and her snarl returned.

Father bristled, gently extracting Solvi and setting her on the ground. His shoulders squared as he faced the man. My hands fell on each of the girls' shoulders and I eased them behind me. My shield was still fastened to my forearm, my sword still in my hand.

The man looked part beast with a broad, hairy chest and limbs as thick as oaks. Father and Mother maneuvered themselves between him and us. Hodor slid his axe from his belt. The man caught the movement. His eyes glittered as they flicked from my brother's axe to my face.

"Your daughter has grown up fine, Hella," he said, still only speaking to Mother and wholly ignoring Father at her side. "*Very* fine," he added, sliding his gaze downward. "She looks just like you."

"Enough!" Father barked.

"She's of age to be married, is she not?" The brute grinned, finally locking eyes with Father.

"Not to the likes of *you*," he snarled. "Nor to your *kind*."

"My kind?" The behemoth laughed. "And what kind would that be?"

"Mutts," my mother snapped harshly. "If you come near her, I'll chop you limb from limb, starting with the one you value most."

The man did not have a retort for her threat, but his beady eyes narrowed.

"Come along, children," she said to us, her eyes warning me to stay close.

Hodor kept hold of his axe as he and I herded Gunnar, Ingrid, and Solvi closer to our parents, forming a protective ring around them as we followed Mother through the crowd.

"Come," she urged as she carved a quick path far away from the smelly lout.

"I'm hungry," Solvi complained, clutching her stomach, blissfully unaware of what had just happened.

"Who was that man?" I asked, pushing closer to Mother.

She threw a sharp look over her shoulder. "He is no one you should concern yourself with."

Father's steps were angry. He forged ahead, leading us to tables teeming with all sorts of food. Gunnar, Ingrid, and Solvi plucked small loaves of bread and hunks of meat from the bounty, while Father and Mother found bowls to heap their dinners upon.

Stars sparkled overhead.

I began to feel a pull, a strange sensation washing over me that tugged me toward the shore... The völva was near.

Hodor's brows pinched together as he filled a bowl of his own. "What's wrong?" he mouthed.

I shook my head. I'd tell him later.

Mother stood beside me. "Does she call to you?" she asked.

I nodded, placing a hand over the hollow of my stomach. "How did you know?"

"My mother," she said simply.

The truth was an arrow to the heart.

"She was a—?"

Mother nodded. "A witch, yes."

Mother always kept us away from seeresses. I guessed now I knew why.

"You must go to her, but keep your wits about you, Liv, and don't speak unless you consider your words carefully. She may use them against you. Remember the warnings I taught you."

I nodded and let my feet follow the strange feeling unfurling in my stomach, all the while worrying I might say something foolish or damning.

I found her near the shore. The Jarl in his heavy, fine clothes, a coyote pelt gathered around his shoulders, stood at her side as if she was the Queen and he her servant. I'd never seen him so gracious with his manners, or his things.

32

A small crowd huddled in front of the völva, who was seated on an ornately carved chair, twin dragon's heads curling toward her as if they might swallow her whole. And yet, even if the beasts were real, if they poured fire down upon her, she wouldn't have been singed. Power radiated from her; a strange energy I couldn't explain, but could potently feel.

Her hair was as shiny and black as a raven's wing as she stood, her eyes honing in on me from afar. I kept my steps steady as I made my way to her, allowing her magic to reel in the line that held me, like a fish being dragged above the water's surface.

Rings that lined her fingers glinted in the light cast from a nearby fire as she waved me forward. She whispered to the Jarl and he gave a command for the crowd to disperse. Those who surrounded her, men, women, and young children, obeyed, trickling away.

Their eyes searched me as I passed. They must have wondered what the witch wanted with me. I stopped in front of her, keeping several feet between us. Soon we were alone, the witch and I. My shield was on my back, but the heavy weight didn't comfort me. Neither did the weight of the sword tucked into my belt.

"You fought well," she said as her eyes quickly combed over me. Once. Twice. Her voice was coarse, as if she rarely spoke.

I inclined my head, afraid to speak, Mother's warning ringing in my head.

She wasn't old, nor was she young. She was, perhaps, Mother's age – the sweet place between the two stages of life. But she was no warrior. There were no hard edges about her. No scars upon her flawless, moonlit skin.

Her clothing was fine, her dress stitched from thick, crimson fabric and her matching gloves lined with snowy white fur. She'd drawn runes on her face. Some I recognized easily, and some I didn't know and had never seen.

She took the opportunity to study me as intently as I did her, much more deeply than her first glances. I wondered what she thought of me. If she thought I was a good fighter, or perhaps she considered me a warrior. Now, a shield maiden – like my mother had announced. I hoped she was afraid of me and that she saw nothing but fearlessness in my face.

"Words hold power," she finally said, taking up a long, wooden staff and walking toward me, closing the distance between us. I realized it was her wand, not a staff. The tip looked woven, like strands in a basket, but even as they bowed from the staff itself, they rejoined to make a fine tip. They said witches could use their wands to spin the fates of lesser men.

I wasn't lesser. My eyes narrowed at her closeness.

"Few realize that," she continued, undeterred. "They waste what little power they have by wagging their tongues too much." She smiled as she approached, stopping only when the bottom of her crimson skirts brushed the tops of my boots. "But not you. You observe first and speak only when it's necessary. Even when your mother *doesn't* warn you beforehand."

I swallowed thickly as she lifted a hand and let her thumb ghost down the lumps and bumps of my braid, pausing over the iron serpent coiled around it. She took in my shield. "I need you to come with me now, Liv." She turned her back to me and began walking away from the shore.

"How do you know my name?" I asked, refusing to follow her retreating form as she walked toward the wood.

She turned with a knowing smile on her lips. "Because someone very important has a message for you."

She continued her trek, using her wand to help her up the slope, weaving herself into the oaks and pines as if she was a scarlet thread in the forest's vast tapestry.

My feet followed her.

The coppery scent of blood filled the air and we entered the spot where the animals had been slain. They hung from thick branches in the trees above us, their blood leaking into pots and jugs, buckets and bowls. "We must sit amongst them," she said, laying down her wand. She gathered her fine gown and sat on the forest floor. "On Winternights especially, there is more power in the dead than in the living."

Hodor had stood there earlier. He split his rope to hang each of the animals we brought to later smoke and preserve.

I recognized each of them. The scrawny lamb that was born too late in the year and wouldn't survive the cold, the goat with the lame hoof, the runty piglet who was born months ago, but wouldn't grow despite the amount of food she ate.

Now they were dead, hanging limply from branches, and the witch wanted me to sit with her beneath them, surrounded by captured puddles of their blood.

Silently, she stared at me and waited for me to comply with her request. I slowly walked forward, the wind stirring the strands of hair escaping my braids as I stepped beneath the animals. The moment my backside touched the forest floor, a strange energy washed through the air.

The dead animals hanging above us began to writhe. The lamb let out a pitiful bleat and the pig weakly grunted. The cocks flapped their wings and flew in circles. Blood droplets landed on us. I ducked and shielded my head with my arms, looking to the witch as goosebumps erupted over my skin.

She sat calmly, completely unaffected. Her cool, brown eyes were fixed on me.

The animals went still again as a gust of wind tore their spirits away once more. My heart fluttered as I watched them rock back and forth, the ropes that held their weight creaking on the rough limbs until they finally went still.

Splat.

Splat. Splat.

More droplets of blood splashed into the containers beneath them, wrung out by spirit and wind.

A slow smile spread over the völva's berry-stained lips. "There is power in blood and bone," the witch offered.

Power in words.

Power in blood and bone.

Power in the slain.

For me, Winternights had always been a raucous mixture of celebration and spine-tingling fear. The dead walked the earth and joined us as we bade farewell to summer and greeted the frigid winter, bade farewell to the earth's life and let death claim it again, as it had claimed our kinsmen. We were nearer to them on this night, for they dwelt in the coldness of death now after their walks in the sun, among the living.

"Why did you ask for me?"

"I told you. Someone has a message for you."

She untied a small pouch from the belt at her waist and withdrew a wad of leaves, placing them in her mouth and chewing them. She rolled her neck. Her silken hair fell over her shoulders as she rocked forward and back, forward and back. Her movements, once smooth, became jerky and erratic. Her breathing became labored. She wrung her hands. Her legs fidgeted.

A burning smell filled the air. Not one of oak chips or firewood, but one that smelled of sizzling flesh.

I scooted away from her.

Her hand clamped onto my ankle. "No!" she snapped. "Do not retreat. *She* is near."

I looked over my shoulders, all around the shadowy wood. If someone was close, I couldn't sense her. No branches snapped. No leaves rustled.

She removed another small bundle of herbs from her pouch and offered it to me. "Chew."

I shook my head when she insistently pushed it toward me. I didn't take it from her. "It is the gateway to the weavers... to the norns."

Blood whooshed through my head, through my ears. "The norns?" I asked breathlessly. *The weavers called for me? By name?*

"Skuld wishes to speak with you. This is the only way."

The witch dipped her fingernails into a pot of lamb's blood and flicked it toward my face. Small droplets sprayed my skin.

She shoved the wad of blood-soaked leaves into my hand. My clammy palm wrapped around them, then unfurled. It wasn't wise to eat certain plants. Some would cause visions, but some... some killed. And völva often sacrificed humans to the norns and to the gods.

They would drug them, and when they did not know their head from their feet, the witches would tear the heart from their chest and hold it, still beating, in their hands, calling out to the gods to show what they'd done for them.

"I won't eat it."

"But, Skuld—" The witch's voice cut off. Her breath hitched, then a squeak escaped her throat. My mother stood behind her, the tip of her knife biting into the woman's skin, her knee in the witch's back.

The runes began to writhe on her forehead, cheeks, and throat as she called upon her magic, but my mother didn't care. She held her blade tightly and refused to relent.

What is she doing? The witch will kill us both! Or Skuld may decide to clip the threads of our lives for refusing her... I leapt to my feet.

"I believe she declined your request," Mother gritted.

The völva's dark eyes locked on mine. "You are making a mistake. You've seen the first sign of what is to come."

The first sign... *Does she mean Hodor's dream?* "Tor?"

The woman managed a small nod, her eyes pleading with me. Her lips trembled.

Mother fisted the woman's hair. "Leave this village now. Do not stop for your entourage of faithful dogs. If you return, if you come for my family, you will taste my blade at the back of your throat. Do you understand?"

The woman's face mottled, whether from fear or shame, I wasn't sure. "I'll take my leave."

Mother smiled cruelly. She waited until the völva stood and pointed north, away from the village. "Go."

The witch reached for the wooden staff, still lying on the ground, but Mother kicked it away, far out of her reach. "But my wand!" she protested.

"Make a new one," Mother insisted. "I know you can."

The völva looked toward the pooled blood. She needed the animal blood for her spells. I wiped at my face, dragging the droplets across my skin.

Mother cursed, then kicked each container over. "What part of 'go' do you not understand?"

The woman gasped and growled at her, a glint of hatred in her dark eyes.

"I told you to leave. I will not repeat myself again." The leather on the handle of her knife protested as she gripped it tighter.

The witch flicked her eyes toward the blade clenched in my mother's hand. Mother's brows rose as she waited for the woman to flee. When the witch finally turned her back on us and walked north, I could breathe again, though not easier.

She walked quickly across barley and wheat fields, through patches of wood. Every time she stepped from shadow into the open, into the full moonlight, her crimson dress could be seen like a bloodstain on snow.

The further she walked, the easier my stomach felt. The cord she'd drawn me in with had been severed.

"Go to the house, Liv," Mother said, still watching the völva. She crouched down and took up the witch's wand. Her fingers gripped the wand so tightly, they turned white.

"Aren't you coming?"

Mother shot me a harsh glare. "Go. Home."

40

FIVE

I didn't sleep well that night. Father left, grumbling about going to look for Mother. After Mother returned, he still hadn't.

A fierce wind roared through the valley, sweeping off the mountains and cutting toward the fjord. It tore at the thatching on our roof and more than once I braced, expecting it to peel completely off.

My bed, which I shared with Solvi, lined the wall closest to the mountains. Ingrid's bed was at our heads, and Gunnar and Hodor slept in the bed closest to our feet. Mother and Father had a small, private room at the far end of the house.

I was not looking forward to the winter when the animals would have to be kept inside with us, lest they freeze. No matter how often we cleaned, the smell was horrible. Not even wind like this could drag it out of the house.

The hearth crackled and smoked with every gust. I got up, careful not to wake Solvi and crossed the room to add a few logs. The flames caught and soon the fire was more than just flickering embers and the room warmed between the gusts. I looked back at my vacated bed and decided to sit by the fire for a while.

"Why are you awake?" Hodor asked quietly as he climbed out of bed and came to sit with me.

I pointed to the roof.

"It'll hold," he whispered.

I shrugged.

His cool eyes met mine. Flame flickered within the hollows. "What did the völva want with you?" Hodor's brow wrinkled.

"She said Skuld wanted to talk to me."

His eyes widened and he scooted closer. "What did Skuld say?"

I shook my head. "I didn't speak to her."

I could see the question in his eyes, but I had no answers to give.

The norns were the weavers of fate.

Urd. Verdandi. Skuld.

Past. Present. Future.

No one dared deny them anything they wanted, not that they often spoke with humans. And now that I'd likely insulted Skuld, I worried my life might be cut short.

I flicked a meaningful glance toward Mother and Father's room and his eyes widened further. I mouthed the word 'Mother.'

"I *knew* she went after you! Did she threaten the völva?" he asked. I nodded. "That was unwise," he said so faintly I almost didn't hear him.

No. What had been unwise was her hunting the witch down.

Pointing to the tall, twisting wooden staff in the corner, I listened as he exhaled sharply. Dried blood coated the witch's wand, and it hadn't come from one of the farm animals.

Mother was as good a tracker as she was a shield maiden, and the witch was as good as dead the moment she tried to get me to eat the bundle of leaves.

"Liv, this is bad."

As he and I stared at the bloody wand, a dreadful feeling settled into my stomach.

At some point, I fell asleep near the hearth beside my brother. Before daybreak, Hodor woke me. He and I dressed quickly and walked outside into the cool, blue twilight. Stars still sparkled over the waters of the fjord, but little by little, the blue lightened with the dawn that rose brilliant and golden above us.

The wind whipped my hair as we climbed the nearest hill to check the roof's thatching without climbing atop and waking the others. "Looks fine," Hodor said. He scrubbed a hand down his face. "If the Jarl finds out what she did, he'll–"

"He won't. Mother will make sure of it."

The witch's warning slid through me like a shiver. "Hodor, she mentioned something before we parted ways... The völva said that I'd seen the first sign of what is to come. I think she meant Tor's death."

Hodor tensed. "It was a coincidence. Nothing more," he said, tearing apart a piece of tall grass with his stubbed nails. His cool eyes scanned the fjord. It was sunny, not a trace of fog over the water.

Coincidences had never bothered him so badly before. Yesterday, he was shaken. This morning, he brushed it off as if he was trying to pretend he'd never dreamed any of it. He gained his shield and seemingly forgot the dream entirely. I refused to let him forget. The witch pointed it out for a reason.

"Did you know that Mother's mother was a völva?"

He flicked a surprised glance at me. "How would I know? She doesn't speak of her past."

"She was. You could have her gift, Hodor."

"If that's the truth, any of us could, Liv, but that doesn't mean we do. It was merely a dream, and I am a warrior, not a witch." He put a finger on my chest. "Don't ever accuse me of being one again."

I batted his hand away. "I wasn't accusing you."

It was a dream... yet Tor was rotting halfway up the closest mountain in the spot where Hodor had seen him fall in his dream. It may have been a dream, but the witch knew my name and revealed that Skuld herself wanted to speak with me.

What if none of this was coincidence? What if it was the beginning of something larger, a tumble of snow that would build and bury us all?

I knew what Hodor's fears were about the second sight. Male völva were considered unnatural, and while they were respected out of fear, they were also shamed for their gifts. Hodor didn't want any such shame to hang on his shoulders or besmirch the name of our family.

Hodor stood. "While you were with the witch, Father took me to pledge myself to the Jarl. I leave in the spring with the first ship. I choose to be a warrior, Liv. You can choose the same."

Could I?

"What if Father says I must take a husband?" The memory of the man who'd stopped my parents after the sparring matches came to mind. I just hoped Father remembered his refusal to wed me to that... mutt.

"He won't force your hand before spring."

I hugged myself. How did he know that? I swallowed angrily. I did *not* want to marry. Not now, maybe never.

"Since you didn't get to pledge yourself to the Jarl because the witch demanded to speak with you, you will get another chance to meet with him."

"This morning? Before he leaves for town?"

Hodor shook his head. "You'll meet with him in the spring, when the winter breaks."

That was months from now. Would he still put me on a ship then, or forget me entirely? I wanted to sail with Hodor so we could fight at one another's backs and keep each other alive.

"Father wanted to force the issue of you marrying, but Mother forbade it," he said softly. "I heard them talking before Mother left to find you. Nothing will be decided about your fate until the winter breaks and you talk with our chieftain, Liv. Calm down. You have several long, harsh months to survive before worrying about that."

Father was strong, but not brave enough to risk Mother's wrath. If she forbade it, he wouldn't cross her. Deep down, our behemoth of a father feared his wife.

The woman who fought alongside men, who slew those who opposed her, who put a knife to a witch's throat, ignored the wishes of a norn, and then tracked the woman down and killed her with her own wand...

Mother was a force of nature all her own.

Untamable. Unstoppable.

Father would see the völva's wand coated in her blood and know his fate would be far worse if he crossed her.

Hodor and I sat on our favorite boulder. He brushed ochre into the swirl he'd outlined in charcoal on his blank, wooden shield. I sat with him, quietly watching his careful strokes. When his brush traveled outside the careful lines, he used his thumbnail to scrape off the errant paint and started again. Hodor was patient and his work painstaking. Winternights left everyone with headaches and sour stomachs, so we'd done our chores and Father said we could take the afternoon for ourselves – as long as we stayed outside. The children skipped rocks from the shore, trying to see whose bounced the farthest.

"What will you paint on yours?" he asked, eyes flicking to me just for a moment.

"I'm not sure yet."

Hodor was drawing something pleasing to the eye, but his design held no more meaning than a collection of pretty lines. I wanted my shield to represent me – my heart and my life. If it was going to protect me, I wanted it to be an extension of me.

I toyed with the iron serpent still coiled in yesterday's braid and watched him drag a brush made of horsehair over the wood. The color soaked in and dried, the vibrant orange dulling before my eyes.

When he finished all the ochre lines swirling from the center, he stood and washed his brush in the cool waters. Next, he would fill in the spaces with the dark gray paint he'd made. He squeezed excess water from the brush and dipped it into the bowl.

"You seem troubled," he said.

"I am." I wasn't sure why exactly. I could've pointed to Hodor's dream or to the fact that Tor was dead. I could've said it was because of the witch or Mother's actions toward her. It was all those things and none of them, but I wasn't sure how to explain that to him.

"I'm troubled, too," he confided. He didn't elaborate and I didn't press him. How could I, when I couldn't explain my own feelings?

I watched as he finished painting and waited with him while the paint dried, the echo of children's laughter as they chased each other over the rocky shore the only other sound. And then, just like last night, a leaden feeling settled into my stomach. The feeling pulled me behind the house and beyond our fields to a small piece of land sheltered beneath a tall pine tree, its boughs laden with needles that dripped with sadness, and where a patch of soil had been disturbed.

"Tor rests there," Hodor said from behind me, making me jump.

My fingers drifted over the overturned dirt. "How did you find time to bury him?"

"When someone truly wants to do something, they find the time, or make it."

I wondered how long it took him to dig a hole deep enough in the frost-packed dirt. I imagined he had to chop through many tangled roots and move countless rocks to place his beloved friend beneath this tree.

He raised his hands and took hold of a low branch, bracing himself against it. "The wind is already dragging winter to us. I don't look forward to a single cold day."

Neither did I, but no amount of dread would stop it from coming.

"I couldn't just leave him up there," he said, crouching down to brush the clumped earth flat.

I was about to tell him that I understood, when Solvi shrieked for Mother. I rushed from the tree through the barley field toward the water, counting the children's heads.

Solvi, Ingrid... Where is Gunnar?

"Gunnar?" I screamed.

Hodor ran beside me. "He's there." He pointed farther down the shore.

Mother and Father met us on the rocky beach along with a few clansmen. "What is it?" I asked, gasping when I finally reached them. They'd huddled around something large that had washed up. I expected it to be a chunk of dead whale swept in on the current from the ocean beyond, but it was no sea creature.

It was a man. A mutt, my mother had called him.

The man's body was bloated, and his skin was as pale as ice. His lips, toes, and fingers were blue, but there were no

47

visible wounds on his body. The whites of his eyes were red, which was the only thing that seemed strange.

"It's Jarl Wolf. He and the völva traveled here with our chieftain as his guests. Didn't you have words with him, Erik?" asked Arne, who lived closest to us. Our clansmen looked to Father.

My mind struggled to put together the pieces. *Wolf... Jarl Wolf. Chieftain of Clan Wolf. Mutt.*

My heart thundered as I glanced furtively at Mother, whose back was straight as she stared emotionlessly upon the body. Ingrid and Solvi came to me. Each clung to one of my legs, peeking out from around them to watch the dead man as if he might spring up from the afterlife. Gunnar, on the other hand, stood proudly between his mother and big sister.

Across from us, Father crouched to look the dead man over, shaking his head as if it were a pity he lay dead on the shore like a beached carcass. "A brief, meaningless exchange after our sparring matches," Father said almost innocently.

But I knew the words between them weren't empty. They were so cold they burned, filled with threats and ire, even though they were few.

Arne didn't question any further. He accepted my father's word as truth and rolled the hefty man onto his side and glanced over him, raising his arm and easing it back down, looking up at us all. "No wounds. The drunkard probably drowned trying to climb back into the ship. He helped himself to half the mead we put out."

He let Wolf's body flop backward, then pressed his eyelids closed. "I'll tell the Jarl. Will you help me drag him from the water?" he asked Father.

Ingrid and Solvi backed up with me, giving the men wide berth to do their deed. Arne hooked his arms under both of Jarl Wolf's while Father waded into the water and took up his feet. The man's head lolled as they moved him onto the beach out of the water's reach and lay him back on the rocky ground.

Their ghastly task complete, they walked together toward Leif's house, who was hosting our Jarl. His house was located farther up the fjord, the largest of our small village and the best positioned as it sat upon a small ridge overlooking the fjord.

Jarls were kings, also called chieftains, and we were ruled by Jarl Urðr. His grandfather started our clan many years ago after winning a battle for the lands we stood upon. Chieftains weren't born into the position; they fought for it; our chieftain was known as fierce and ruthless in battle.

Sometimes he hosted other chieftains to keep alliances solid and strong. I had a feeling this would weaken the ties our king wanted to keep with Clan Wolf.

A shudder ran through me at his name. A name far more terrifying than the blue, bloated man lying at my feet. Would Hodor still insist his dream was meaningless now?

Mother turned on her heels and left him to lay there, dead and alone. She never looked back as she stepped into the shadows inside our house. She would not give him another thought.

I was unsettled. My ribs cinched around me and would not loosen. My hands shook as I turned to Hodor, who had heard the man's name as clearly as I had.

"Take the children to Tor's grave. I need to speak with Mother," I told Hodor.

He shot me a look of warning. "Alone?"

"Alone. Please, I don't want them to hear what I am about to say."

Hodor pinched his lips together but asked the children if they would like to see where Tor was buried, to perhaps bring him a wildflower or two. They forgot the man's body as quickly as their backs were turned and a more peaceful option was offered.

I stalked to our house and found Mother stoking the fire. "Why did you do it?"

Her flinty eyes narrowed. "If I hadn't killed the witch, she would've killed you."

"You don't know that."

"I do, Liv. And you're welcome."

She grabbed a wooden bowl and placed it on the table, turning to gather some oats from a barrel. I slapped the bowl off the table and it clattered to the floor. She wasn't going to ignore me. Not now.

"Why Jarl *Wolf?* You knew about Hodor's dream! His name and that omen are stitched together by the weavers."

She gritted her teeth and came to stand beside me. "I didn't kill that mutt. I *wish* I would have been the one to do it, but *I didn't kill him*. He deserved a coward's death, Liv. You have no idea the sort of man he was, but your father and I do. Our ships joined his once for a raid the Jarl ordered. We joined with their clan to raid a monastery, and that mutt allowed and committed acts that still turn my stomach. Our clan took what we found and left them alone. Even *we* couldn't watch what they did." She was quiet for a minute. "It is one thing to take from others, to raid and plunder things. It's another to torture, Liv. Not even Odin would condone what they did."

"And the witch?" I rasped.

She shook her head. "You have no idea what she wanted with you. She wanted to cut –"

"My heart out? I considered that, but I don't think she did. She pled with me to talk to Skuld. What if she was being honest, Mother? What then?"

She shook her head. "Völva are not to be trusted. Skuld gives messages through rune stones, dice, or bone. She *does not* speak with mortals. She sits beneath Ygdrassil and spins futures. She doesn't concern herself with present situations. That burden is Verdandi's alone. The witch was lying. She would have killed you. Let me be completely clear with you, Liv, because I'm not sure you know it: You are *my* daughter. *My* firstborn. You grew in my womb and I labored to bring you into the world. I will die before another völva tries to take you out of it."

Her words sank into my stomach like a heavy stone dropped in deep water. "What do you mean, *another* völva?"

Mother regretted the words she'd let loose. I could see it in her eyes as clear as her resolve to make me understand. "My mother, your grandmother, came to us after you were born. She said she was called to you. And while we were sleeping, she tried to smother you with a blanket when you were only weeks old. I caught her and saved you from her. She was frantic, claiming you were dangerous and would one day become a scourge upon the earth."

My breath left me in a rush and it was hard to inhale again. "What did you do to the völva last night?"

Mother's brows rose. "You worry for the one who would've stolen your very breath." She shook her head disappointedly. "Your heart is too soft."

And what about her heart? I was certain that just over her heart was a series of invisible scars that had hardened into nearly impenetrable flesh.

"I *don't* worry for her. I merely want to know the full story." If I worried for anyone, it was for Mother.

Mother smiled at that retort, but it didn't reach her eyes. She bent to pick up the bowl and placed it on the table again where she'd first put it. Then she crossed the room to grab the witch's wand, the wood still coated with her blood.

She threw the wand in the fire. The flames barely licked at the wood at first, almost repelled by it, then something shifted and the wand was consumed in a flash. The entire staff from top to bottom turned to ash, held together as if it were whole until Mother blew them apart.

Mother turned away from the scattered ashes and tamed flames to face me. "You are my daughter, Liv, and I will spend every breath and every ounce of strength in my body to protect you until I am no more. And I will never apologize for it."

51

52

SIX

Father did not sail with the men who rowed our chieftain and Jarl Wolf's body back to Urdr Town where our guest's ship was docked, so that his kinsmen could take him home to be buried among his people. And Mother didn't mention the slain man or the witch again.

My father and Hodor went hunting instead, providing what I hoped was enough meat to last the winter – for us and for the families suffering because someone had to sail the dead chieftain home before the winter made sailing impossible.

While they were gone, Mother and I fished by wading into the shallows with our spears in water so cold, it numbed the skin after only a few minutes. We stayed in as long as we could stand the frigid, paralyzing cold, then we would warm ourselves by a large fire on the shore and wade out again. We caught fish each day, and the children prepared the fish as we caught them. After, Mother and I smoked them, putting the meat away for lean times.

Other women and children fished along the shore as well, doing what they could while their husbands were gone. Some went hunting, leaving their children with other families.

All I could think of with every fish we speared and every carcass my father carried down from the mountain, was that many a family would go hungry this winter. But not ours.

Mother killed the witch, but we weren't yet being punished for it.

I wondered why.

Our parents didn't welcome the returning clansmen home, though much of our small village did. Gunnar ran out to greet them, excited to be part of something so dramatic. He'd talked incessantly about the disgusting bloat of Wolf's body, how *he* was the one who first noticed him and how he *bravely* told Ingrid and Solvi to run to Arne's house.

Many of those returning rushed to their homes, bundled themselves, and took up their spears, bows, and arrows in search of game despite the cold creeping down the mountains.

I told Hodor what Mother told me about witches, including our grandmother and what she tried to do, and that she burned the völva's wand. He didn't reply; he just sat quietly with me next to Tor's grave.

For days, he was quiet. As were our parents.

And then winter began with a roar and we spent our days indoors between chores that called us into the frigid air. We spent our days laughing at Solvi's silliness, at Ingrid's sharp wit, and Gunnar's attempts at proving his manhood, ignoring his failures for now. He was still young.

For weeks the snow poured, let up for a scant breath, then heaped on us again, slowly morphing into weeks that blurred into dismal months. Months so cold, I doubted the spring would ever be able to battle its way back to us. The fjord froze solid a few times and we took advantage, slipping over its icy surface, careful to stay close to the shore in case it fractured and broke.

Gunnar grew taller and Ingrid and Solvi's plump cheeks thinned as the food we'd stored and subsequently shared with our kinsmen got sparser, and we went from consuming two meals each day, to one so thin it didn't begin to fill us.

Father and Mother somehow didn't kill one another, even as the animals huddled in the house close to their room, confined to a small square lined with hay, making noises at all hours of the indescribably long days and nights.

Hodor and I kept the children entertained, helped with chores inside and out, and didn't mention either of our futures while winter roared on.

But soon, winter loosened its grasp and Hodor and I began to wonder how it would be on a boat, how we would fare in the raids we would make for the Jarl. Whether we would sail and fight together or be separated.

In time, the snow melted away and the first crocus bloomed, its bright green shoots pushing through the loamy earth to reveal a beautiful, vibrant purple flower. It was the herald of change.

"The Jarl arrived yesterday evening on a large, new boat. The fjords are thawed, and he is ready to send ships across the sea. You should see the newly built fleet. They're enormous! Each will carry fifty warriors. He is at Leif's house and has called for you both," Father proudly announced the day after I found that flower. He stomped the mud off his leather boots and removed his fur, soaked with rain. "He's likely to send the two of you out on the first ship, considering its size."

Hodor's eyes widened as he tugged on his boots and fastened a fur around his neck and shoulders. I wasn't quite as eager to receive the Jarl's command, and even less eager to pledge my life and allegiance to him.

He was one man. And while he ruled over us and I'd been taught to respect him, I didn't agree with much that he did. Even so, I couldn't avoid the words he would pry from my lips any more than I could avoid the stench of the animals about to be turned out of our home. Not if I wanted to stay in the clan and live upon his lands.

I shrugged a deerskin around my shoulders and pinned it beneath my chin, following Hodor as he pushed out the door. My mother's eyes locked with mine before I ducked outside to follow him. I closed the door behind me and bumped into a frozen Hodor.

He stared over the fjord, or what we could see of it. It was completely enshrouded with a fog so thick that even though I could hear the choppy water, I could not see it, even as it lapped along the shore.

I knew instinctively he was trying to convince himself the fog was nothing, though he'd dreamed of this fog many months before. I stared into it, wondering if I might see a pack of giant wolves racing toward us.

"Let's go, Liv," he prodded, striding decidedly toward the future he wished to claim.

The mud was half-frozen. It would've been easier to walk on if it were a few degrees colder or warmer, but this in-between slush froze my feet and made them wet. I kept watch on the water, a feeling of unease coiling into my stomach like *Jörmungandr*, the great serpent of Midgard, son of the trickster Loki.

The Jarl's proud ships were disappointingly hidden within the mist. Though if they were as large as Father described, I thought I'd catch a glimpse of them anyway. Hodor's steps were rushed. He craved the Jarl's approval in a way I didn't. Or perhaps he wanted to flee the constant sight of the all-encompassing fog and the dark memory contained within.

We hurried past the few houses scattered along the shore onto the ridge where Leif had built a large home, which was where the Jarl was staying. To be honest, I was glad our house was quaint and stuffed full. I wouldn't have enjoyed hosting him, though most coveted the opportunity. Not only would I be worried that my actions weren't gracious enough, I'd have to wait on him hand and foot, bending to his every whim. Jarl was king to us and as his subjects, we were subject to his laws and punishments. Some of the latter made even my iron stomach turn.

The front door of Leif's house was grand, a small eve held up with sturdy beams he'd dragged from the forest and carved by hand. Leif was a master woodworker, and he had a separate building behind his home in which to work. Even though he also farmed, his gardens were far smaller than everyone else's. He had more than enough work to keep his hands full of wood-carving tools and little time to work the land, so if someone needed something from him, he bartered with them for food.

He was a good man, a fair man, Father said. He'd replaced our door just last year when the winter cold had withered it on the hinges.

I turned to look back over the shrouded fjord as we paused at the threshold, squinting when I thought I saw something in the pale, dense depths. I blinked and it was gone. My eyes raked over and over the spot where I thought I'd seen darkness silhouetted against the mist... but nothing was there.

From the fjord, a raven cried. I let out the breath I'd been holding as the animal appeared, then disappeared again as it flew over the water, through the fog.

"Leif!" Hodor called out as we paused outside his door.

There was no answer, so Hodor pushed open the front door. The blissful warmth from inside hit my cheeks and I shuddered.

"Come in," a familiar voice answered.

Our chieftain looked comfortable, seated at a table in the largest house in our small village. Animal skins were laid out on his bench and his hands were wrapped around a cup of steaming liquid. A fire roared and I noticed our neighbor's animals had been turned outside earlier than Father normally allowed, no doubt to spare the Jarl their stench.

Jarl Urðr was not a large man like Father or Arne, but he was a fierce fighter. Father once told me he'd become Jarl, not because of his strength but because of his cunning ways. I retorted that only the weak had to rely on such skills, earning a rare pat on the head.

Little did I know that being cunning was how Hodor would earn his shield from him.

The Jarl's hair at the root was white, leaching to a ruddy brown, neatly combed and pulled back from his face. His broad, white beard hung to cover his stomach. His clothes were finer than anything any man in our village could afford. Like the witch, there were chunky rings on each of his fingers, sometimes more than one squeezed onto the sausage-like appendages. His complexion was mottled and his nose and ears had begun to sag from age.

"Young Hodor Eriksson!" he greeted my brother with a booming voice, waving him forward. I wondered where his hosts, our neighbors, were since the house was otherwise empty. "Come and sit with me." Hodor followed his command with a puffed out chest, sitting on the bare bench across the table from our leader. He glanced at me, eyes beseeching me to sit, too, even though I had not been addressed. I eased onto the bench.

I wondered if he thought I killed the witch, or perhaps ran her off. I was the last to see her, as far as he knew. My palms began to sweat.

"You must be Liv. I've heard a great deal about you," he said, his sky blue eyes sharpening. I wondered if the völva told him more than she was able to tell me. Worse than that, I wondered if she told him the same thing my grandmother had seen of my future. That I would one day become *a scourge upon the earth.*

I supposed if shield maidens were scourges, I would certainly be that. A scourge was only considered as such if you received their wrath.

"You both fought well at Winternights," he began, crossing his hands in front of him and leaning forward. "I couldn't believe how quickly you bested Erik," he praised Hodor. "Or how interesting your strategy to win against Hella was, Liv. Tell me, did you plan it beforehand or did the notion to strike her hand come to you during the match?"

"I did not plan anything beforehand," I rasped, clearing my throat afterward. I'd seen an opportunity, realized it might be the only one I would get, and took it.

Jarl Urðr stared at me in silence, making me fight the urge to squirm under his hawk-eyed scrutiny.

Suddenly the door flew open, the force ricocheting the heavy wood against the wall. A tall stranger stepped inside, his shield up and axe raised. His greasy, sweat-soaked hair hung to his shoulders as he panted in the doorway, a sinister smile spreading across his lips.

This can't be happening again. Not again. My first thought was of our younger siblings, and then I realized we were unarmed, save for the knives tucked into our boots. A knife would not stop a swinging axe.

Working together, Hodor and I overturned the bench we'd sat upon and made for the fire, each taking up an iron poker. Bile burnt the back of my throat with the memory of how I plunged one of these through another attacker's stomach when I was far younger.

"Who are you?" the Jarl barked, standing up to face the intruder.

The man barreled into the room, letting out a battle cry before slashing at Hodor, then me, then the Jarl who had drawn his own sword. As the man focused on the Jarl, Hodor and I circled behind him and stabbed him from behind. I thrust the cold poker close to his spine and Hodor skewered his heart. He fell to his knees, the iron handles sticking out of his back.

Hodor rushed to the Jarl's side as he collapsed, but quickly realized the attacker had dealt a death blow. Blood seeped from the middle of our king's stomach and cascaded to the floor, pouring in thick ribbons to soak the boards. Hodor held his hand tightly to the wound to staunch the flow, but it was too late. Even the Jarl knew it. His sharp eyes slid to me. "You've earned your shields," he said, a bloody bubble growing and popping on his lips. "Go and fight. Odin calls me home."

I jerked the poker from the attacker's back, tearing through muscle and spine with a sickening sound. Then I ran toward our home, assuming Hodor would follow. From the ridge, I could see the Jarl's great ships because they were burning, towering columns of smoke reaching dark tendrils into the sky. I couldn't see the fight unfolding below, but the roofs of the two houses between Leif's and Arne's were already aflame, the fire ripping across the thatching as if it were a live beast desperate to devour those secured within their walls. Snarls and yells rose from the valley. The sounds of metal biting metal rose, startling the birds in the trees.

I pushed harder, pumping my arms, sliding down the hill where the mud would allow, pushing far past the point of fiery leg muscles and lungs.

Standing in front of his home, Arne fought off a man with an axe in one hand and a sword in the other. While he was occupied, another man snuck behind the house and threw a torch to the roof. The flame caught and spread swiftly. Within seconds, the entire structure was engulfed.

The sun burnt off the fog little by little, but our house was still too far away and the fog too thick around it for me to see. It was not on fire, though. Not yet. There was no smoke.

A scream rose from the valley. From our home. Mother's scream.

My pulse pounded in my ears.

"Hodor!"

"I heard!"

60

They're not dead. There is still hope. Fear tore through my veins, heating them and pushing me to run faster. I wished I could grow Valkyrie wings and fly to them... I wished I could cut down our enemies from above, to slay every bastard laying waste to our homes and cutting down our clansmen.

Hodor raced past me. In his strong grip was the iron implement he'd used alongside me as we killed the man who killed our Jarl.

An unfamiliar ship bobbed in the harbor, the currents pushing it flush against the shore. The sail was white with a black figure painted on it. A wolf.

Gods, no.

Smoke poured from every direction, mingling with the thick fog our enemy had hidden within. Screams rent the air and a chorus of anguish ripped from the throats of men, women, and children. I pleaded with the Aesir to keep my family alive. We were almost there...

I pushed myself to keep up with Hodor, pulling the knife from my boot and preparing to fight for them. I imagined the pale hair of my little brother, the delicate bones of my sisters. Their laughter reduced to terror and shrieks.

Fear fueled my steps. Not honor or pride.

Pure, unadulterated fear.

And boatloads of fury.

Hodor let out a guttural roar. He worked himself into a rage that already boiled beneath my skin, one I wanted to keep every ounce of, refusing to unleash it until I faced the enemy who had come to kill us all.

We ran past our clansmen, past our neighbors to our home, toward Mother's scream. But by the time we got close, she'd gone quiet.

Everything had.

Hodor and I ground to a stop as two men as tall as Father exited our house, throwing a torch onto the thatched straw roof. I started toward it, quickly realizing it was too late.

It caught fast, despite the dampness that had seeped into everything it touched. Our roof was soon ablaze, bleeding plumes of smoke into the clear, blue sky.

There was no sound but the whoosh of fast-spreading flame. No lambs bleated. No horses whinnied. They had all been slaughtered. Their fur and wool was stained red, their blood seeping crimson into the brook that emptied into the fjord.

Hodor held his hand out from across the earth. We were still too far away. He realized it the moment I did. The stone in his throat bobbed when he swallowed.

I took a step toward the house, but Hodor stopped me by making a cutting gesture. Three more men emerged from the animal pens, their swords and clothes coated in blood. One of the attackers' eyes danced between us as if he wasn't sure whom to kill first. When they settled on Hodor, my stomach dropped.

"Who are you?" my brother gritted.

I couldn't stop staring as the flames danced on our roof and a thin section at the top caved in. Nothing inside stirred. Through the doorway, I saw nothing but billowing plumes of smoke.

The man ticked his head to the side, revealing three puckered scars on his forehead, one bisecting his golden brow. "My name is Fenris Wolf. My father was killed by someone in your village after he attended Winternights to celebrate with you. I have come to avenge him. Since no one will admit to murdering him, I claim *all* your lives as retribution. His was worth much more, I assure you."

"Mother!" I shouted, easing closer. No sounds came from inside. I knew in my heart she hadn't fled. Even for the children's sake. She would have fought and defended our home to her dying breath, as would Father.

Fenris Wolf's eyes flicked to me.

Hodor made another motion to get my attention. *Run,* he mouthed.

I shook my head. *No.*

I couldn't leave him. I wouldn't flee like a coward. Valhalla be damned, he was my brother and I would stand beside him. If he took another step forward, so would I. If he raised his weapon, I would raise mine. If he fought and died, I would fight and die at his side.

Maybe that was what being a warrior, being brave, really meant. It meant staying loyal no matter what. It meant facing Fenris Wolf, and my fate, without flinching away.

I gripped my knife tightly with my left hand. In my right was the poker.

Fenris was neither as old as Father, nor as young as me and Hodor. His beard and the tips of his long hair were soaked with blood, his forehead splattered with it. He adjusted his grip on his sword, holding his shield in front of him, speculatively eyeing the iron in Hodor's hand and in mine. Eyeing my knife.

Hodor gritted his teeth. "For the love of the gods, RUN!" he roared at me. But my feet did not move. I refused to leave him. I swallowed thickly as agony slid over his features along with a final plea.

I focused back on our enemy.

Despite his pale hair, Fenris's eyes were dark.

"Is this your home, boy?" Fenris asked Hodor, gesturing to our burning house, slowly easing toward us, his men falling in step behind him like a pack.

The ship that bobbed in the fjord floated sideways. The Jarl's favorite ship's bow had been fashioned to look like a dragon, complete with a ferocious head to lead the way through the misty waters. The head of Fenris's ship was a wolf, complete with a gaping maw and canines ready to snap.

A shiver slid down my spine. My brother dreamed this. All of it. Down to the ship in the form of a wolf that sailed across the sea…

I gripped the poker, knowing it couldn't withstand a blow from Fenris's thick sword, and held tight to my knife, wishing my shield wasn't inside the burning house. Wishing I could hear my mother, father, or siblings inside…

"I asked you a question," he said firmly, addressing Hodor again. He'd moved closer, too close to Hodor without me even noticing.

But Hodor noticed and was ready. "Liv, run!" he shouted.

Finished with their bloody chores, the enemy clansmen had gathered on the shore to watch us die. There was no way we could fight this many men. I knew we would not survive this attack.

"Is this your sister?" Fenris taunted him with an arched brow, hooking his thumb toward me.

Hodor answered by lunging forward, slicing the tip of the poker across Fenris's neck and chest. The poker cracked his skin but left nothing more than a small, jagged gouge. Blood slowly pooled in the wound, then oozed down the skin of his throat.

With a slow, terrible grin, Fenris brought his hand to the spot my brother had left. He looked at the blood on his fingers and dragged them across the leather breastplate he wore, an intricate, howling wolf carved into the dark hide.

Then Fenris laughed. His clansmen laughed with him. My skin prickled.

Hodor launched at Fenris again, but Fenris easily deflected the blow and tore the poker from Hodor's hand in the same moment he launched my brother at his men, who had moved steadily closer without us noticing. They held his arms and hair tight before Fenris used his sword to cut my brother's throat in a sickeningly sharp slit.

I couldn't move. Couldn't breathe.

For a moment Hodor was still, his eyes wide and rolling in fear. Then a terrible gurgling sound came from his throat.

"Hodor!" I yelled, running toward him but stopping short. The sight of blood spurting and flowing like a river down the front of his shirt before they let him tumble to the ground told me he was already dead.

I didn't want to die.

My heart thundered and I wondered if Thor felt the tremors from Asgard. I pondered if Odin had already come for Hodor, if the Valkyrie were already dragging his spirit into the sky. I wondered how this could be real. It didn't *feel* real, yet my heart knew it was. It started grieving for him the moment he fell, the second he stopped moving, the instant his chest went still.

Fenris's eyes were focused on me. "You're a pretty thing." He stepped closer, pinning me between him and the men who killed Hodor. Angry tears filled my eyes. I wasn't supposed to cry.

I should have run like Hodor asked. I might have been able to outrun the behemoths. I knew this country and they did not. Either way, my brother would still be lying dead. I gulped in several deep breaths, unable to settle my heart or get enough air to satisfy my lungs.

I don't want to die.

I wasn't supposed to feel this way. I was supposed to crave a warrior's death. But I wasn't sure death was what Wolf had in mind just yet... A glint of something far more torturous glimmered in his eyes. I stared at his scar. It looked as though he'd been clawed by a wolf, and I wondered if the mark was accidental or if it had been put there on purpose.

"Come along," he said, reaching his hand out for me like a child. I raised my poker.

With one deft blow of his sword, he cut the metal off just above my hand.

65

I threw what was left of the iron to the shore and transferred my knife to my dominant hand, ready to fight again. I would fight him, and I would not stop fighting until I lay on the beach like Hodor or like my family inside our house. I knew their bodies were in there… enshrouded by the smoke that billowed out.

As a larger section of roof fell in with a loud crash, I flinched from the sound.

My teeth chattered.

The young wolf eased closer, extending his hand. I sliced it, raking the blade cleanly over his palm. He hissed and clutched it to his chest, then flexed it and watched as his blood dripped onto the rocky shore.

"You didn't learn from your brother's misfortune." He let out a mirthless laugh. "That was the worst mistake of your life. Your very *short* life…"

His sword sliced the air, bringing that horrible noise to my ears.

I tried to fight him, but my knife blade was no match for the edge of his sword. His blade bit into my side, lodging there. He jerked it free, raking it from my back through my stomach.

I couldn't move. I couldn't scream.

My breath was caught in my chest. I felt the weight of his sword. Felt it tear through my skin, through muscle, but stunned by the pain, I could feel nothing.

Suddenly, like a gust of tormented wind, I felt everything in a series of blind flashes.

I sucked in a deep, wet breath and clutched my side to keep my body from falling apart, knowing I had been cleaved in the middle. My lips fell open and my breath escaped all at once.

I fell to my knees, then onto my side. The pain made a cold sweat pebble over my skin. A raven swam through my vision as I stared up at the sky, unable to turn my head to face the one who'd cut me down. Were they sent by Odin? Was he coming for me, too?

Fenris's face came into focus. His scars. Three lines of puckered, shiny skin. "You're very pale," he noted, mocking me as he crouched down to draw one of my tears onto his finger. He brought it to his mouth and tasted, then smiled.

"Kill me, you coward," I managed to rasp, my lips straining to release the words.

He shook his head. "You will die knowing that you and *your people* will never enter Valhalla. The Aesir hate your clan *almost* as much as I do. Why do you think they sent me here? They filled my sails with their breath and pushed me across the sea. The gods gave *me* their blessing, and now that I have avenged my father and killed his killers, I fear nothing."

I blinked up at his cool, dark eyes and watched him lazily drift in and out of focus. "But you will..." I weakly promised. "I *curse* you, Fenris Wolf."

"Is that so?" He smiled cruelly. He stood and took hold of my arms, dragging me toward the shore, my side screaming with the tugging and with every bump and rock I was hauled over. I screamed as my body was torn further apart. My head lolled, eyes catching on the thick trail of my blood he painted over the land as he arced toward the fjord.

His boots splashed into the shallows and he left me right at the water's edge where the icy water bit at my head, dragging my hair and braids into it.

"If you don't die first, the tide will carry you away for the creatures of the deep to devour – if the carrion don't eat you bite by bite, that is," he promised quietly, crouching and tasting another of my tears. "They're starving when they wake after such a harsh winter, such as the one we've had."

He stood, a dark, undefined form silhouetted against the bright sky. At his command, his men trudged toward their ship, which had drifted close to the shore. Or maybe he only dragged me here so I could watch them sling themselves inside, hang their shields along the rail, and take up the oars. The wolf's head bobbed menacingly overhead, just as its master had.

The wake from their rowing made the water choppy. It lapped at my face.

Maybe the gods did favor them and wish us all dead...

They cut through the water soundlessly and disappeared as fast as they'd come. Soon, I could no longer hear oars pushing the water or orders being shouted. Nothing but the lapping of waves and silence.

Tears fell, though I wasn't sure how I could still be alive when my entire family was dead. I cried for the children, knowing full well how terrified they must've been.

My body relaxed, blissfully falling numb.

Feeling tired.

It was hard to keep my eyes open.

But then I heard the fire still crackling from our home. I heard the stillness. The lack of laughter. The splashing waves of the fjord. I heard the flapping of wings, the cry of a raven. More than likely it was there to feed from the dead, but if there was any chance it was one of Odin's, Muninn or Huginn, come to look over us until he arrived...

I licked my cracked, dry lips. "Odin, save me," I mouthed, staring into the bright white sky.

The bird did not come close. It didn't soar over me, but kept to the trees nearby, crying out incessantly.

"Freyja," I tried, but the goddess did not answer or come for me.

I attempted another. "Frigg? Goddess of wisdom..."

My vision became hazy around the edges.

"Thor. Please. Is this the fate you wanted for me? I refuse it. I deserve better. We *all* did." My voice was rusty, barely there. Not numb, but drained, like my body of blood.

A colder wind cut across me.

The fjord was slowly rising, gurgling at my ears, filling them with water.

The Aesir weren't going to save me.

But maybe one other would consider it… "Sku—"

I choked on her name.

Skuld… Fenris Wolf deserves a fate worse than death. I curse him. I curse his men. I curse his clan and his ship and his name. And if you save me, I will end him. I will battle him, cut him down, carve him up and let the pigs devour him.

Weave a new destiny for me. Weave a future where I can taste his tears and watch the light bleed from his eyes.

The frigid water rose to cover my throat and flowed over my eyes. Only my nose and mouth remained above it. It rose to my lips. I clamped them shut.

Fenris knew he'd dealt a death blow, but he left me like this so I would have to slowly endure, knowing I would drown before succumbing.

I refuse this fate. Weave a new thread, I demanded. *Stop Fenris Wolf. Let me be your hands. Let me be your shield, your blade. I will live as your vengeance. Then I will be content to die.*

Water trickled into my nose.

He left me to drown.

To die.

To give up.

I refuse this fate.

70

SEVEN

A strong hand clamped onto my ankles. Water drained from my eyes and ears. I was too weak to cough. My hair dragged the ground as I looked up. Two ravens circled one another; one black as night, one white as the snow capping the mountains.

Odin?

I saw no great wings flapping. No warrior woman carrying me into the sky. The Valkyries hadn't claimed me yet. Was he near, or was he claiming Hodor first? Father and Mother? Gunnar, Ingrid, and Solvi? Our clansmen? The Jarl? Would they be chosen to feast in Valhalla with the Alfather, too?

The back of my head bumped the ground as I was dragged back across the pebbles. I couldn't raise it. Couldn't tell who or what had saved me. But pain flared in my side, which meant I wasn't dead. Yet.

"Liv Eriksson," a thousand voices hissed over me, "I accept your bargain."

"Who are you?" I wasn't sure if I said or thought the words as the person kept dragging me. Finally, they released my ankles and my legs and feet hit the ground, completely limp.

"Be gone, Odin," the voices shouted. "Do not be greedy. I claim her as *my own*." The pale and dark crows circling overhead flapped their wings slowly, so very slowly, then flew away.

Who was brave enough, or strong enough, to chase away a god?

A form crouched beside me, moving closer until they blocked the clouded, bright sky. My eyes widened as I sucked in a long, terrified breath.

"You dared call my name? You refuse death?" she asked, pushing the tattered, dark hood away from her face. My lips gaped. She was me, but somehow looked a few years older. She wore similar honey-blonde hair, down to the braids Hodor had twisted along either side of my head and down the center, my tattered apron-dress, just a little too small at the hips and chest. She wore my glacial eyes and raked them over me, catching on the wound cut deeply into my left side.

"How?" I whispered. "How do you look like me?"

She stared, never blinking. "You begged for a future my sister did not want for you. I almost didn't come for you. You were foolish to refuse me when I sent *my own* to you. If *you* had taken my völva's life, we wouldn't be speaking now. I would have come to carve a new völva from your flesh and bone to replace the one taken from me."

"Skuld," my dried mouth formed.

"Yes, girl. Skuld. And I come to you in *this* form to answer your plea and reveal your destiny. I wear the skin of the woman you are destined to be, and *I accept your bargain*," she said slowly, intentionally. The power of those words washed over me. "Fenris Wolf is destined to bring Ragnarök to our people, to every land and every clan in his bid for power, and

72

you are destined to stop him. Your mother warned you that her mother, *my own* and your very blood, said you would be a scourge upon this earth." Her lips curved upward – my lips. Full and strong and knowing... Wise lips. "And you will be. You will be *my* scourge. You will protect the future of the warriors of the north, and you will wipe Fenris Wolf and his entire clan from Midgard, one sharp blow at a time."

I was dying. I could not fight for her, or even for myself. Though I desperately wanted to untether the nearest boat and row until my arms couldn't row anymore, to chase down the wolves and make them bleed, to skin them and wear their pelts so that all might see what became of those who took away everything I held dear, I didn't have the strength.

My skin was cold. My bones were frigid. If my body could have, it would be trembling furiously, making me look like a fish flopping just out of reach of the water. But I could not so much as quiver.

Yet because of Skuld, I had not died. I felt the steady thrum of power pulsing from her. It tickled my nose and skin.

"You will *not* die this day, Liv. I claim you. I call you *my own*. Today, you become my eyes, my hands, my fists and my fury. I will weave a thread and call it Liv. I will place her through the needle's eye and point her at our common enemy, and I will watch her pierce them in penance for all the havoc they hope to wreak. Havoc the norns have forbidden and not ordained."

As my eyes drifted closed, I felt the ends of her hair drape onto my shoulder.

"Völva," she whispered, her cold lips brushing my ear. "I will knit you back together piece by piece and make you stronger than you were before *he* cut you down. Then I will show you how to end him."

My eyes opened, then fluttered closed as I tried to focus on what she was doing. She plucked long hairs from her head… hairs that looked identical to mine. Then she took a needle out of a small leather pouch. "What are you doing?" I slurred.

She smiled at me with my mouth and with my voice, told me to keep still.

I screamed as her needle began the difficult work of stitching my flesh together. I screamed until my voice went raw, until Skuld disappeared and nothing but quiet darkness remained.

I woke lying on the ground on my stomach, gritty rock and sand biting into my cheek. I raised my head from the earth to see tiny plumes of smoke trickling into the air in the distance, but closer, I saw that everything had been incinerated. I could smell the charred wood in my hair and clothes. I used my palms to push myself up onto my knees and saw Hodor lying dead, his mouth open, eyes unfocused, staring at me.

It wasn't yet sunset when I stood up, as clumsy as a newborn fawn, but I wasn't sure how long I'd lain on the shore. My side did not ache or burn. Through the gaping hole of my dress, I felt my skin and a new scar, clean and straight and healed.

The mud on my leather boots had dried. It crumbled from the soles as I walked toward my brother, holding a hand over my nose. The stench was overwhelming. I gagged twice on the way to Hodor.

A tear leaked from my eye as I approached him. Stray hairs had escaped his braids and flailed helplessly in the soft breeze. Flies swarmed him. I shooed them from his eyes and mouth. I swatted the air, but they only buzzed around and returned.

"I'll bury you properly, Hodor. I will," my voice broke. "I swear it." I crouched down and reached my thumb and forefinger toward his face, closing his wide eyes. From me. From the flies. From the world he could no longer see. His soft lashes brushed my fingers and I pulled my hand away. "I'm sorry. I'm sorry I couldn't stop them. I'm sorry I wasn't strong enough," I cried. Sobs poured from my chest, stemming from a chasm that sprouted tendrils so dark and full of hatred I couldn't believe I hadn't noticed them before now. "I will make sure I'm strong enough now."

I hated Fenris Wolf with every fiber of my being.

I stood and strode toward the house, leaving the sickening sound of flies buzzing behind me.

What if the children survived? What if they escaped to the mountain to hide? They must be terrified.

If I had been with them, I would've pushed them to safety. Surely Father and Mother either sent them for help or told them to hide and stay hidden until Hodor or I came for them. Hope began to bubble in my chest as I rushed toward the house.

"Ingrid! Gunnar! Solvi!" I yelled through cupped hands, toward the near mountain and the tree under which Tor was buried. My feet carried me closer to our home, though I kept watch on the mountainside for movement. There was only a stray white cat crouched in the fallen leaves. None of my siblings emerged. I yelled for each of them again, louder this time.

What if they can't hear me? What if they ran to another village for help?

The roof of our home was gone, parts of the walls, too. The jagged, charred wooden planks that were left jutted from the ground like a desiccated rib cage. The new door Leif crafted for us had been burned away. Only charred pieces limply attached at the hinges remained. I stepped over what used to be the threshold and surveyed the stone hearth that was always burning, the heart of our home, where Mother baked and cooked our meals, lying cold and dormant. Not even a wisp of smoke rose from it.

I walked to the left, toward the far corner where our beds used to be. The beds were burned away, but in the ashes of the bed Hodor and Gunnar shared lay Gunnar's favorite bone flute, charred and bleached whiter from the heat of the fire, but intact. I plucked it from the ash and clutched it tightly.

From the bed I shared with Solvi, I saw a row of teeth… from Solvi's bone comb, the one I used to brush her unruly curls. I raked the row over the pad of my thumb, then traced the fine designs Father had carved into it.

A tear leaked from my eye.

While our home had always been dim and dark, it was full of life. Now that it was laid bare to the sun above, it was empty, full of ash and despair, the fragment of dreams that burnt away.

"Solvi!" I yelled again, my voice shrilling.

Near what used to be our dining table lay a charred, round shield. Swirled ochre and dark gray clung to the edges, nearest the ring of iron Father had bent around it. I reached out for it, finding my shield laying beneath it. It wasn't singed. No flame had touched it because Hodor's protected it.

As he tried to protect me.

And his shield died in battle, just as my brother had.

"Gunnar!" I turned and yelled weakly toward the mountain looming above me. Clutching his flute and Solvi's comb in one hand, I took up both shields and held them against my chest.

"Ingri—!"

My words died when I saw my mother's charred legs and feet lying just inside where the door to her bedroom used to be. I rushed to her, dropping to my knees, dropping all the things I'd salvaged.

I screamed.

And I would not stop screaming.

Father lay dead beside her, his body also half-burned and still smoldering. The children lay on their bed. They had been slain before the fire took them. Solvi's tiny chest was split open, the edges of the wound charred. Her soft, blonde hair was burned away.

Ingrid... her arm and side...

Gunnar's neck, chopped from the side, almost severed.

I couldn't look at them.

I could only clench my eyes tightly shut as I rocked and screamed.

EIGHT

I rowed a small fishing boat that should have been manned by at least six from where it was tethered along the shore below the ridge where Leif's house sat. Behind it, I towed another even smaller one, fastened together with the strongest rope I could find, one I took from Arne's animal pen. He'd used it to tie a sick heifer to the fence the other day to keep her apart from the herd. The heifer was dead, like everything else in our village. She no longer needed it. The blood-soaked fibers of the rope were taut, creaking as it strained between the bobbing vessels.

The Wolfs tried to burn the boats, but something put out the flame. Each bore char marks on their hulls, but the wood wasn't damaged. I just needed them to float, for the rope to hold… for a short trip.

The water was calm, gently lapping the boat's bottom as I urged it along.

As I rowed… Rowed… Rowed…

After leaving the massacre at my house I checked every house belonging to my clan. There were no survivors, and nothing remained but ash, bone, and metal from buckles and weapons the fire didn't consume. I couldn't bury those who were already ash, but I could bury our clansmen who had been left on the shore to rot – Arne and his brother, Olav. They and my family were all that hadn't been consumed by dust and ash.

I will give them... a proper... burial... I vowed with each stroke.

The salty air stung my already stinging eyes, but I rowed until the bottom of the boat ran aground near the spot where Hodor lay, the wooden planks raking across the rocky shore. I threw the moor line over the prow.

I'd seen my share of burials and remembered Oskar's with disturbing clarity, but I'd never had to bury anyone myself. I jumped over the side of the boat and landed in the frigid water with a splash. The sudden coldness bit into my calves and dragged at my skirts. The material at my side gaped open where it had been torn by the thrust of a sword; it was stiff to the hem where my blood had soaked into and dried against the fibers. The wind made what was left of my dress flap like a tattered, useless sail.

I walked to Hodor, unsure of how to go about this, wishing I could hear his voice one more time. Watch him laugh and toss a stick to Tor, who would bolt wherever it landed, tail wagging. Hodor would laugh and call him back and Tor would eagerly jump into Hodor's hands, waiting to be praised and scratched for a job well done.

I missed his presence more than anything. Hodor was always there. Dependable. True. Honorable. And despite it being a trait that was considered by most to be worthless, Hodor was kind.

The two of us should be leaving on a longship together, off on a grand new adventure. I shouldn't be burying him.

My heart ached with a soul-wrenching pain that wouldn't allow it to rest.

I tried to lift his arm, but his body was stiff and I was afraid that if I picked him up, he might crumble. His was the only one of our family whose body remained whole, though he'd begun to smell and flies still buzzed and picked at his wounds.

Anger welled in my stomach at the sight of those buzzing black bodies.

"Leave him!" I shouted. The flies departed and did not return.

My heart raced at the sudden quietness. The droning served as an incessant reminder of what I lost, and now that it had finally ceased, all I heard was the water of the fjord and the ships' hulls occasionally scraping the rock beneath. I was consumed with an inferno of hatred and something even more powerful that simmered beneath my skin.

Hodor was larger than me, built like Father. I bit my lip as I drew near, trying and failing not to cry again as I crouched beside him. My head hit my chest. "Skuld, help me lift him."

The hair at the back of my neck stood on end.

I hooked an arm under his knees, slid the other under his back, and rose. Somehow, he was no heavier than a feather. I silently thanked her. Tears flowed as I waded into the water and placed him gently in the shallow, bobbing boat. It was hard to see through my tears, and my shuddering sobs made it hard to breathe.

Holding to the rail, I tried to stop the boat's rocking and calm myself, stop the tears, and get my breath. When I lifted my hand from the wood, a charred imprint of my fingers and palm remained.

My breath caught.

I clutched my hand to my chest and then dunked it into the water, where steam wafted from the warmth of my skin against the chill of the frosty fjord.

I tore myself from the water and forced my steps back to our home where I carried my family, one by one, and laid them in the boat with Hodor. As I did, I realized that nothing, no god, not even Skuld herself, could stop the grief I felt from consuming me. The state of their bodies in their damaged, broken state shattered my heart so that it lay in pieces as they did.

At least Hodor was whole. Mother, Father, Gunnar, Ingrid, and tiny Solvi... were not.

But I collected them and lay them with Hodor.

Father's once strong body threatened to crumble in my arms, while Mother's face was unrecognizable. And I couldn't bear to look at the children. I sifted through memories of them while taking one step at a time toward the boat, trying not to look down at their faces or feel their loosened skin as the motion jostled them.

I was strong as I carried Gunnar and Ingrid, somehow managing not to look. I knew their wounds; they were seared into my mind. Looking would do nothing but hurt me worse, and I wasn't sure I could withstand anything worse right now.

But when I took Solvi into my arms and a tiny, untouched patch of hair tickled my arm, I lost myself. I hugged her to me and sobbed. "I am so sorry, my little bee. I promise to kill the ones who did this to you. I'll make them pay for this a thousand times over. As I do, I hope you watch from the sky from your seat at Odin's table, and that Ingrid is with you toying with your beautiful hair. I hope you see me claim their lives for you and know they'll never come near you again, in body or spirit."

Eventually I managed to let her go and placed her in the boat with the rest of our family. The soft current rocked them as a mother would rock a child to sleep, the very waves death's lullaby.

The charred smell of what was left of my family's cloth-ing, skin, and hair infused itself into my hair. Their blood and fluids seeped into my dress, the last part of them attaching to me.

The burial was all I could give them. Their spirits were elsewhere, but their bodies remained. I would see them buried as warriors, not left to rot for carrion to further tear them apart and scatter over the mountains.

I carried Arne and Olav to their own boat and placed the bodies beside one another, then left them to walk the fields and gather every wildflower I could find. The land hadn't fully woken from winter's clutches and though I combed it, I found only a small bunch that barely filled my palm. I divided the blooms and scattered them in each boat atop the dead.

In our small village we were all karls; not noble, but still free men and women in charge of our own destinies. We were subject to the Jarl's rules as long as we lived on his land, but those were fair enough to follow. Karls were typically buried in the earth to replenish it. When Oskar died, Father insisted he have a ship burial like a noble, a warrior, because he fought and died like one.

Ship burials were reserved for nobles, like the Jarl and his family, but the Jarl was gone and I agreed with my father. My family deserved it as much as he. I knew deep in my heart that this would please my parents and siblings.

Arne and Olav deserved no less.

There was no oil to pour over them, so I could only hope my instincts were right when I untethered the ships, loosening the knot I'd made. I clasped the railing of Arne and Olav's ship and allowed the blistering hatred I felt for Fenris and his men to flow through my veins, through my palms, and onto the boards. In moments, fire licked and popped, the eye-watering dry heat searing my face. The ship was fully ablaze when I pushed it out into the water. It drifted into the deep but ambled left, toward Arne's house, as if it knew who it carried… and honored their sacrifice.

I slogged to my family's ship, closing my eyes as I gripped the rail until the wood scorched and caught fire. The flames spread across the ship with a vengeance – *mine*.

When I could no longer stand the heat, I dug my feet into the water's rocky underbelly and pushed the heavy ship into the fjord.

Sitting on the boulder we'd perched on more times than I could count, I curled my knees to my chest and listened to the wood of each ship pop and groan. I heard the flames lick and roar and consume, followed by the gurgle of angry water that had risen a few feet with the tide.

Fire caught on the rope tethering the boats and ate it in two. The vessels drifted from one another, bobbing over the water as helplessly as I felt.

The sky dimmed, fading into deep purple before sliding into indigo. The stars winked above, as if they honored the dead. The only clouds in the sky were from the twin plumes emerging from the fjord. And I, the only one alive to bear witness to their deaths, watched as they burned.

The small boat carrying Arne and Olav was the first to sink.

One of the sides crumbled, allowing water to seep in. The sea overtook the ship and it slid beneath the small, now-choppy waves with a hiss, releasing a final puff of steam.

I watched the ship my family was in burn in an unwavering blaze, a flaming torch over the dark water, feeding smoke into the midnight sky. But the beams never collapsed, and the boat didn't capsize. It bobbed and crackled, slowly drifting closer to the shore as the hours of my grisly vigil passed. The sky progressed from indigo to the blackest navy and a harsh wind began to roar from the mountain; wind that should have carried them further away instead of bringing them toward me...

I stared at the flames still licking far into the sky, vowing not to move until I knew the exact spot they slipped beneath the water. I needed to remember – for them, for me – so I could describe it to Fenris Wolf as I slowly tore him apart.

So I could still see the ripples, as I could for Oskar.

A sudden gale streamed over the water and pushed the ship closer to me, the silhouette of the serpent head protruding from the bow seeming to coil and stretch toward me. My fingers touched the iron snake wound into my braid.

I stood and prepared to push the boat out of the shallows, jumping down from the boulder and wading into the fjord. The wind blew my hair and stiffly-dried clothing back, plastering it to my body as the bottom half of me was soaked through. The boat raced across the surface as if called by my presence, stopping before me. When my hand stopped it from coming further ashore, the flames died with a whoosh.

My heart thundered.

Somehow the ship's wood hadn't been touched by my flames. The hewn planks weren't charred. The ship looked exactly as it had before I pushed it into the water many hours ago, except my family's bodies were gone and, in the hull, lay nothing but ash and bright white, intact bones that shone starkly in the moonlight.

"How?"

A shiver ran up my spine. This was an offering from Skuld. I could feel it in my blood.

"There is power in words," the völva had said. *"Power in blood…"*

There is power in rage, in death, and in ash.

There is power in shield and ink and bone.

The words rushed over me like a stiff gust of wind, her voice smooth as silk in my ear.

Skuld promised to guide me, and I allowed her to direct my steps. I ran to the garden behind our house and took up a small pot and lid I'd told Ingrid she could use to make mud cakes with, then brought them back to the fjord where I rinsed the pot and lid. Twilight painted the sky from the darkest navy to a slightly softer azure shade, slowly fading to lavender streaked with golden clouds. As the colorful tapestry unfolded above me, I sifted through the ash and removed the bones of my loved ones, then scooped their ashes into the pot, thankful they all fit inside.

This was how I would take them with me.

A bind rune formed in my mind, stroke by careful stroke, consisting of a complex line of protection runes, some I recognized and one I instinctively knew belonged to Skuld. I wet my finger, dipped it into the ash, and drew the rune line on the ash pot. A slash of a line with two intertwined arrows, one pointing east, one pointing west… Skuld's deadly mark at the tip. Then runes for prosperity, protection, perseverance. Three slashes to infuse them with power.

The rune darkened as it settled into the pot's clay. When I tried to smear it, it wouldn't budge. I fitted the lid and sealed it as an image filled my mind.

A young woman with honey-gold hair braided away from her face stared at a choppy, gray sea. The wind tore at her hair and clothes, but she didn't yield. She clutched a tall staff lined with vertebrae. The entire thing undulated like the skeleton of a serpent creeping over the ground. At the top of the staff, a spinner had been formed from fused rib bones.

Angry clouds billowed over her head and lightning slithered across the clouds, forking to the sea and earth all around her. Inexplicably, I felt a deep and profound urge to run to her.

When she turned to look at me over her shoulder, my heart thundered.

The girl was me.

NINE

The greatest mistake Fenris Wolf ever made was not killing me.

Now I would spend my days making sure he regretted it for the rest of his. When he stared up at me, wrath embodied, and drew his last breath, I would make sure he saw the Valkyries comb futilely over the ground, finding his clansmen wanting, finding him undeserving and leaving him to rot atop the earth the way he left Hodor, the way he left my parents, Gunnar, Ingrid, and little Solvi. The way he tried to leave me. He would watch as I came for him. His eyes would widen in the moments before his soul withered and I would drag him to Hel, even if stepping foot there meant I could never ascend to be with my loved ones in the hereafter.

It would all be worth it.

Just to see him burn. With fear and with flame.

88

TEN

Skuld faced me as we sat on our knees on the shore long after the sun had set, the pebbles cradling our knees, shins, and the tops of our feet. The moon shone full overhead, bathing everything it touched in cool, silvery light. The strongest stars flickered overhead, defying the full moon's brightness. The wind off the fjord was cool and crisp, slipping over the land toward the mountains still capped in snow.

Crickets sang from the fields behind the remnants of our homes. It was the first I'd heard them since just after Winternights. Ingrid would have loved to sit out here and listen with me, or to run through the fields to catch them as they sprang over the land. She loved animals, small and large.

The attack was real and my family was gone, but my mind refused to accept it. Every so often I'd catch myself searching the hills for the children, listening for their laughter. It still caught me off guard to peer through the space where the houses should be standing, or to study the fields and find them empty save for the spring grasses that wouldn't be eaten. I wondered when I would be able to look on this place and feel anything but the bone-deep ache in my chest. I wondered when my mind would finally accept it and allow me to look over the voids, for my ears to stop seeking out what they wanted to hear, my eyes what they wanted to see.

Skuld leaned toward me and took hold of my hands. First they were like icicles, but she held on while I adjusted my fingers around hers, and a shift occurred. Her skin heated and the warmth from her fingers flooded my palms and streaked up my forearms to my shoulders, spilling down my back, chest, stomach and legs, until it reached my toes and filled me from their tips to my scalp. The weaver of future wore my ruined dress as if she needed to feel the cruelty of my past. She wore my face, but her expressions and the keenness in her eyes were not mine.

"If Fenris Wolf intended to avenge his father's death with *only* the lives of those from Amrok Village, I would not have saved you, Liv," she asserted bluntly. "But the moment he saw his father's bloated body and the evidence that he'd been murdered, his hatred began to boil. The moment he called for his best warriors and boarded the ship, his intentions were set. Now, his hatred has bubbled over and scalds the innocent. More importantly, his intentions now conflict with mine, something I neither appreciate, nor take lightly."

Something in her tone made me want to squirm, but I kept still.

"What proof did he have that his father was murdered?" I remembered how he looked, washed up on the shore. His skin and lips were tinted blue, but Arne looked him over and found no wounds.

"Your people delivered him home as quickly as they could, but even they couldn't deny the dark bruises that crept and blossomed over his throat as they sailed north."

Mother was strong, but not strong enough to strangle Jarl Wolf with her bare hands. That honor fell to someone else.

While I didn't know who, I wasn't sure it mattered. If one of our warriors died at the hands of someone in another clan, our Jarl would've called for *one* life in exchange for what was lost. He wouldn't have sought to end the lives of an entire people.

The pleasant warmth radiating from her hands into mine ignited, flooding my body with dry heat I could feel inside and out, like my skin was too close to a fire and shrank as it dried over my bones.

My bones felt molten, malleable as iron in a forge.

My blood boiled, and I hated that I knew how Fenris felt when he found the bruised marks on his father's neck.

"That feeling – that anger and fire? You will nurture it inside until it is time to unleash it. Fenris will feel your flame, girl, and he will wish he'd never sparked it."

She looked upon me proudly, and I could see how much I favored my mother, and how much Skuld's frosty ire reminded me of Mother's hardness.

"What I am about to show you will establish your path," she said, squeezing my hands. "You asked me to spare you so that you could end him, but those who fight with him must die, too. You will fight Fenris and you will raise an army to destroy his clan and eradicate the threat they pose to all. It is the only way to put out the fire that burns within you, Liv. And while I could wipe them all off the earth with a whisper, I want to give you this chance. You deserve nothing less. Since creation, never has a human cried out for me, Liv. No one has had the courage to refuse me, let along strike a bargain with me. You are stronger than the mightiest warrior the gods have ever dragged into Asgard, and you are *my own* now. Until the day you die, you belong to me. I will see you victorious. Let go of your fears and trust me."

Trust a norn? My entire life I was taught to fear them, especially Skuld, because she had the power to clip the threads of one's life or to weave a future that was torturous, one that drove a person mad, one that a person would do anything to escape.

The thought of trusting her terrified me, but I was hers now. She'd answered my pleas when no one else would. My life was in her hands before, but it was wholly hers now. I had no other choice than to trust her.

A challenge glittered in her eyes as if she could hear the battle raging inside my mind. This moment would no doubt push and test me. Her full lips parted as she squeezed my hands again encouragingly, then clamped down, holding them tight. Something inside writhed to pull away, but I grasped hers just as tightly and vowed to go wherever she took me.

"Where we are going, Liv, your body will not follow. Release your spirit and come with me."

With a gasp, I realized I was standing with her on the shore, still clinging to her hands while my body sat still as a statue on the shore. My palms lay flat on my thighs. The wind whipped my hair and the torn dress I wore flapped like a blood-stained pennant. My eyes were fixed and unblinking, staring at the spot Skuld had occupied. I looked to her. "Where are you?"

"I'm going with you. I am not spirit and flesh, Liv. I am norn."

She guided me toward the water and stepped onto the waves, urging me forward. Together, we walked across the water until sky and sea merged and I couldn't tell up from down, earth from stars. We might have walked a thousand steps or ten thousand. All was a blur until a ship appeared, bobbing near a distant shore.

"Fenris," I growled, taking in the pristine white fabric of their raised sail.

When it was unfurled, a carefully painted dark silhouette – a howling wolf, its maw raised to the sky – could be seen, one to match the wolf carved into the prow's wooden head. I remembered seeing it afloat on the fjord that fateful morning, bobbing in the shallows. When they sailed onto our shore, they didn't even bother raising the sail. They ran aground hard onto the shore, wedging their ship in the rock. Fenris's men had to work to push it back out onto the water when they left me for carrion.

The fire inside flared. "Where is he?" I growled.

Skuld pointed to the shore where a longhouse's roof burned. Flame crept from the roof down the planks, spreading down the wood, eating it bite by bite.

The sounds of battle raged from the village. I recognized some of the warriors from the attack on my family. Some of the mongrels who encircled my brother now cornered other men and women determined to fight for their homes, their children, their lives...

"Where are we?" I asked, wishing my body was here. Wishing I could cut them all down.

Skuld walked further into the village. "This is Skögar Village."

My brows kissed. "Clan Bjern? How have they wronged the Wolfs?"

The pack took the Bjern man down, hacking at him from all sides. We were so close, his blood spurted toward us. I jerked reflexively to avoid the spray, but it passed through me. Still, I could almost feel its warm wetness on my skin. When he let out a final groan and the breath left his body, the men who killed him didn't notice. They were already scenting their next victim, running together deeper into the village.

I wanted them dead. I started after them when Skuld's hand fell on my shoulder.

"No one in this village wronged Fenris, or his clan," Skuld said carefully. "His thirst for revenge was sated with your clan's death, yet still he massacres. He takes what isn't his, what belongs to me. You know more intimately than most that it is *I* who decides when a life is to end, when a clan is to rise and when one is destined to fall."

My blood boiled. I tore away from Skuld, determined to find Fenris. How could anyone take so many innocent lives?

I found him amid the houses his men were trying to burn, shouting something at his warriors. I walked toward him, every step fueled with wrath and purpose. His eyes caught on me and they widened. He blinked and backed away, then rubbed his lids and looked for me again. This time, his eyes darted left and right. He turned in a fast circle, searching for me.

I wanted him to cower, to run. To know I was coming for him and that I wouldn't stop until he was no more, a wisp of a memory told to frighten children.

He jogged away to help a clansman who was losing the battle he fought against an oak tree of a man. The behemoth nearly took both of their heads off as he cleaved a thick axe in an arc beneath their chins.

I was on my way to him when something remarkable caught my eye.

A small line of young children scurried up the hillside. The older among them held the smaller children's hands and rushed up the hill with them so they didn't wander or get lost. An older man with a pronounced limp guided them into the trees, hurrying them along with gestures and urgent words.

A large hound quietly herded the little ones onto safe paths as a trio of young warriors from Bjern poured down the hillside, clashing with the Wolf raiders who had finally cut down everyone in the valley below and were chasing after the kids. They would've killed the limping man if the three hadn't reached him in time.

The hound pounced at one of the Wolf brutes, clamping his jaw onto one of the attacker's arms and dragging him to the ground. He yelped when the Wolf fighter caught his leg with the tip of his sword.

The three men from the wood worked efficiently, cutting down every Wolf that ran at them. With axe and blades and sword they cut through their enemy, one soul at a time.

The Bjern man with the axe planted his blade in the forehead of the man who'd hurt the dog, and when he was dead, put his boot on the felled Wolf's jaw and jerked the axe blade free from his skull. The axeman's hair was as flaming red as glowing hot embers, and his chest was as broad as his axe blows were sharp and decisive, indefensible. He cut through the pack as they tried to take him down, taking the legs off one of the men who'd encircled my brother. Blood pulsed from what was left of his ruined legs, hacked off just above the knee.

His anguished screams made my heart pound, my lips turning upward in a smile.

I drank in his misery and wished I could multiply it a hundred-fold.

Hodor didn't have the chance to make a sound after Fenris cut him. Even as he fell, his fading, bewildered eyes begged me to run.

Another of the Bjern men's hair shone white as the pale moon as three Wolfs roared from the shadows, coming to aid their fallen kinsmen. The pale-haired man flung one glinting knife after another with such precision, I thought he could split hairs with his blade until no more threats could be seen.

I rushed toward them to see a sword erupt from the back of one of Fenris's mutts. I was so close, it would have pierced my chest if I had been more than a spirit bystander.

The Bjern swordsman twisted his blade, roaring as he pushed the Wolf away, tearing his blade from his belly. His face and shield were spattered with blood, his square jaw ticking in anger as the wounded collapsed with a thud, banging his head on the earth. But the man didn't die immediately; the Wolf begged for mercy.

"Kill me."

The swordsman crouched beside him, blood dripping from his hair. I could see it was neither pale nor dark, a shade of brown-blonde the moon and fire didn't quite wholly reveal. "You've shown us no mercy, and so mercy is the last thing you'll receive."

He stood and rejoined his friends, who were fighting at one another's backs like Hodor and I had planned to do.

Skuld stared at the three Bjern warriors. "You need men and women like them in your army, Liv. They aren't fearless. They're terrified. Terrified that someone they love might be hurt. Terrified that their way of life will be annihilated. They have much to fight for and much to defend."

Studying the Bjern swordsman, I marveled at his graceful movements. They weren't sloppy or desperate. He looked like a god fighting a monster, muscles rippling beneath his shirt, snapping beneath his forearms. He never tired. If he thought of quitting, it didn't show.

I had forgotten Skuld until she spoke, startling me. "Fenris fears the other clans. If Urðr killed his father, who is to stop another from killing him now that he will be Jarl?"

Skuld studied the swordsman my eyes kept gravitating toward. His shield was scarred. His brown-blonde hair was sweat-soaked from exertion. He was clever, quietly creeping up on one of Fenris's men who was holding a torch to the roof of a longhouse, trying to fan the flame so it caught. The swordsman slid his slick blade across the intruder's throat and the man slumped, dropping the torch and gagging on his own blood.

I closed my eyes and tried to push the sound away.

The Bjern swordsman called for his two friends, the pale-haired bladesman and his flame-haired axeman. "I'm going to set their ship on fire," he panted. "It'll draw them out. We can't let them reach the houses in the hills. Keep my father alive," he told them. "Keep the Wolfs in the valley."

The two friends agreed. As the swordsman sprinted away, the flame-haired man barked at the pale one to guard someone named Armund, whom I supposed was the swordsman's father. They raced toward the base of the hill where the limping man – Armund – still defended those who'd fled into the woods above. With a worn shield strapped to one arm and an axe in his grip, he was ready to fight, to die if needed. I'd seen that look in my father's eyes before, as well as my mother's. And for the briefest moment, in Hodor's.

Casting my eyes back to the shore, I watched as the swordsman tore off his shield, ripped his shirt over his head, and grabbed a nearby rake, snapping it over his knee. He wrapped and tied the shirt on the end.

I looked to Skuld, who smiled. "You want to see if he succeeds?"

I didn't want that. I mean, I wanted him to succeed, but… that wasn't enough. "I want to protect him."

"My power flows through your veins now. You only need to wield it." She gestured for me to follow him and I did.

I couldn't bear to leave the man who wanted to light Fenris's only way out of here on fire. If the Wolfs caught him, I knew what would happen – but his plan, if he could execute it, would work.

I could almost feel him running at my side, pushing faster, harder, focusing on the target swaying on the sea.

The warrior paused at the longhouse burning closest to shore to light his torch, then rushed across the pebbles and waded into the sea, holding the torch above the surface while stroking toward the ship. But the fabric burned quickly and the sea spray dampened the fire he'd captured. The torch was dying as he reached the vessel.

Refusing to give up, he eased the torch over the edge and gently let it fall before pulling himself into the hull, careful not to splash water onto what was left of the fire. He worked quickly to unfurl the sail. The wind caught it, filling the wool and easing him further out to sea.

The breeze wasn't strong, but it put the tiny remaining flame out. The warrior held the flickering, dying torch to the sail, but the fabric of his tunic had burned away, leaving only charred remnants that glowed in small tendrils like fiery snail trails.

He didn't need embers; he needed flame.

The warrior wiped his brow and kept trying, holding the guttering torch to the wool. Water sluiced off his skin and hair, dripping onto the planks at his feet. "Come on," he growled at the torch. He looked to the shore and naked fear shone on his face. If this didn't work…

I had to help him. I'd scorched the ship that held my family; I could set fire to this sail.

I walked over the water's surface, breezing through the ship's hull planks, and placed my hand on the sail where he held his torch, fiery fury pouring from my palm.

The woolen sail ignited with a whoosh. Flames tore across its width and raced upward until the entire sail was ablaze. The middle quickly burned away and the boat rocked when the wind raced through the hole in the sail.

The swordsman let out a relieved gasp and backed away to watch the fire spread, then searched the shore for signs of the Wolfs noticing the inferno wrecking their sail. I placed my hands on the damp mast and encouraged it to burn, leaving charred handprints where I'd gripped the towering oak beam.

A column of smoke dragged across the water. Skuld flicked her wrist and pushed it ashore, smiling at me sinisterly. "I will make sure they know."

Suddenly, Skuld was gone.

I spotted her walking on the shore, winding between the burning homes, into the melee… then bending to whisper in

Fenris's ear. He scanned his surroundings, his eyes catching on the burning sail.

I turned to see if the swordsman had made it back to shore, but he hadn't moved. He stared at me with wide eyes as if he could see me. He tilted his head, lips parting, and reached out for me. His fingers drifted through.

Skuld laughed, and I heard my voice echoing from the shoreline. The Wolfs were retreating to the ship... but the young man was still stunned, still standing and staring at me.

"You have to run!" I shouted. Now I knew what it was to want to save someone the only way you could and have them refuse. "Run!" I yelled. "They're coming."

His brows furrowed and he slowly shook his head as if in a trance. I pointed toward the enemy who rushed toward him. His eyes tracked my finger, widening when he realized what I was saying. The Wolfs were already swimming toward him, some cutting through the water as if their bodies were slick and finned.

He flicked a final glance at me, climbed to the ship's rail, and dove into the sea. He stayed beneath the surface so long, I feared he might have drowned. What he'd done, his plan, was brave and cunning and I envied him for having thought of it. He used their most obvious vulnerability against them. No ship meant no escape.

The Bjern swordsman finally surfaced and swam furiously toward the far shore where the hills emptied into the sea. Relief poured over me the moment his feet found purchase. He pushed himself from the heavy water and fell onto the bank, still staring in my direction. Whether he marveled at the fire and the Wolf warriors reaching the ship and trying to put it out by gathering water in their shields and flinging it onto the flames, or still saw me standing their midst, I didn't know.

But I couldn't look away from him, either... until a volley of arrows zipped through the sky, finding a few targets among those swimming for the listless ship. Fenris held his shield to the back of his head and stroked toward the boat, shouting at his men to put the fire out. They yelled back that they were trying.

Warriors were pulled from the sea into the hull and chaos ensued as I walked circles around their ship, smiling at their difficulties.

When Fenris was hauled over the ship's rail, I waited and watched until the fire was mostly extinguished by their efforts, allowing it to die away so he could focus on something else. I let him think he had control of the situation again.

And then, in the moonlight, I felt something powerful erupt from my spirit. His eyes caught on me and he startled. He tripped over one of his men, quickly righting himself, then watched as I walked between his ship and the shoreline.

"Should we row back to shore?" one of his warriors asked him as he helped him up. "Finish this?"

I stood between them and shore.

Between his intentions and safety.

"No. We sail," he ordered his men, scanning the sea to catch sight of me again, too afraid to finish what he set out to do here. Afraid he'd step ashore and I would be there to meet him.

Skuld was suddenly beside me. "Every choice he makes is like a shovel full of the earthen hole that will soon be his grave."

ELEVEN

When Skuld rejoined my spirit with my body on the shore of Amrok Village, it felt like my skin might not be able to contain it anymore. I'd left my body behind, infused with Skuld's warmth, but returned with an inferno that was all mine. Before she left, Skuld walked with me to my ruined house where she dipped her finger into the pot of ash and cinders. Her eyes locked on mine. "Watch, Liv. Learn every stroke. Feel the energy of each. You'll need them all."

On the outside of my parent's room, down the wall that had only half-burned, she drew a powerful bind rune line. A thick vertical slash where runes of protection, strength, and bravery were stacked atop one another. At its tip: malice. Skuld's forked symbol.

"What holds this mark is sealed with my protection *and* yours," she added before straightening. "I have duties I can neglect no more. Prepare yourself, Vengeance. A glorious battle looms before you."

I thanked her and she smiled sinisterly, pointing to the pot of ashes. "There is power in *ink*."

She left me with a whoosh of wind that tore my hair and dress sideways. Skuld truly did seem to favor me. She thought I was brave when I thought calling on her was weak. She showed me the hearts of the men and women I needed to fight by my side and where to find them. Then she gifted me with her mark and told me what to draw it with to make it so potent, Fenris would never be able to erase it.

I took up the pot and brought it to the fjord. The cold water disappeared into the ash, rendering a vibrantly dark ink, thick as butter on my fingertips.

There is power in ash.

I could feel it course through me. With the ink, I drew the rune mark on the ground and felt it tremble beneath me in response. I drew it on the boulder I loved, pressing my palm against the unyielding surface to feel it hum, then drew it on the trunks of trees surrounding the village. If Fenris, or anyone but I sought to make this land theirs, my bind rune would repel them. I could almost feel the sick feeling it would leave in their gut. The kind that sent shivers up a person's spine and made them shrink away, compelling them to find another place that didn't feel so haunted and cold.

In a makeshift bag made from a remnant of gathered leather I found beneath my parents' bed, I carried Solvi's comb, Gunnar's bone flute, the head of Mother's axe along with the spike that once fit the handle's bottom, my sword, Hodor's and my shields, the pot of ink, and the rest of the bones I hadn't used to make my wand.

I walked toward Skögar Village over moonlit hills, over the paths the völva my mother killed took the night she died. Did the witch know she was being stalked? Did Skuld reveal she would die, and did she take the path I walked now when the moment of death arrived?

My finished wand glowed in the moonlight. With the fire in me, I'd heated my loved ones' rib bones. I only had to hold them in my palms until they were pliant, then I pulled and formed them into a flared spinner for the top of my wand. The ribs met to form a sharp tip, one with which I planned to pierce Fenris's dark plans. And perhaps his blackened heart.

I found my father's sword when I found the leather hide. It had clattered beneath the bed and when I touched it, I saw flashes of the moment he was cut down. I heard the desperation in his breaths as he told the children to hide beneath the bed. The cry he let out when Mother fell, and as one by one, his children's lives were cut short.

His sword was strong, difficult and stubborn as he. It was only fitting that his weapon was the backbone of my wand. He was the backbone of our family, and our mother its heart. I worked and stretched it into a long staff that stood a foot taller than me when it was finished. Then I pulled the iron on either side to make the straight iron slink left and right, back and forth before carefully threading the vertebrae of my father, mother, and siblings onto it. I knew by feel to whom each bone belonged.

There is power in bone.

I walked steadily north toward Bjern lands as the sky lightened and the sun rose golden through the light mist that crept through and settled in the woods. My dress was damp and hung from my body, worse on the side Fenris had cleaved. My fingers found the puckered scar and traced the uneven bumps.

When the paths that led to Urðr town widened and the mist began to burn away, hooves pounded the trail I walked along. I waited atop a hill to see who approached, clutching my staff tightly. The bones fed me their power and I drank it in.

I was prepared for the horse and expected a rider, but I did not expect *him*.

The Bjern swordsman pulled on his white-gray gelding's reins when he saw me, his forearms flexing, knuckles tightly gripping the leather. His lips parted as the horse slowed, then trotted, then stopped, nervously cantering in a circle. The horse's ears pinned back and he snorted, pawing the dirt. His back hollowed, ready to bolt.

"Stop," I said quietly, trying to calm the animal. "I won't harm you." The gelding's muscles relaxed. His ears flicked and his back rounded again.

The swordsman slowly dismounted and guided his horse to a nearby tree, carelessly lashing it to a low-hanging limb, keeping a wary eye on me.

The hair on his forearms stood on end as he took his hands away. "I saw you," he said. The scent of smoke still clung to his shirt, wafting from him as he came closer. There were circles under his eyes. He hadn't slept.

"I saw you, too. What's your name, swordsman?"

His hand found the handle of his sword at the mention of it. "Calder," he answered.

Calder. He'd been named for harsh, cold waters, the very color of his eyes reminiscent of clear glaciers.

The moonlight hadn't lied. His hair was the color of bark after the rain had soaked it. Not brown or blonde, but a conglomeration of many rich shades trapped in between. No matter what else I looked at, I kept returning to his eyes. They were the exact silvery blue of the fjord when it froze solid so fast the water couldn't cloud with sediment. So clear I could almost see through them.

He watched the wind catch my hair and rattle the stiff fabric where my dress gaped. His eyes trailed my scar, then tracked the blood stained around the slit at my side to the hem, then raked over my ruined boots. Then he took in my wand, his startling eyes catching on every vertebra. "Did you pass through Amrok Village, völva?" he rasped.

"Why did you leave Skögar?" I asked.

"To warn your clan. Urðr Village lies in ruin. I thought I might be able to warn Amrok." He regarded the blood stains on my skirt again. "Were you there when they attacked?"

A knot the size of my shield formed in my throat. "I was."

"Did anyone else survive?"

"The Wolfs left no one alive."

He let out a harsh breath. "Did your power keep you safe from them?"

"No," I answered honestly. "I died in Amrok Village, too."

His brows furrowed. "With respect, völva, I don't understand. You are alive and standing before me."

"There is a vast difference between living and existing," I answered, leaving him to consider my words.

The muscle in his square jaw ticked.

He likely had more questions. As if any answer I could provide would make sense of what Fenris Wolf had done to his people. I felt guilty that the actions of someone in Urðr had fed an inferno that had engulfed Bjern as well.

According to Skuld, Fenris would not stop with Urðr. He would not stop with Bjern. Skuld said his hatred would boil over on all the clans in the land. No one would be safe until he and those who fought with him lay dead.

A warm wind slid through my bones as I took in Calder.

His linen shirt was half untucked, the v at his neck dipping toward a muscular chest. He had no beard, like most men coveted. His expressions were unconcealed. His sword hung at his right side. At his left was a knife whose handle had been forged to resemble a raven's head.

My body hadn't died in Amrok Village, but there were many levels of death beyond the physical body. My heart died that day along with my parents, Hodor and Gunnar, Ingrid and tiny Solvi. The only thing I had to live for now was the promise of battling Fenris Wolf.

Let me be your hands. Let me be your shield, your blade. I will live as your vengeance.

I hiked my makeshift leather bag onto my shoulders when it slid off them once more. It was heavy, but everything in it precious.

The rounded edges of Hodor's and my shields raked the back of my head. From the corner of my eye, I could see the handle of my sword and the bubbled joint of a thigh bone.

"Where are you walking?" he asked softly.

"To find you."

He scrubbed a hand over his lightly stubbled jaw. "Why me?"

"Because I need your help. Skuld chose me to end Fenris Wolf, but I'll need an army strong enough to meet his. He won't stop with Skögar, Calder. He won't stop killing until I kill him."

He weighed my words. "Are you Skuld's chosen?" he said fearfully, reverently. His eyes darted all around us as a chill wind slid through the trees.

I stood taller, turning my spine into iron. "I am her vengeance, and I am mine. Fenris Wolf took everything from me, and I intend to repay the favor a hundred-fold. He will choke on my blade and know that he created the fury from which I was forged."

I wasn't sure which was stronger – Skuld's needs or my thirst for Fenris's screams. I wanted him to feel what it was like to burn so that only a tuft of grizzled hair remained on his head; to be abandoned at the water's edge and feel the water trickling into his nose and mouth; to feel a blade sink into his flesh and lodge in his bone; to watch those he loved bleed to death, knowing deep within there was nothing he could do to save them. I wanted to see him watch the life drain from their eyes and wounds and watch helplessly as their chests stilled. I wanted him to hear their last gasps, followed by the parting sigh that came when the spirit separated from their body.

And after he had tasted every horrible thing he'd inflicted, I would drink in his last breath, bind his spirit, and ferry it to a place so dark and terrifying, his soul would forever scream.

Calder was quiet for several long moments. He hesitated so long, I thought he would turn away from me and head back to his family and his people. I imagined myself watching the blades of his shoulders flex as he strode toward his horse, mounted and kicked the gelding to urge him to run home as fast as it could run.

But he didn't do any of those things. His eyes hardened as his lips thinned. "I would love to witness you end him. May I carry your bag, völva?" he finally said, extending his hand.

My fingers curled around the leather straps and held tight. I couldn't bring myself to move them, to peel the straps away and hand it over to someone I barely knew. This bag held all I had left of the ones I loved.

"Please," he said softly. "I'll carry it on my back and you can ride in front of me. I'll give it to you the second you ask for it to be returned."

It was the tenderness in his voice that eased the weighty feeling holding me down, the sincerity in his eyes that strengthened my resolve.

"Thank you," I rasped, then tugged off the straps. He took the heavy bag. The weight didn't seem to bother him as he shrugged it on.

TWELVE

Calder's horse didn't bolt as I approached. The animal watched me carefully but didn't move so much as a step backward. I reached out to smooth a hand down the gelding's neck. His ears perked when I whispered, "Are you able to carry both of us?"

I unlashed the gelding's reins and ran a hand down his silken mane the color of silver. The horse lowered his head, leaned forward while keeping his back straight, and bowed. Calder's jaw slackened for a moment.

I gave him a slight smile and ran a hand through the gelding's mane. "He's tired, but I will strengthen him."

"Thank you, völva."

It was strange to hear him call me that. It was what I was now, but I wasn't sure I'd accepted the title any more than I'd fully come to understand the limits of the power Skuld had given me.

"Do you need help climbing onto his back?" he asked, his hand already extending.

I ignored the offer and mounted with ease, wand-in-hand, a small grin tugging at the corner of my lips. "Do you?"

A laugh escaped his chest before he gave me a quizzical look, a smile still tugging at the corners of his lips.

He swung onto the gelding's back and settled behind me, then reached around me to take the reins. Shivers slid over my skin as his forearms brushed against my waist. He guided the horse toward his home while I tried to ignore the warmth that radiated from him, how my curves settled against his muscular frame, and every bump that brought us closer. I leaned forward to whisper something into his horse's ear, stopping short. "What's his name?" I asked, glancing at Calder over my shoulder.

He shrugged. "I haven't named him. My father considers it bad luck to name livestock because a name bonds them to you. I traded a neighbor for him at *Winternights,* and though we've gotten to know and trust each other over the frigid months, nothing I come up with seems to fit him." His eyes shimmered. "What is *your* name?"

I whispered to the horse, strengthening his legs, ankles, and back, telling him to run faster and transport us home as quickly as he could. To jump high over obstacles and race fearlessly over the land.

The gelding took off, darting through the trees where the path was no longer visible, and barreling down a steep hill. Calder's hand clamped onto my side, his fingers biting into my scar.

My body tensed beneath his touch. I expected the scar to hurt under the pressure of his fingers, but something warm rushed to the skin where his hand lay. He took his hand away as the gelding raced ahead onto flatter ground.

"I had to steady myself," he assured me apologetically. "I didn't mean to touch your skin…"

I knew he didn't. As respectfully as he'd treated me thus far, there was a healthy amount of fear in him, too. Völva were the things of stories told around fires when the women and men had too much ale. Their tales stretched like shadows onto the walls of longhouses, the witches morphing into monsters who stole children and drank blood, who killed for the bones they wanted to cast.

The tension between me and Calder melted away the further from Amrok we traveled. I'd never left home, never even traveled to town for celebrations. Father and Mother said there was too much work to be done at home to think about leaving for any amount of time, but I think that keeping us close was their way of shielding us.

"You never gave me your name. Völva have names, don't they?"

I looked over my shoulder at his smirk. "I will give it to you once you give one to your horse."

He shook his head, fighting a smile.

I urged the gray gelding faster and Calder leaned into me. His chest pressed hard against my back and his face hovered over my shoulder.

I craned my head to look at him. "What are you doing?"

"Trying not to choke on your hair."

I couldn't help but laugh. He joined me and the timbre of his voice was as warm and comforting as the heat still radiating from his skin.

The sun boiled high in the sky when we reached Urðr Town. The hatred inside bubbled uncontrollably when I saw the destruction there. The town had been ten times the size of our small village. Maybe larger. But every house was burned to the ground. Only the outlines of the once proud homes were visible, the land cleared of all that had painstakingly been built.

"No one survived," Calder said gravely.

I told the horse to stop and leapt from his back. "I need my bag," I demanded. He slid off and handed it to me, watching as I rifled inside and pulled out the pot of ink. I drew the bind rune throughout the town, on boulders, tree trunks, what was left of houses and fences. Calder followed along behind me, noticing the earth quaking, but never commenting on it. When I was finished, I replaced the lid and handed it back to him before walking to the water's edge to rub the ink from my fingertips.

I climbed back onto the horse's back and waited for Calder, trying to calm myself, worrying that if I didn't, I might scorch the beautiful gelding. Calder pulled the bag onto his back and settled behind me again, and we rode north, passing the harbor. The skeletons of many knorrs – merchant ships – could be seen just beneath the surface. "Where are the longships?"

He took a deep breath. "I think they took them."

Knorrs were for trade, to ferry goods across the sea. Longships ferried warriors. It seemed Fenris was building his army and providing ships to carry them across the sea to ravage other clans and lands. His men and women would use Urðr ships to accomplish his plan. The thought boiled my bones.

"Skögar has no harbor," he said.

"Did they strike Bjern Town?"

Calder flicked the reins and gave a kick. "A friend of mine rode to find out. We'll know their fate soon enough."

The gelding carried us into the hills and away from Urðr Town. Away from the ruined town and its ruined harbor. For a long time, Calder was quiet. Then, from out of nowhere, with the familiar hint of playfulness in his voice, he asked, "What would *you* name the horse?"

I smiled. "I'm not sure I know him well enough to give him a name."

"You don't have to know him to know his nature. You already seem connected to him in a way I'll never be," he mused. "Perhaps you'd name him after a warrior you once knew? He certainly is strong," he carried on, as if speaking to himself, though he knew I listened. "Tor, perhaps?" he asked, prodding my side.

My body stiffened at the name he suggested. The memories of Hodor and Tor, Tor's death-stiffened body, and Tor's grave flashed through my mind.

Was it coincidence that Calder chose that name, or were Skuld and her sisters busy weaving? Urd was the weaver of past, Verdandi wove the present, and Skuld carefully crafted futures. It seemed all three were working together and Calder and I were trapped in their tapestry. I wondered what vibrant threads they used for us, and whether our souls screamed upon their loom.

I will weave a thread and call it Liv.

"Are you okay?" he asked cautiously, as if sensing my discomfort.

An image was painted in my mind of a glorious silver gelding wading into the waters of the fjord just in front of where my home had been, just in front of our boulder. The vision was gone as quickly as it came. I blinked rapidly to clear my mind.

"Call him Mordi," I rasped. "I've had a vision of him wading into fjord waters, and Mordi means 'to wade.'"

Calder shifted uncomfortably behind me. "Mordi suits him. Thank you."

He didn't speak again until Mordi carried us across the foothills of the Grandys Mountains and into the forests surrounding Skögar Village, drawing closer to his home as the sun set.

"My house is full," he said. "I had planned to stay with a friend, but I'd like for you to meet someone before you decide what you're most comfortable with – if you don't mind."

My eyes locked with his as I peered over my shoulder. "Who?"

"My father."

His father, the one who saved the children despite the limp that caused him pain. *Armund,* I remembered.

"Okay." I wanted to speak with him, to tell him how brave he was and how wise to save those who could never have defended themselves against the brute strength of a fully grown warrior. Children were a clan's living, breathing future, the lineage of the warriors before them, and their pride. They would be raised to be warriors. Taught to fight. But when they were small, they shouldn't be expected to battle someone twice their size. They shouldn't be expected to die. I wished my father had learned that lesson with Oskar's death. Instead, he lost far more than he would have gained had he saved my siblings. Though, I was starting to wonder if I was just assuming things about what happened. Maybe they caught them unawares and the children had no other place to escape but into Mother and Father's room. Our parents were closest to the door, as if they'd been guarding it.

Maybe I knew nothing and wanted to blame someone other than Fenris for their deaths. I could just as easily blame myself. I wasn't there to help fight and defend them. I was too busy chasing a future I wouldn't have.

"My horse has a name," he mentioned with a gentle nudge after I whispered to Mordi to stop.

I slid off the horse clutching my staff, then took my bag from him. I shook my head. Calder was cunning, I'd give him that. "*That's* why you wanted me to name him?"

He nodded, an ornery glimmer in his eye as he swung down from Mordi's back, only to face me. The swordsman who outsmarted Fenris Wolf had also tricked me... A name for a name. That was our bargain. And I intimately knew how solid a bargain was once struck.

"Very well. My name is Liv."

114

"Liv," he said softly. "It suits you."

"How do you know it does?" I asked, stroking Mordi's mane.

"Because *you* lived, when no one else was strong enough to."

The strength he spoke of didn't come from me. It came from fear and from Skuld.

"Calder," I said, growing uncomfortable when his eyes searched mine too deeply for something I wasn't sure I wanted him to see. "Take me to Armund."

He went still. His lips slowly parted and his head tilted. "What did you say?"

"I asked you to take me to your father."

"You called him Armund." I clutched my staff tighter. The bones twisted and clacked together. "How did you know his name?"

"I saw you and your friends during the attack. One of them shouted his name." He knew I'd been there, though I hadn't told him how much I'd seen or how long my spirit walked among them. How badly I wanted to be there in body, to fight with them.

As I walked toward Armund through the forest's shadows where the setting sun couldn't breach, Skuld showed me a vision of Calder's father being wounded. Just a flash of a glinting sword sweeping through the air and catching in his kneecap. Of Armund crumpling once the sword was jerked free.

Calder followed at a careful distance as I carved a path straight to Armund, feeling him amongst the trees. His house was one of many in the wood, but stood closest to the village.

The wood of Armund's longhouse was somewhat weathered, but stood strong, pine needles blanketing his thatched roof. Moss crept from the ground up the foundation stones, walls, and up either side of the door. I paused outside as the sun finally set and the fireflies winked through the darkening forest. Inside, only steady, rhythmic breaths could be heard.

"What's wrong?" Calder asked, placing a hand on my lower back for the briefest moment, kindling the fire under my skin.

I turned toward him and his hand fell away. "He sleeps. I don't want to wake him."

His hand found my lower back again as he gestured to the door. "He won't mind, Liv."

Calder's touch made my heart thunder, but when my name passed his lips so purposefully, it was like he wanted me to know he saw me instead of my wand, the girl instead of the witch.

It meant more to me than he'd ever know.

He stepped around me to the door and knocked, waiting patiently. The door was wrenched open and a man with the same icy eyes as Calder stood in the doorway. My father would have grunted and turned away, returning to his nap, but Calder's father was different. A relieved smile stretched over his face. He limped outside and hugged Calder, clapping him on the shoulder, but stiffened when he saw me.

"Who is this?" He looked me over, his smile falling away when he noticed my staff. "A völva..."

"Father," Calder said, gesturing toward me, "this is Liv."

The older man's brows furrowed. "My goodness... I can sense Skuld in you. Most völva are only distantly connected to the norn. But you're filled with her power, aren't you?"

My mouth gaped.

Calder ticked his head toward his father. "He has a gift."

Armund's eyes hooked onto my side, traveling over the dried blood stiffening the fabric of my dress. He suddenly strode into the house, leaving the door wide open. Inside, the hearth's embers glowed red-orange. It was warm and comfortable. I saw a small table and a couple of wooden chairs, but couldn't see beyond those without stepping inside.

"Father, has Fell returned?" Calder asked so his father could hear him.

Armund reappeared in the doorway holding a smooth walking stick as tall as his chest, with a knot in its middle. "Fell has not returned, but we expect him any time. Tyr is still sleeping," he explained quietly as he closed the door behind him. "He's been working nonstop and gave his house up for the others. The boy fell asleep after dinner and I didn't rouse him. He's worn out."

Calder scrubbed his face. Worry settled in thin lines around his mouth and eyes. "Where is Sig?"

"Muryak's dog is in heat. Where do you think he is?"

Calder groaned as Armund laughed. I smiled at their easy banter.

"He has an elkhound that's smarter than I am," Armund confided loud enough for Calder to hear. I remembered the smoke-gray dog, a warrior's companion in every way, one that fought alongside him.

"Fell's house is also occupied, but the four of you are welcome to stay with me. As long as you're comfortable with that arrangement, Liv," he added with a deferential nod to me. "Or would you rather I address you by your title?"

"I prefer Liv, and I appreciate you letting me stay in your home." Typically, a völva stayed where she wanted, with whom and wherever she wanted. It was considered an honor for one to sup with a family, doubly so for a völva to seek shelter under your roof.

Mother wouldn't have allowed it. I knew why now. But our Jarl hosted them at every opportunity. He would lavish them with gifts and delicacies and riches in the hope that in exchange, they would speak kindly of him to the one who weaved his future. And perhaps, she would give him a little insight, a taste of what was to come. A warning, or perhaps news of good fortune. A völva could also influence where he chose to send his warriors to raid. I remembered Mother grumbling about changed plans more than once.

Armund smiled kindly and ticked his head to his house. "Calder, why don't you go inside and rest?" he told his son over his shoulder as he walked to me. "I need a few moments alone to speak with Liv."

He limped past me and started down a smooth path that led upward, deeper into the forest. I quickly caught up, finding that I wasn't as tired as I should be.

Thin trails of smoke slithered from each home, settling in the tall pines and budding trees. Armund was quiet as we walked down the trail. Calder watched us from the doorway of his father's home, leaning a forearm on the facing.

"My son is a good man," Armund said suddenly, stopping to watch my reaction as I stopped beside him.

"He is," I agreed.

"Did he find you in Urðr Town?"

I shook my head, adjusting the grip on my staff. "He found me on the path to Amrok Village. He'd ridden to warn our Jarl at Urðr, but they'd already been attacked. Calder kept riding to warn Amrok." When anyone else would've returned home where he was no doubt needed, Calder kept hope that someone had survived. That he could help someone avoid the tragedy he'd endured.

"So you were staying in Amrok Village?"

"It was my home," I told him.

Armund's expression turned sad. "How many survived the attack on Amrok, Liv?"

I swallowed thickly, remembering the tickle of the tiny tuft of Solvi's hair. My bottom lip quivered, traitorous to my thoughts to quell the swell of emotions trying to free themselves.

He placed a hand on his chest, immediately intuiting what I couldn't bring myself to voice. "I can't imagine what you've been through, but I'm glad *you're* here with us. I want you to know that."

"Thank you," I rasped.

He nodded once, pursing his lips, then continued climbing the path. His shoulders were almost as broad as Calder's, but climbing hurt Armund worse than walking on straight paths did. He tried to hide the pain, but when the path steepened, he stopped to take a break, leaning into his knobby walking stick.

"I'm slow," he said to apologize.

"I'm growing tired, so slow is good."

He gave me a kind smile, his pale eyes glittering with thanks. Armund was so warm, so different from my father. He began the climb again, this time at a slower pace. "Did your magic save you from Clan Wolf?"

I hesitated. "I had no magic before the attack."

His back straightened as he stopped again. This time it wasn't for a break, but to face me as he very carefully asked, "What do you mean?" His brows drew in like Calder's when he was concerned or confused.

My grip on my wand tightened and I shifted my weight from one foot to the other. "It's a very long story," I hedged.

"I would very much like to hear it – when you're rested, maybe?" he suggested, thankfully dropping the matter. For now, at least.

Armund hiked toward a house that sat in a ring of towering pines, their needles dripping toward the ground to form a spongey carpet. I peered down at the valley below, noting that it skirted around and climbed the other side of its horseshoe shaped hills. Armund glanced at the vertebrae on my wand as he knocked on the door of the home. "Some will fear you," he warned.

I knew they would and was prepared for it. To be honest, I didn't care how uncomfortable I made them; I needed an army to fight with me, and if I didn't inspire respect or duty, maybe fear would encourage their allegiance.

A woman came to the door. She was slightly younger than Armund, with a sweet smile and fading golden hair. "Armund," she greeted warmly. But the warmth bled from her when she saw me waiting behind him. Her eyes took in my wand and she glanced from it to Armund, whom she trusted. "A völva is in our village, I see." She dusted the ground wheat from her hands and joined us outside, closing the door softly behind her.

Armund waved a hand toward me. "Hilda, this is Liv. She is from Amrok Village. Amrok and Urðr Town were also attacked. She is in need of a dress."

"Of course," she breathed, keeping her eyes on Armund. "Would you like to come in?"

Armund limped forward with a placating smile, shaking his head. "No need to rouse the children if they're settling for bed. They've been working very hard."

"Yes, they have," she agreed, her voice sharpening. She slipped inside and returned a few moments later with an arm full of folded clothing. "I hope these will do."

I reached out to accept them, but she handed the clothing to Armund.

"Thank you," I told her as he handed them to me. He echoed my thanks and she watched as we left her home and retraced our steps down the steep path, Armund much more careful as we descended.

"I'm going to show you to a spot where you can wash privately, although the water is still cold. Hilda tucked a piece of soap in among the clothes she gave you. That woman has a heart of gold when she's not holding an axe." I could hear his smile as he described her.

"You were right. She was afraid of me."

"Oh, everyone will be, dear."

"*You're* not."

He glanced over his shoulder with a kind smile. "Because I can sense your heart, Liv. The norn might have claimed you, but you've kept your heart from her. I'm not sure how, but you have."

I wasn't sure that was true. And if it was, I wasn't sure Skuld wouldn't still take it in the end. What good was a scourge whose heart made her weak?

He led me to the valley where the homes had been torched. It was unsettling how every town and village bore the same scars, each feeling as empty and haunted as the last. Maybe it was the sadness of those who lived. Or maybe there were spirits in these places that refused to settle, who wanted to see Fenris rue the day he stepped on their shores.

My feet drew me away from Armund. I stopped on the shore, just out of reach of the lapping waves in a place where the rocks were charred. Armund joined me a moment later. "This was where the pyre was built," he explained. "We burned our dead this morning."

"Calder helped build it?" I asked, though I knew the answer. I could feel him here, see him stacking the wood.

Armund gave a hum to affirm. "He didn't stay to watch them burn. A warning is only good if it's delivered in time to make a difference."

"The Wolf Clan attacked at dawn..." I began in a raspy voice. "They left our shores and must have sailed north to Urðr Town, then to Skögar."

"Do you know why they attacked, Liv?" Armund asked carefully.

"Their Jarl died in our village on the eve of Winternights. He was murdered."

Armund was quiet as he pondered the information. He pursed his lips together. "What did Bjern have to do with it?"

"Nothing. Fenris wants to wipe all threats from the land. He plans to claim the title of chieftain but fears the same fate could happen to him."

"So he has painted everyone an enemy…"

I crouched on the shore, holding my staff, but dragging my fingers over the rocks. There was power here, nestled within the pale chips of bone littering the ashes the wind hadn't been strong enough to scatter.

I sat down, placed my wand over my lap, and closed my eyes. I saw in my mind how the pyre had looked, how the red-haired axeman Calder fought with last night reverently brought the torch down upon the oil-soaked wood, how the children bravely stood to send their parents into the afterlife, and how the breeze carried the smoke trail sideways out to sea.

"I saw you after the battle was over and the Wolfs rowed away; not as you are, but as you will be," Armund noted quietly, standing behind me. My eyes opened.

"What was I like?"

"I thought you were terrible, but I see the full picture now that I've met you, Liv. *You* aren't terrible, but you will lead a terrible army. You are Skuld's vengeance embodied."

"Yes, I am," I whispered. "She even calls me Vengeance, as if it's my name as much as Liv is."

I knew he wanted to know how I'd become her own, but I wasn't ready to speak about what had happened.

Thankfully, Armund didn't push.

He waited until I stood and then led me around the shore to a small secluded spot where hill met shore. "No one will bother you," he promised, laying the soap and clothing down on a small boulder. "Do you remember the way to my house?"

I nodded.

"Will you come back to it when you're finished? I'll make something for you to eat and find a warm place for you to sleep."

I nodded again, fighting tears that stung my eyes. Exhaustion had finally claimed my muscles and I was bone tired. I felt like I could sleep for years.

He pursed his lips into a thin smile, then limped away to give me privacy.

124

THIRTEEN

It took half the sliver of soap to remove the blood, dirt, and soot, but finally my skin and hair were clean. So were my hands, though they still bore stains. It didn't matter. They would be stained again soon enough. I would protect this place, these people, from further harm. I didn't mind the frigid temperature of the water until I waded from it and the harsh wind hit me. I dressed quickly, reveling in the feel of the soft woolen dress that covered me and was neither stiff nor torn.

At the tide line, I scrubbed my boots clean and tugged them on wet, then took up my wand and clothes and the small, serpent hair charm Hodor had given me and headed up the winding paths into the hills.

Armund was waiting for me outside his house with another of his smiles. He had many. This one was knowing. His eyes lit up with excitement as he wagged a finger at me. "I believe I know your mother. I was trying to place your face, and I think I've got it. Hella?" he asked.

"Yes." I tried to smile back, suddenly feeling her absence as a hollow in my chest.

"And your father?" he asked softly.

"His name was Erik."

Armund's brows shot up. "I knew him, too. Even fought with him once. He was a strong fighter. Very strong."

If Father could be described as anything, it was that. He was strong. He fought well. When I was young like Gunnar, I thought he was stronger than ten men. I still wondered how many it had taken to cut him down. There was no way Fenris Wolf had done it alone.

"I'm sorry they were taken from you."

The aching hollow filled with hatred. "Not as sorry as Fenris Wolf will be."

Armund nodded slowly. "I have no doubt you'll make him feel every inch of the scar he left you."

I would. I'd make him pay for it.

"I've made a place for you to sleep." He gestured to the door and I followed him over the threshold, stepping into the comforting warmth of Armund's longhouse. Calder sat up when I walked in and my face heated at his perusal. Sitting in a nest of blankets in the far-left corner of the room, his forearms were propped on his knees and he looked me over so unabashedly my cheeks caught fire.

"Would you like some bread?" Armund offered a palm-sized loaf that was charred on its bottom. I gladly accepted it and bit into the bread, chewing until I could swallow. "It's all I have to offer for now, but tomorrow... tomorrow, I'll make something hearty."

"I appreciate the bread."

Armund gave a small smile and limped away, passing the warm hearth built into the room's middle. I wanted to stay in the halo of that warmth but was pleased to see the nest he'd made for me was directly across from Calder.

Someone snored from the other end of the room. I assumed it was the friend Armund mentioned earlier, Tyr. "I hope this will be comfortable enough," Armund said.

I crouched to pull back the top blankets so I could climb in and tucked my wand close to the wall. Though I wanted to curl into the darkness and face the wall as I did back home, curling around Solvi, I wasn't sure everyone in Skögar was friendly. I would have to watch my back, not expose it. So, I turned to face Calder and pulled the quilts tightly around me.

He laid down. His eyes met mine before they drifted closed.

Armund offered a quiet goodnight from the far end of the room, to which Calder quietly replied.

I was used to snoring. Father snored louder than a den of bears. And I was used to Solvi watching me as we tried to fall asleep. But this was not home, and these people were not my family.

A fly's feet tickled the hair on my cheek as I slowly begin to slip from beneath sleep's spell. Startling, the creature lifted and buzzed around the room.

"Should I wake her?" Calder asked in a low tone.

Armund rustled around doing something. "Let her rest."

"She's slept all night and day. It's almost dusk," he argued.

"She will wake when she's ready. Why are you so anxious to see her?" His tone was teasing.

"Father..." Calder warned.

"She's lovely," Armund baited.

"She is. Anyone can see that. Even one as old as you."

Something thumped and Calder started chuckling.

The smell of wood burning in the hearth and the scent of blood had my eyes popping open, but I stayed in the nest of covers, watching and listening.

Calder and Armund sat at the table using sharp knives to skin a pair of hares, peeling the fur away.

Armund's hair lay wet over his shoulders, soaking his clean tunic. He stood and raked some meat off a plate into a pot of boiling water. He had a spring in his step. He wasn't limping badly at all.

"You like having her here," he said to Calder.

His hand and knife stilled. "We barely know her."

Armund's brow quirked.

"But yes," Calder said. "I'm glad she's here."

The front door creaked open and orange sunlight spilled over the floor. The pale-haired bladesman stood in the door. "Tyr," Calder greeted.

I sat up, watching him. One flick of his wrist and he could send one of those blades sailing. His eyes caught on me and he frowned before turning to Calder again. "I'm going to Bjern Town. Fell should've been back by now."

My long, sun-kissed hair was a tangled mess and my borrowed dress was wrinkled, but Calder looked me over and the memory of the conversation he'd just had with Armund made my cheeks heat. I stood up, quickly straightening my clothes. "Your friend hasn't returned?" I asked, walking toward the three men.

"I wasn't speaking to you," the pale-haired Tyr snipped.

"Liv is my guest," Armund said sternly. "And as such, she is someone you will respect while you're in my house."

Tyr's temper calmed. "Of course, Armund." He nodded toward me, though I could tell it was the last thing he wanted to do.

"Do you have something of his? Something personal?" I asked them.

"I can get something," Calder offered. "Let me run to his house." He began tugging a boot on when Tyr stopped him by placing a hand on his shoulder.

"I have one of his knives." Tyr drew one of his friend's knives from the bag he'd already packed. He walked to me and slapped the handle in my palm.

I sucked in a breath the moment the iron hit my skin. "Red hair. Favors an axe. He lit the torch for the pyre." I could see him. "He's alive… he's walking through the woods. It's getting dark where he is. In the forest. He's leaning against a broken pine… It was struck by lightning and bears char marks where the fire spread up its trunk."

Tyr and Calder ran out of the house, sprinting further up the hill and deeper into the wood in a direction I wasn't familiar with. I grabbed my wand and Armund and I hurried after them.

"He's hurt!" I yelled before they came to the top of the nearest hill.

My heart sank. Had Fenris struck Bjern Town, too?

Holding my wand, I filled the forest's shadows with whispers, allowing Calder and Tyr to push faster, run harder, for their vision to sharpen and their feet to stay true. My voice murmured through the trees. Armund glanced all around us as he limped beside me.

They found him leaning against a broken pine just as I'd seen, panting, wincing, with blood and soot on his face. "Fell!" Calder yelled, sprinting down a hill toward his friend with Tyr on his heels.

"Thank the gods," Fell wheezed, holding a hand to his ribs.

"What happened to you?" Calder asked.

"Clan Wolf… had already attacked… Bjern Town. There were no survivors."

"How did you get away?" Tyr asked, taking one of Fell's arms and trying to loop it over his shoulder.

Fell cried out in pain, drawing his arm back into his core. He leaned his head on the bark of the broken tree and shook his head. "I didn't encounter them... Horse threw me. I landed on a boulder. Cracked some ribs." There was no sign of the horse. "He's gone. Bastard bolted and ran north," Fell gritted, standing up straight and hobbling a few steps.

He clamped a hand over his ribs and let out a painful cough. Specks of blood flew from his mouth. Armund limped closer.

Fell's eyes widened at the sight of me, then at the sight of my wand. "Völva," he wheezed, trying to stand up straighter.

"She's a friend," Armund assured him.

His eyes begged for more of an explanation, but I was fixated on what was broken inside him. I could see through his skin somehow, see where the bone had splintered and broken. I raised my hand. "May I?"

He nodded, wiping away a sheen of urgent sweat coating his brow. It was slick again in seconds. I pointed my wand's bony tip toward his body and cupped his wound with my free hand, closing my eyes and imploring Skuld for the power to heal him. Warmth flowed through my palm and into Fell's skin and I could hear the bone knit, the pieces that had broken and wandered returned, fusing stronger than they had been before. It wasn't painless, though. Fell winced, gritted his teeth, and let out a pained growl.

Then suddenly, he surprised us both with a relieved and surprised gasp. "It doesn't hurt anymore," he marveled. I took my hand and wand away.

He pressed on the injury through his tunic, then raised it to push on his skin, feeling the bone beneath it. "Thank you," he said, breathing easier. He wiped the speckles of blood off his lip with his thumb. Fell's eyes combed over me. He flicked a questioning look to Tyr and Calder.

Tyr glowered, looking at me like Mother had looked at the völva in the woods at *Winternights*, like I was a danger he needed to eliminate.

"This is Liv. She survived the attack on Amrok Village," Calder explained.

"Amrok?" Fell asked. "I thought you were going to Urðr Town?"

"It was already destroyed, so I rode on to try to warn Amrok. She and I met on the trail."

"Liv," he said reverently. "Thank you for healing me."

I inclined my head and looked back to Armund, who smiled proudly at me as he patted my back. "You did well."

I offered him a smile and accepted the arm he proffered. Armund and I walked back up the hill, darkness blanketing us. Crickets sang and night animals scurried through the fallen, dried leaves all around us. A moth fluttered through the air, crossing our path. Armund told me about the storm that brought the lightning that split that tree. They'd been walking nearby, heading home after chopping firewood, when it struck. "I thought I'd been hit. That's how close it was. The hair on my neck stood up and I thought we were done for."

I laughed, then latched onto a conversation taking place behind us.

"Calder," Tyr said in a careful tone. "She is völva."

"I know," he assured.

"Then stop looking at her like she's anything but," Tyr fired back.

My heart thundered. I glanced at Armund, who shook his head. "Ignore them. They've fought like this since childhood."

The three caught up with us. Fell took in the bag thrown over Tyr's shoulder. "Were you coming for me?"

"Yes, but then the witch saw you near this tree."

"Her name is Liv," Calder corrected. Tyr's greenish eyes crackled with the same warning he'd voiced a moment ago.

"She may be völva, but she's also a human with a name. Use it."

Fell's eyes darted between the four of us, no doubt sensing the tension hanging in the air like humidity. "Whelp, I'm starving," he said, thankfully changing the subject.

"Father was about to make stew from two hares we managed to snare. There's bread until it's finished," Calder told him.

"Stew sounds amazing, after I wash up. I burned the dead," he admitted, adding, "The Wolfs took the longships and left the knorrs. They sank most of those, but there was one still afloat, though charred. It held everyone, but that's what took me so long."

"They did the same at Urðr harbor," I divulged.

Fell let out a colorful curse. "I should've taken Starr, but I was afraid the Jarl would send me home by ship and keep her for his stables." He looked at me and further explained, "Starr is my favorite mare. She's dependable, and listens. She never would have thrown me. Nor would she have run off. Instead I took Ren…"

He'd walked a long way in the shape he was in. Given the way he was having trouble breathing and the blood in his spittle, I wondered if he would've made it home despite how close he was.

"It looks like I have a lot to catch up on," Fell said, a weary but thankful expression on his face. His eyes slid over my wand again. "Thank you again, Liv."

FOURTEEN

Armund and Calder finished preparing the stew while Fell rested. When we'd eaten, Tyr and Calder walked with Fell to his house to retrieve some of his clothes and belongings. While they were gone, Armund and I finished washing the bowls and spoons and set them out to dry. I sat next to the hearth, keeping my wand in sight. It wasn't cold outside, but the warmth and the mingling scents and sounds of popping wood reminded me of home.

"I think it's time I tell you my story," Armund said, easing into a chair close by. "You know about my knee, but that's superficial, isn't it? Everyone can see that I don't walk well. So, let me tell you about my sister instead. She was völva," he revealed. "Skuld's own."

"But you're not?" I asked. He certainly possessed abilities of some kind. If he wasn't a witch, was he a seer?

"I wasn't chosen by the norns, but by Odin himself. I have second sight, which means I can sense things, but have no influence over them," he answered simply.

"How did you meet Odin?"

"Through Skuld, in a roundabout way. Skuld spoke to my sister through rune stones she cast, and my sister often carried messages to the gods on behalf of Skuld. She called on Odin so often, I came to recognize the feel of him. Odin gave his eye in order to obtain great wisdom, and sometimes, he gifts hints of his knowledge to humans. I'm fortunate he trusts me."

I drew my knees in, laying my cheek on them. "Do you know all the gods?"

He shook his head, leaning his elbows onto his knees and staring at the glowing red embers as they flared and cooled. "I know when a god or goddess is in my presence, but other than Odin, distinguishing them is difficult. Other than Thor," he laughed. "Thor's language is derived from storm."

If Armund had been in Amrok, would he have sensed the gods circling me as I lay dying, crying out for them to spare me? Had Odin come for the warriors? Did he come for me? I remembered seeing ravens circling overhead.

Suddenly, the vision of a woman walking through this room with her back to us entered my mind. "Armund, is Calder's mother dead?"

"No," he answered, then paused. "She left when Calder was only a boy. Old enough to remember her, unfortunately. Often, I wished he couldn't. He tends to blame himself for her absence, when the truth is that it was never his fault. Wounds like that fester. They never heal."

Armund changed the subject, telling me that growing up, he was the only boy in a house full of girls, save for his father. He chuckled, admitting his four sisters were tougher than any brother he might have been brought up with. They never went easy on him, though they taught him to fight as soon as he could grip a sword. From them, he learned to never let his guard down. He was a light sleeper because of it. It was how he heard the screams from the village the night of the attack.

Armund's uncanny eyes met mine. "If you want to defeat Fenris Wolf and those who fight for him, you must accept all of Skuld's power. I can sense what simmers just under your skin, but Skuld has given you a well of immeasurable depth. You just have to tap it."

There were moments I could feel that cavern and what writhed within it. I knew that what I felt now was only the tip of a much larger iceberg, the bulk hidden beneath the water. "How?" I rasped.

Skuld stirred the air in the room and the fire in the hearth blew sideways. The air thickened, becoming humid and heavy. A sheen of sweat bubbled over my skin.

Armund smiled knowingly. It was refreshing that he knew so much, and fortunate for me because I knew very little about völva. "You have to trust her. You must give yourself completely over to her. You are still thinking as the Liv you were before Fenris and his men came ashore. You have to leave that girl behind and become the Liv you are destined to be. The völva you were chosen to be. You're ready, Liv."

Mother once told me that while the harshest lessons were learned fast, they were most important. The lessons that came gently didn't threaten or seem as dire as the ones that tried to pull us underwater and never let go.

"Most witches, like my youngest sister, are chosen at a very young age, so their power matures as their bodies and minds do. You did not have that opportunity. Accepting yourself and the power Skuld wants you to have will likely overwhelm you. Just know that Skuld chose you for this task, and she will give you the strength to endure it."

I owed it to my family. I owed it to everyone who'd lost someone they loved to Fenris Wolf and his pack of ruthless mutts. "How can I reach the power I need?"

His pale blue eyes met mine. "Liv, you have to tell your story. Your power lies in your tragedy."

My body hummed as despair once again swelled through it, an overwhelming wave lapping just beneath my skin. There it was in the middle of my stomach, the pit I was afraid I'd never come out of once I went in. "I'm afraid of what will happen when I do."

"What will happen to others if you don't, Liv?" The question hung between us, the air thickening with his unanswered plea.

I wanted to avenge my family. I wanted Fenris Wolf to die. I couldn't afford to be frightened but I was, and it was the worst feeling in the world. Mother valued hardness and Father valued strength. They would have taken Skuld's power the second she offered it. And so would I.

"I'll tell you, but not here. If something happens, I'd rather be someplace where I can't hurt anyone or anything, and the village is already ruined."

Armund grabbed his walking stick and stood stiffly, waiting for me. I hooked my heavy bag over my shoulder and took up my wand and walked out the door, traveling down the trodden pathways and into the village situated in the valley.

Armund didn't complain about the long walk or his pain, or comment when I sat in the middle of a burnt down longhouse. I chose the space because it reminded me of home. The structure faced the sea the same way mine had the fjord waters. It was about the same size, given the foundation stones.

The cool moonlight slid over our skin as Armund sat across from me, keeping his damaged knee bent, but stretching it toward the bright water. He was quiet and patient, waiting until I was ready to speak.

Gritting my teeth and positioning my bag in front of me, I pulled out the two shields. Mine was barely marked, while Hodor's bore deep scars and was charred. I ran my thumbs over the wood and metal, remembering the day he painted the swirling pattern.

"This belonged to my oldest brother." I traced the swirled pattern that had been mostly burnt away but was still engrained in my memory. "His name was Hodor."

A cool breeze blew from over the water. Calming. Steady.

I first revealed how we were attacked when we were younger, how Hodor and I survived, but our younger brother Oskar didn't. He was as much a part of my story as my other siblings. I told him how we buried him, how he sank beneath the water, and how I knew the exact spot and would never forget it. How I tried to bury my family the same way and was confused when the boat didn't burn, instead returning to me with nothing but ash and bone in the unblemished hull.

I told him about Gunnar, Ingrid, and my little bumble bee, Solvi.

From my bag, I withdrew a smaller leather pouch containing the burnt tuft of her hair, the only remnant of her except for her comb. I should've buried it with her, but I wasn't strong enough to part with it. I removed the soft, downy hair and wound it around my finger. A tear slid from my eye.

"She and I shared a bed. She was often my shadow, but I didn't mind. She was wild and her laughter could make everyone in the room smile."

Armund pressed his lips together, nodding. Listening.

"Ingrid was equally sweet. Unlike Solvi, she tended to mind Mother and Father. She loved helping Mother in the kitchen and fishing with Father, though she hated touching the fish she caught. Gunnar wasn't afraid to touch them, so they fished together most of the time. He was so little, but he was braver than all of us and thought himself a splendid warrior." My throat closed and tears began to fall.

I remembered seeing Armund shepherding the children up the paths that led to safety and my heart split in two.

My lips quivered. "I thought I'd find them hiding in the woods... I screamed for them when I woke."

My hands trembled with anger.

"I found them inside our home, dead, their butchered bodies within a house only half-burned down. This small tuft of hair, along with their ash and bones, is all I have left of them now."

The earth beneath us began to vibrate. Armund braced his hands against it, but he nodded at me, encouraging me to continue.

My chest heaved, feeling like it might burst. There wasn't enough air in the world to fill my lungs as they desperately tried to fill themselves with something other than pain. "Fenris Wolf lost his father, but I lost... everything."

Clouds covered the moon, thickening, racing across the sky. I could barely see Armund, but I could sense him. As I could sense Skuld with me now.

"What happened to Fenris's father, Liv?" he asked, his voice steady.

"On Winternights, Jarl Urðr had hosted two people in Amrok. He always came to the countryside because of the feast we prepared, and because the forests beyond our village were the best to hold the great hunt that would follow the celebration. He brought the chieftain from the north, Jarl Wolf, and a völva. I did not learn her name."

I told him what happened to both, beginning with how the witch said Skuld wished to speak to me, and how she knew my name even though she'd never met me. Then I told him how Mother intervened, and of the bloody wand that at first refused to burn.

I shared the exchange between my parents and Jarl Wolf after Hodor and I'd fought for and earned our shields, and how Gunnar found the chieftain of Clan Wolf washed up on the shore. How Mother denied killing him.

"Hella was fiercely protective when I knew her," he offered softly, clearly shaken by what she'd done to the witch.

"Not protective enough," I gritted, unwinding Solvi's hair and winding it tighter around my finger. "I couldn't save them. On Winternights, the Jarl told Hodor he would leave with the first raiding ship of the spring. When he called me and Hodor to him with the first thaw of spring, we expected him to tell me the same and tell us when we would leave. We climbed the hill to see him at our neighbor's house and had just sat down to discuss our futures. We didn't know Clan Wolf had sailed in through a dense fog and were already attacking.

"One of Fenris's men busted in and killed our Jarl moments before we ran him through. But by the time Hodor and I ran back home, it was too late. Fenris and his men met us on the shore..." I closed my eyes, unable to stop the image of Hodor's crumpled form or the sound of his blood as it gurgled in his throat. "They killed Hodor right in front of me, and I was powerless to stop it." I sobbed, swiping angrily at the tears that fell.

"You were the only one left alive?" Armund prodded gently.

I nodded, cupping my scarred side. "What I remember most is how empty and silent everything was. The animals stopped crying out. The screams of men ceased. Only the rhythmic water lapping the shore and the sound of boots crunching on the pebbled bank remained. Fenris Wolf... I fought him. I just wasn't strong enough to kill him. He cleaved my side, but the blow didn't kill me right away. I cursed him, calling him a coward. So, he dragged me to the fjord so I would drown if I didn't bleed to death first. As I lay there with the water creeping steadily up my face, I heard him and his men slog into the fjord and push their ship off the shore. I listened as the oars sliced into the water, carrying them away. Then sea filled my ears, my eyes, and..."

I pressed my eyes closed. I could almost feel it trickling into my nose and edging down my throat. Armund leaned forward and steadied me with a hand on my shoulder. My eyes snapped to his.

"I begged the Aesir to spare me, begged them for my life. When they refused, I cried out to Skuld. She alone came. She saved me."

"Tell me about your wand," Armund asked softly.

I glanced down at it proudly. "Made from the bones of my family, and I will use it to spin Fenris Wolf's demise. I will find him. Then I will end him."

I reveled in the feeling of liquid fire as it poured through my veins, but within moments it was replaced with something colder, something that felt more ice than flame. I rocked back and forth as a multitude of emotions filled me to the brink. I'd fallen into Skuld's powerful well, and there was no coming back now.

The entire world – the air, the land, the sea – vibrated beneath and around me.

"Liv!" Armund cried out. He felt it, too, his head darting in every direction. Ravens poured from the trees in a roiling black mass and flew overhead in tightening circles, forming a kinetic funnel above us.

Armund's mouth gaped, his eyes widening as he watched the flapping of their wings and listened to the raucous caws, waiting for them to fly away. They didn't, because I would not allow it.

I held them close.

Closing my eyes, I let the memories burst from behind the wall I'd dammed them with, until all I could see was Fenris's smug smile as he tossed my brother to his friends. I heard the splatter of Hodor's life blood pouring out, spurting with every beat of his heart. I felt my knees hit the rocky shore, the helpless feeling of the water threatening to drown me, inch by terrible inch.

I let the crushing sensations churn through me until I didn't feel helpless anymore. Suddenly, I felt like I could split a tree, cleave the mountains, and fly with the crows above using nothing but the power of my rage.

My eyes flew open and I jumped to my feet and spun in a slow circle. I could feel the heartbeat of every living thing in the forest, village, and every person in the hills. Every fish in the sea, every swish of every fin. Every insect, their scuttling legs. I heard their song, listened as they sprang between blades of grass.

It was incredible.

Impossible.

Vipers poured from nearby boulders, painting the earth black, their scales glistening. They sped over the ground toward us, stopping short and forming a circle of serpents around the remnants of the house in which we sat.

"Liv!" Armund guarded his head with his arms and shouted. "*Enough.*"

The air pulsed with unspeakable fury. My eardrums throbbed, my eyes blurred, and Armund faded away. When I blinked and my vision cleared, Skuld was there, sitting where Armund had sat, wearing my face again. Wearing my blood-stained dress that gaped at her side – the one Armund insisted I burn. Wearing my scar.

I studied the slightly older version of myself as the norn spoke with my voice. "You have the power to move oceans, raze forests, and call upon every living beast. Now, what will you do with it?"

"I will end Fenris Wolf and the entire Wolf Clan."

She smiled. "Yes, you will. What began as Fenris's violence will end with yours."

Calder's face flitted into my mind. His strong jaw, the stubble that dusted his chin, his clear, cool eyes. They blazed with anger as he strode toward the enemy, blood streaked across his face, my bind rune emblazoned on his forehead.

I imagined Armund running easily along the shore, slashing his axe head at one of the mutts, then watching as two ravens – one dark and one stark white – circled overhead before diving and clawing his enemy's eyes and face.

I saw a vision of Calder's fair-haired friend Tyr wearing a serious expression as he battled with axe and sword, but still managed to fling blades that always hit their targets. Of Fell with the fiery hair, fighting with a shield strapped to his arm, snarling as his axe cut through the air, stopping in the torso of our common enemy.

Each of the men in the vision Skuld sent wore my bind rune on their foreheads… dark and infused with magic and my urgent intent to protect the wearer.

"Is this our future?" I asked.

"It is," she confirmed. "He left survivors in Skögar, Liv. Today, he returns with more men and ships than he came with the first time. But Fenris Wolf will not die today. He will see you and his fear will drive him back to the sea. He will return home to gather even more warriors and head south-ward along the opposite shore. That is where you will meet him for the battle to end all battles. On the southernmost shore. What I just showed you is the battle to be fought on Grandys soil."

I bristled at her words. I wanted Fenris dead now. "Why, when I can end him now and save time and trouble?"

A growl rumbled in Skuld's chest. "Today is a small battle in what will be a much larger war. Today, you let him taste your anger. Save your fury for when he's close enough for your sword to strike. When the time comes for you to fight and you pluck up your sword, I will strengthen its sharp blade. When your body tires, I will reinvigorate it. When you falter, I will straighten you. I accepted your bargain of vengeance and I will see you victorious. But this war will be fought on *my* terms, not yours."

Her blonde hair dripped toward her waist where her dress gaped, the scar on her side on full display. When she straight-ened, her clothing was different. She wore the dress I wore now, the dress I'd been given. Her hands were stained with ink. There was a tuft of hair wound around her forefinger. That finger gripped my sword, and on her left arm was my shield, the bind rune spiraling from its metal center in every direction.

"Prepare those whose path has merged with yours, and when the Wolf tucks his tail and flees from you, lead them south. Cross the mountains and gather your army, Vengeance. That is where Fenris will go, where you will battle him face to face, only a blade's song away."

With those prophetic words, her voice faded and she disappeared, leaving me staring at the horizon.

I blinked when fingers wrapped tightly around my upper arms and someone shook me, hard. When I could see again, I was staring into Calder's wild eyes. He was shouting something, but I couldn't make out the words.

"What?" I asked, breathless.

All around us was darkness, but the darkness had substance. It moved in a frenzied column. We were surrounded by the funneling ravens.

"Depart," I whispered, and they peeled away to reveal the shore and those gathered on it. The ravens flew into the trees and perched on limbs close by, waiting for any other command I would utter. The carpet of writhing serpents slithered away, tucking themselves among the rocks again.

Armund was there.

A freshly scrubbed Fell, who looked spooked.

Tyr's pale hair whipped about his face, his mouth set in a grim line.

I looked back at Calder, so close I could smell his fresh scent. He still held my arms in his hands. I clutched his waist to steady myself. "What happened?"

Armund spoke, limping closer. "Skuld was here."

"I know."

It felt like a dream, but I knew it wasn't. My skin felt like it held a storm, crackling with forked fire and lightning. I pursed my lips and held my hand beneath my mouth, blowing a breath toward the heavens. The clouds that had built thinned and evaporated over the sky. Moonlight drenched us all, but it wasn't enough light. Fenris was coming and I wanted him to see me.

My hands clutched Calder's arms, mirroring his pose. "Warriors from Wolf are coming back to finish what they started."

"When?"

I sent a single raven to search the sea, closing my eyes and watching through hers as she flew low over the sea. She didn't have to fly far before she saw the pale sail. "They're almost here."

"No…" he breathed.

"I won't let them reach the shore this day. Skuld wants the final battle to be fought on southern shores, Grandys lands…"

His lips parted and he gave me a lingering, apologetic look. Over his shoulder, he called to Tyr and Fell. "See that the children and elderly are safe, then return to shore and prepare for battle." He locked eyes with me. "I can't risk them," he said. "I hope you understand. I trust you, but we have to be prepared."

"Don't apologize for protecting your people, Calder. It's what I would do if the circumstances were reversed."

He inclined his head and brushed an errant strand of hair from where it caught on my lashes, his knuckle brushing my cheek.

Armund limped over. "How can I help?"

I plucked a certain bone from my bag and ran my thumb over the smooth surface, instinctively knowing it was Father's. I asked Calder for a knife and he placed the raven-headed handle in my palm. Pushing it against Father's bone, I carved a piece to perfectly fill the void in Armund's knee.

He and Calder watched in rapt fascination while I worked. I brought the piece of bone to Armund. Holding it in my palm, I let him look at the bone's new shape. "This belonged to my father." Armund's chapped lips parted as realization dawned. "I want you to have it. I want to heal you, Armund, but part of your bone is gone. Only bone mends bone."

He glanced at Calder, who blew out a long, tense breath.

"I healed Fell. Trust me," I begged. His icy, clear eyes clouded with emotion as he fought against what he knew and what he couldn't fathom.

Something passed between father and son, but in the end, Armund nodded.

I grabbed my wand and knelt beside him, Calder watching as I rolled up the leg of his father's trousers. I fitted the bone to the divot in his skin and closed my eyes, imagining the fragment seamlessly sinking into his flesh. Warm blood flowed under my fingers, cooling in the breeze. Under them, the smooth fragment met with the damaged bone, fitting itself inside the space the sword had left and fusing seamlessly with it. I held my hand over his knee and waited as the skin healed, then scabbed. When I retracted my fingers, there was nothing but smooth skin and smears of blood left behind.

Armund put his weight on the limb and gave a surprised laugh, then bent his knee and straightened it again.

I stood and spoke to Calder. "Skuld gave me a bind rune that contains her deadly mark." I drew it on my forearm so he could see. The ash ink darkened. Then I held my finger between us. "Let me draw it on you. It will protect and strengthen you," I begged.

"You said they wouldn't reach the shore," he argued.

A ghost of a smile traced my lips. "And yet you sent Fell to hide the vulnerable. This is no different. If something happens and I make a mistake, this is protection. The rune marks you as a member of Skuld's army. As long as I breathe, it won't falter or fade unless I will it to."

Silently granting me permission, he bent and let me draw my bind rune from his hairline to the bridge of his nose, his crystalline eyes never leaving my face.

T
W
⊘

WITH INK

FIFTEEN

His attention made it hard to concentrate. It wasn't because he was looking at me, but rather the intensity in his stare. Not fearfully. Not in awe. Curiously. And I wondered what it would be like to have him stare at me another way: with need or want in his eyes.

Tamping down those thoughts, I meticulously drew the powerful line of runes on Calder's forehead and the ink seeped darker into his skin, like it was made from night itself.

With every stroke, a new sensation came. A tingling in my finger, an awareness of the raven still flying between us and Fenris, a connection between me and the sky above, the earth under my feet and every creature on land and sea that was close. The air smelled fresh and dangerous, like the ozone crackle in the air just before a storm.

Calder cleared his throat. "I hope you know how much it means to me and to him… what you did for my father."

"Having power is pointless if you don't use it wisely. Your father deserves to be whole, and not only because he can fight, but because he's kind. He – and you – treat me like I'm still a person."

His brows furrowed. "You *are* a pers—"

"A ship!" Fell yelled into cupped hands from the hill he raced down. He pointed toward the sea to a spot where something white bobbed in the distance.

I darted to Armund and drew the rune on his head with smooth, precise strokes, then unwound Solvi's blonde hair from my finger and gently tucked the cut sliver into a small leather pouch, returning it to my bag and withdrawing our shields from the rucksack.

"Armund?" I offered, holding Hodor's shield out to him.

"I would be honored," Armund said, rushing to take it from my hand. He moved so freely, it was hard to believe we were about to be attacked once again. I grabbed my sword from the bag and handed it to him as well. "My father had this sword made for me," I told him. "It's probably lighter than what you're used to, but I would like you to use it."

He pursed his lips and inclined his head. "Thank you, Liv."

I laid my wand against my shield and cupped my ink pot again. As the stiff breeze caught the invaders' sail and dragged them closer, the wand above and below my hand began to writhe as if it was alive, slithering back and forth the way a serpent slid over land, just as I'd seen in the vision Skuld gave me. The vertebrae clacked together where they met, a macabre tone raking over the land. It grew louder as Fenris sailed nearer.

Another ship appeared on the horizon to the left of Fenris's. Then a third sailed into view to the right.

Fell reached Calder just as he tied his hair back with a piece of leather, handing him his sword and shield. An enormous elkhound bounded down the hill and stood beside Calder, wiggling as Calder greeted him. "This is Sig," he told me.

I reached out to pet him, but Sig tucked his tail and whimpered as he began to back away. "I wouldn't hurt you," I told him. "You remind me of someone special." I could see that he loved his master with the same unwavering loyalty as Tor had loved Hodor.

Sig sensed the danger on the sea and went still, his large eyes watching the three threats approach. A growl tore from his gritted teeth.

Tyr joined us, armed to the teeth. As the ships sailed closer, the men onboard began to shout, working themselves into a berserker rage.

The remaining Bjern kinsmen and women rushed to the shore, but they shied away from me when I offered to paint the protection rune on their skin.

I rushed across the pebbles, Calder falling in step beside me. "Can I hold it for you?"

"Thank you." I placed the pot in his hand, hoping the people's trust for him outweighed their fear of me.

Calder met a young couple and waved them toward me. "Liv, meet Brux and Elga. Elga just gave birth to a daughter." There was sharpness to his words.

"Save your judgment, Calder. If *I* don't fight for her, what kind of mother am I?" she gritted, staring at the ships approaching with such hatred and ferocity, I thought she might stop them using only the heat of her glare.

When Calder explained the purpose of the bind rune, the behemoth Brux bent to let me draw it on his broad forehead. Elga allowed me to draw it on hers, though she watched me carefully, her hand braced on the handle of an easily accessible knife.

Fell jogged over to receive his, but Tyr stayed planted on the shore.

"Tyr!" Calder yelled. "Do you want the bind rune?"

"No," he bit out over his shoulder, glaring at me.

Calder started toward him, his mouth opened to argue, but I placed a restraining hand on his chest. He stopped at the touch. "It's fine; he doesn't want it."

Sig barked at the ships and the roars of the men they held. The first time they attacked, they came quietly. Now, Fenris wanted his targets to know they were about to die.

I drew the rune on Sig's back as Calder petted him and told him to keep still. Sig was smart and had a remarkable bond with Calder. My brother's dog was a good herder, but he didn't listen and wasn't as aware of the world around him as Sig seemed to be. And he was a dog who had already seen his share of fighting.

The wind began to gust, carrying Fenris and his ships closer. Sig bared his teeth as the moonlight lit our enemy, revealing a bone white sail with a solid black wolf silhouette drawn onto the wool. A man stood proudly at its prow. Ready to lead. Ready to take what wasn't his.

"Fenris," I hissed. Calder slid the ash pot into my bag as I strapped my shield to my arm and took up my wand. In my hand, it came alive again, the bones clacking together as the wand itself undulated.

Calder stood beside me and drew his sword, watching the Wolfs. "What is the ink made of?" he asked, sliding a hand over Sig's bristly fur. The ink didn't budge or smear. "I've never seen ink so rich and dark. And it dried so fast."

I watched the one responsible for the ash. The Wolfs spotted us on the shore and began howling when Fenris told them their prey was waiting. He was almost close enough to see my face... "It's made from my family's ashes. It will not fade until I will it."

"My gods," he slowly breathed. I could feel his icy eyes appraising me, but couldn't take my eyes off the threat in front of us. The one I wanted dead more than anything in the world.

"With shield and ink and bone, I will have my vengeance," I whispered, staring at the mutt watching us from the ship's prow.

The wind died completely, and our breath plumed as Skuld's frost filled the air. Armund stood nearby with Hilda, the woman who'd given me her dress. He nodded to me once, indicating he'd sensed the shift. Skuld wasn't there in front of me, but I could feel her breath over my shoulder, almost hear her whisper to me: *Show him who you are, Vengeance.*

I called upon the ravens in the forest and sent them wheeling to the ships, as dense as a thundercloud. One by one, the birds began to dive and claw at Wolf and his men. They shouted, flailing like children and using their shields to cover their heads.

Only days had passed since Fenris and his men came to Amrok, but it felt like an eternity. I needed him closer. He needed to see me.

I felt the life teeming beneath the ocean's choppy surface. The eels and fish sensed me and obeyed as I urged them toward my enemy. The large ships rocked beneath the writhing mass gathered thickly beneath them. The sea life dragged the ship carrying Fenris into shallower water, while another mass of creatures held his other two ships back. If any of his cowards jumped overboard, they would be able to slip and stumble on the wriggling backs of fish and eels all the way to the shore. The hull rocked over their undulating bodies until they brought Wolf close enough that I could see his harsh features.

I walked onto the water and called more fish and eels, allowing them to carry me over the surface, my footsteps steady and sure across their slippery bodies as they writhed under my feet. Fenris gripped the ship's rail, watching warily as I approached.

The hatred in my stomach warmed the moment he recognized me.

"You…" he breathed, his voice sliding over the water. "You should be dead!"

I laughed without humor. "Fenris Wolf, the worst mistake of your life – your very *short* life…" he scowled at me for using his own words against him, "…was not killing me when you had the chance."

His kinsmen were spooked by the scene unfolding before them. They looked over the ship rails and shouted, clubbing at the sea creatures with their oars, still trying to guard themselves from the ravens attacking from above.

Through the tumult and clamor that raged around him, Fenris kept his eyes on the greater threat. He kept them on me.

My staff writhed in my hand as I drew nearer.

Fenris spat toward me. "Völva."

"You may call me Vengeance. Skuld sends her regards, Fenris Wolf."

I released my grip on the sea and sent the ravens toward the shore where they circled the Bjern survivors. His ship began to bob on the waves once it was released by the denizens of the deep. His men could see me and slowly, the ship went still. Not even a murmur could be heard as they carefully watched me and listened. "Row your boat closer if you aren't a coward, Fenris Wolf. Or would you rather tuck your tail and run like the mutt you are?"

His face contorted in rage and his complexion took on a mottled shade of red. He pointed a finger at me and threatened, "I'll see you again." He sharply commanded his men to turn the ships about, which they managed with incredible haste.

"I believe you are frightened, Fenris. I *will* see you again; I promise you that. I will count the hours until our fates reconvene."

I blew over my palm and sent a fierce wind that pushed them far out to sea, taking the other ships with them. A tumult of emotions roared through me as I walked back to the shoreline.

I wanted Fenris dead.

Why should we cross mountains and gather an army when I could end him now?

When I was almost to the rocky shore, I started back toward Fenris. No matter what Skuld said, I would end this. Today.

Armund's steady gait echoed behind me as he crossed the shore's smooth pebbles. "Liv. Don't test her." His beard blew sideways as he approached, hands out. He waved me toward him. "Come back to us."

I stood atop the sea, unsure whether I should return to shore or run after Fenris and drown him here. Skuld sent a foreboding shiver up my spine. She wanted him dead, but not yet. I just wasn't sure why.

"Liv," Armund continued, his steps and words refocusing me and drawing my attention away from Wolf, "what must we do now? Did Skuld reveal anything more to you?"

I watched as the three ships shrank into the distance, becoming mere specks on the horizon, until they were nothing. Only then did I return to the shore and speak. "First, I will paint my protection over this entire place. Then, those who are willing to fight with me will ride into the mountains to Clan Grandys. From there, we'll inform Jarl Grandys what the Wolfs have done and what they plan to do. We'll send word to the clans he hasn't massacred yet, and each one will have to decide whether to join Skuld's army or stand against the Wolfs alone. The battle will take place on the southernmost of Grandys's shores."

My feet carried me to Calder where he stood beside his father. Once I stepped foot on dry land, my wand stopped writhing. The Bjern warriors murmured as they peeled away, heading back to the hills. Asking any of them to come with me was hard. They'd already lost so much, and now I was asking them to leave the home they needed to rebuild, a task that seemed impossible, given the depth of destruction. Worse than that, I was asking them to separate from those who survived and needed them here.

Armund gently caught my arm. "This is Ragnarök, isn't it?" he asked so softly, only Calder and I would hear.

My brother's words echoed back to me. He thought his dream felt like the world's end because everything he held dear was gone. Hodor's foreboding dream had come to life, but his dream ended when he died. It didn't include what happened afterward. We had Skuld behind us now.

"No, this isn't Ragnarök. Skuld wouldn't have resurrected me if she planned to allow the world to end."

Calder's steely eyes met mine. I'd told him once that I died during the attack on Amrok Village, that I'd died with my family, and I wasn't lying. I *did* die that day. If not bodily, then part of my heart and soul had withered. Skuld stitched me back together with the sole purpose of facing Fenris again, this time victoriously. But sometimes, when Calder looked at me, I wondered what it would be like after the battle and whether he might play a role in my future.

Calder raked his teeth over his bottom lip. "If we don't fight, if we don't help you stop this, we might as well invite them to end us all," he said, loud enough for all to hear. Those walking the paths into the hills stopped, the moonlight glinting across their weapons, catching on white garments. "I'll fight with you."

Armund quickly agreed, as did Fell. Tyr was more reluctant, but I knew he would come with us in the end. They were family, and family protected each other.

As for the others, I wasn't sure if any would come with us. Only time would tell.

SIXTEEN

I slept like the dead but rose with the dawn as if I was home and a list of morning chores awaited. Calder was lacing his boots when I sat up and smoothed my twisted dress. "Where are you going?" I asked.

He flicked a lazy grin at me. "Tyr, Fell, and I are going to down a few trees. Right now, most of the livestock Father saved from the village are herded so tightly into one of the houses, there's barely room for them to move. Not to mention it'll take a year for their stench to waft away. We're going to build a new pen up here, where it'll be easier to care for them until we rebuild. Father and several others are trying to clean up what's left of the village and salvage what we can."

I nodded. "I'll find him. I'd like to help."

"I'm sure they'd appreciate another set of hands."

He finished lacing his boot as I stood up. I tugged on my boots and met him just outside the door where the first rays of sun shone through the canopy, peppering the ground with dappled light. His eyes slowly raked over me and my heart began to gallop. He gave a small smile.

"Your hair is the color of sunshine," he said softly. "It's beautiful."

"Thank you."

He propped the head of a broad axe on his shoulder. "I'll be back soon," he promised with a small smile, brushing a strand of hair from my forehead, letting his fingers drift to my jaw as he traced it.

The gesture was quick and to him was probably meaningless, but it made my heart skip a beat.

Calder strode into the forest as I made my way into the village. A few older men and several women were hard at work tearing down fence posts and boards that weren't burnt or broken. Children shoveled debris, ferrying it to the beach where the tide would claim it. Some made sport of it, racing one another to the water.

Armund and Hilda were raking through the debris of one home, adding a knife to a small pile of salvaged things. I told him I wanted to help, and he happily pointed me to a few shovels lying on the ground nearby. He showed me the house they'd just combed through and asked if I'd care to start shoveling there.

I poured myself into my work, enjoying the familiarity of holding a sturdy tool in my hand, shoveling ash and cinders into a bucket. Whenever thoughts of the attack wandered into my mind, I resolutely pushed them away, giving them to the sea with the debris of the homes and lives that once thrived here.

For a while, Armund and Hilda worked quietly together, but as the sun lifted, their lips loosened. I couldn't help but listen.

"Will you send word to Jorah?" she asked.

"Liv said all the clans would be informed."

"That's not what I meant."

"I feel nothing for her," Armund said quietly, never stopping his task. His rake's head found metal and he pulled an oval brooch from the ashes. He brushed it off with his thumbs, a small smile tugging at his lips. "Something so fine should be worn by a woman even finer," he flirted, bringing it to Hilda and slipping it into her palm.

Her face glowed under his attention. She pinned it to her dress. "Some of the others won't go, Armund. I've tried to talk to them, but they don't trust the völva."

"Even after what they saw? After she defended us all?"

Hilda grimaced. "Especially after that. They're frightened. They've just lost everything, and the wounds are so new."

"Will you stay, then? With Elga and the baby?"

She shook her head, her eyes meeting mine for a second. "No, I'll fight."

The new fences were in place and the livestock herded into their new pen. Sig helped to herd them into the broad gate. Among the trees they had room to move, new things to chew, and novel places to explore. The goats especially enjoyed gnawing the leaves. The hogs rooted and wallowed, finding cool dirt. The lambs bleated. Cattle still roamed, but they stayed together for the most part. They would be fenced soon enough. That was the next project those who stayed behind would tackle.

The children ran around the pen, holding out tufts of sweet grass for the animals to eat. One little girl giggled as a goat found her offering, shrilling when his lips brushed her fingers. "He tried to eat me!"

Far from deterred from her brush with goat's teeth, she ran to get more grass.

Calder found me near the animal pen, his eyes lighting. "Hey."

I smiled. "Hey."

He'd just bathed. His hair was wet and unplaited. He smelled like pine and harsh, cold waters. Fell joined us a moment later, also bathed. He nodded my way and greeted, "Liv."

Tyr passed us by with determined steps, continuing into the wood, fully armed. Fell flicked an irritated glance at Calder, who said, "I take it he won't be joining us for dinner."

I tried not to let Tyr bother me. I offered to cook for the village tonight when I told Armund we would need to leave in the morning. We'd accomplished so much together in a day, but it was all I could spare. Every time I turned around, my attention fell on the mountains. Skuld wanted me in Grandys.

"Never mind him," Fell said, waving his friend off. "I'm starving, and I hear you're baking bread for us."

I smiled. "Don't get too excited. I'm not known for my skill in the kitchen."

Armund walked over and clapped Fell on the shoulder. "Tonight, we will eat lamb. I could use some help."

Fell nodded. "Of course."

He looked to Calder, who gestured toward me. "I'll stay and help Liv."

Fell's brow quirked, but he didn't say anything else before leaving to catch up with Armund.

Calder and I walked to Armund's house.

A few aged barrels sat in a dark corner, one with a little oat left at the bottom, the other with barely any wheat flour. The winter hadn't been kind in Skögar. I leaned far in to reach what was left.

Calder laughed as I teetered on the edge of the barrel. "Would you like some help?"

"I can reach it," I gritted, stubbornly raking what I could into a bowl.

"I'll help with the dough, then," he said decidedly, rolling the sleeves of his tunic up to his elbows.

I climbed from the barrel and smirked. "I didn't know men could bake." My father would've died rather than work in the kitchen.

He smiled, shrugging a shoulder. "Men are capable enough. Father has been baking since I was a boy, and he taught me once I was old enough to help."

I rummaged through the shelves until I found honey and butter.

"If there is milk left from this morning, it's out back. I'll get it." Calder slipped out to find the small, covered bowl tucked into the shaded side of a barrel.

We worked in comfortable silence as we created dough out of the ingredients, working them into sticky messes that would soon form loaves.

"Making bread – it seems so ordinary after what you demonstrated on the beach," he finally mused.

"It *is* ordinary, but I'm grateful for this bit of domesticity. Nothing feels like it did before…"

"Do *you* feel differently?"

I wasn't sure if he meant before the attack or before I reached the well of Skuld's power, but the answer to both was the same. I pressed my lips into a thin line. "Sometimes. Sometimes I don't recognize myself, my life, or anything in it at all."

Sig nosed the door open and curled near the hearth, exhaling loudly. I couldn't help but laugh.

Calder laughed, too. "He's spending his nights with a kinsmen's dog – she's in heat."

"Chasing girls is exhausting work, huh?" I teased him. He chuckled and shook his head. I studied his profile for a moment before adding, "You, Fell, and Tyr seem more like brothers than friends."

"That's because we are brothers by choice."

I wiped my hands when my dough was smooth and formed, then turned to stoke the fire, spreading the embers so the bread would cook evenly.

"Did you have siblings?" Calder suddenly asked.

I froze, then took a deep breath. "The shield your father used belonged to my eldest brother, Hodor. My younger brother Oskar died a few years ago, and I had a younger brother named Gunnar whom I lost in the attack, along with two younger sisters, Ingrid and Solvi."

My voice broke on Solvi's name.

"I'm sorry," he said. "I shouldn't have –"

"The sword I loaned Armund and the shield I wore are mine. My shield was tucked beneath my brother's in our house when it was set ablaze. As such, it was mostly unharmed. My brother tried to protect me before they killed him, and his shield protected mine even as he lay dead and I lay dying."

Calder was quiet for a long moment as he worked his dough into a matching loaf.

"There were no survivors in Bjern Town. My mother is likely among the dead," he confided. "She, uh… she left when I was young and never looked back. I haven't told my father that I know where she is. He still thinks she lives in the south. She did for a time, after marrying someone from Clan Layrk, but for whatever reason she moved back to Bjern." He shook his head and gripped the table's edge. "I saw her on a trip to see the Jarl once. She was washing clothes outside her home. She saw me, too, but either didn't know who I was or was too much of a coward to speak my name."

"She shouldn't have left you. Either of you."

"No, she shouldn't have, but that didn't stop her," he said. "I don't think my father loves her now, he hasn't for some time, but part of him is connected to her in a way that a husband is linked to his wife. If she's dead, it would hurt him. Besides, I don't know for sure."

"Fell said he'd burned the dead in Bjern Town. Would he recognize her if she was among them?"

He shook his head. "He's a little younger than me. Probably about your age…"

"Seventeen," I supplied.

"I'm nineteen."

I caught him watching me as I picked up my dough and placed it in a large pan. Without warning, he flicked a bit of dough at me. It landed on my cheek. I scoffed indignantly and tore a fat glob from my loaf, launching it at him. It hit his jaw with a wet smack. "If you had a beard it would be stuck," I teased, smiling.

"Do you prefer beards?" he asked seriously, his grin falling away.

"Not on you."

"On others, though?" he pressed.

"It suits some men, I suppose. Fell would look strange without it. Tyr… his is short, but it fits his features."

"My father hates that I won't grow one. He teases Tyr about his short beard constantly."

"Don't grow one," I said. "You look good without it."

"Good?" he groaned, smiling at me.

"Why is good bad? What should I have said?"

"Handsome."

"You certainly *are* handsome, Calder, but you don't need me to tell you that. I'm sure you've broken your share of hearts."

He locked eyes with me. "Actually, I haven't. Were you promised to someone in Amrok?"

Surprised by his abrupt question, I answered honestly. "No. My father mentioned marriage a few times when I was younger, but Mother refused to consider it. Recently he'd started pushing the issue more often, but my mother insisted I become a shield maiden first so I could live on my own terms before settling down with someone else and living on theirs." I cleared my throat, sliding the bread pan into the coals. "And now, neither of those futures will happen. I belong to Skuld now."

The thought of never finding love and having children of my own bothered me. I tried to push the dampening feeling away as Calder slid his pan into the coals and settled it next to mine.

What would my future look like after I killed Fenris Wolf? Would Skuld insist I live the rest of my years as a völva, or could I dream that she would consider our bargain fully paid and set me free?

SEVENTEEN

We sat beneath the stars and passed platters of deliciously charred lamb, cheese Armund made days ago, and thick pieces of the loaves Calder and I baked. We drank mead while the children enjoyed milk, sipping from horns to be more like us.

Some were carefree, running around pretending to be dragons who breathed fire and soared through the skies. But others sat among the adults with forced smiles. I could feel their heartache, their loss, and their pain because it was also mine.

It made every swallow more difficult than the last.

I learned that Hilda, the woman who gave me this dress and to whom Armund gave the pendant, was Brux's mother. Though he towered over her, I could see her features on his firm face. She and Elga sat together, cooing over the baby. Elga watched me carefully.

I didn't blame her. I'd heard stories of völva stealing infants.

Many who came kept their distance from me, their wariness as thick as the wood smoke in the air. They avoided my eyes and refused to come close or allow their children near me. When the child wandered, they were carefully rerouted to a safer spot.

If I asked any one of them for something, they would give it to me without hesitation. I had little doubt they feared Skuld and by extension, me enough to comply. But fear wasn't how a *warrior* led people into war. That required trust and respect, something I wondered if they'd be able to give a völva. I just wished that for once they could see me, the girl who cried out to the gods and norns, begging for a chance to avenge her family, and not the witch with the wand of bone.

I sat on a stump beside Calder. Next to him sat a little boy that reminded me of Gunnar. He was shorter, perhaps younger, but as he tried to be brave and fit in, a tear slipped from his eyes and his bottom lip quivered. Calder saw and scooted off his seat to crouch next to the boy.

"Don't let them have your tears," he told the child. "They've taken everything else. Don't give them a single other thing."

The boy wiped his face and straightened, puffing his chest out the way my brother used to. I stood abruptly and walked into the darkness at the side of the house to compose myself.

It wasn't just the boy that shook me. There was one quiet girl whose eyes sparkled the way Ingrid's did when she was happy, watching what unfolded around her, from the fluttering of a butterfly's wings to a sibling's antics. And then there was a child, who though months younger, reminded me of my little bumble bee, Solvi. Her hair was a curled nest on her head and her bare feet were quick and nimble.

Watching the children broke me.

It was a stark reminder that I would never comb Solvi's sweet hair or have her jump on my back unexpectedly. I'd never parry swords with her or pretend to be *Jormungandr*, the great serpent so large he encircled the world and gnashed at his own tail. I wouldn't make fangs out of my fingers and chase her around the house, leaping over the backs of goats who then started jumping all over the walls and even over the backs of other animals in their mindless urgency to flee the commotion.

Ingrid would never hand me a fist full of fresh-picked flowers or share her honey with me because she knew it was my favorite.

And Gunnar would never team up with Hodor against me and the girls to see who could reach a certain mighty tree we called Yggdrasil, fighting battles of the Aesir versus giants, or Valkyries versus the dead, or elves versus dwarves. Gunnar was Thor no matter what, of course. He had a small wooden hammer Father made him when he was barely toddling around. Though he thought he was getting too big for the small hammer, he still played with it.

As my ribs tightened with thoughts of my slain siblings, the side Fenris chopped began to throb. I placed my palm over the raised skin, holding it together to be sure the scar was still there. That I was still whole.

If the little ones were here with me, Gunnar would spar with any other little boy sitting around the fire near Armund's house. Ingrid would be toying with another girl's hair, and Solvi would probably try to leap the fire just to see if she could, and giggle when I caught her in midair so she wouldn't get burned.

In my mind they still lived, swimming in thoughts of what should be and the life from which they were robbed.

A twig snapped behind me. I calmed my breathing and wiped my tears, turning to find Calder. I knew it was him before his clean pine scent wrapped around me, before my eyes met his, because I could feel his presence. It was becoming familiar, like home.

How could someone who'd only been in your life for a few days make such a heavy impression? Could the norns be weaving the two of us closer?

I took a deep breath and waited for him to speak.

"It's hard for you to see," he said quietly, intuiting my sadness.

A tear slid from my eye – a tear I was giving Fenris Wolf, though I hated myself for it. I held myself tightly, as if that might keep me together as securely as the strands of hair with which Skuld stitched me.

"It's not just that. I'm so glad *they're* alive," I croaked, unable to tell him that I just wished my siblings were, too. I squeezed my eyes shut, the pungent scent of Solvi's charred skin and hair lingering in the air.

Two arms wrapped around me and I tensed, blinking up into Calder's unwavering eyes. "I am your friend," he said. "And friends care for one another." His hands were warm and strong and sure as they stroked up and down my back, then settled, holding me tightly. "You are not alone, Liv."

It felt like I was. Even in his arms, I felt completely alone.

Alone and weak. Sometimes I wondered if I'd made a mistake in begging for my life and striking a bargain with Skuld. Maybe I was meant to die on the banks of the fjord and my horrid memories were the price for my cowardice. Then again… there were moments like when Fenris Wolf saw my face and realized who I was. Moments that my supernaturally extended life and new purpose made perfect sense. Moments I reveled in and felt perfectly comfortable and ready for.

My fisted hands slid around Calder's back and for a moment, I uncurled them and pressed him closer. His warmth radiated through his shirt into my palms.

I needed this. To feel his strong arms, his steadfast strength, his heart…

Footsteps came from around the house and we parted just before Armund appeared, glancing between me and his son. "Is everything okay, Liv?"

I avoided Calder's eyes. "Yes, thank you."

He nodded slowly, then looked to his son, hands clasped behind his back as he rocked forward. "Calder, perhaps you should find Tyr."

Calder pressed his lips into a thin line but walked into the darkness, but not before throwing a lingering glance in my direction.

Armund watched his son until we couldn't see him anymore, then he turned to me. "Now that dinner's over, most are heading home to get some rest. I didn't know if you wanted or needed it, but I saved the lamb's blood for you."

My mouth went dry at the thought, and I didn't know why, but I *did* need it.

"Where?" was all I could croak.

He waved me forward and we walked around the house where Hilda, Brux, and Elga stood. She cradled their infant, coolly watching me. Brux thanked us for the meal, even nodding to me briefly.

"Where's Calder?" Brux asked, his deep voice rumbling.

"Off to find Tyr," Armund answered.

"I wondered how the boy would take your presence, Liv. I don't mean you any offense by saying it, though."

"What do you mean?" I asked.

Brux frowned. "Tyr's mother died birthing a second child, but his father died in battle. I was with him."

It was then I noticed that Brux was older than Elga by a few years.

"Clan Varsyk used to control part of the Grandys Mountains, partly because their Jarl used a völva to sway his battles in their favor. Before his father fell, the witch cursed him. She knew his name, used it, and he was cut down almost immediately. You remember, don't you, Armund?"

"I do," he said quietly, turning to me. "He's heard the story, and over the years whenever a völva came here with the Jarl, he left the village until they returned home."

I felt horrible. I didn't want Tyr to feel uncomfortable because of my presence. This was his home, not mine.

"Don't worry, Liv. He'll come around. Not every völva is as that witch was," Brux said, pointedly nudging his wife's elbow, only to be met with a scowl.

"Aren't they, though?" I rasped. Hilda's brow furrowed, and Brux's bent the same way as his mother's. "I need an army to finish off the Wolfs. If you fight with me, *I'll* be the witch cutting down someone else's father."

Everyone went still for a moment. Elga's eyes narrowed on me, but she swayed the child as she started fussing.

"This is different," Brux argued. "Clan Wolf *must* be stopped. Armund said if we don't stop them, they will wipe all the clans away and claim the lands as their own."

"You need more than the few you can pluck from what's left of Bjern Clan," Elga said spitefully, meeting my eye unflinchingly.

"What I *need* is an army that can stand against the one Fenris is amassing. You saw the ships. He brought more this time. Ships he stole from my people and yours. He will keep building. Keep killing. He must be stopped, as must all who fight alongside him."

She nodded, looking up at her husband.

A cool wind slid over me, passing through the pines toward the Grandys Mountains. That was our path. Skuld would protect us on the journey. I could use my power to bolster our horses for the expedition, but we needed to leave. Soon.

The vision of a vibrant orange and golden dawn filled my mind and I knew what Skuld wanted.

"Anyone coming with me should be ready to leave for the Grandys stronghold at sunrise."

Elga's brows rose. "Dawn?"

"The mountain passes should be thawing by now," Brux pondered, stroking his long beard. He was bulky like my father, gruff and fearsome, but not nearly as cold or aloof. Brux cared for his wife and their new child, and it showed. He would protect them if he could, and if he couldn't, he would fight alongside her. He searched her eyes for her decision. "We could reach the stronghold in two days if we move quickly," Brux tossed out.

"We'll make it in one," I answered.

His head ticked to the side and he quirked a smile. "Impossible. I've crossed the Grandys mountains in spring many a time, and—"

"I can strengthen the horses, make them faster, fearless."

He nodded and grinned, immediately trusting my guidance. "One day to Grandys. Sounds like a fun ride. Brux shrugged to his mother, a silent conversation passing between their eyes and features.

Armund looked among the small group, the firelight flickering over his features. "Then we should all get some rest. Those who are going with Liv should prepare tonight and leave with her in the morning."

Brux offered to spread the word to those who'd left in case any chose to leave and fight with us, but even he knew no one else would join us.

Armund turned to me. "You need rest, too."

"I need the blood worse." I wasn't sure why, but since he'd mentioned it, the thought of blood had drenched the back of my mind and my fingers twitched to calm the itch his words invoked. Skuld wanted me to have the blood, though I wasn't sure what to do with it.

Armund led me inside and took a rag off the top of a bucket. Crimson stained the thin, pale fabric. "I'll take it outside, thank you," I said, reaching for the handle.

He swayed the bucket away from me. "Stay inside, Liv."

"Why?"

He shook his head. "Some conversations are best kept private."

I nodded and he sat the bucket down just beside the hearth. I dropped to my knees in front of it.

There is power in words.

There is power in blood.

And shield.

And ink.

And bone.

Armund retrieved a large fur and held it out to me. "If you get this bloody, I can get the stains out. But nothing will save your dress."

With a grateful nod, I draped it over my lap. In my mind, I saw a vision of myself cupping my hands, plunging them into the blood, and holding them there. So, that was what I did.

The second my skin touched the lamb's blood, something within me shifted.

EIGHTEEN

I sat on the near mountain next to Hodor as he tossed pebbles into the glacial lake we sometimes used for fresh water when the streams dried up. It was as pure and clear as Calder's eyes. At the thought of his eyes, I wondered where he was.

"Where is Calder?" I asked Hodor.

His brows twitched. "Who?"

He tossed another pebble. It broke the surface, spreading ripples across it, but they didn't travel across the water. They lingered like they didn't want to die away.

I studied my brother. Watched his chest rise and fall. Took in the familiar, easy way he sat with one knee on the ground and the other pointed toward the heavens. A forearm rested on the raised knee, but his other hand sifted through the pebbles we sat upon to find the perfect one.

Did he know he was dead?

"Where are you, Hodor?"

He snorted and gave me a half-smile. "I'm right here, Liv."

Of all our siblings, he and I favored one another the most. My features were more delicate, but we shared expressions and fears, told one another things we had never told anyone else. Things we wouldn't trust to anyone else.

Hodor was sitting with me. It was really him. I'd stake my life on it.

"Where are you when you aren't here with me?" I pressed.

"I'm content."

Words truly did have power, because those two, simple words made it easier for me to breathe. They made the clenched fist around my heart relax. It made it easier to look at him and not look away. Most of the time, my guilt wasn't worn like a blanket, lying heavily on my shoulders. It was a thick, wet clay that I sank further into with each step, one I couldn't back out of no matter how hard I tried. One day, I knew it would smother me.

"I miss you," I told him.

"How can you miss me when I'm sitting right next to you?"

"You aren't always," I answered, also sifting through the pebbles.

He threw one and the strange, slow ripples slid over the pond, lethargic and unhurried. "Aren't I?" he asked. "I'm never far."

Two ravens appeared and circled us. One stark white. The other dark as the midnight sky. Muninn and Huginn. Odin's ravens.

My spine straightened. "Are you with the Alfather?"

Hodor gave a single nod, then leaned back and watched the ravens circle us.

So Odin had been there after Fenris Wolf and his clansmen left me to die. I saw his birds, but Odin didn't want to save me. He wouldn't listen to my pleas. He refused to spare my life, but took my brother to Asgard to live amongst the gods. He led him into the great hall of warriors, Valhalla, and invited him to his table to feast among the fiercest warriors to have lived.

My brother deserved to be taken into Odin's care. He deserved much more than the violent death I wasn't strong enough to prevent.

My lips parted. I wanted to tell him I was sorry for not listening when he told me to run, sorry he died, sorry we weren't sailing across the sea together, preparing for our first raid. I wanted to tell him how his shield protected mine against the fire that consumed the largest part of our home. I wanted to say all those things, but when I looked beside me, he was gone.

I glanced up, but the sky was empty. The ravens left with him. I wondered if they had carried him to me. If they might do it again.

All that was left was the fresh-smelling wind, the pebbles beneath my fingers, and the crystal-clear lake.

A sapling sprouted from the water. Its small, green leaves unfurled and widened, becoming as broad as clouds. The trunk stretched taller and expanded until it consumed the lake itself and there was nothing but trunk, branches, and gnarled roots punching through the sky and ground. Yggdrasil.

I stood and followed the only sound – whispers that came from the other side of the enormous tree's trunk. I crept closer, letting my fingers drift along the bumps and ridges of its smooth bark, walking until I saw three tall women huddled around something on the ground.

One of them turned to me.

Skuld wore my face. "Welcome, Liv." She waved me over.

At their feet was a spring inlaid with smooth, gray rock. "Urðarbrunnr," Skuld began, "waters Ygdrassil. The spring keeps her healthy. On Midgard, it nourishes the living and allows them to complete the purposes we create for them."

Her sisters were beautiful. One boasted hair the color of dark, rich earth with skin as pale as moonlight. Her dress was simple, comprised of translucent shades of dew-covered spider webs at dawn. She crouched near the well, cupping her hands to capture the spring water before gently applying it to the tree's trunk. It soaked into the rough bark, darkening the wood. "Urd tends the trunk, where the past of all those who live and have lived is held."

The second sister had hair as red as a fox's. It hung in waves to her calves and fanned around her somber dress as she bent and collected damp soil from around the spring and applied it to the thick base of the roots springing from the tree's trunk. "Verdandi tends the soil blanketing every root that springs from the tree. The soil gives the root what it needs most right now. She tends the present of every living thing."

"And you?" I asked. "What do you look after?"

Skuld smiled with my mouth and brought an axe out from behind her back. The iron was strong and the edge glinted as she regarded her weapon. "I determine when a root will no longer grow. When it has outlived its purpose and causes more harm than good to Ygdrassil."

She clasped my hand and drew me away from her sisters, to the far side of the tree. I watched my back over my shoulder, but the sisters kept to their tasks; Urd watering the bark and Verdandi applying mud to the base where the roots began to stretch and separate.

When I turned forward again, I saw the charred remnants of our home. A twisted root curled toward Amrok Village. I could see it beyond the tree, the root slithering through the rocky soil like a great worm. It split and forked too many times to count, spreading necrotic tendrils over the ground, greedily taking hold of the soil.

"This root belongs to Fenris Wolf," she said with a gleam in her eye. She crouched beside it, her fingers – my fingers – sliding across every bump on the root's surface. She stared up at me. "Tell me what you feel."

I ran my fingertips across the root.

There was strength.

There was life.

There was darkness.

Malicious hatred.

Greed.

Violence.

Bloodthirst.

"How does it help the tree?" she prompted.

My hand drifted along the root toward the tree, but all I could feel was hollowness. "It does not help the tree."

She let out a confirming hum. "Because it serves itself now. It is almost time to rid the tree of this parasitic root." Skuld smiled. She stood and waited until I stood with her, then held out her axe to me.

"I offer you a gift, but it comes with a warning." I swallowed thickly. "Do not let harsh, cold waters draw you away from your destiny."

Calder?

My fingers wrapped around the leather handle and my eyes slid up to the delicate axe head, tracing the familiar arc. At the base of the handle was a sharp spear I knew by heart.

"And now for your gift," she said. "A reminder… of what you lost and what you stand to gain when you fulfill the bargain we struck. And a reminder that I will cleave any *root that diverts from the tree to serve itself, Liv."*

I blinked, trying to focus and make sense of what I'd seen. My mother's axe lay beside me, the wood her hands had worn intact. Not even a char mark marred the handle. Blood-smeared bones were strewn from my bag to a black tunic on which a needle lay threaded with my hair. Someone had worked the bones, stretched and arranged them over the tunic's fabric, layering them like… like armor. But they weren't affixed to the garment.

A blood-sopped fur lay haphazardly across my lap and my arms were submerged in a bucket of warm, wet blood. My forearms were stained where I'd pushed them deeper into the bucket, the blood rising higher up my skin.

What was happening?

Calder opened the door, took one look at me and rushed across the room, dropping to his knees. "What happened?"

"Don't interrupt her, son," Armund chastised.

Suddenly the air turned frigid and our breath plumed. Armund's eyes met mine. "She's coming."

"Who?" Calder demanded. My teeth began to chatter as the blood filling the bucket before me froze. He tugged at my hands, but they wouldn't come free. The ice hurt. It burned my skin. I began to pant as I tried vainly to move my fingers. Desperate to be free, I lifted the bucket and brought it down hard on the ground, crying out when the impact cut all the way to my bones.

Sig whined and paced back and forth behind Calder. He shrank as the fire in the hearth went cold.

As our eyes gradually adjusted to the low light, a strange feeling crept over me. It started in my fingers and spread up my arms, clawed at my throat and slid down my spine, down to my toes. I tried to scream, but no sound would come. I tried to move and couldn't. I was trapped in my body, while another presence was trapped inside with me.

"Calder Armundsssson," Skuld hissed from my mouth. This time, she used her own voice, the one I recognized when she called my name as she pulled me from the shore's edge. "The thread of your future is entwined with hers, but *she is mine*."

Before me, Calder's eyes shimmered with fear and then something hotter, more akin to anger.

The bucket of frozen blood that trapped my hands thawed in an instant, the blood sloshing as I jerked my hands free. Calder covered them with his, feeding them warmth, but like wading into warm water with cold feet, my fingers stung and burned at his touch.

NINETEEN

Armund, Fell, and Calder were busy packing their things when I woke, each rummaging for this and that, stuffing leather bags and satchels full of what they might need. Tyr was nowhere to be seen.

Neither Armund nor Calder mentioned what happened the night before, and I didn't bring it up. Instead, I stretched my fingers and peered out the open door to see the sky was still stained as dark as the ash ink in my pot.

I sat up, my eyes catching on the bone-laden tunic. Someone had cleaned the mess up. The floor had been scrubbed and the bucket removed. It sat clean just inside the door. The bones that had littered the house were tucked back in my bag. My mother's axe lay beside me, unblemished and whole, but how was that possible? I'd taken the charred spike and axe head from the ruins of our house. I rifled through my bag, confused about the item that lay beside me.

Had Skuld given me one that looked like hers? Or had she used Mother's axe to build it anew?

My hands came up empty. Skuld had truly given me my mother's axe, replacing what had burned away and was destroyed.

"A reminder… of what you lost and what you stand to gain by fulfilling the bargain we struck."

Hodor was in Valhalla.

I didn't know where Father, Mother, Oskar, Gunnar, Ingrid, and Solvi were spending their afterlives. I could have kicked myself for not asking Hodor if he knew what had become of them.

Scrubbing a hand down my face, my heart thundered. With more blood, would I see Hodor again?

"Liv?" Armund asked from across the room as he cinched his bag of clothes. "Where did you get that axe?" Fell watched me as he tied his leather boots. Calder's hands stilled as he clutched his shield.

"It was my mother's," I croaked. "It was burned. Ruined. But Skuld returned it to me."

Armund studied me closely. "You remember her being here?"

"Bits and pieces."

"She spoke through you."

"That I remember," I told him, suppressing a shudder.

Armund hiked the bag he'd packed onto his shoulder. "I imagine it was difficult to bear the giantess inside you."

"She doesn't feel or appear like a giantess when I see her. She wears my face," I admitted. There was something about her that frightened me. Maybe it was the calculating gleam in her eye or the wicked glint of her axe. But mostly I was just grateful to her, for her presence. If it wasn't for her, I never would have come to Bjern, never would have met Calder or Armund, or Fell or Sig, or any of the others.

Armund went still. "She appears *as you* when she visits?"

I nodded, examining Mother's axe, turning it left and right, running my fingers down the handle and spear, pausing on the point. "You sensed her the same moment I did," I told him.

Armund nodded slowly. "Skuld feels nothing like you, Liv. She feels like a cold so deep, it burns the skin."

"How do *I* feel?" I asked him.

It wasn't he who answered. Calder spoke instead. "You feel like light rain in sunshine, and the Bifrost that arches the sky on a warm spring day."

The Bifrost was delicate, comprised of red that blended to orange and yellow, morphing to green, blue, and purple. It didn't appear often, but when it did... everyone stopped what they were doing to watch and stare until it faded away again.

I was taken aback by his answer.

Fell cleared his throat, claiming my attention. He tucked his axe into a loop on his belt. "He's right. You feel like everything beautiful and good in this world, and none of the bad in it."

Calder flayed him with a sharp glare before Fell hurriedly took up his pack and left the house.

Armund waved his son outside. "Let's give Liv some space to ready herself." Calder stood, gathered his things and left the room, only the doorway severing his stare. "We'll prepare the horses," Armund promised, leaving me alone in his house.

Sig sat just outside, rising when I closed the door behind me, then trotted over to where Calder stood. Dawn was just beginning to brighten the cloud-filled sky. It would rain today. I could smell it on the breeze that toyed with my hair.

Tyr was ready and waiting for the others, wearing more knives than I could count. He scowled at me and turned his attention back to his horse, patting her thick neck.

Fell gave a friendly nod from where he spoke with Brux and Hilda. Son and mother, both willing to fight. It caused a leaden weight in my stomach when I thought about them leaving Elga and the infant alone while they traveled with us, yet I needed them.

Armund left Calder to hold the reins of three horses and made his way to me. "Liv," he greeted with a smile. "Many are not willing to leave their children, so I'm afraid this is it."

"I appreciate every one of you and don't fault anyone for wanting to stay," I told the assembled group truthfully.

I wore a dark cloak and a thicker, pine green dress I found folded near my bag. Had Hilda loaned me another?

She chatted with Brux and Fell. I was thankful for the sturdy, tightly woven wool. There was a chill in the morning air, but this was nothing compared to what we would face when we made our way into the mountains.

"Calder prepared a horse for you," Armund said, gesturing toward his son.

Calder's crystal blue eyes were already watching me. He had not stopped since I stepped outside. He wore a thick eggshell tunic, brown trousers, and a fox skin across his shoulders. It was the same shade as Verdandi's hair, and a shiver ran up my spine at the thought. My hand tightened on my staff.

I recognized Mordi when I approached. The horse stepped left to get a better look at me, calming the moment he recognized me. "Mordi," I greeted. "You look well. Are you ready for another adventure?"

He dipped his head and raked the ground with heavy hooves in response.

"I hope you'll be comfortable riding Mordi. You named him, after all," Calder said, appearing on the opposite side of Mordi's neck. I smoothed a hand down his silvery mane, inhaling sharply when Calder's finger grazed mine. He was also stroking Mordi, but I could almost swear I felt his touch drift down my neck and back.

"But he's yours," I argued weakly.

Calder smiled. "I'm not so sure of that anymore. He's quite taken by you."

His words hung in the air like the grin clinging to his lips. My face warmed and I shifted on my feet, hoping he meant what I thought he was implying.

For one, selfish moment, I wished I was simply a girl who could revel in his wit and charm. For a moment, I wished my life was mine and not Skuld's…

I never should have let the thought linger. I should've pushed it away. Skuld plucked at the hair binding me and a sharp pain zipped through my scar.

I managed not to scream, though I inhaled sharply and pressed against the raised slash.

With magic whispered in the ear of each horse to bolster speed and strength, we made our way into the mountains in a serpentine line of travelers whose horses' hooves quickly ate up the ground. The instant we left the lower forests and crossed the invisible line between warmth and frost, the terrain changed. The trees became sparser, only the hardest and sturdiest pines able to withstand the unforgiving cold, snow, and wind.

The passes were mostly melted, though a few snow-slickened places remained. The horses never slipped, but remained steady, focused, and determined. Tyr and Brux led the way, having traveled to the Grandys stronghold more times than either could count.

With spring's arrival, travel would soon resume, the trade routes opening between clan lands and over the wide, salty sea. Tyr's almost-white hair flapped behind him, a pale pennant announcing our party to the gods and nature and anyone else who might happen upon us.

Brux's horse was enormous. It had to be to carry him. With a wiry beard that covered his thick chest, his head was freshly shaved on either side, a thick, golden braid sweeping down the middle of his head. Neat and tidy. Like the gleaming axes strapped to his back, easy to access.

His mother, Hilda was covered in a large fur, her golden hair tucked beneath a knitted hood. She and I rode behind Tyr and Brux, with Fell, Armund, and Calder behind us. Sig ran alongside Calder and his mud-brown mare, easily keeping pace with long, loping strides. I'd whispered magic to him, too.

Snow-capped mountains surrounded us in every direction, like the teeth of a great beast rising from the earth to devour us. The air was crisp and cold, but the more distance we put between us and Skögar Village, the more relieved I felt. It was like taking a breath after holding one in for far too long.

It was how I knew Skuld, though she was watching the tip of every root from Ygdrassil, all the while sharpening her axe, was with us.

Our horses drove down a steep mountainside with us clinging to their necks. When we drew near to the bottom where a shallow stream lay, I whispered for them to stop. They slowed and then obeyed. After hours of riding, they needed water and food and we needed to stretch and take a short break.

Fell cursed light-heartedly. "I didn't think there was any way we'd make it to the stronghold by nightfall, but I'm glad you're proving me wrong, Liv."

I led Mordi to the water.

Armund brought some oats for him. I couldn't help but laugh as Mordi inhaled them. "He loves to eat," Armund told me, "but he's greedy. Aren't you, boy?" he teased the horse.

When not even a single oat remained in his hands, Armund returned to get oats for each of the other horses. Though I was making them strong with the magic Skuld had given me, true strength came from within. They needed nourishment. Beyond that, no amount of magic provided the comfort in knowing we would care for them despite the punishing pace we asked them to endure while carrying us and our belongings.

Hilda brought smoked fish around to everyone. I accepted a piece and thanked her. It seemed those were the only words we could speak to one another.

Tyr glowered as he passed us on his way to Fell and Calder, where the three spoke in hushed tones. Armund and Brux wandered into the pines to relieve themselves, leaving me and Hilda alone for a moment. Hilda watched them go, then turned to me.

"Don't let Tyr upset you," she offered, brushing wild strands of hair from her face.

"He doesn't."

"He can be very untrusting of newcomers."

"And witches," I added. "But I don't blame him, given his past. And I would rather feel his ire than have him hide it and have it explode when I least expect it."

Hilda nodded. "My last husband could be violent when he was drunk," she said. "That's why I poisoned him."

Our eyes met, and in her steely blues swam a thousand unpleasant memories. She brushed her horse's mane, running comforting fingers through the dark strands. "Brux doesn't know."

"I won't tell him."

She inclined her head respectfully.

My mark was on her brow. It was on all their brows… except for Tyr's. He refused it again before we left Skögar. I explained the power of the bind rune, and he explained that he didn't want me to touch him. And that was that.

"He would have hurt my child," she said, strength and surety in her voice.

"Some roots were meant to be clipped," I told her, bolstering her with Skuld's wisdom.

I remembered being a child and watching Father stalk toward Mother, his face mottled and red with fury. I remembered cowering into Hodor's side, closing my eyes only to open them again to make sure she was okay when the shouts and grunts began. My mother was nothing to trifle with, and she showed Father that more than a few times before he learned it well enough not to test her again.

That night, he almost lost an eye to the sharp blade of her knife. The next time, she split the top of his ear. The last time he crossed her, she almost killed him. If he hadn't begged, lying on his back with his hands up in surrender, apologizing all over himself, I think she would've split more than his ear in two.

That time, Oskar huddled against *my* side and I held him tight. I could still remember the feel of his thin, trembling body. After Oskar died, things between my parents settled. Perhaps grief was responsible for calming their tempers. Perhaps it was time. Whatever accomplished it, I was grateful.

When Hilda walked into the woods, I leaped the stream and picked my way into the trees on the opposite side. The frigid wind roared, rattling the pine needles and blowing them sideways before dying down again. I relieved myself and returned to where the others were resting. Tyr stood beside his stallion, tying his bags on tighter. He watched me carefully as I emerged from the copse of stubborn trees, stopping beside Mordi.

His eyes were an unusual shade of green. Not dark or light, but something in between. The hue was muted, but there was a bright vividness in the way he combed over every detail around him.

"If you're wondering why I came, it's to protect them from you," he said, ticking his head toward Fell, Armund, and Calder.

"From me?"

He nodded once. "From you." He paused. "And anything else that threatens them."

"I won't hurt them."

He snorted derisively. "Not purposely. But there are ways a man can hurt when no one lays a fist or blade to him."

I knew that. Gods, did I know it well.

"I won't hurt them," I repeated.

His features hardened. "Then stay away from them. Fell believes you're some sort of Valkyrie come to save him and lead us into battle. He'd lick the leather soles of your shoes if you asked. And Calder…" He shook his head, disgusted. "Just keep away from him. You needed warriors, and here we are. Don't believe we are anything more than that to you. When Fenris Wolf lays dead, all this," he gestured to his clansmen, how they jovially laughed and teased, "…will end for you. You'll never be part of us."

I nodded my head, feeling the sincerity of his words ring through my soul.

I turned away from him and swung onto Mordi's back as Sig loped between the horses, eager to run again. Taking my cue, the others mounted and prepared to ride. I infused all the animals with strength and told them to run, to keep their steps sure, and to keep pushing forward. We would make it to Clan Grandys's stronghold before the sun set behind the thick blanket of pale gray clouds.

192

TWENTY

We rode hard, up and down the steep, hoof-worn paths, some of which were barely passable, until one particular pathway widened and curved upward, choosing one of the mountains from the midst of so many. The road was well maintained, with no ruts, holes, or bumps.

Tyr and Brux led us up the mountainside along winding trails that switched back and forth up the slope, toward the stronghold. The walls of the fortification were built of hewn rock provided by the mountain itself, and the men keeping watch atop the walls saw us and were ready when the earth gradually flattened at the base of the fortress. We approached a pair of enormous wooden doors boasting carved, intertwined dragons, their scales intricately and painstakingly crafted. Even the fire they breathed seemed to lick from the wood.

"What business have you with Clan Grandys?" one man shouted from the top of the wall.

Armund answered him; as the eldest among us, it was his duty. "We come to you from Skögar Village, from Clan

Bjern, with news for your chieftain." He brought his horse around to ride next to me as the men from Grandys prepared to open the door for us. "They will know what you are and ask things of you, Liv."

"I know." Jarls always sought favor with völvas.

He inclined his head, pursing his lips. "Their Jarl is known for his skill in battle. If you can secure his favor, his warriors would be a great addition to your army."

The wooden doors creaked and groaned as they parted. Tyr and Brux led the way into a courtyard, the hooves of our horses crunching the fine, dark rock underfoot. Several young boys and girls waited eagerly to take our horses to the stables. I gave Mordi a parting stroke and told him I'd see him soon.

The young boy holding Mordi's reins went still as he took in my staff. An older man with a dark gray, grizzled beard pushed him away and told him to run along. He waited, guardedly watching me. "The Jarl will want to know a völva is in our midst." He waved me forward. "Come with me."

"Where she goes, I go," Calder insisted, stepping forward to stand with me, close enough that his shoulder brushed mine.

"We *all* go," Armund amended, scratching Sig behind the ear as they stood on my other side.

The man huffed a laugh and scrutinized our party, his eyes catching on Brux above my head. "Very well. *All of you* can follow me."

He led us through a herd of goats contentedly chomping on hay, their rectangular pupils watching disinterestedly as we passed through the courtyard. After another set of carved wooden doors opened for us, we were ushered inside and led down a long, straight hallway. In the middle of the corridor, we turned left into a great room. Mounted animal skulls adorned the walls, their horns sharp and pointed. The chieftain of Clan Grandys sat in a massive wooden chair, draped with deer and bear skin. His eyes raked over me, flicking to Sig who sat protectively against my leg.

"We come with news, Jarl Grandys," Armund addressed him.

"What news?" Jarl Grandys was taller than most men, even as he was seated. His legs were long and muscular, and his body was broad and strong. In his thirties, he was still a formidable warrior, one who rarely lost a battle. But more than that, he held power because of his central territory and the mountains that allowed him to fiercely protect it.

"Clan Wolf has attacked towns and villages belonging to Clans Urðr and Bjern. He has plans to decimate towns along the western coast, and we have reason to believe they will soon turn their attention south. Your people in the towns and villages along the coast are in danger."

He stroked his dark beard once before leaning forward and planting his elbows on his knees. "No one will breach the stronghold we have built," Jarl Grandys boasted, dismissing our worry.

"Do you not care for your people who live outside this fortress? They'll all be slaughtered," I spoke, stepping forward.

Along the path, Tyr told how he'd visited Grandys last year and spoke of the mysterious circumstances that surrounded the elderly Jarl's death. His son took the position, challenging anyone who stood against him, and won handily. He said that Ivor Grandys was neither kind nor fair, but was the sort of man who aligned with whomever was most powerful.

He pursed his thin lips and sat up straighter, amusement glinting in his eyes. "You finally speak, *smár ormr*," he laughed. "I wondered what your voice sounded like." *Little serpent*, he called me, his eyes raking hungrily down the vertebra lining my staff. "I thought it might be *your* backbone lining your wand. But clearly, yours is intact."

My fingers tightened on the bones and I walked forward until I stood directly in front of the Jarl. Sig's toenails clicked the floor behind me as he paced.

When I took hold of his arm rests and bent to stare him square in the eye, he had the good sense to lean back in his chair. Startled, he muttered a curse at something he saw in me. After a few ponderous moments, I slowly told him, "An insult to me is an insult to Skuld herself. Watch your tongue, or I'll carve it out and offer it to her in penance."

His fingers tightened on the upper length of the chair's arms. "What do you want from my clan?"

"I want every man and woman warrior you can spare to join the army I will lead against Fenris Wolf. We need to make our way south. Fenris Wolf is already sailing there. The battle will take place on your shores, and I am positive that if you aren't willing to leave your safe fortress to defend the vulnerable who've pledged fealty to you, Skuld will replace you with one who is."

"How do you know Fenris Wolf's plans?" the Jarl asked curiously, the conceit he'd once dripped like venom evaporating at my threat.

"The same way I know your seeress is standing just outside," I told him, standing up straight again.

The chieftain choked on a laugh. He nodded to a broad-shouldered man in the back who opened one of the doors from which we'd entered. Sig's hackles raised as a seemingly frail old woman shuffled into the room. Her hair was coarse and gray, lying in tangled snarls on her head.

Deep wrinkles covered her face and neck. Her dress was stark white, reminding me of the snow that covered this mountain. Some of it still lay in great piles outside after being cleared by hand so people in the stronghold could move about. The weathered woman's eyes were cloudy, like milk in water. The seeress made her way across the room, one of her hips popping each time she put weight on it.

"She is what she claims," the woman announced, her brittle voice crackling over the room before she even reached me. And when she did, she was short of breath and took a moment to catch it. The woman was blind, but still... she could see. She looked me over and shook her head. "My gods," was all she could say. Over and over. "My gods."

Ivor Grandys stood from his broad chair, a deerskin slipping carelessly onto the stone floor at his feet. "Velda, tell me what you see of Clan Wolf."

The seeress Velda tilted her head to the side, staring over my shoulder, beyond this room, to someplace none of us could see. I glanced at Armund, wondering if he could sense what she saw. His features and muscles were rigid as he waited to hear what she said.

"They ride the waves... bloodthirsty and ready for battle. Skuld affords you an opportunity through *her own*. You'd be wise to listen to the girl." Velda's milky eyes fell on Ivor. "You should give her anything she needs, otherwise, prepare to taste your death. The Wolf won't stop at the shore when he craves the mountain."

Ivor did not like the vision his seeress painted any more than he liked imagining himself dead, his power stolen from him by another.

Velda stared at me and I at Velda.

Neither of us moved.

Neither shifted their weight.

Neither breathed.

Until suddenly, Velda looked away, turned, and slowly shuffled back across the room to the door she'd entered by.

"Have you nothing more to say?" Ivor shouted after her.

She ignored him and kept walking.

He scrubbed a hand down his face. The weight of his people's future pressed his shoulders down. "Most of the rooms here are taken. You'll have to share," he offered gruffly. "I'll have something brought up for you to eat," he said, his voice low and pensive. He was still likely considering what to do now that his seeress had confirmed my dire claims.

"Thank you, Jarl Grandys," Armund answered graciously.

"How long do I have to consider what you've said?" he asked, his hungry eyes trained on me again.

"We leave at sunrise," I answered.

His mouth dropped and he sputtered, "That's too soon to gather an army!"

Fell and Calder shared a knowing glance, their eyes flicking to me. If he was talking about gathering his men, it meant he was with us.

"How long would it take?" I asked.

"Days."

I shook my head. "Your people along the coast don't have days. We leave at sunrise and we ride south as fast as the horses will carry us."

Tyr interjected, "Our horses need rest."

"They will be rested, Tyr," I promised. "They will be ready."

Ivor Grandys stood, stretching as tall as an elm. "I'll do what I can."

We were given two rooms to split and share, straw and skins to make beds with, thick, spicy porridge to fill our empty stomachs, and plenty of fresh water that tasted like and probably was melted snow. It was so pure and clean I almost drank it all at once.

Armund stayed in the drafty stone room with me and Hilda while Brux, Fell, Tyr, and Calder took the room next to ours. Sig kept watch in the hallway between the two, curling into a ball, ready for sleep.

Within moments of settling in, each person in our weary party had cuddled into their beds. Exhaustion overcame us quickly after a hard day's ride and the promise of an even harder trek tomorrow. Armund's soft snoring kept me awake at first, but soon lulled me to sleep. Just knowing he and Hilda were in the room made it easier to relax.

In the dead of night, Sig's low growl woke me. I threw the deerskin off and padded to the door to find the seeress waiting outside for me. She reached out to pet Sig and quietly shushed him, but he would not stop the low growl tearing from his chest and throat. "Sig," I whispered. "Stop."

Sig obeyed but continued to watch Velda closely.

The woman waved for me to join her and then shuffled further down the hall, turned left, and hobbled down another dark corridor. She led me into a room lined with tables. On their tops were crystals, bundled herbs, littered animal bones, eggshells, a pile of dusty, unused rune stones, and more bottles than I could count.

There were no chairs in the room, just a circle-like nest of blankets and goose down pillows, bristly feathers poking out of one of them. "Sit," she said, gathering a few things among her many tables. They varied in height, build, and function, but she knew what each held without the gift of physical sight. As slow as she seemed, she made quick work picking through what she needed and didn't.

"Do you know much about seeresses?" she asked as she worked.

"No."

"Most don't," she agreed. "But your mother kept you from them, and from völva. Among her children, she was especially protective of you. Do you know why?" she asked conversationally.

Because her own mother thought I'd become a scourge upon the earth. Or maybe she thought Skuld might one day choose me and she'd have to put me down, too.

"She may have wondered if you might share her mother's... inclinations," the old woman plucked the thoughts from my head, "but that is not why she guarded you so fiercely, Liv."

"Then why?"

"Because she saw herself in you. You were so much like her, and she wanted to keep you from the awful things she experienced in her youth."

I opened my mouth, wondering if I should ask what had happened to her, when Velda answered. "You don't want to know them. Don't taint her memory with such ugliness. Just know that she was justified in her protectiveness. Any woman who'd endured such things would've been the same way, if not far worse, as a mother." Velda made her way to yet another table and searched it for something... I wasn't sure what. "Völva are Skuld's own. Seeresses, on the other hand, belong to Urd. We see the past when she allows it."

"Who does Verdandi claim?" I asked.

"The living. Everyone has the gift of knowing what is happening now."

She shuffled across the floor and her hip creaked when she lifted it over a pillow. She sat down slowly, finally falling on the pillow across from me, ignoring my outstretched hands. I'd jerked to my knees to assist, but she didn't want or need my help getting down. I wondered if it would be different when she needed to stand.

"You have rune stones. Those are not used to view the past..." I led.

She chuckled. "Do you see the layers of dirt? They were a gift from Ivor once he became our chieftain, before he understood how witches and seeresses differed. He was disappointed when I told him I couldn't use them to predict his future. The only thing I *can* view are the pathways of the past. From those routes, sometimes one can get a sense of what the future could be, even though I can't see it. It's like standing in the middle of a stream. If you can only see upstream, your instincts will tell you what downstream might look like for a time. Of course, it's a very small glimpse, as streams often carve unexpected paths, twisting and turning where they can. The past and future are no different. The past does not change, but the future is always ready to."

My brows kissed as I struggled to follow her logic.

She wagged an arthritic finger at me. "You're different, though. One look through your past and I knew your future, even without the ability to read it. Snap a stick and one can fit the pieces back together. The piece of your past line up with the pieces of your future. The sliver of air where they meet in the middle... that's your present."

Velda held out her hands. I cupped mine beneath them and she let the rune stones fall into my palms. A rush of energy pushed the breath from my lungs. The stones turned hot and I cupped my hand around them. Somehow their heat met the flame in me and became comfortable.

Velda smiled, her pale eyes seeming to focus on me. "Yes," she said. "They warm to you." She rifled through a collection of bowls, smiling when she found what she was looking for. She scooped leaves into a small pouch and handed it to me as well. "Henbane."

"For what?"

"In case you need to go to Skuld in a hurry, child."

Henbane was poisonous.

As if she read my mind, she added, "Just chew a tiny pinch. Skuld will keep you." She was quiet for a long moment before speaking again. "Your bind rune... would you draw it on me? And if Jarl Ivor chooses to send his men with you, will you protect this place with it?"

I nodded. "Of course."

She smiled and closed her eyes. "With shield and ink and bone, you will have your vengeance, Liv. It is what you said, and so it will be. But it won't be as easy as you think it will. There is a secret on your brow, one you keep even from Skuld. What are you planning?"

201

I swallowed and pushed the thought away, locking it in the darkness where it belonged.

Velda's milky eyes assessed me, but she didn't prod. She lit a bundle of herbs and let the smoke billow upward, a wave of fragrant smoke bursting and pluming across the ceiling in every direction. She told me how she envied me for visiting Ygdrassil and watching the fate weavers work at the tree of life, then admitted she pitied me for what I'd endured by Fenris's hand.

I didn't want her pity.

Pity wouldn't bring my family back.

I wanted Fenris to bleed. I wanted to hear him scream, to beg, for his lungs to gurgle with blood. I wanted to listen as he suffocated. His death wouldn't bring them back either, but knowing he was dead and couldn't ruin another life would comfort me through whatever time I had left on this earth.

When Velda was satisfied with the blessings she spoke over me, she told me to go and get some rest while I still could. Dawn would come soon enough, and I'd have to race off toward my destiny.

Could a person's destiny be one *thing* – one defining moment – that was the only thing you were born for and the only thing that mattered? Or was destiny a tightly woven fabric made of many moments of fine threads, each as important as the one beside it?

Calder waited in the hall outside our rooms, comforting Sig by petting his back. Both perked when they heard my footsteps.

"I didn't mean to wake you."

He smiled slightly. "Sig was concerned."

"Only Sig?" I teased before I could stop myself.

"No," he answered seriously. "Not only Sig." He stood from where he crouched beside the gray elkhound. He raked his knuckle down my cheek, then used it to raise my chin, his touch soft and warm.

"You shouldn't," I whispered.

He leaned in so that his warm breath fanned the shell of my ear. "Saying a man shouldn't do something doesn't keep him from doing it. Just like telling a man he shouldn't feel a certain way won't stop him from feeling it."

I steadied myself by gripping his forearms, feeling them flex under my hands. His found my back and pulled me closer.

"I worry for you," he said. "I shouldn't, but I do. And I can't stop. I've tried."

A twinge of pain rushed across my scar as Skuld reminded me, once again, that I belonged to her. And while I was hers, I could never belong to him.

If things were different, I would have placed my palm on his stubbled jaw and hoped he would lean into it. And if he had, I would have drawn his lips to mine and placed a slow, chaste kiss upon them, infused with everything I felt for him so he could taste what was slowly building between us, what had begun churning in me since my spirit met him that fateful night.

His eyes glittered in the darkness, illuminated only by a torch far down the hall.

"You should rest," he said, breaking the tense silence.

He wanted more than I could give him, more than Skuld would allow. And so did I. The two of us were hopeless. Tyr warned me that I would hurt him and I wondered if, in the end, he'd be right about that.

I slipped back into my room and settled into my bed. When I pulled the deerskin over my body, I thought of Calder. His steadfastness. The honesty in his crystalline eyes. The way he cared. The feel of his hands, his breath. I imagined what his lips would feel like, and then wondered if I should push him away to protect his heart, and what was left of mine, before Skuld shredded them both.

Now that my family was gone, I didn't matter to anyone beyond what I might do for them. That was even true of Skuld.

But it wasn't true of Calder.

To him, I mattered.

And Calder now mattered to me. I couldn't have pushed my feelings for him away if I tried, and I wasn't nearly strong enough to do that.

TWENTY-ONE

Jarl Ivor Grandys met us in the stronghold's courtyard before dawn, every inch of the rocky soil filled with his men and their horses. It had snowed overnight and the light coating glistened in the morning sun.

Draped with a sumptuous blue cloak, fine skins around his neck, and wearing cat fur gloves, Ivor Grandys looked every ounce the noble chieftain. His shield and axe lay beneath the layers, the fine, silver double blade sticking out.

A falcon was perched on his arm, a small piece of parchment tied to his leg. He raised his arm and the bird took flight, screeching as it flew north over the mountains.

Our horses were brought out, looking rested, satiated, and ready for the arduous journey ahead. I swung onto Mordi's back and steadied my wand over my thighs as I tied my bag onto my shoulders. Mother's axe poked through a hole I'd made for it, careful to make it just large enough and not stretch the animal hide further. I didn't want to lose anything out of my bag as we rode.

Jarl Grandys found me right away. He was almost as tall on foot as I was seated on Mordi's back. The wind tugged his dark beard sideways as he walked toward me. "These are all the men I can spare. Some will remain behind for protection."

In case Wolf prevails and sets his sights on the stronghold, was his unspoken explanation.

"I understand. And this is a formidable force. Thank you for trusting me."

He smiled. "I trust my grandmother."

My eyes flicked toward the stronghold where at the nearest door, Velda waited and watched, a blanket wrapped around her frail body to fend off the cold. She raised a hand to wave goodbye. I waved back, knowing that somehow she knew I did.

The rune stones she'd given me hummed in the pocket of my gray trousers, and the bones I'd begun to knit into armor warmed against my back beneath my plain cloak and the furs Jarl Grandys gifted as thanks for warning him and potentially saving lives and his land.

He grinned. "She is my mother's mother. If you're wondering whether I favor her, I'm afraid I take after my father."

His eyes flicked over my shoulder. I turned to see what he was looking at. Calder, Armund, Fell, and Tyr maneuvered their horses closer to me. Hilda was tying her leather boot on tighter as she chattered with Brux about the descent and how it would be one to remember if it was as fast as the climb yesterday.

Sig paced where he could, avoiding hooves and swishing tails, excited to run again.

"They say you can make the horses fearless, fast, and unbreakable."

"I can."

He nodded. "Please do. I'd like to reach the coast as quickly as possible. Sterg Village is in the foothills. We could stop there to rest, then continue on tomorrow."

"We'll stop there by midday and make it to the coast by sundown," I amended.

His mouth gaped. Then he laughed. "There is no possible way."

"Armund told me about your lands. Korg Village has fewer people than your twin coastal towns. We should go to Sten Town or Ragyr Town."

"I'll send a rider to Korg. He can split from our group near the coast and tell them to either join us in Sten or flee to the stronghold. Since Sten Town lies between the two, I say we make our stand there."

"Very well."

"I'm sending messages to the other chieftains, to warn them and ask their warriors to join us in Sten Town."

I traced the path through the sky carved by his falcon.

"Are you sending the falcon to all of the jarls?"

"Just to one. To the others, I'm dispatching my fastest riders. They'll lead the other clans' warriors to Sten Town."

I nodded, though there was something in the sly way he smiled that made me think of the screech of a mountain lion.

"I'll lead the way down the mountain, völva," he asserted, giving Mordi a pat. "Let's see what you're capable of."

Armund guided his horse beside mine and shook his head. "That man is a mountain himself. No wonder he chooses to live in them."

Ivor Grandys was exactly that, and I had a feeling that like these icy topped spires, he was just as deadly and unforgiving when he wanted to be. In fact, I was counting on it.

"It's good he's warning the other clans," Calder said from my right, watching as the doors of the stronghold parted for us.

I hummed an assent, still watching Ivor as he swung onto the back of an enormous black stallion. When everyone was on horseback, he called for the gates to open.

Jarl Grandys rode through the outer wall of the stronghold first, followed by too many men and women on horseback to count. Our smaller group was tucked into the middle of them and from there, I spoke the words that bolstered the horses, urging them to run faster, keep their steps steady, and ignore the icy ground.

Armund and Fell rode in the front, Calder and Sig at my side, and Brux, Hilda, and Tyr trailed behind us. "We stay together," Armund had told everyone as we gathered outside the rooms at dawn. Fell, Tyr, and Calder had immediately replied in tandem: "Fight as one, live as one," to which Armund gave an approving nod.

These people were family. They took care of one another. They fought for one another. Back to back. Swords toward their enemies. Ready to fight, bleed, and die to protect the others.

Hodor and I were like that. If Fenris Wolf had never come ashore, at this moment he and I might be sailing across the open sea, preparing to strap our shields on and raid for riches. To fight together and survive together before returning home as true warriors, tested and tried and emerging victoriously. Bringing our Jarl silver, gold, and jewels. We would be rewarded for our journey and bravery, and then congratulated with a share of the spoils.

When we had raced from Leif's house toward our own, Hodor and I made a grave mistake. We forgot one another. We were so focused on the same goal – protecting *the rest* of our family – that we forgot each other. I couldn't help but wonder, if we had stayed together, would it have made a difference? With so many of our people dead and so many of their warriors unscathed, in the end, maybe it wouldn't have mattered at all.

But things would have ended differently. I wouldn't have watched as Fenris's men surrounded my older brother, slit his throat, and let him collapse on the shore we walked since birth. I wouldn't have watched his life drain away.

I *shouldn't* have run like he shouted. Like he begged. But I should have stayed close so I could fight beside him. So we wouldn't be separated, then or now.

Snow trickled from the sky, flurrying down and catching on my hair, eyelashes, skin, and fur as our horses raced down the mountain pass so fast my eyes burned and watered against the bracing air.

Our horses carried us over rock and ice with sure hooves, over solid ground and soft earth that gave little by little and slipped off the mountainside. We climbed, descended, and climbed again. Surrounded by so many capped mountains that all looked similar, I wondered how we would escape them, or if we would ever find our way south and out of the cold and snow and ice.

As we rode along the side of another peak, a sudden clap of thunder sounded overhead, startling Mordi, even startling me. I shrank down, hunkering against his back. He didn't rear, but he did slow. Most of the horses did. Then they huddled together with darting eyes and pinned ears, frightened.

Snow flurried from above.

"Thundersnow," was murmured throughout the group. As well as, "Thor."

Fell cursed from behind us as he and Tyr studied the sky. Tyr quietly spoke to his friends and warned them, "The mountains have their own weather, much like the sea. Storms relentlessly weather these peaks, common as waves rolling onto the shore."

I stared up at their jagged tips, wondering how they were still pointed after so many years... or maybe the wind was more like a whet stone, sharpening them into something even the snow and ice couldn't stick to.

Calder spoke to Sig in a calming voice and for a moment, I envied the dog because I was anything but calm. This high up, the lightning that accompanied the thundersnow was terrifyingly close to our heads.

Some of the horses balked and refused to go forward, backing into others, turning in circles where there was little room to do so. I whispered for them to calm down.

Another clap of thunder.

Snow and rock trickled down the mountain above and below us.

Jarl Grandys shouted, "We need to get off this path and out of the storm!" He urged his horse forward again, but we remained still as the horses carrying his clansmen and women in front of us were slow to peel away.

Sig tucked his tail and whimpered a moment before another low rumble rolled across the clouds.

The only warnings I received was the hair on my arms raising and the taste of fire in the air before a bolt of lightning plunged from the sky, striking a tall, thin pine on the hill just above us. The pine let out a harsh crack and fire quickly consumed its trunk. "Tyr, move!" I screamed.

Tyr was alone. He'd doubled back to check on Armund, who saw the strike and pushed forward. But Tyr was going to be crushed. The tree would not stay upright for long.

I leapt from Mordi's back and ran as fast as I could toward the tree.

"Liv!" Calder shouted. I could hear barking and heavy footsteps behind me pounding the earth.

The tree teetered, then with a groan, began to fall.

I caught it with my staff, calling on Skuld for help. The trunk hovered in the air over my head as the lightning fire spread. Branches and needles raked my clothes and tore at my face. Bark and ash peeled away and fell onto me. Heat from the fire slid over my skin. I gritted my teeth, holding the tall, heavy tree as high as I could.

Skuld flooded me with her strength, taking the burden from my arms. In that moment, it felt like I could hold a mountain up if I needed to.

I could feel her in the bones in the bag on my back and in the bones threaded onto my wand, in its ribcage spinner. I sensed her on the wind and in rock underfoot. In the fire consuming the pine. In the ash and in the frigid air and ice that surrounded us. She was everywhere and nowhere and with me.

Tyr ducked his head and rode beneath the tree as fast as his horse would carry him. Once he was clear and out of danger, I stepped back and let the pine fall. It crashed to the ground, making the earth tremble. Loose rock and more ice skittered down the slope.

The tree lay across the trail. Jarl Grandys stared with wide eyes from atop his horse from where he'd stopped to see what the commotion was.

Steam hissed as fire met snow and ice and flame was snuffed out. Plumes billowed into the air and soon, the fire was put out and the plumes dissipated.

Calder wrapped me in his strong arms, laying his chin on my head. "How did you do that?"

"I didn't want him to get hurt."

Calder let out a shuddering breath. "Thank you."

Tyr dismounted nearby, all of us crammed on a piece of level earth along the path too small to hold us. Taking a few seconds to compose himself, his pale hair flinging back and forth by the wind, he finally calmed and focused on me, pointing a finger at my chest.

I wasn't sure if his gesture was accusatory or a strange way of thanking me, but I didn't explore it. If he thought I sent the bolt and called it down so I could pretend to save him, he was wrong. And I didn't feel like hearing the venom I thought might spew from his mouth.

More thunder rolled overhead. Lightning split the sky again and again, forking sideways over the darkening clouds. "Jarl Grandys!" I yelled. "You need to lead them down this mountain as fast as you can."

His horse cantered nervously in a circle, but he kept his eyes trained on me, seated above the pile of men, women, and beasts though he was downslope.

"Go!" I screamed as the sky turned green and my hair rose again. I could hear my name on the frigid wind. Someone was calling for me, and it wasn't Skuld.

My eyes flicked to Calder's. "It's not safe for you here."

"And it's safe for you?" he challenged, the muscle in his chiseled jaw flickering.

I didn't have time for his stubbornness or his honor. Looking over his shoulder, I found an ally. One who respected me and loved him. "Armund, tell him to go."

"Liv, I sense Thor," Armund warned. "Calder!" he barked. "This is something she must face. Alone."

I looked to Fell and Tyr and they appeared beside Calder, each pushing a shoulder backward. "I'll be fine," I promised as he was carried away by his friends. Their horses hauled them further down the mountain, out of harm's way.

Wind blistered my face, peeled the fastened fur from my shoulders and sent it flying up the peak, leaving me shivering, but my bag stayed on my shoulders. Skuld quickly filled me with warmth. Did Thor want to stop me? Did the gods favor Fenris Wolf? If the gods entered the battle, would they or Skuld prevail?

Lightning bolted to the ground from every direction, searing rock and ice as the bolts traced a fiery circle around me.

Snow stung my face. Thunder shook the earth.

At the peak above me, a drift of snow began to slide down the mountainside when a jagged bolt melted and loosened the snow. I ran as the snow and ice gathered, building into a frigid wave as it raced toward me. It was too wide and fast to outrun, and when I realized that running wouldn't help, I planted my feet and held out my staff. If I was going to face Fenris Wolf, I had to be brave enough to stand against a

212

collapsing mountain of frost, or the wrath of a god, because *he* was far scarier. Far more destructive.

The barreling snow and ice would last seconds. Fenris could kill for as long as he drew breath. And if I was going to best Fenris, I had to trust Skuld. I had to finally trust myself and believe I was the warrior my mother had seen, the girl she handed the shield to the evening that felt like a lifetime ago. Worthy and fierce.

The mass of snow uprooted trees as it picked up speed, plucking them as easily as errant weeds as it skinned the peak. It roared like the storm that threatened to scalp our home the night Mother killed the witch.

I wouldn't be brought down today, even by the mighty god Thor.

My staff began to writhe, the bones clacking as they touched, separated, and touched again. Power flowed through my veins, white hot and deadly. I set my feet and screamed as it roared closer, closer, and as it hit.

Though the white ball of fury slammed against me, it was as if I was encapsulated within an invisible wall, impenetrable and true. When my surprise wore off, I couldn't help but laugh. My chest felt free for the first time in so long.

Why did I doubt what my purpose was? *This.* This was my purpose.

Vengeance embodied.

The living vessel of the norn of future.

The snow fell away, leaving a pile in front and behind me that covered the trail, but I climbed over it, careful of my steps. I laughed again, relishing the feeling of absolute freedom.

"Fenris Wolf is a plague upon this earth, and he will die at my hand!" I shouted to the sky, to Asgard.

Thunder crashed again and a great bolt of lightning forked down. I caught it with my wand and it coursed through my skin, evaporating as quickly as it came. My wrist burned, but my clothes were intact. My heart thundered in time with the sky.

I was alive.

I was struck by lightning and survived… though my inner wrist still burned like it was on fire.

I pushed up the sleeve as much as I could, revealing skin that was angry, red, and blistered. My mouth parted in a silent scream as the burning intensified. Tears leaked from the corners of my eyes and my breaths became shallow hisses. I was afraid to touch the wound but needed relief. I plunged it in the snowbank left in the snow slip's wake and cried out when my skin burned against the ice. Steam poured when hot met cold and the snow around my arm melted until only a cavernous hole remained.

My heartbeat calmed as the pain ebbed. I brought my arm away from the bank, thankful the pain was gone.

A strong wind kicked up, threatening to drag me off the mountain as it pushed every tall thunderhead from the sky, clearing it almost as instantly as night gave way to the day. When the sun shone down upon me and I could see the mark left on my forearm, I noticed a white scar in a shape I intimately knew. *Ygdrassil.*

Footsteps crunched the snow behind me. I whirled around and came face to face with myself. *Skuld.* "Well done."

I stared at her, energy still pulsing through me with every beat of my heart. The wind howled around us. Unsettled.

She jutted her chin toward the blazing scar on my wrist. "Thor sought to kill you by wiping you off the mountainside, but you believed in me and showed him that you are worthy of my favor. The Aesir meddle in affairs that are not their concern. I will remind them of their place, and none will dare bother you again." I swallowed thickly, staring between her and the white scar of Ygdrassil. "It's a mark of respect," she continued, "and all who see it will know you are favored by Thor."

"I didn't seek his favor. I just want a chance to end Fenris Wolf," I rasped.

She smiled with my lips. "I know. And so you will have it." Just then, she turned and crouched down, catching Sig as he leapt into her outstretched arms. Startled, he bellowed and jumped away, looking between the two of us. He took several steps back, tucking his tail and letting out a low growl.

I soothed, "Sig. It's me."

Skuld laughed as she stood. "You are *my own*. You don't need him at your side."

I knew I didn't need him. But just the knowledge that Calder was near made me turn from her and look for him through the strands of hair lashing my face.

He appeared on the path, his hair the color of wet sand whipping in the gusts of wind that hadn't yet died down.

He saw me. He saw Skuld.

He stopped in his tracks, panting to catch his breath, darting his eyes between us.

"Liv?" When his eyes fixed on me, the fact that he knew me made my heart thunder harder than the skies had only moments ago.

Skuld gave me a look of warning, a stern, unyielding hardness in her eyes. She raised the edge of her tunic, sliding her fingernails to the scar on her side and slipping one under the hair that held the skin together, plucking at it. A slicing pain filled my side before she vanished.

Calder ran to me, catching me as I fell, a hand pressed to my side. His frantic hands pushed strands of hair from my face. "Tell me what to do!"

My teeth chattered from the pain.

"Is my side bleeding?" I managed. "My scar…"

He raised my tunic and gingerly ran a thumb over the scar. He shook his head. "No. It's whole."

It didn't feel whole.

He held me as the pain ebbed. When it was gone, he hugged me to him. "I'm terrified for you."

"*Of* me, you mean." I was afraid that any moment something I did would frighten him away, that maybe it just had. Yet… he was here with me. Worrying over me.

His hand stilled on the back of my head. "I meant what I said."

TWENTY-TWO

Once we traveled below the frost line, the tension bled from the shoulders of those who rode ahead of me as they released the collective breath they'd been holding. My own muscles relaxed and Mordi's did, too. I felt his steps lighten even as we continued the hard ride down, over and around the hills that formed a seemingly unending labyrinth of dark stone, emerald pines, and arctic gusts of wind.

The sun guided our way, not a cloud entering the sky. The frigid air bled away with the melting ice and snow and the sparse trees thickened into a proper forest as we descended. Once the thin trails became wider, the spirits of the warriors in our party seemed to lift.

What remained were the whispers, mostly about me.

They saw me catch the tree and watched as I held it aloft until Tyr was free of it. I'd earned their respect, but somehow something worse shimmered in their eyes. Swirls of admiration and awe, yes, but also fear.

Calder was silent as he rode at my right and Sig flanked me to the left, easily keeping pace with Mordi. Brux and Hilda rode ahead of us, while Fell, Tyr, and Armund rode behind. We made it to Sterg Village just as the midday sun reached its apex.

Jarl Ivor Grandys wasted little time and words. The faces of the villagers lit up at the sight of him, but when he told them why we'd come, their smiles quickly faded.

Children brought water and fed our horses while we took the chance to stretch our legs, eat a quick bite of whatever was offered, and relieve ourselves. The day's ride wasn't over. We still needed to reach the coast. From here, two riders would diverge from our group, heading to Korg Village and Ragyr Town, while we plunged ahead, heading straight for the heart of the coastal settlements Clan Grandys lay claim to: Sten Town.

Children pointed at my wand, then at the bones wrapped around my heart, ribs, back, and arms. Women whispered behind covered mouths. I ignored them and withdrew the pot of ash ink from my bag and began painting the bind rune, moving from house to house. A hush fell over the busy town, even as they rushed to attend their Jarl and clansmen. I felt their eyes tracking me as I moved, examining every swipe of my finger.

A child approached, her wheat-colored hair carefully braided. She held her hands behind her back but withdrew a brush. "Would this help?" she asked, her innocent blue eyes wide. She feared me, but not enough to keep her from bringing me a gift.

I crouched down as I would have done for Gunnar, Ingrid, or Solvi and saw the faces of my young siblings reflected in the leanness of her cheeks. Winters were always hard, no matter how much a family packed away to prepare for it. There was something about the cold days that seemed to stretch on when the food wouldn't. The harsh wind and meager provisions robbed children of the roundness of their faces far too soon.

I smiled and she did, too.

"It would help me very much. Thank you…" I waited for her name.

"Lofn," she said, holding out the brush.

I took it from her small hand. "Thank you, Lofn."

She bounced on her feet but didn't leave. "May I watch you?"

I smiled at her puffed out chest. She reminded me of Gunnar in the confident way she held herself, but her eyes burned like Ingrid's. So seriously. Firmly. "Of course you may."

Dipping her brush into the pot of ink, the horsehair came out as black as the night sky. I used her gift to paint the rune on everything I could, as quickly as I could. The brush made the strokes sharper, more potent. As I moved around the village, I heard the Jarl telling his people to gather what they could and move to the stronghold, to take tools to dig through the snow slip, and to go quickly.

He told them what Clan Wolf had done to my village, Urðr Town, and to my people. He told them about Clan Bjern's losses at Bjern Town and Skögar Village. Then he told them about the agreement he'd made with me… that through Skuld, I would protect them all. He pointed to my bind rune and told them it was evidence the norn favored me and them.

Even though Lofn had watched me carefully, her little ears were listening to her Jarl. "Skuld?" she whispered. "Do you speak with the norn who weaves our futures?"

I turned so she could see my face. "I do."

"Is she beautiful?" she asked innocently.

I wasn't sure how to answer that. She'd always worn my face each time I saw her.

"She wears many faces."

The girl's eyes widened, then her mother called her name and she quickly told me goodbye, thanking me for keeping her safe before running home. "Do you need your brush back?" I yelled.

She stopped and shook her head. "You need it."

She took off again. I watched her pale hair stream behind her as she ran, her homespun apron dress flaring at her feet as she dashed away.

My sisters did the same whenever our mother called for them.

I went back to my task with a lighter heart and finished painting the bind rune on all the longhouses, moving quickly around the tree line to form a circle of protection around the village itself. That was where I saw Tyr... in the woods.

"I suppose I owe you now," he said as he leaned against a tree, picking beneath his nails with a sharp knife.

I shook my head and dipped my new brush into the pot. "I didn't do it so you would be beholden to me, or even stop hating me for someone else's deeds long enough to give me a chance to prove I'm not like the witch who cursed your father." He stood upright, deftly tucking the knife into a sheath. I watched him and he watched me just as carefully. "I saved you because I could, and because you didn't deserve to die for a trial meant for me."

He was quiet, his eyes locked on mine with a storm roiling in his greenish eyes. The wind stirred his pale hair, his short beard.

"I gave my word to protect you, and I will keep it," I vowed. "I grow tired of death." The exhaustion I felt down to my soul leaked into my voice.

"Yet you crave it," he challenged. "For Fenris and his clansmen."

"As you crave it for all völva, and for Clan Varsyk's chieftain for calling her wrath down upon your father, Tyr. Yes, I crave death as much as I loathe it. Vengeance is a razor sharp, double-bladed axe, and I will wield it against my enemy. Will you?"

His throat bobbed as he swallowed, then he quietly walked toward the village.

Tyr wanted me dead, but he wouldn't kill me. He wouldn't risk upsetting his family. I just wondered if he'd attack during the battle. An opportunity and a well-thrown blade was all he needed.

When I returned to Mordi, I noticed Calder and Armund in a heated argument. As I placed the small pot back into my bag I tried not to listen, but couldn't help it as their voices raised. Sig stood, watching the men's argument escalate. I brushed a comforting hand down the back of his head. He looked up at me, wanting to help but not knowing how. I felt the same way.

"Don't, Calder," Armund fumed, placing a restraining hand on his son's chest.

"And why shouldn't I? They insulted you!" He started toward a group from Clan Grandys who stood amongst their horses, chuckling and nodding toward Armund and Calder.

"Because it doesn't matter," Armund asserted wearily.

"It matters to *me*," Calder gritted, pushing past his father. I stepped out in time to catch him.

"What happened?"

Calder's nostrils flared. His skin was flushed with anger. Fell and Tyr rushed to his side, pushing him back toward Armund. Calder withdrew his knife and pointed it at the four men who'd angered him. A promise of death.

His friends removed him from the men's sight as I walked after them with Armund. He scrubbed a hand down his face.

"What happened?" I asked Armund.

"Some people do not understand second sight. They think it's a gift for women. Many know I have it, so they say things... things spoken in ignorance. I learned long ago to ignore it. My wife was unable to endure it, even in our own village, and Calder struggles with it as well."

I shook my head, protesting, "But everyone seemed so kind there."

"You only met a few survivors, Liv. Most of them weren't warm to you, either."

"I'm sorry." Sorry people weren't kinder, yet sorry Calder hadn't reached the men. The balance between peace and war within me was always teetering in an uneasy truce.

He placed his hands on his hips and stretched his back, then stroked his horse's mane. "It's not Calder's fault. He's been fighting for me since he was a boy. Did he ever tell you that he ran away to find his mother once?"

I shook my head.

"He found her, though he doesn't know I know. He told me that he searched high and low and she was nowhere to be found, but a friend of mine kept watch over him while he was in her town. Calder learned a valuable lesson in seeking her." Armund paused for a long moment before continuing. "He learned that I was not to blame for her choices, and neither was he. That she'd *chosen* to leave. I gave her everything she asked for and more, and in the end, it wasn't enough. But that was not my fault. It was hers.

"She was never satisfied with anything. Not a stable home, a husband who loved her, a son who needed her... Nothing. And she will never be satisfied or content with her life because she always believes she needs more. Nothing will ever fill the void that lives inside that woman."

Calder thought Armund would be hurt to hear she might be dead, but I didn't think so.

Armund blew out a tense breath and looked to the blue sky. I wondered if he needed a friend. I knew how to be a sister and a daughter, but a friend was something I'd never strived to be before now.

Without speaking, I wrapped my arms around him, hugging his neck. He clasped his around me and patted my back. "You are a good man, Armund. An honorable one. And you were blessed with a gift that can't be understood by lesser men." He hugged me tighter.

We parted and he gave me a grateful smile. "Thank you for stopping him. For being a friend to us both, Liv. And I'm sorry lesser men and women don't understand you either."

I watched him go, then retraced my steps, easily finding the four who'd insulted him. When they saw me approaching, they stiffened and stood up straighter, their laughter dying away.

I stood there for a beat and scrutinized the men's faces, allowing them to feel the full weight of my glare. "If you speak of him again, I'll cut out your tongues. If you look at him again, I'll carve out your eyes."

Fear shone in their eyes. What mighty warriors they were… cowering before a young girl. I might have Skuld's powers resting in my bones, but it was the spirit of my mother who stirred within me now. Her protective heart. The firm grip of her hand on the handle of her axe. My threat was not without substance. I hoped they saw the truth of it in my eyes.

I turned and left them, returning to Mordi before Armund, Calder, and the others returned to their horses. The men I threatened moved closer to their Jarl like scolded children clinging to their mother's skirts.

Jarl Grandys looked from them to me with his brow wrinkled quizzically, then shouted for his clansmen to prepare to ride out. Warriors from Sterg Village joined our ranks and together, we raced toward the shore. I just hoped we weren't too late.

Sten Town was unharmed when we arrived, and still abuzz with activity as the sun sank west. Jarl Grandys was visibly relieved, smiling at those who greeted him and took his horse away to tend. If Sten Town was fine, then perhaps Korg Village and Ragyr Town were as well.

A small boy came to collect our horses, leading them into a large pen. I took my staff and bag and stood, unsure what to do or where to go.

We were at the mercy of the Jarl.

Armund was still angry with Calder for losing his temper, so the rest of us kept quiet, too, though we stayed together.

Jarl Ivor Grandys sent someone to fetch us and usher us through the town where the houses were tucked tightly against one another, breaking the sea winds that rolled off the water. We walked past the impressive harbor where ships and their masts and tucked sails bobbed, ready to be boarded and sailed across the water upon their chieftain's word. We followed the messenger onto a slope where the rock abruptly stopped, having fallen into the water long ago, the cliffs remaining steadfast and strong. From there, we stepped into the largest longhouse I'd ever seen.

Jarl Grandys sat at the head of a thick wooden table, already sipping from his spoon, a steaming plate of fish stew in front of him. He dipped a loaf of bread into the stew and bit off the hunk, chewing loudly. His eyes fastened on me.

"Smár ormr, *little serpent*, welcome to my home. You are welcome to stay with me as my guest," he said. "And your friends as well," he added, gesturing with another chunk of bread.

I narrowed my eyes, but thanked him.

"Please," he gestured to the table, "sit. Food will be brought out right away."

Jarl Grandys insisted I sit at his right hand, in a seat of honor. Fell managed to skirt around the table to sit on my other side, so Calder settled across from me. Tyr sat on Calder's left and Armund sat beside him. Brux and Hilda took the seats on either side at the end.

"Are you married, Jarl Grandys?" I asked, gesturing to the empty seat at the table's other end.

He gave a saccharine smile. "Indeed, I am not. But I could be persuaded…"

The innuendo hung heavily in the air and I fought the urge to gag until steaming bowls of stew were placed in front of us. My stomach hurt it was so empty. I was sure everyone else felt the same way. The table was quiet as we satiated our hunger and thirst, gulping the mead that was served next.

"Have you traveled outside of Clan Urðr lands before, Liv?" Jarl Grandys asked, taking a measured drink of mead and watching me carefully over the rim.

"I had never left my village, but just before we were attacked, I met with Jarl Urðr. I was talking to him when the Wolfs ran aground. I think he was about to tell me that I would sail for the first time this spring to raid with the warriors of our clan, along with my brother."

"Then you'd earned your shield."

"Yes." My hands tightened around my cup.

He raked his hand down his beard and asked me to explain how Clan Wolf attacked Amrok Village. I told him the onslaught was swift and violent, the fight short and decisive. Clan Wolf sailed to shore cloaked in a heavy fog. The village didn't know they were there until they were cutting people down.

He asked us how they'd attacked Skögar.

Calder told him about how they came ashore at night, how Armund woke him, and how the people seated with him now rushed from their homes in the hills to fight back.

Tyr spoke up. "If it weren't for Calder, our village would have been devastated, like Amrok."

My eyes locked with Calder's as Tyr elaborated, telling the Jarl how he swam into the sea, then climbed aboard and lit their ship and sail on fire. How the flames drew the vermin from our shores and sent them scrambling away. I'd seen it with my own eyes and with my soul, and he'd seen me there with him. No one knew that but him and I.

"Clever," Jarl Ivor complimented Calder as a shapely young woman poured more mead into his cup. His eyes raked over the girl and she blushed.

"I hope you come up with something equally as clever when Clan Wolf comes to these shores. Which," he began, turning his attention to me... "will be *when*, exactly?"

"I'm not sure."

"There are two völva who spent the winter in Ragyr Town. I asked the rider who went to warn them to ask them to come here and assist you in any way they can."

He effectively ended the conversation when he caught the young woman who'd served him mead and tugged her further into the house, into a private room. Uncomfortable, we left his house to give them privacy I wasn't sure they wanted or cared about.

Armund, Tyr, and Fell went to get the lay of the village while Brux and Hilda went to search for one of her cousins who had married a man from Sten Town. Sig was waiting for Calder outside the Jarl's house. I scratched behind his ear and his leg thumped the ground. The setting sun warmed my skin, casting it in gold tones.

Calder's eyes were already on me when I looked up.

"Calder, what you did to save your people..."

"Happened to work. Nothing more."

I shook my head. "You're too modest. Jarl Ivor was right. It *was* clever."

"Cleverness might save you once, but it does not win wars."

"I'm more than aware that you've a body for fighting, Calder." My eyes raked over his chest. He'd removed his tunic after we ate, intending to bathe and change. His muscles and scars were on full display, gilded by the sun.

His breath caught in his chest as my fingers traced the scars on his upper arms, on the back of his hand. I suddenly wished he had more scars to enjoy.

He tipped my chin up. "And you do as well. I'm aware of that, too, Liv." His thumb grazed the faint scar on my cheek and the one just beneath my ear. I wanted to draw him in and press my lips against his, to learn his taste and feel his heartbeat against my chest.

But Skuld sent a lightning bolt to my side so strong my knees almost buckled. I tried not to let him see.

"I can't, Calder," I whispered, pulling away.

He looked away. "Can't, or won't?"

"Does it matter?"

"It does."

I stared out over the sea, picking up a rock and sending it hurtling over the cliff on which the Jarl's house was perched. "I want to, if that matters at all. I want you. But I can't."

My heart sank, flooding like one of the *knorrs* Clan Wolf had put under the tides.

He stood quietly with me as the sun disappeared, leaving us drenched in twilight.

"Calder," I began, pausing for a long moment. I wanted to throw caution to the wind and pull him back to me, but I couldn't hurt him like that. Anything we started couldn't be finished. But there was something I needed, and I trusted Calder to be there for me. "I need help from someone I trust."

"Name it and it is yours."

I removed a small pouch from my side. "I need to speak with Skuld to see when Fenris and his clansmen will arrive. This is a quick way to her."

"What is that?" he asked as I pinched some herb from inside and held it between my thumb and forefinger.

"Henbane."

His lips parted. "Henbane is –"

"Poisonous, I know. But this will not hurt me."

"How do you know? Did Skuld give it to you?" he asked.

"Velda did. The seeress from Clan Grandys."

"How do you know she can be trusted?"

I placed a hand on his chest, over his heart. "I feel it. The same way I felt it when I saw you that night on Fenris's ship."

The muscle in his jaw ticked. "Is this the *only* way?"

"There is blood." He pinched the bridge of his nose. "But I think this way is best. I just need you to watch over me while I go to her."

He nodded decidedly. "Then that is what I'll do."

I placed a hand on his cheek. "Thank you, Calder."

He caught it as I let it drift away and brought it to his lips. They were soft and supple, and the kiss sent warmth up my arm. I clasped his hand and drew him toward the sea, toward the cliff, where I sat and pulled him down to sit with me. I kept my eyes on Calder's crystal ones as I placed the pinch of henbane on my tongue.

At first, nothing happened. Then everything happened *too* fast.

I could only see through a small tunnel.

My eyes darted, looking through the hole of a needle, seeing nothing. Where was Skuld?

My pulse raced and my breaths turned shallow.

"Liv?" Calder said, concern lacing his voice.

He eased me into his lap and held me tight, raking hands down the side of my face, my hair. "Calm down," he urged, whispering into my ear. "Find Skuld, Liv. Is she there with you?"

Helplessness overwhelmed me, an angry wave crashing over a ship's hull, as I began to tremble and my skin heated like iron in a forge.

All I could do was scream.

TWENTY-THREE

Skuld was ice.

She turned to face me, still wearing my face. Perhaps everyone she came to regarded their future selves through her. It made sense, as she was the keeper of their future.

"Liv."

"Where is the spring?" I asked, searching the base of Ygdrassil for the life-giving water. For Urd's dark tresses and Verdandi's long, fox-fur mane.

Skuld stood alone, as tall as a pine in front of a great loom nearly as wide as Yggdrasil's trunk. Urd emerged from the back of the loom while Verdandi slipped up from behind me to join her sisters.

"The past has been woven," Urd explained. "I do not need to tend the loom… though I do enjoy revisiting the patterns in the fabric." She ran her hand down the intricate detail, sand threads interlaced with midnight blue ones.

"The present," Verdandi slyly smiled, "is the thread on the shuttle." She pushed the shuttle through the threads and pushed the weaving bar down, squashing the thread she'd spoken of into the others. "And then with a quick pass, it's gone and belongs to Urd."

"But the future…" Skuld said, "is full of possibilities." She plucked the strands strung across the loom's top.

"We made it to Sten Town. Jarl Grandys joined us. With his help, we have a small army with which to face Clan Wolf. He sent word to the other clans so they can prepare and join us."

"You've done well, Vengeance. You wish to know when he will arrive?" Skuld intuited.

I nodded.

"And what will you do with the time I allow you? Prepare for battle, or spend it on the boy you pine for?" Skuld smiled, but it did not reach her eyes… my eyes. "What if I told you that you will die *with* Fenris, that the time you borrowed from me would end when you end his life? Would you still kill him?"

Calder's kind eyes and soft lips crawled into my mind. The steady feel of his hand on mine. Though I wanted a future with him, I knew I would give it up in a heartbeat so he and his family could live.

"Yes."

Skuld observed me shrewdly. "You are thinking of him even now. The boy's future is entwined with yours."

"I don't want him to die with me. I'd rather you clip and part us than for that to happen. Calder deserves to live."

Skuld's eyes glittered as she looked from each sister to me. "You care for him."

"It doesn't matter. If I'm going to die after I serve your purpose, my feelings for Calder and the fondness I feel for his family and clansmen don't matter."

"Your feelings for him, however fledgling, are *everything*," Skuld argued, her sisters ignoring me completely; Urd inspecting the woven fabric pooling at the bottom of the loom, and Verdandi moving the shuttle tirelessly through the cords of spun wool. "Do you know the only thing more powerful than hatred?" I shook my head. "It is love."

I wasn't sure what to say or how to respond, so I remained silent.

"When you begged for your life, for a new fate, you did so because you were filled with hatred for Fenris Wolf and what he had done to you and your family. But you will prevail against him, not because of that hate, but because you will do anything to protect those you care about. You are very much your mother's daughter, Liv. And very much your father's."

Ygdrassil groaned. The great tree's roots stretched further into the soil, nudging at my boots. I moved to give them room, then looked back at the norn wearing my face.

"Hella killed *my own*. And Erik killed Jarl Wolf."

My lips fell open. "Father killed him?"

"To protect your honor, if that lessens the blow." It did, but it didn't. If he'd just let him sail away. If he'd just dropped the matter... he wouldn't have brought this down on us. It was his fault, and it wasn't. Fenris had done far more than simply avenge his father.

"Verdandi, though she wanted you to die on the shore of the fjord and urged me not to save your life, sees value in your new purpose. She's a romantic, and so she weaves a thread for you and Calder, however short that thread might be."

"A romantic thread now? For days, you've been tearing my side apart, warning me away from him," I reminded her.

She gave a small smile. "And *now* I am telling you that Clan Wolf will not attack your shores for days, and that those days are all you have left, Liv. You should make the most of them."

She was insane and was only encouraging me because she wanted my feelings to grow, so my love for these people – *for*

231

him – would make my rage explode over Clan Wolf and Fenris, who sought to harm them.

She sent me to Calder and his family because she wanted them as warriors, because they had something to fight for. Now, she wanted to give me something, too, but would tear it away almost as fast.

But if I only had days with Calder, I wanted every second. "How many days?"

"You have five sunsets before they come in the night, Liv. As wolves do," Skuld answered, pointing to the dark fabric that Verdandi was finished weaving.

She removed it from the loom and held it up. Skuld grew in height, stretching into the giantess Armund knew. She shook the fabric and the bottom flapped toward me. The entire thing was black. Every thread. I wasn't sure how they told one from the next, until in the dark depths emerged a vision. Ships... so many ships, sailed through the night.

I covered my mouth.

"They will overtake Clan Nyerk tonight and rest there before carrying on," Skuld revealed. "Then they will sail south around the land, devouring everyone left in their path, until they reach you."

We were too late in reaching Nyerk. A rock formed in the pit of my stomach, turning over and over at the thought of what they were about to experience. "Will our messengers reach the other clans in time?"

"With you strengthening them, they already have. Jarl Grandys lied to you. He did not send a missive to Clan Nyerk because of the bad blood between them, but the others received their warnings and will heed them. The weak will retreat to the stronghold as the Jarl's letter instructed. Many will come and fight. Your army will be formidable."

I hoped so, because Fenris's certainly was.

"You're not upset about Clan Nyerk being decimated?" I asked carefully.

"There are casualties in every war, Liv."

A question tore through my chest. "Why must I be one? Why must I die if I cut Fenris down?"

"Liv," Skuld said sternly, slicing me with my own eyes, "I accepted *your* bargain. The terms *you* set."

My heart sank.

At that time, while lying on the shore dying, I was consumed by hatred and wanted to live just long enough to kill Fenris. Now, I wanted to live because Calder planted something else in my heart.

Hope.

But there was no hope in Skuld's eyes. I felt the plant already withering. My side, where she'd stitched me, began to ache.

I would fall apart again in five sunsets.

I would not see a sixth.

My body felt heavy. I couldn't lift my arms.

Something grazed my mouth. "My gods. You're breathing. Stay with me, Liv."

I couldn't see him. He sounded so far away, like my ears were full of water...

"I am a scourge upon the earth," I muttered. "Skuld... Fenris Wolf deserves a fate worse than death. I curse him. I curse his men. I curse his clan and his ship and his name. If you save me, I will end him. I will battle him, cut him down, carve him up and let the pigs devour him. Weave a new destiny for me. Weave a future where I can see him dead."

A cool wind toyed with wayward strands of my dampened hair. Tears fell from the corners of my eyes, trailing over my skin and disappearing into my braids as I finished the bargain I'd struck with a whisper, "I refuse this fate. Weave a new thread. Stop Fenris Wolf. Let me be your hands. Let me be your shield, your blade. I will live as your vengeance. Then I will be content to die."

I saw Skuld drag me from the water, my side screaming with every bump along the ground.

"Liv, please," Calder begged. Warm lips pressed against my temple. "Come back to me, Liv, please."

Skuld's voice brushed my mind. "Find Calder, Liv. Open your eyes."

They *were* open. Weren't they?

I blinked, weakly raising my hand and finding Calder's stubbled jaw. "Calder."

Gathering me in his arms, he stood and carried me to the Jarl's house, walking straight to Armund. "What happened?" he asked, rushing to help.

"She took henbane."

Armund's thin lips fell open. "How much?"

"Enough to reach Skuld. It was only a small pinch."

Armund gasped. "A small pinch would kill a man as large as the Jarl."

Calder's eyes flicked to the man he'd spoken of, who strode over and hovered over me. "She got her instructions from *your* seeress," he accused.

Ivor straightened. "A seeress who would *never dare* harm one of Skuld's völva. The girl will be fine. She just needs to rest."

TWENTY-FOUR

I woke in a dark, unfamiliar room filled with strange smells, along with smoked meat and something masculine.

I was sweaty and hot, yet cold at the same time.

Five sunsets.

That was all we had left. All *I* had left.

Someone had removed my tunic and trousers and dressed me in an apron dress the color of the deep sea. I tugged at the fabric twisted around me. Early rays of sun peeked through the door on the other side of the room.

Tyr sat against the wall across the room, his green eyes watching me like I was the threat he believed me to be.

I looked around, surprised to see he was the only one in here with me. "Where is Calder?" I asked with a voice rusty from disuse, standing and waiting for his answer.

He took a bite from the smoked fish in his hand. "He thought you were dead. You scared him."

"I didn't mean to scare him."

"He asked me to look after you so he could attend Jarl Ivor's meeting. Said he'd fill me in later."

"What meeting?" I asked.

Tyr ignored the question. "You spoke in your sleep after Calder left." I waited to see if he would elaborate. "You said that you would die once you killed Fenris."

I swallowed thickly.

"So it's true."

"Are you going to tell him?" I asked.

"No," he said before taking another bite. "He'll get himself killed trying to prevent it. I don't want that to happen. I take it you don't want him to know?" I shook my head. "Very well. I will repay you with my silence," he said, offering a rare smile. "We're even now."

I took up my wand and left him in the longhouse, then rushed down the hill toward the busy town where the Jarl had gathered his warriors.

"We need a plan," one man clamored. "They'll likely bring several ships with fifty men in each…"

"Their ships are twice that size, and they stole the longships from Clans Urðr and Bjern. They'll fill those as well," Armund shouted.

The crowd of men and women went silent as each considered the sheer number of berserkers that could spill upon their shores.

Jarl Grandys watched me walk toward them, wand in hand. "Liv," he greeted me with a nod.

Startled heads turned to face me, and people moved aside as I walked toward the Jarl. "I have news from Skuld," I rasped.

The Jarl's dark beard blew sideways. "What news?"

"Clan Wolf will come ashore at night. We have five sunsets until they attack." I waited for the tumult to die down before adding, "They have many, many full ships. They will attack Clan Nyerk tonight and stay on their land to rest

236

before making their way south, skirting around the shore. Your messages have been delivered…" He could tell by my expression that I knew he lied about sending the message to Nyerk. I enjoyed watching him squirm. "The weak will retreat to the stronghold. Those who can fight are already on their way here."

He nodded, turning his attention back to his warriors.

"Jarl Grand—"

His head swiveled to me again. "You may call me Ivor, Liv. Please."

I swallowed, conscious of all those watching us. "Very well. Ivor, we need to prepare. We need archers on the cliffs. Fires on the shores. We need Calder to figure out a way to sink their ships. I don't want them to be able to sail away, regroup, and attack again. It ends here."

He slowly nodded. "It ends here." He looked around at the men and women who would fight, commanding, "Let's see that it does."

A roar of approval rose from the crowd.

Ivor avoided me after his little speech. He knew that I knew who the real serpent was.

For hours I painted my bind rune on the foreheads of stout men and strong women, studying their eyes as I drew the strokes that would protect them. "Will I sweat it off?" a woman asked cautiously.

I smiled. "It won't budge until I allow it."

Her eyes were hard. "They say it'll protect all who wear it."

"It will."

"*It* will, or *you* will?"

I locked eyes with her. "One and the same."

She snorted. "Good. I don't plan to die. I'm about to be married."

I smiled, happy for her. "Who is your husband-to-be?"

"Like I'd tell a witch. The last one that came to the village bedded half the men during her stay."

"I wasn't asking because of that…"

She made a sound of derision and turned, leaving me reeling in her wake. *What else do these people think of me?*

There was no one waiting for the rune, so I packed up Lofn's paint brush and my ash ink pot and tucked both in my bag. I found Armund waiting at the Jarl's house with a plate full of food. "I was about to bring this down to you, Liv."

I smiled. "Thank you, Armund."

"What's the matter?"

Ugh. I could hide nothing from the man. It was both a relief and a curse. "One of the women warriors. She said she was about to be married, but wouldn't tell me to whom because she said the last völva who came to her village slept with half the men in town."

His mouth fell open, but he quickly recovered. "I am aware that some are freer with their bodies than others, but I know you aren't."

I gave a wry grin. "I guess not everyone knows that." Taking the plate he held, I brought a chunk of turnip to my mouth. As the spicy flavor exploded on my tongue, I groaned at the burst of taste. Maybe I was hungrier than I realized.

"Lesser men… *and* women," he said, reminding me of our prior conversation. "Liv," Armund began gently, "let's talk about the henbane."

"What about it?" I asked around a mouth full of food.

"There are safer ways to reach the norn," he chastised gently.

"None as fast, though," I teased.

"No, but blood, for instance, is effective and doesn't drag you to death's door to bring you to Skuld."

"You're right," I admitted. "I'll be more careful in the future unless there is a strong reason for quickness."

He nodded and smiled. "Thank you. It's strange; I know we haven't known you long, but you're one of us now. You're like one of my kids, Liv, and I still take care of them when they'll let me, now that they're grown. I hope you'll trust me to look after you, too."

A knot formed in my throat. Unable to speak, I nodded once.

He smiled and excused himself to go outside.

Fell waved me over to where he sat at the table, eating. "The sun has kissed your skin," he noted with a blush that made his ruddy cheeks redder. He had freckles, which complimented the softness of his strawberry blond hair.

"Am I burnt?" I asked.

He shook his head. "Just… you have new freckles along your nose and cheeks."

"Well, that won't do. How am I supposed to scare Fenris with innocent freckles?" He laughed and took a heavy drink of mead. "Where is everyone?" I asked as I took a seat and set my plate on the table to eat.

"You'll have to be more specific, unless you'd like to know where everyone in our party is. Brux, Tyr, and Hilda are training some of the young to fight. Armund is wherever he just went. Probably going to join them now that his knee is good as new. Calder is assisting Jarl Grandys in making 'clever' plans of attack. And you and I are here."

"What about Sig?"

"With Calder, last I saw him."

I ate a few boiled carrots, thoroughly enjoying the Jarl's stores. Winter never depleted the food supply of a jarl.

"Fell, what do you think of Ivor?"

I couldn't help it; there was something about him that bothered me. We needed him. Needed his warriors. But I wasn't sure his reasons for joining us were selfless. If he took

Clan Wolf lands, he would effectively divide the continent… and if he sought to settle the land remaining to Clan Bjern or Urðr … he would conquer half of the Norse lands.

"Ivor is as cunning as Calder is clever. He wants our lands *and* Wolf's, just as you probably suspect. He'll expect you to grant it all to him once this is over. If his clansmen put their lives on the line, he'll want something in return."

He looked around the lushly appointed room appreciatively. I joined him, taking in the mounted horns, the furs, the ornately carved furnishings and space. "Would you ever want to be Jarl?" I asked. Someone would have to take over for Clan Bjern to survive.

"Hel no," he swore.

"Why?"

"Sure, the food and houses are plentiful, but they come with a hefty price. The wellbeing of all your people lays like a yoke on your shoulders and a target is always drawn on your back. Many men clamor for power, but Jarls are killed and replaced with the passing of seasons. Only the ruthless see their gray years." He took a sip of mead. "I'd bet my favorite axe that Ivor won't see many more winters."

I'd bet the same.

"So, you'd rather be a raider? A warrior for someone else?"

He leaned back in his chair and took a drink. "Nah. What I'd prefer would be to find someone I could relate to, speak easy with, and then have children and a farm with plenty of animals roaming around. Loads of land. That isn't possible without sacrifice, however. A man is always subject to his Jarl."

"As is a woman," I challenged.

He raised his glass, waited for me to do the same, and together we drank. "Can I ask you a question? You can choose not to answer it, of course."

I inclined my head and waited.

His brown eyes burned with curiosity as he swilled the mead in his cup. "Do you think of Calder as someone you might want to make a life with?"

I opened my mouth to speak, carefully mulling over my answer.

If things were different, my answer would have been an emphatic *yes*. I could see myself building a life with Calder. But things were *not* different. My fate seemed unfair now, regardless of the words I spoke as I lay dying.

"I'm not sure he would want that," I admitted softly.

Fell laughed. "Oh, he would. Trust me, he would. Tyr says you're going to hurt him in the end. That you can't be with him, but I wonder if that's true. You weren't born to this life. Maybe the laws of the norns don't apply to you the same way they do the other völva. You're certainly unlike any I've seen."

"I don't want to hurt him."

But I'm selfish. I knew my days were numbered, but I didn't want him to know. Didn't want to sully the few remaining moments I might have with him. And Tyr was right. If Calder knew, he'd try to prevent it even when it was impossible. Skuld seemed intent on holding me to the bargain I struck with her.

Fell gave a friendly smile and shrugged. "Then don't."

I tried to smile back, but the effect was forced.

"I didn't mean to upset you," he said gently. "I… Since you saved me, I've thought you were the most beautiful thing I've ever seen. I wanted to see how you felt about men in general, but especially about Calder. I see the way you look at each other sometimes, and I'd never hurt my friend. I want you to know that. And know that if the two of you don't… well, I'm here for you."

"I…" I was speechless. "Thanks."

He took a bite of bread, chewing and swallowing before speaking again. "I told Calder last night that I wished I'd known you before Fenris Wolf began tearing us all apart. Do you know what he said?"

I shook my head.

"He lay beside you with his hands folded under his head, staring at the ceiling like it was the sky of stars, and said he *knew* you. He could imagine you before and after, even though he hadn't met you yet. He knew your heart, your smile. And in his mind, he could see you walking the shores with your brothers and sisters, working in the gardens behind your house, tending your family's animals, fighting for your shield... He could see it all, even though you hadn't yet met." A tear fell from my eye, making Fell curse. "Aw, I'm sorry, Liv."

I shook my head. "Thank you. It's good to know that someone can see the me I was *before*, because sometimes I forget her completely."

Just then, a pounding commotion erupted outside the long house. Sig barked ferociously. Fell and I both jumped from our seats and rushed outside to see Calder smashing the face of one of the men who'd taunted his father earlier, his fist pummeling the man mercilessly as others tried to pull him off.

"Calder!" Armund shouted. Sig growled as he bristled and sought a way into the fight.

Fell cursed again and ran into the fray to help Armund defend Calder as the man's friends ran toward the two wrestling on the grass. Each man held a knife at the ready.

I knew why Calder was fighting.

Fury bolted into my heart, hotter than the bolt sent by Thor. My vision darkened, and in its absence, I felt every root and creeping thing in the soil. Sensing a nearby alder rising into the sky, I reached my hand toward its roots and called them to me. When they stretched, groaning as Ygdrassil had when I last saw Skuld, I urged them toward Calder's foe.

The roots reared out of the soil and quickly wrapped around the man's torso, pinning his arms to his sides. Calder snapped out of his rage, watching in disbelief as the roots twisted and tightened like a serpent around its prey.

Calder stepped away, watching the roots lift the man into the air with wide eyes, his boots scrabbling for ground they would not find. Sig steadfastly planted himself beside his owner.

I walked toward the man, passing Fell. "Your knife," I demanded, palm open. He slapped the handle into my hand and gave me an amused, encouraging smile as I wrapped my fingers around it. The man's nose bled into his mouth, dripping down his chin and splattering the twining roots, his tunic, and the ground. His brow was split, and his face was already bruising and swelling.

"I believe I told you what would happen if you wagged your tongue against Armund again."

A crowd was forming, growing with each second that passed. Jarl Ivor, the man's chieftain, stood behind me. This was his subject. He crossed his arms over his broad chest. "And what did you tell him would happen, *smár ormr?*" he asked, sternly glaring at his man. *Little serpent.* Maybe he was right in his assessment of me.

"I told him I'd remove his tongue."

"Liv," Calder said, coming to stand beside me and wiping the sweat from his brow. "Don't."

Sig brushed against my legs as if to calm me.

Jarl Ivor stepped forward to stand between me and Calder. "What was he wagging his tongue about?"

"He insults Armund, and an insult to Armund is an insult to me. Armund is like family," I explained.

Armund thanked me with a glance, but gave a single shake of his hand. He didn't want me to hurt him. He wanted me to show mercy.

Skuld was right. I protected those I cared for, and I cared for Armund's feelings.

I spoke to the crowd so they would all understand as I understood. "If a man is granted second sight, it is because Odin himself wills it. Without question, Armund will be ushered into Valhalla. He will never have to wonder where he'll spend the afterlife. He is Aesir blessed. But you..." I whirled to face the man. "Men like *you* will *never* enter Odin's great hall."

It was so still, one might hear a leaf fall.

Jarl Ivor nodded. "I give you permission to take his tongue."

I didn't need his permission. Skuld's fury filled my veins as I gripped the knife's handle.

A hand fell onto my shoulder and Calder's fresh pine scent wrapped around me. His fingers flexed gently. "Don't, Liv."

I jerked away from him and stalked to the man, whispering words that Skuld wove through my mind. His mouth opened, though I could see him straining to close it, his eyes wide and wild as I lifted the knife. I drew it across his tongue, not enough to sever it, but enough to draw blood, enough that he knew there would be no third chance for him.

"The next time you speak of Armund or anyone I care about, I won't bother with your tongue. I'll carve out your heart instead." I raked the blade between the gnarled roots of the tree that held him mercilessly aloft, then dragged the tip over where his heart beat a staccato rhythm in his chest, piercing his tunic, causing a thin line of blood to streak down his flesh. "Do you understand?"

Anger burned in his eyes, but a stronger feeling of fear and self-preservation churned within them, too. I loosened my grip on his jaw so he could speak. "Yes," he said quickly. His cheeks puffed with every breath he exhaled.

"Good." I handed Fell's knife back. "The warning applies to everyone. To defeat Clan Wolf, we must be a people who stand together, ignoring our divisions. How can we stand against a common enemy if we spend precious energy fighting amongst ourselves?"

I recalled the roots and they retracted into the ground, lowering the man's feet to the grass again.

Ivor barked at his men. "You're lucky she was merciful. I would not have been. Now get out of my sight." The tall Jarl held my eyes for a beat before turning away to enter his house.

Fell sheathed his knife and huffed a laugh as the Grandys men and women walked cautiously back into the town. "I'm damn glad you're on our side, Liv."

"I don't want you all getting into scraps because of me," Armund chastised, glancing between me and Calder.

"My mother would've gutted him," I breathed. "She wouldn't have hesitated."

Armund cleared his throat. "There's nothing wrong with you learning lessons your parents didn't, or you solving a dispute like they wouldn't have. We're all formed by the scars we earn, and no two people wear the same lines. There's nothing wrong with forging your own path. For what it's worth, I'm glad you didn't gut them."

"Some men are grown, yet still act like children," Tyr added from behind. I hadn't even heard him approach.

"I regret nothing," Calder said, flexing his fist. His knuckles were split, angry, and red.

"Then you learned nothing," Armund said, his temper rising again.

"Calder?" I asked, yearning to defuse the situation. He turned his attention to me. "Will you come with me?"

Anger still flared within his icy eyes, but he nodded once.

Fell gave me a look as if to remind me that what he said about Calder was true. Even though it might only be the short threads Verdandi wove together for me and Calder, I wanted to spend the next five sunsets with him, if he'd allow it.

I clasped his hand and tugged him down the path that skirted the cliff and led to the sea, memorizing the feel of every callous and rough place that adorned his palm. The way his fingers made mine seem small. The strength in his grip.

Sig ran alongside us to the shore, running excitedly through the small waves that lapped the rock. Calder and I stared out at the water, separately but together.

I finally broke the silence. "On the shore just beyond our house was a large boulder."

"I remember," he rasped.

"Hodor, Oskar, and I spent hours climbing all over it as children. Sometimes we pretended it was a ship and we were sailing into battle, and other times we pretended it was a dragon and we tamed it, forever its riders."

Calder's lips curled on one side. "When we were boys, Fell, Tyr, and I had a place like that, but ours was a tree. It had grown sideways so the trunk twisted over the ground before rising to the sky. We spent many hours imagining fierce battles and daring rescues. It was our dragon, and sometimes our ship."

We were silent for a beat before I spoke again. "On the evening we fought for our shields, I braided Hodor's hair as he sat on that boulder, and then he braided mine."

Just then, the loss of him and my family filled me with despair so dark and deep, I felt like I was drowning. Like the salty fjord water was still stinging my nose and leaking down my throat.

He squeezed my hand. "Liv, you are not alone. When your hair needs braided, I'll braid it. And I'd be honored if you braided mine."

A tear fell from my eyes. I pressed them closed, listening to the soothing cadence of the water, accented by the playful slaps and splashes of Sig romping in it. "Sig reminds me of Tor, my brother's dog. He wasn't as smart as Sig, but he was a good herder. He would fetch sticks we threw, too. Hodor loved Tor the way you love Sig. I remember..." I smiled. "I remember the little ones feeding Tor bones under the table and Father grumbling that we were spoiling him, making him weak so that he wouldn't hunt for himself. But we didn't care. He loved bones." Sig jumped into a wave and swam out into the water. "But Tor couldn't swim. Not like Sig. I'm glad he was with you the night of the attack."

Calder cleared his throat. "He's brave. That night, he took down a man twice my size, then helped Brux's wife carry their newborn to safety. He watches out for Father. He's one of us. I've always thought he was. Always treated him like one of our family."

I let go of his hand and watched his expression. He blinked, curious by my open perusal. "Do you want to swim with me, Calder?"

A warm breeze pressed my dress against my legs. His blood-stained tunic hugged his muscled chest.

He nodded. "I do."

I took hold of the dress and underdress and pulled them over my head, leaving only my *serkr* on. It was pale linen and fell to the skin above my knee. Calder looked me over unabashedly, removing his own shirt and placing it on top of my dress at our feet. He clasped my hand and we waded into the water.

"It's cold," he warned.

"It's always cold," I answered as I let him tug me into the frigid, salty sea.

My skin pebbled. His did, too. Gooseflesh spread over his chest and neck. My fingers ran across it.

He studied me. "Why the sudden change? You've been holding me at arm's length since we met."

I shrugged and loosened the braids in his hair, using the seawater to wash the blood away, then scrubbed it from his skin.

247

He dipped beneath the water and came up glistening, water sluicing from his skin. His long lashes were clumped. "Your turn." He let out my braids and combed his fingers through my long hair. "Why?" he asked again.

"What do you mean?"

"Why did you bring me down here? Just to swim?"

I smiled. "Because it's sunny and beautiful, and we should enjoy as much of the day as we can. We can't let anyone ruin it. You never know how many days you might have left."

Five.

His icy eyes drilled into mine. "Spoken by someone who has tasted death and fought for life."

And will taste it again sooner than you realize.

Sig swam to shore and lay on the warm stones to dry. Almost before it should've been possible, he was asleep and snoring.

Calder smiled. "He falls asleep so fast. I envy that."

"I do too," I told him.

"I was afraid last night," he said. "I thought I was losing you. I was going berserk trying to find a way to bring you back."

I swallowed thickly. "I'm fine."

"Will you do me a favor?" he asked, hope swimming in his expression.

"What's that?"

He pulled me close and kissed my temple, his lips moving against my skin. "Never use henbane again."

I laughed. "How can I promise that? I may have to."

"Only if you must, then. I don't want to lose you."

"What makes you so sure you have me?" I teased, moving away just to splash him.

His look turned predatory and I backed up a step, smiling and hoping he chased. He splashed me back, and the wave he sent fell over my chest but didn't hit my face. When his eyes were drawn to where the water landed, I was suddenly conscious of the fact that my *serkr* was thin and he could likely see through it. I covered myself, squeezing my arms together.

Calder stepped forward. "I want to kiss you."

My lips fell open. I wanted that, too. More than anything. "Why do you want *me*? We barely know each other."

"Life is harsh, and tomorrow isn't promised. So if we see something we like, something that calls to us, we need to go after it *now*. No hesitation. Or it'll slip through our fingers like sea water." He raised a cupped hand and separated his fingers, letting the water fall away.

He was absolutely right.

This time when he prowled forward, I planted my feet and let him catch me. His arm snaked around my back and drew my chest against his.

The remaining time I had was a gift from Skuld. I could have been lying dead among my clan in Amrok village, but instead I was alive. Alive and enjoying a few sunsets with a boy who was everything I wanted and couldn't have, nor did I deserve. Every moment with him was a precious gift. I vowed not to squander a second.

I pressed my lips to his.

His eyes fluttered closed as we moved against one another, drinking in one another's tastes. Neither hesitating.

250

TWENTY-FIVE

That night, the Jarl announced a great feast. Tables from all the homes were carried outside, along with chairs and benches. Sliced loaves of bread and mounds of venison, lamb, and pork lined the tables, along with steaming pots of stews and roasted vegetables. Mead flowed like waterfalls into outstretched cups. Roaring fires were placed all around, the flames casting a warm glow over the faces of those who would fight alongside me.

Calder sat across from me, and at the Jarl's request, I sat at his right hand.

"Velda has died," he said abruptly, even as he chuckled at a joke from the next table over.

My heart skipped to a stop. "What happened?"

"Age."

"You don't seem upset," I bit.

He turned to face me. "She will be missed, but this winter she told me she wasn't long for this world. Though she couldn't see the future, she knew her own body. I've had time

251

to accept it. And now, though I miss her, I know she is at peace. You, on the other hand, do seem upset. Why?"

"Because she's gone."

"Nothing is forever, Liv," he said, softening his voice.

"I know." I took a drink to wash down the rich food I could no longer chew. "I know that better than most."

"How did you get word?" I asked.

He pointed to a cage just outside the entrance to his longhouse. I'd seen it inside, empty. Now, it housed a falcon. "He is trained well to send and receive messages for me. The falconer stole and raised him from the nest. He trained me as he trained the bird."

Lofty pine boughs and alder leaves swayed in the cool night air, causing the fire to flicker with each gust. The smells of food and popping, crackling wood mingled with the briny sea air. I tried to commit it all to memory. Every flavor. Every scent. Every feeling. Even when the hair on the back of my neck stood, the result of cold and thoughts of the looming battle.

I memorized Calder's expressions as he spoke and laughed with his father and friends. Hilda snorted when she laughed hard. The skin around Armund's eyes wrinkled, as did the lines around his mouth. Fell cursed incessantly and laughed with abandon. Even Tyr looked happy, as long as he didn't catch me looking at him.

Since our talk this morning, things between he and I had settled into an uneasy truce.

As I relaxed, watching my friends and half-listening to Ivor's hunting stories, footsteps pounded the ground from the forest. Someone rushed from the darkness and ran straight to Ivor. "Jarl Grandys," he greeted. "Warriors from Clans Bjord, Naturk, Laryk, and Wonruck are approaching."

"Varsyk, too?" Ivor asked. Tyr tensed at the name of the Clan that had attacked his, the clan who worked with the witch who cursed his father and took him away.

The messenger shrugged noncommittally. "I can't be sure."

Ivor stood and searched the darkness as the sound of hooves striking the ground filled the land behind us. "They came together, stronger as one." He nodded to his clansmen. "Welcome them to our tables."

There was more than enough food left, even as we stood to give our seats so our allies could rest and eat. Men and women poured from the forests with shields on their backs, armor glinting in the moonlight and then in the firelight as they drew close.

The Jarls made their way to Ivor, who greeted each with claps on the back and praise. He offered them seats, ordering that mead be brought out, along with fresh plates.

Sig and the other village dogs were in heaven, having crunched and eaten every bone that had been tossed to the ground. Calder petted his dog behind the ears and his back paw thumped the ground so fast I could barely see it.

I walked to Calder. "Would you take a walk with me?"

He stood, his eyes twinkling. "If it's anything like swimming with you, there's nothing I'd like more."

"Nothing?" I teased.

He laughed. "Well... maybe a *few* things. I'll show you."

He pulled me away from the crowd and we sank into the darkness, pulled by a magnetic force to the shore again, where we kissed until we were drunk on one another.

Until we swayed on our feet and could do nothing but smile.

Until we kissed again...

On the cliffs above, the storyteller's fanciful stories floated down to us on the salty wind, fading as the sounds of tents being pitched overtook the lilting voices. "We should probably go help them," Calder noted.

I nodded, smiling. "We should."

But his hands held me tight against him and I didn't pull away.

So we kissed and swayed in one another's arms until the hammering stopped and the storyteller finished his tales, and the sounds of talking and laughter faded away. Until the lapping waves were the only thing making noise around us.

There was the sea and there was Calder, and for a short time, nothing else existed.

It was perfect.

I woke just before dawn to find Calder watching me, one side of his lips curled happily. Tyr was already awake. Tyr lowered his voice. "With all the Jarls here, it'll be a wonder if any of *us* survive to battle Clan Wolf."

"What do you mean?" I asked.

Tyr went silent when I joined the conversation, ignoring me altogether.

Fell sat up. "They're already discussing how they might conquer Wolf's lands and divide it up. They don't want Grandys swooping in and taking it all. They each want a piece."

"They'll want Bjern and Urðr," Calder said, sitting up.

"Our clans and land aren't theirs to take. We need to appoint someone to Jarl. We have survivors. It's our right to appoint a new chieftain," Fell said hotly, "and to take what's rightfully ours, by force, if needs be." He gestured at me, asking me to weigh in.

"He's right," I said.

Tyr stared at Calder. "It has to be Armund."

Fell nodded his assent. "Armund."

"He won't like this," Calder warned.

"What choice is there, Calder, other than losing your homes?" I asked. "Or swearing fealty to a Jarl who doesn't deserve to rule over you?"

Fell stood and straightened his clothes. "I'll get Brux and Hilda. You find your father," he said to Calder. "Let's meet on the shore, away from those who might overhear."

His eyes scanned the long house. Empty as it seemed, we didn't know all its secrets; we didn't want anyone knowing our plan just yet.

"It'll take all of us to convince him," Fell added before walking toward the door and disappearing outside.

"The chieftains circle like sharks at the first hint of blood in the water," Tyr said, rising and striding away.

Calder turned to me, scrubbing his hands down his face. "The gods might have to intervene in this conversation."

I glanced toward my wrist, to the mark Thor left there. "I hope not."

At the shoreline, Sig splashed in the water, barking and chasing the tiny schools of fish that rode the waves toward the rock and then rode them back out again. The wind was brisk this morning, the sky cloudy and gray.

Hilda and Brux waited with Fell, Tyr, and Armund. He had no idea what we were about to ask him. His face was relaxed, open.

"Would someone like to explain what's going on?" Armund finally asked.

All eyes fell on Calder.

He cleared his throat. I squeezed his hand encouragingly, letting go when Tyr's eyes hardened at the gesture.

"Father, the other clans are already discussing how they will push toward and claim Clan Wolf's lands after this battle. They are also discussing taking the land that belonged to Clan Urðr, as well as our Bjern land. As the eldest survivor among us and the eldest of our clan, we would like you to accept the honor of being our Jarl."

For a long moment, Armund didn't move. He stared at Calder, then he stared at me, scrubbing his beard and mustache.

"Before I even consider such a thing, I need to speak to you," he told me. "*Alone.*"

"But," Brux began to argue.

Armund held his hand up. "But, nothing. I haven't been able to pry her away from her duties or my son, and I wish to speak to her now. Once we're finished, we will come and discuss this again."

I walked to Armund, giving Calder an encouraging look, ticking my head toward the town. Reluctantly, he left us on the shore. All of them did. Hilda shot me a 'good luck' look and threaded her arm through her son's. Brux walked with her behind a nearby longhouse.

He crossed his arms and watched patiently as his sons and clansmen walked away from us, Sig bounding along behind them before splitting from the group, chasing a fawn-colored hound. The two took turns pouncing on one another play-fully, chewing on each other's ears, splashing in the water and running between longhouses.

Armund's graying hair floated up on the wind before it laid back down. "Liv," he said cautiously, "what has changed?"

"What do you mean?" I asked, trying not to look at him.

"Calder has been affected by you since he brought you home, but now you can't get enough of him. Initially I thought it was your grief, but now... You're acting as though these days are your last, or *our* last. Tell me true – is my son going to die? Will I lose him in this battle?" he croaked, unable to cloak the emotion crashing over him.

"No," I assured him, looking him squarely in the eye. "I will protect him. I swear it on my own life, Armund."

He loosed a pent-up breath. "Then he will survive the battle?"

"Yes."

Armund swallowed, the knot in his throat bouncing up and down. "Then is it *you* who will die?"

I studiously avoided his question. "Why do you think anyone but Fenris Wolf will die?"

His shrewd eyes fastened on mine. "Because death hangs heavily in the air here for someone, and Fenris isn't here yet. Do you not feel it? Smell it? It's waiting, biding its time. Death isn't patient, Liv."

"Armund, no matter what happens during the battle, your people need a voice for afterward. They need a strong leader."

He gave me a cunning smile. "Then that means Clan Urðr *also* needs a voice. And you are its only survivor."

I gave an unladylike snort. "A clan of one? Jarl by default?"

He shrugged a shoulder. "Unless we merge clans and land."

My eyes darted to his. "And save them both."

He placed a hand on my upper arm and gave it a gentle squeeze. "No Jarl on his own, or all of them together, would dare cross you, Liv. Claim your clan and lands, and I will claim ours. We will announce our merging tonight at the feast and ruin all their careful plans." A sly smile graced his lips.

"Now I know where Calder gets his cleverness."

He laughed. "This is not an honor I would ever have fought for, but if all of you feel I should be Jarl, then Jarl I shall be. I won't let you down."

I hugged him as a daughter would a loving father. "I know you won't."

"Shall we go get the others?" he asked, holding his arm out for me to take.

"Wait." I stopped him, my mind spinning with the implications of our plan. If we announced this, Armund and I would be targeted. For now, I could protect him from any scheming and attempts on his life, but what about after I killed Fenris? Who would protect him then? "You have to promise me something," I told him.

"What is that?"

"As soon as Fenris is dead, collect your family and leave before anyone knows you're gone."

His brows furrowed. "You mean *we* collect *our* family and leave together before anyone knows we're gone."

"I might have to stay behind, like I did on the mountain, Armund," I replied cagily. "But I can take care of myself. You have to trust me."

He scrubbed a hand at the back of his neck. "Very well. I don't like it, but I trust you. I give you my word."

This time when he extended his arm for me to take, I wrapped my hand around it and we walked to get our kinsmen. I felt awful for lying to Armund, like I'd become exactly the *smár ormr* Ivor had always accused me of being.

Armund's free hand patted mine. "Take a breath. Skuld will keep you safe and you can keep the rest of us safe."

It took a moment to sink in, but I wasn't alone anymore. I was part of a merged clan. A new one. A better one for the man who would lead it, and for the men and women who would fight for it. Suddenly things looked brighter, despite the gloom of the day and death's frigid breath on the back of my neck. In the midst of darkness, I could see the norns weaving a future that would be bright for the people I had so quickly come to love.

I wished I could live to see him revive our clans.

I wished I could be one of his for longer than four more sunsets.

"Liv?" he said before we rounded the corner of a house. "Thank you."

"I don't understand."

He gave me a kind smile, deep wrinkles fanning around the outer corner of his eyes. "Calder is happy. Calder smiles because of you. He hasn't done that in a very long time."

The others were surprised that Armund agreed to become their Jarl and chieftain so easily, but more surprised that I planned to claim Clan Urðr lands and then combine them with Bjern's. This alliance would protect our homes and those still trying to rebuild in Skögar Village; the men, women, and children we left behind.

Everyone supported me and Armund making the announcement at the feast planned for tonight, even with the knowledge that we would have to watch one another's backs from now on. A feast was planned for every night until the battle. Thanks to Skuld, we were in a unique position of knowing when the Wolfs would reach our shores and could prepare.

The clans pooled resources and built circles of stone along the cliff. Once Clan Wolf was close to shore, fires would be built inside for the archers' arrows. Casks of oil were gathered at the tide line. Men could smash them on the hulls of the Wolf ships and archers on the cliffs would fire lit arrows to light them.

There was an odd sense of excitement in the town, almost as if this were a great gathering to celebrate the change of seasons, or for Jarls to bless new marriages. The warriors from one clan good naturedly challenged warriors from another to spars and games.

I was busy painting my rune of protection on the foreheads of anyone new who wanted to accept it, when a familiar face sat down before me and pushed his pale hair away from his head.

"I thought you didn't want the bind rune."

Tyr smiled. "I want to live. If taking the rune helps, so be it."

"Then we aren't so different after all," I told him, dipping my brush into the ash ink.

His smile fell away. "How so?"

"I wanted to live, and as I lay dying on the beach, I made a bargain. The bargain, like the bind rune, helped me stay alive."

"For a time," he added with a cruel glint in his eye.

Calder's laughter rang out from where a boy no older than Gunnar chased him, slashing at him with a sword too heavy to lift. My first thought was, *Why is this boy, so young, not in the stronghold?* My second was one of realization. As mine often did, Tyr's eyes found Calder. A smile played at his lips. Not because of the boy... because of Calder.

My mouth fell open and my hand stilled. Tyr's green eyes met mine and hardened. "Are you finished?"

I added the last mark and nodded. "I'm finished."

"Good," he spat before stalking away.

My gods... Tyr was in love with Calder. *That* was why he hated me. Why he took the mark, despite his hatred for the witch who cursed his father. Why he wanted to live when he knew I would die.

His pale hair flew behind him as he quickly strode away, disappearing between houses.

THREE

WITH BONE

264

TWENTY-SIX

The Jarls sat together at the table we'd eaten at last night, Ivor insisting again that I sit at his right hand. The man wanted the status that having the most powerful völva in the land by his side would bring. The two witches Ivor had mentioned he would send word for had arrived from Ragyr Town.

They were twins, dressed in similar fine gowns, made of expensive fabric that billowed with the slightest winds and accentuated their womanly forms. The dark-haired beauties, mysterious and observant, sat across from me, fawning over Ivor's every word. He told them how I'd come to him on the mountain, how his grandmother had taken to me and told him to listen to what I advised. He told them Skuld had told me Clan Wolf's ships would soon run aground in the shallows. How their blood would fill the waves that lapped the shore.

Their dark eyes glittered at the gruesome scene he painted.

They hadn't come with Ivor's warriors, but had taken their time crossing the countryside to gather bounty from the forests to prepare themselves for the battle. They said that before word from Ivor reached them, Skuld had revealed my existence to them. "How?" I asked.

"Through bone and blood," they answered in tandem.

I wanted to ask them questions about Skuld, about how she spoke to them. Was it only through blood and bone? Did she ever visit them? Did she wear their faces, too?

But Ivor loved attention and commanding conversations, and the völva twins marveled at his every word, toying with their hair and batting their lashes as they told him how wise he was to listen to a völva such as me. I would bet my sword he'd already bedded them. Probably together.

I kept watch on my friends, who ate at a table nearby.

"Your attention, Liv, keeps diverting toward your friends. Or is one of them more than that…?"

I narrowed my eyes at Ivor. "My *attention* is none of your concern."

He laughed, raising his cup for someone to fill. "You know you care for someone when you worry for their safety even as they are safe."

The chieftains at the table's other end went quiet. Some leaned in to better hear our conversation. The murmured word *Urðr* caught my ear. I met Calder's eyes, then Armund's. It was time.

"Actually, I'd like to speak to all of you about my clan," I said, waving Armund over. "As well as Clan Bjern." I stood with Armund, behind my chair, my hands on its back threatening to char the wood. Every warrior at every table, from every clan noticed, shifting to better see and hear us before going quiet.

"As the sole survivor and only one qualified, I claim Clan Urðr lands," I declared, "as well as the position of Jarl."

The men around the table glowered at me. Ivor chuckled under his breath, sipping from his mead cup again. I was glad I amused him. "You never cease to surprise me, *smár ormr.*"

"Never has a woman been Jarl," the chieftain of Varsyk snarled. He and his warriors had arrived with the other clans. I could feel rage waft from Tyr, just feet away.

Grease from his dinner slickened the Varsyk chieftain's graying beard as he blustered about a woman's place. Thrumming metal filled the air and I looked toward Tyr. He'd stabbed the table with his knife, likely to stop himself from letting it fly.

Armund stood tall as he faced the table full of greedy men. "And I claim the position of Jarl of Clan Bjern, and all the land belonging to it."

"What gives *you* the right?" Jarl Wonruk, a broad-chested, stocky man demanded, pushing his chair back from the table.

"We do!" Brux shouted as he stood. Wonruk's eyes slid up Brux's tree-tall body before darting around the table to Hilda, Tyr, Fell, then Calder. They returned to Armund.

"What?" Wonruk pushed, half-laughing. "The five of you?"

"There are others," Father asserted calmly.

Wonruk looked to Jarl Naturk at his side. Naturk was the eldest at their table, still fit despite his age, but withering year by year. His grizzled, wiry gray hair stood out from his head in unruly tufts and wide, open eyes gave him the look of an owl, though he was certainly not the wisest. He chuckled. "What's to stop *us* from claiming them? A handful of you versus the might of this collection of Jarls?" He waved a hand to the warriors seated all around, warriors quietly listening to the exchange with bated breaths.

"Me," I offered. "*I* will stop you. Do what you wish with Clan Wolf and their lands after we slaughter them, but leave our people and lands out of it."

The völva twins smiled sinisterly. "We would love to see what you are capable of," one said carefully.

Ivor rapped the table with his knuckle. "I told you what happened on the mountain," he told his equals. "Do not think for one second that she is incapable of doing anything she wishes. Skuld stands behind her and Thor favors her from Asgard."

The chieftains were silent. They sized up our small party, not caring about Skuld or Thor, but about their dashed plans to conquer and divide the spoils. But our homes weren't gold they could plunder from lands far away. They weren't something left unprotected. If they wanted a fight, I would bring one they'd never forget.

Ivor was quiet, studying us both. Armund stood proudly and never faltered. A few minutes later, Ivor grabbed the nearest serving girl and sat her on his lap, signaling he was done with the conversation.

The twin witches smiled approvingly at me as I sat back down. Armund returned to his seat, eyes from every direction tracking him like prey. If anyone dared hurt him, I'd incinerate them on the spot.

I took a drink of mead and a small amount of steam escaped my nostrils and mouth after I swallowed. The fire inside me raged more every time I got angry, every day that brought Fenris and his army closer.

The Jarls slowly left the table to rejoin their own kinsmen.

"How does Skuld speak to you?" one of the völva asked. "We can sense you from afar, as if you're one of the norns or gods."

"Have you never seen her?" I volleyed.

The closest witch leaned toward me, her ample breasts resting on the tabletop. She put her petite hand on mine, her wide eyes glimmering with ambition. "Have you spoken directly with Skuld?"

"I have. Sometimes I hear her whispers, or she'll send a message I know is hers." I didn't mention my ruptured side or Skuld tugging the hair that held it together when she felt I needed a reminder of my place. "But sometimes she comes to me. Other times, she brings me to her."

The woman sat back, almost pouting. "We've tried henbane, animal blood, human blood, the dirt from fresh graves – everything – but she has never come to us or allowed us to visit her. Have you seen her sisters?"

I nodded, sipping my mead. I wasn't sure I wanted to divulge too much in front of Ivor. Though he seemed engrossed in kissing the girl still on his lap, he was listening. His eyes drifted to us often. The witches noticed, too.

"The three of us should take a walk, and we can show you how we reach Skuld," one offered with a smile.

The two witches waited for me where the waves lapped their bare feet. Their fine dresses rippled in the light breeze coming off the water. Each held a wand of pale pine with spinners of twisted grapevine. Each surveyed my plain apron dress, the ink on my fingers, and my wand.

"A wand of bone," the woman on the right marveled. "How did you form the spinner so?"

"With the fire in my veins," I answered.

"Skuld's fire?" The other smiled excitedly. "We've never felt it."

The wind whipped our hair and blew the fires around the feast sideways, the gusts pressing our dresses tight to our bodies. The women were strange, and I got a feeling in the pit of my stomach that something was amiss, but then I thought that the thing out of place here was probably me. Perhaps Skuld wasn't fond of directly speaking with her own. Perhaps she and I were closer because she'd saved me, and because my purpose would soon be fulfilled. Maybe she wanted to see through what she'd started by stealing me from death's grip.

Armund said he could feel death in this place, lingering, watching, waiting…

"Come with us. We will call on Skuld among the trees," the woman on the right said, smiling at me and gesturing for me to follow them as they made a path across the town and into the dark woods.

Animal bones littered the thick, pine-needle covered ground as we strode closer to the thicket of trees. They graciously answered my questions. I wanted to know how I differed from them, and how I was the same. From their mannerisms, I couldn't have been more different than if I were the moon and they the sun.

They were beholden to no clan, wandered where they liked, slept where they pleased, ate what they wanted when they wanted it. They were free as the wind because no one would dare deny them anything, lest they be cursed.

Chieftains and common people showered them with gifts, like the dresses on their backs and the glittering jewelry ornamenting their hands and necks.

They knew how to cast and read rune stones and felt Skuld's power in all the things in nature. They could tell a person if their livestock would last the winter, or if they should slaughter more before the frigid air fell over the land and the snows came, to put away more food so they wouldn't starve. And, they could use their wands and spinners to fix bad blood between clansmen, help women conceive or survive a difficult birth, or curse someone.

They were so open and answered everything I asked, right up until the moment they pulled knives from their boots once we were fully cloaked by foliage and shadow. The moonlight peeked through the canopy when the wind shuffled the leaves, glinting across their wicked blades.

I clenched my jaw and raised my staff. "Why?"

The witch to the right answered with a calculating smile that sent a chill over my skin. "We have waited in vain our entire lives to speak with Skuld herself; now we see *you* are the way to her. With your blood, we will finally reach her at the base of Ygdrassil and drink from urðbrunnr, the well of fate. With you gone, *we* will be the strongest of her own."

My fist tightened on the bones of my staff. "You will anger Skuld, but worse than her, if you attack me, I will kill you both."

My warning was ignored. They separated, each walking her own half of a circle around me. Angry wind tore through the trees and howled over the land as it tore toward the sea. The witches looked up but didn't stop their predatory dance around me.

"Did Ivor put you up to this?" I asked.

The women laughed. "Ivor does not own us."

The witch to my left struck first, and it became apparent that these women were no warriors. Her stab was tentative, as if she meant to quickly stick an animal in the neck and let it bleed out.

I was no innocent lamb. And I certainly would not be a sacrifice for them to use to contact Skuld.

I cracked my staff against her wrist and the knife fell to the ground with a thud. She cried out, holding her flayed skin together where my family's bones had split her flesh. Blood poured from the gash, running between her fingers and splattering the pine needles.

Keeping the injured sister in sight, I bent and picked the discarded knife up by its tip. Her sister didn't even realize I'd thrown it until she was choking on her own blood, the quivering blade lodged vertically in the base of her throat.

Her twin rushed to her, screeching as she ran to catch her before she fell. The one I'd skewered sank to her knees and slumped onto her side. The knife she clenched in her hand dropped to the ground as her grip relaxed. The gurgling noise in her throat and chest bubbled as she tried to cough, to breathe, to live.

I knew what she was feeling.

And as sorry as I was that it came to this, I was no victim.

I was a warrior.

A shield maiden.

Though I'd begged Skuld for the chance to live long enough to end Fenris Wolf, I was no coward. She knew that when she accepted my bargain, as she knew that my mother raised me to fight, be strong, and defend myself at all costs.

The living twin watched the life bleed from her sister's face with a horrified expression. She roared at me, jerked the blade from her sister's throat, and vaulted toward me with it raised, her wrist still bleeding, cut to the bone by the bone of my staff. Tears welled in her eyes. She couldn't see clearly through them and sliced clumsily through the air between us. "You took her! You took her away from me," she sobbed.

I answered calmly, "It was her or me. I chose me."

"Now it is you and I," she growled, cutting through the air, stepping closer.

"I still choose me," I told her, waiting until she swiped again, her own momentum throwing her balance to the side. I slipped up behind her and used her own hand to stab the side of her throat where the blood would flow fast and free.

I jerked it out of her neck, as she'd done to her sister only moments ago, and she fell like a tree with shallow, weak roots in a heavy storm. The two lay dead, their blood flowing over the ground in crimson rivulets. It called to me.

I bathed my hands in it, lavishing in the power it immediately gave me, and then grabbed each by an ankle.

These women may have been honest with me. They might have seen me as a way to bolster their own power, using my death as a direct path to Skuld herself. But they could have been lying. Someone may have asked them to kill me.

Since Armund and I had made our intentions known, there were targets on both our backs. He knew the risk as well as I did.

Did these women carry out a larger plan for one of the chieftains?

It could've been any of them. It could've been Ivor.

Fury flooded my veins as I tugged the dead weight from the wood.

Sig barked when he saw me and came running toward me in the darkness. He scented the blood when he came close, sniffing the ground as he circled me. Their bodies left wide, bloody trails across the grass and soil. I carved a gruesome path through the longhouses, only stopping when I reached the shore.

I walked back to the wood to get my wand. And to get both of theirs.

When I returned, warriors from every clan waited with their Jarls for an explanation I didn't owe them but would freely give.

"Let them serve as a warning to anyone who thinks I'm weak, or that beyond the power Skuld gave me, I can't fight or defend myself." I planted their wands in the pebbles of the rocky shore and with my hands, warmed the wood of each until both caught fire, the flames licking up the staffs and into the air, thin smoky trails snaking into the night sky.

Ivor crossed his arms, his expression landing someplace between annoyed and amused. "And what did *they* do to deserve your wrath, Liv?"

"They tried to kill me to reach Skuld."

He laughed, shaking his head and relaxing his stance. "Hella taught her daughter well, and Skuld recognized her ferocity," he said to everyone, his voice loud and strong.

I didn't like the look he gave me. It was almost challenging.

My hands began to shake. My teeth began to chatter.

Their blood was sticky on my face, neck, and hands.

Armund eased toward Ivor, placed his hands on the behemoth's shoulders, and said something that none of us could hear.

Ivor watched me carefully, then announced, "The hour is late. Most of you are drunk. Let's go and rest. We have much more work ahead of us in the days to come. Rest easy, knowing we have the strongest völva to ever live in our midst."

Three sunsets.

They were all that was left until Fenris and his clansmen stepped foot on these very pebbles. Until the rocks would be slick with the blood of his kinsmen.

The witches' blood seeped into the stones and trailed into the water, tainting it red. They lost most of it in the wood, and more as I dragged them. How was there still so much blood?

I felt the power it held all the way to my marrow, but I felt something else, too. Something that felt hollow and empty deep down. Like I'd lost something of myself.

These twin women were the first people I'd ever killed. And though they deserved it, though I would do it all over again, I was changed.

My eyes found Calder's. I'd avoided his icy blues until this moment, but found I couldn't any longer. He knew what I'd done, what I was. I couldn't hide it from him.

As people trickled away from the shore and returned to their houses and tents, my friends waited for me on the shore. "Fell, Tyr, and Brux," Armund snapped. "Bury them. Put large stones over the soil of their graves so they don't rise again." He moved to Hilda and quietly asked her to go fetch me clean clothes. She hurried to Ivor's longhouse.

Calder eased toward me, his steps tentative and cautious. "Liv?"

"Yes," I answered, my voice croaking.

"I was making sure it was you."

"It's me."

"Will you swim with me?" he asked, brows raised.

I nodded, my teeth chattering.

He caught my hands and spun me from the shore, away from the sight of the völvas' bodies, and drew me into the cleansing, briny sea where their blood was washed from my bare feet.

Armund helped Brux, Tyr, and Fell move the women's bodies away, Sig's padded feet lumbering into the night with them. Hilda soon returned and placed a bundle of clothes just out of the water's reach. Calling out that she was going to help the others, she followed the path they'd taken.

A few men lingered, watching our friends as they disappeared over a small embankment, then they carefully watched us. "Eyes on me," Calder said. "They don't matter."

No, they didn't.

We stepped deeper into the water where he scrubbed the blood from my throat, cheeks, chin, and forehead. He scoured the blood from my hair, washing until nothing stained the strands. Moonlight kissed his skin and his muscles rippled as he worked.

"I thought it would feel different," he admitted quietly, sensing where my thoughts hovered. "When we were attacked, I fought to stay alive, to defend myself, our home, Father... Even though it was honorable and I was justified in killing the few I managed to, it didn't feel that way. I couldn't help but feel guilty. They meant something to someone."

"I don't feel guilty for killing them." I wasn't sure what it said about me, but I wasn't. I'd meant what I told them. If it came down to them or me, I'd choose me every time.

He hissed when my hands found his sides, tugging his shirt up so I could feel his taut skin. I peeled his shirt up and he helped me tug it off, then helped me with the cumbersome dress I was getting tangled in. Wading back to the shore, he deposited our things and swam back to me.

"You're shaking," he said in a gravelly voice as his hands found my waist.

"I can't stop."

He tilted his head to the side. "We'll see about that."

Then he kissed me.

I closed my eyes to shut out the men watching, the blood swirling around us, the moon above us. For a precious, fleeting moment, there was only Calder, his strong arms, his lips on mine, and me.

TWENTY-SEVEN

Calder waited with his back turned as I tugged the new dress on, then waded from the water. Lit hearths and campfires still burned all over the town. The wind dragged their smoke trails sideways where they mingled together over the sea.

With my staff in one hand and the other firmly wrapped around Calder's, we walked quietly to Jarl Ivor's longhouse and slipped inside, laying down next to one another. He covered us with his furs and the warmth radiating from his body stopped the trembling I felt to my bones, despite how cold the water had been. His hand settled on the scar I bore on my side as if he, and not fragile strands of hair, held me together.

Skuld sent no pain, no warning. I could almost feel her nudge us closer.

He folded one arm beneath his head and watched me as I watched him. Though we weren't alone, it felt like we were.

Despite the stirring of others, the occasional cough, and snores from those who'd already fallen asleep, in that moment, I knew all that mattered was Calder and me and the three sunsets we had left.

A troubled wrinkle formed between his brows and I wondered what he was thinking, and if he could somehow tell I was keeping a secret from him. If he somehow knew I was going to die.

And if he'd worry if he knew what I was planning...

Soon, my eyes drifted shut. I snuggled into Calder's chest, resting in his warmth, before sleep claimed me.

Skuld sat on the boulder on the shore in front of our house, a house that was intact and had never been burned, still wearing my face. "You killed two of my own," she said simply, glancing from me to the fjord's placid blue water, using my voice. I didn't bother defending myself. She knew what had happened. "Well done," she added with a smile. My smile.

I didn't thank her for her praise. I only did what I had to do to save my life; she knew intimately well how much I valued it.

"Fenris Wolf and those who sail with him will leave the shores of Clan Nyerk at daybreak. They will carve a path around the land, but won't find a welcome place, thanks to your cunning plan."

It worked, then.

In Jarl Grandys' messages to the other clans, he allowed me to include a drawing of my rune and instructions for how to draw it onto anything they wished to protect. That way, they would have houses to come home to when this was all over.

He told them to inscribe the rune in blood, someplace the rain wouldn't wash it away. Inside homes and buildings. To carve it into trees all around the towns and villages they wanted to return to – whole.

It was the least I could do for those willing to join me in fighting Clan Wolf, and another subtle way to destroy Fenris' plans.

"You grow restless," she observed.

"My time is slipping away," I told her. Like water through my fingers... as Calder had shown me.

"Your beloved will survive. Is that not enough?" she asked, turning to face me again.

It was enough. Yet it would never be.

I loved Calder. I loved his father's kindness and his friends' laughter. I loved his kinsmen and his home and land. I loved my home, this place so dear to my heart. I missed it already.

In this dream, it smelled familiar, like my childhood. The brine. The scents from livestock. The earthy smell of mud. Of wildflowers. They bloomed now beyond the houses; on the bottoms of the hills they swayed in the wind.

"I've never met someone so desperately in love with her own life, despite the tragedy in it, Liv."

"I am," I told her.

"How do you know that you won't enjoy the rest death provides as well?" she asked. "Your brother told you about it."

Hodor was content.

Death was probably peaceful in a way I couldn't understand as I lived and breathed, but that didn't make me ready for it. It certainly didn't make me ready to leave Calder when he and I had only just begun.

"Would you like to see the future I've woven for Calder in your absence?"

I wasn't sure I did but couldn't help but nod.

She stood from the boulder and the shoreline disappeared. We stood beneath Ygdrassil once more at the norns' loom. In the fabric, I saw Calder's magnetic smile. Saw him tossing a young child into the air, playfully catching him again. His son. I could see a structure behind him, an enormous longhouse. "Fit for a Jarl, no?" Skuld asked.

"What about Armund?"

"No one lives forever," she replied. "Everyone's days are numbered. I am sorry, Liv, but so are yours. You have three sunsets and the moments leading up to Fenris's death, and no more."

279

I woke upset. Tears flowed from my eyes and trickled into my hair as I stared at the sloped ceiling planks. I wanted Calder to smile, for him to find happiness, to have a family and sons and daughters.

As a chieftain, I knew he would rebuild what Fenris had so ruthlessly destroyed. Then it would all be worth it.

But my heart ached with the knowledge that I wouldn't see it. That it would not be me who would be his wife and bear his children. That it would not be me fighting at his back against the world and anyone in it who opposed us.

Begging Skuld to save me would be worth it when I watched the light bleed from Fenris's eyes, but it was also worth it because of Calder. Through the thick mist of pain and loss and heartache and hatred, he emerged. Knowing him, loving him was everything I never had and didn't realize was missing.

How would I stop from unraveling *before* Fenris stepped ashore? How could I hold myself together when it felt like the strands were taut and ready to snap? How would I look into Calder's eyes as death came for me? I knew he would be close, probably with Fell and Tyr watching out for one another. How could I tell him how sorry I was for leaving? How much I wished I could stay?

He turned from one side to the other as I lay in tattered pieces beside him. I pinched my lips closed as my ribs shook from the sobs I vainly tried to hold in.

A few moments later, when I'd calmed down again, Armund whispered. "Liv?"

I glanced up to find him sitting up, watching as the orange firelight from the hearth danced over the room.

"Walk with me?" he asked quietly.

I nodded and eased from under the skin covering us, shivering in the absence of Calder's comforting warmth. Armund and I softly padded across the dark room and slipped outside.

The air had a chill to it. Overhead, clouds and stars battled one another for control of the sky. I crossed my arms over my chest and held my ribs.

"Did you dream?" he asked.

I nodded.

"Was Skuld there?"

I nodded again.

He tilted his head to the side, his graying hair drifting down his chest and arms. "Why are you crying?"

Swiping at my cheek, I gave a pitiful laugh. "I didn't know I was."

"Was she angry because you killed her völva?"

"Angry? No, she commended me for doing it."

Armund folded his hands behind him and was quiet for a long moment, staring off the cliff to the lapping waves below.

Unable to keep the bitterness from my voice, I pondered, "I'm so tired of feeling like a piece on the gods' and norns' game board, when it's apparent our lives are worth absolutely nothing to them."

"We all are pieces, being moved around with each choice we or they make," he mused darkly.

His dark blue tunic was wrinkled. His trousers, too. *Did he sleep, or was he too afraid to?* He saw my eyes rake over him.

"Tyr felt it would be best that one of us stay awake to watch the others. He took the first watch. It's my turn now."

"Why didn't you tell us?" I asked.

"You came in quite late. Brux, Fell, and Hilda were already sleeping. Tyr was awake when you came in. I was too, even though it wasn't my turn to watch. I have trouble sleeping sometimes. It gets worse with age. Babies and the aged sleep often but never deeply," he said with a smile and a wink.

Armund wasn't that old, but sometimes in his eyes there was a tiredness that looked bone deep. It never fully went away.

281

I'd heard of maladies taking years to kill a man and hoped Armund didn't die by that. He would go to Valhalla. I knew that as intimately as I knew the grass was green and the sea deep. Not every warrior slain was taken up to Odin's great hall, but a warrior who survived every battle he fought and lived to slip into the afterlife in his sleep deserved the honor of Odin's table more than the rest, if you asked me.

"Liv –" he began and stopped just to begin again. "I sense a change around you. I know you were affected after killing the witches, but I feel this is something deeper." I swallowed thickly as he continued. "Dread wafts from you night and day, during sleep and during all your waking hours, unless you are blissfully busy spending time with my son. What is the matter? Is it Fenris? Are you afraid to face him? Are you no longer confident that you can protect us?"

"No, I am sure of that, Armund," I answered his final question, ignoring his earlier observations.

"You don't have to tell me anything. But if you want to let me help you shoulder your burden, I gladly will," he said.

I gave him a grateful smile and a quiet thank you. He inclined his head, but disappointment weighed down his brow at my continued silence. "Armund?" I said. He perked up. "No matter what happens in the battle, please protect Calder. Make sure Fell and Tyr fight with him. Don't let him come near me. The power I have is… volatile."

His brows furrowed. "I always do. But what about you, Liv?"

"I will handle Fenris, but I need to do it on my own. Calder can be… protective."

"Yes, he can," he said softly. "I can't make promises, but I will try, Liv."

I thanked him. I knew there was little he could do to restrain his son if he was fighting as well. Even less if Calder set his mind to something.

"And remember your promise... as soon as the battle looks like it's swayed in our favor, you gather them all and run."

Concern wrinkled his skin.

"Tell them the plan beforehand."

"Is it my death you see?" he asked, searching me for the truth I kept hidden.

"No, but given the opportunity, the Jarls will attack you if I'm otherwise occupied and can't help."

He hugged me into his side. "I know you can do this, Liv. The Jarls think they lead their warriors, but it is *your* bind rune marking their heads, *you* who will sense the wolves descending, *you* who will light the fires and shout to the archers to draw their strings back. It is *you* who will be waiting on the shore, ready to face Fenris. You would face them all and never cower, but remember that you don't have to. You're not alone. You are part of our family now, and though I'm sure we're a poor substitution for your blood, we fight with you."

They *were* my family now. Skuld had given me a precious gift, not only of time, but of someone to love, something else to fight for and defend. I would kill Fenris to avenge my family. Blood spilled for blood spilled. But having someone to fight for, someone living, changed things. And fighting for someone I loved... changed everything.

Skuld and her sisters were wise to unleash my heart.

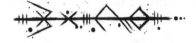

I wondered if I would ever finish painting runes on the heads of the newcomers. There seemed to be a constant flow of them with no end in sight. The sun peeked out between puffy clouds that shadowed the ground where it wasn't lit. A cool breeze slid lazily over the land, ruffling the blades of grass and bending the taller weeds.

A woman sat before me and I wondered why she looked familiar. She was thin but strong, as old as Armund, if not older. The lines on her face didn't disappear when she stopped smiling. I painted my bind rune on her forehead, uneasy as she studied me, staying silent until I had finished. "My son is in love with you," she finally said.

My fingers tightened on the brush.

What right does she have to claim him as hers after she abandoned him? "He thinks you are dead," I answered.

"I've kept my distance since arriving here. Last he saw me, I was in Bjern Town. I heard the entire town was killed," she said, her voice devoid of emotion.

I saw traces of her features in Calder, where Armund ended and she began. In the fullness of her lips. Calder's were much fuller than Armund's. In the shape of her eyes, though he took the ultramarine color from his father. Her eyes were blue, but many shades darker.

"I knew your mother," she said, watching me carefully.

"Everyone knew of my mother," I answered. For the first time, I was grateful for my mother's strength, for her sharpness, because it had sharpened me. "Why are you here?"

"Because my Jarl ordered it," she answered. "I moved to Clan Wonruk as soon as winter let up so that ships could sail around the southern shores. I must have just been spared by the attack from Clan Wolf."

"How fortunate for you."

She laughed without humor, brushing her light brown hair behind her ears. "It turned out to be."

"Did you marry into the clan?"

"I won't marry again," she said as easily as one would brush a fly from their shoulder. "I fight where I am given the most riches. The chieftain at Wonruk is generous with his warriors. He sanctions many raids and we are all given silver, gold, and jewels." She rattled the silver bracelets on her wrist and wiggled her ring-covered fingers.

"You didn't deserve them," I told her as she stood from the plain wooden chair. "And though it hurt them both, I'm glad you left. They're better without you."

Her lips parted. For a moment, I thought she might smack me. But shame swallowed her words and she finally nodded. "You're right. I was never meant to stay in one place, or with one man or child. I am a seed, blown on the wind, subject to its whims."

"A bad seed. Stay away from Calder and Armund."

She smiled. "Or what?"

"Or I will melt your rune away and let the wolves devour you while I protect your husband and son the way you should have done."

She weighed my words and turned, leaving me to paint my rune on another.

286

TWENTY-EIGHT

Calder, Fell, and I sat on stumps near Jarl Grandys's long-house, but far enough away that we could speak freely. We sharpened our weapons with borrowed whetstones. *A smooth stone means a smooth, sharp blade*, Father said the day he gave me my sword. I raked the rock across my blade.

"Tyr is missing again," Fell said quietly.

"Again?" Calder asked.

"I didn't expect you to notice. Liv seems to be all you can see these days," he teased, winking in my direction. "But yes. He's been going off on his own during the day."

Calder's hands stopped their work. "Why are you concerned?"

"Because of who he's watching. He's studying Jarl Varsyk."

Fell's brown eyes locked with Calder's. We knew what it meant, just as we knew it would eventually happen. Tyr would finally avenge his father. He might not be able to kill the völva who cursed him on the field of battle, but he would end the man who encouraged her to speak the weighty words.

Tyr was likely learning the man. His habits. His preferences for weapons. Who he kept near to guard him.

Now that Armund had announced himself as our Jarl, Brux and Hilda insisted on guarding him.

Tyr could slip away without anyone knowing. Except his brothers…

The chieftain of Varsyk likely had no idea Tyr was stalking him, but I was certain Tyr wouldn't kill him before the battle we faced with Clan Wolf. There were many who aligned with Clan Varsyk here, who respected or at least feared their Jarl, while there were only a handful of us banded together. The roles, land, and power Armund and I claimed were tentative. If they managed to keep it in their hands after this battle, they would have to be careful with it. As careful as I was with the whetstone as a young girl.

"He won't strike until the battle," Calder said.

"I know," Fell agreed, "but if someone sees him and ties it back to all of us… I just want you to be ready to fight our way out of here or run. I will see our home again, Calder. I will see your father as Jarl, even if it means fleeing instead of fighting our way through it."

I nodded in agreement.

"Armund said that as soon as Fenris and Liv begin to fight, we need to slip out of the battle, mount our horses, and make for home."

Calder's jaw dropped and he gaped at me. "He wants us to leave you?"

Fell nodded and glanced at me. "He said this is something she has to face alone, that Skuld is with her and that it's what she wants. She wants us safe and on the way home before anyone can attack us for our lands. For *her* land, too, Calder."

I fought the urge to meet Calder's eyes, though I knew he was drilling holes into my forehead as I studiously sharpened my blade. Truthfully, I didn't know how I would pry myself away from him now that he was dear to me. I knew I could fight Fenris and win with Skuld's magic bolstering my veins, but when I battled him, it would be just me and him. No magic. No Skuld. *I* wanted to avenge my family. If nothing else, I was a stubborn warrior.

"I knew you'd fight it," I hinted casually as I raked my mother's axe across the stone clenched in my left hand. "But this is a battle no one can fight for me. You've seen what I'm capable of. The fury I feel makes me want to kill him with my bare hands, but if I falter, if it looks like I might not win, I will use Skuld's power. I want him dead more than I value my pride. Not only to avenge my people, but to keep everyone I've painstakingly painted the rune onto alive. I want a future without Fenris Wolf, and I'll have it. I have no doubt about my purpose. Neither should you."

Calder's eyes softened. "I know you do, and that you will. I'm just not sure I can ride away without you and leave you behind."

Breaking the tension, Fell joked, "Besides, if she starts using the seiðr magic, she may not be able to stop, and this whole thing might end before it begins. She could sink their ships at the first sight of them, then all we would have to do is finish off any stragglers that made it to shore."

I shook my head and gave a grim laugh. "I need them on land, though I'm not sure why. Maybe it's just to look in Fenris's eyes when I kill him, or maybe this is how Skuld wants it to be. This battle must be fought, not just won."

Fell nodded pensively. "I believe you when you say you're able to protect us, but I can't imagine no one dying in this."

"We fight as one. We live as one," Calder said. Words his father had spoken a hundred times.

Fell quirked a brow. "Then we trust Liv to do her part and ride out of here together."

Sig trotted to Calder and laid down at his feet, his tongue hanging out. The fawn-colored elkhound must have worn him out. Calder scratched his back as he caught his breath, keeping his thoughts to himself.

Armund and his former wife were in a heated discussion behind one of the longhouses. I carried my brush and pot and left my position. No one was waiting for the mark, as most had already taken it.

My feet strode toward him.

Did she seek him out after I warned her to leave him and Calder alone?

My teeth ground together.

The scent of smoking fish mingled with wood smoke as I passed a campfire, walking into the plume and out just as fast. She saw me approaching and her eyes hardened in a way Calder's didn't. When he was angry, his burned with fury. They never turned cold.

"I told you not to seek them out," I seethed, standing next to him.

Armund's eyes flicked to mine questioningly. "How did you know her?"

"She made herself known as I painted the bind rune."

Brux and Hilda strode by, her eyes catching on Armund, then on his former wife. Trouble flitted over Hilda's face before Brux eased her away from the unfolding scene.

"You had no right to approach Liv," he blustered toward the one who deserted him when he and their son needed her most.

"I have *every* right," she countered hotly.

"You lost any claim to him or me when you walked away," he challenged, stepping toward her. "I want you to leave this place."

She laughed and shook her head. "My Jarl brought me here. I'm under *his* command."

"No, you aren't," I told her, waiting as she flicked her eyes toward me. "*I* command this army."

"I will go nowhere unless my chieftain gives me the order," she stubbornly refused.

"Very well," I said, giving Armund a look of promise as I started off toward Jarl Grandys's house where the chieftains were meeting inside. I didn't mind disturbing them. Stopping short, I turned to Armund. "What's her name?"

I'd overheard Hilda say it once, but forgot it just as quickly. To me, her name was as insignificant as she was.

Armund's brows kissed, then relaxed as he chuckled, running fingers over his mustache and trailing down his beard. "Jorah," he answered.

I smiled at her without warmth. "If I were you, I'd gather your things."

Calder's mother snarled at me, her lip curled. "You are nothing. You have no power over me, *witch*."

The ground underfoot vibrated as fire churned in my belly. I wanted to blast her with a column of flame she'd never escape from, but losing my temper and using my power would just draw Calder's attention, and I didn't want him to see her.

"We'll see," I retorted with a knowing smile.

I strode up the hill toward the longhouse and pushed the doors open, interrupting the Jarls as they talked amongst themselves. Ivor stood and crossed his arms. "*Smár ormr*, do come in."

The chieftain of Wonruk stood at the end of the room with one leg propped on a stool, leaning forward, his arms braced on the bent leg. He straightened and brought the leg down when I stormed toward him. "What do *you* want with *me*?" he spat, rearing back when I stopped in front of him.

Ivor tsked. "You'd be wise to speak to her a little more respectfully."

I'd already bristled at the stocky man's tone. "I want you to send Jorah away."

"She's one of my best."

"No, she's your worst."

"In battle, she is a strong fighter. One of the strongest I brought," he argued.

I didn't tell him that she was a weak, pathetic excuse for a woman. That she might be able to fight with axe or sword, but was a distraction for my friends that they didn't need.

I lifted my chin defiantly. "I want her gone. Now."

Jarl Wonruk blustered, his sandy beard trembling with anger as Ivor watched with a trace of amusement. Wonruk met me toe to toe. "Who are you to give me orders?" His hand fell on the handle of his sword.

"The woman who will tear you apart before you have time to draw your weapon, that's who," I snapped. "I'll say this once more: *I want her gone*. This is my army, my battle. I saved your entire clan by asking Ivor to pen that message. You owe me this, if not much, much more."

His hand gradually relaxed until it fell to his side. Ivor and the others were tense as they watched our battle of wills unfold. Suddenly, Jarl Wonruk's shoulders eased. "I'll find her," he finally agreed. "But she won't go easily."

I smiled. "I promise you she will, or I will gladly motivate her. She's right outside."

His eyes widened slightly. He strode from the room, pushing around me, but not quite touching me. The desire to plant his fist in my mouth was emblazoned in his eyes.

Ivor Grandys laughed as the angry Jarl shoved out the door. "You have quite a way of motivating people, Liv. I am glad we are allies."

Allies. Was that what we were? Did allies attempt to conquer the lands of their friends? Did they plot to overtake the most vulnerable in the alliance?

I didn't think so.

I followed the angry chieftain out the door. By the time I reached Armund, Wonruk had ordered Jorah to leave

Grandys' lands and return home. She had already left to pack her things and ready her horse, cursing my name on her way out.

Not that it would do her any good. She was no witch, and I was already going to die.

Armund turned and grabbed two fish spears mounted on the side of a nearby house. "I'm starving and the smoked fish smells delicious. Would you like to fish with me?" he asked as if nothing had ever happened.

I nodded and started walking with him to the shore. "I'd be happy to help, but you should spend a little time with Hilda when we're finished, maybe ask her to help you cook them up."

"Why?" he asked, his brows furrowing.

I smiled. "It's funny that you can see what lies between me and your son but can't see that Hilda wants you."

His mouth fell open. "Are you sure? I mean, I'd hoped..."

"As sure as I am that the sea will be here long after you and I depart from this world."

Armund looked relieved. His face relaxed and he gave a soft laugh. Until I added, "She saw you with Jorah."

Armund cursed, looking over his shoulder for Hilda, but she and Brux were nowhere in sight. "That woman ruins everything, even things I don't have yet."

"You like Hilda, then?"

"I've always respected her and thought her beautiful, I just... I had no idea she might have feelings for me." He laughed. "When you worry for everything on your own, it's hard to pay attention to such things, I guess. I felt like I was always working, keeping my head down and staying focused on the tasks I had to do for Calder, Fell, and Tyr. But Calder and the boys are grown now. They are boys no more. They're men. So perhaps it's time I look up once in a while."

On the beach, I tied my skirts so my calves were bare and we waded into the sea, remaining still with our spears at the ready. We were quiet, waiting together for the schools who rode the waves to come close. We stood motionless for a long time before Armund speared the first fish. Silver-scaled, it wriggled on the spear, leaking blood into the water. Armund's eyes watched me carefully. "Will its blood bother you?"

I swallowed. "I don't think so. The sea should scatter it." The sea took the blood away, though I felt the barest trace brushing my calves.

Men and women from other clans watched us warily. It felt like we couldn't go anywhere without their scrutinizing eyes following closely behind. We fished on despite them, and in the end, speared enough fish to feed our small clan.

Hilda helped Armund clean and cook them over a fire he built for her. While the fish skins sizzled and popped, their eyes met time and again and they smiled. The seriousness and worry Armund wore like armor melted away as the two spoke, enjoying one another's company in the comfort of shared domestic activity.

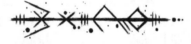

Our small group settled to listen to the storyteller after supper. He was an old man with a long white beard, tan, wrinkled skin, and wispy white hair that stuck up in traces around the crown of his head. He belonged to Clan Laryk and said he'd listened to stories as a boy and made them up as a young man – before he found the value that lay in the truth. Now he told the stories he had once sat and listened to.

His voice was strong and lilting, capturing the tales and making me feel like I was in his stories and not just hearing them.

We'd heard this story a thousand times, but never from him. The storyteller made it new. His gestures, intonation, and the way he spoke of it as if he'd been there to witness it himself helped to weave a mesmerizing tapestry of sight and sound.

"Between Muspelheim, the land of fire so hot it melted iron, like that," he said, snapping his fingers, "...and Niflheim, the land of ice so cold it could freeze a man's heart just as fast, there was a darkness so viscous and thick it consumed all who came near. The darkness was deathly still. Quiet. And empty, though it was full.

"Frost and flame from the two worlds collided in the space between them. The result when they came together was catastrophic. Ymir was the first giant, born in the aftermath of fire melting ice within the great darkness."

Calder leaned back on his hands beside me. His eyes flicked to mine when he caught me watching. He nudged his knee against mine and gave me a secret smile.

"From the melting frost, Audhumla was born, a great cow that nourished Ymir. From him, other giants were born until Odin and his brothers, Villi and Vi, emerged. Odin would become the Alfather, chief of the Aesir.

"Odin, with the help of his brothers, killed Ymir, and his blood became the seas. His skin and muscles formed the soil. Trees and plants were formed from his hair. His skull formed the sky and from his brains, Odin crafted the clouds.

"Eventually, Ask and Embla, the first man and woman, were made. Ask from the ash tree, Embla from the great elm. Now," he paused, leaning forward, "I ask you this: Why did the Alfather slay Ymir?"

There were mutterings among all the clans, but no one shouted an answer.

The storyteller continued, "Either Ymir was evil, or he was not. Could he have provoked Odin and his brothers? We do not know. If he was evil, then Odin and his brothers killed him out of honor. But what if he was not evil at all? What reason would they have to slay the first giant?"

Everyone was still.

The storyteller grinned and stroked his beard, enjoying the rapt silence he commanded with his audience.

"Perhaps, and this is just the musing of an old man, but *perhaps* they slew him, not because he deserved it, but because he had to die. Perhaps Ymir was sacrificed so that Midgard could exist. And because there was no other way to make it but through him, perhaps he lives on in the sky above us, in the clouds that roll over it. Perhaps he feels us when we are buried within the soil, or when we fell a tree to build our homes or a fence to pen up our animals."

He continued his musing and when the tale was finished, got up and walked into the shadows toward the Laryk encampment.

"Do you believe that?" I asked Calder as people began to leave the grass.

"I've never thought of it that way. I always assumed Ymir had done something to deserve death."

"Maybe he was born so that he would die... for this world," I said. "Nothing lives forever. Maybe Ymir's purpose was to become what we needed. The weavers... they see what we can't. They make things true that shouldn't be possible."

Calder gave me a troubled look as our clan – Armund, Hilda, Brux, Fell, and Tyr – stood. Fell hooked a thumb over his shoulder. "Are the two of you staying out or going back to the Jarl's with us?"

"Staying out," Calder answered easily.

Fell chuckled and they left us sitting in the grass. Hilda walked with Armund, her hand purposefully brushing his, and my heart felt lighter.

Until it didn't.

Suddenly, it felt like there was a dark chasm between Calder and I, one that a million kisses and embraces couldn't fill. Maybe it was looming death I sensed but couldn't explain. I stood and dusted the skirt of my dress and we walked to the shore that always seemed to call me. Was it because it was made from Ymir's blood?

"Why did the gods make the norns to weave our fates?" he mused, sliding his hand into mine.

"I don't think they did. The gods, too, have fates. Why else would they subject themselves to the whims of another?" I thought about the story. "Frost doesn't creep toward fire. Its nature would be to retreat from it. Something pushed it toward the flames. I think the weavers were there in the darkness before the world was formed, that they set it all in motion and one day, they will end it all." I stared at the sea. "It's calm now, but the night *he* comes, it will foam and froth and churn."

"You've seen it?"

I crossed my arms, fighting off a chill. "I dream of it every night, and sometimes see visions in the middle of the day."

We sat together on the shore. He wrapped an arm around me and I nestled into the crook of his neck. We sat there watching the moon shift until I started drifting off to sleep. Only then did we walk back to the Jarl's house. I would've sat with him all night on that shore, but it wasn't safe if we both fell asleep. Tyr had suggested that someone stay awake and watch over the others. It was the wisest thing to do, given the fact that the bloodthirsty Jarls still circled us like vultures scenting the dead.

Settled together under a wide, thin hide, it took no time for Calder's breathing to soften into a deep rhythm, like a calm sea ebbing and flowing where sea met the land. Where blood met flesh.

298

TWENTY-NINE

Before dawn, I woke and grew restless, unable to sleep anymore. I slipped out from under the hide when I saw Armund motion for me to follow him outside. Tyr watched us, then turned his attention back to his fingernails where he raked beneath them with the tip of his knife. His eyes flicked back to Calder before we slipped outside.

Armund walked toward the cliff. "I never thanked you for sending Jorah away before she could get her talons in Calder. The woman is poison, and Calder doesn't need to worry about her when such a vital battle lies ahead."

"When she revealed herself to me, I told her I was glad she'd left you both because she didn't deserve you in her life, and you were better off without her. And you're right; the woman is poison. I'm sorry you had to endure her, but glad that Calder was the result of your relationship."

He gave a wan smile. "As am I."

"Does he worry about settling down?" I asked carefully. "I would be afraid to find out that I'd married someone like my father. Does he worry his future wife might be like *her*?"

"If he does, he's never said so to me." Armund's eyes searched mine. "I don't know what will become of you after you end Fenris's life, Liv. But if Skuld sets you free and you and Calder decide to make a life together, I would wholeheartedly approve. You are nothing like Jorah. You would never lie to him. You would never leave him. Love doesn't leave, and I can see that you love my son."

Tears welled in my eyes. Unable to speak, I nodded.

In the end, I was *just like* Jorah. I would leave him, though not by choice, but I'd be gone all the same.

And I did love Calder. That was why it hurt so much to even think about letting him go.

Armund pulled me in for a hug. "You're already like a daughter to me."

And just like that, Skuld sent me an image of a sky with two setting suns. That was how many sunsets I had left with Calder.

Skuld had given me Mother's axe, the blade sharpened so fine, it could split one of my hairs. The spear tip so deadly, it could puncture a tree trunk and not get stuck. And while I'd worked to sharpen it the other day, Hilda sat sharpening hers. So, I joined her, taking up my sword. I soaked the stone and raked the blade carefully over it. Here and there in the town, I could hear the rhythmic scraping of other whetstones, too.

The almost carefree feeling that once surrounded this place was evaporating like mist on the mountains in the first rays of sun.

Hilda sat with me, watching me sharpen my sword. She glanced to Mother's axe lying beside me. "Which will you use?" she asked. "Or do you prefer to use both?"

"No, I will wear my shield and fight with my sword. I was never good with Mother's axe, though I'm glad Skuld restored it."

"I thought you might just need your wand. Like before, when the Wolfs returned to kill us."

I swallowed thickly. I'd need my wand for some things, but Fenris would taste my blade.

"May I see it?" she asked. I nodded and watched as she tested the edge, slicing her thumb. She hissed as blood welled in the wound. "It's bad luck to draw blood before a battle," she said, dread lacing her voice.

"Only if it's done with someone else's weapon."

She laughed. "It was."

"I want you to have it." I watched as her lips parted.

She let out a strangled sound. "This is all you have left of her! I couldn't."

"I want you to have it. You clearly appreciate it, and you're about my mother's height and build. You'll wield it easily. Just mind the spear while you learn."

She studied the fine inlaid design along the blade's head. "This is too much."

"Hilda, you have to stop worrying if you and I are even. We are friends. Friends help one another, as you've helped me. You clothed me when I had nothing, and you didn't ask me for anything in return. Sometimes, one friend gives the other a gift. Please accept it."

"I'm sorry if I was frightened of you at first," she said, forgetting the axe to meet my eyes.

"I would have been afraid of me if I were you. There's nothing to apologize for."

She gave me a gracious smile, then examined the axe further. It was a hundred times finer than the axe she brought with her. Weapons were expensive. If Father hadn't gone on raids and been so richly rewarded, Hodor and I would've had to scrape for something that resembled an axe but could barely qualify as one. I wanted Hilda to be able to cleave someone's head clean off their shoulders if they tried to hurt her. This axe would do it. I'd seen it once.

Besides, if I was going to die anyway, I wanted my things to go to people who would cherish them.

Which reminds me...

"Do you know where Armund is?"

"Fishing again. He loved last night's fish, despite the feast Jarl Grandys put on."

"I think he just likes the cook," I told her with a wink.

She blushed and winked at me, chuckling. "I hope so," she admitted.

I met Armund in the waves. They were choppier than they were last night, but they weren't foaming yet. It wasn't churning. I wondered if the blood of giants was clear, not red like the blood of humans. If it looked blue when it was spread across the world, or if the gods had settled it into something more pleasing to the eye and less terrifying.

"Liv," he greeted softly, peering into the water and trying to see a flash of silver scales. He sighed. "This is pointless when the water is so unsettled." Lifting his spear, he waded toward me.

"Armund," I started. "I was wondering if you'd like to use my brother's shield in the battle."

Armund had his own shield, but the wood was dry and the metal edges were bent and chipped in places. It had been some time since he'd worn it in battle. Since the day someone chopped into his knee and ruined him for many battles to come.

"What if it gets ruined? You'll want to preserve it to remember Hodor by."

"The shield is new. It's a little charred, but it's strong. And if you use it, it'll feel like Hodor is still with me. If it gets ruined, so be it. Hodor would rather it help in the fight than for it to go to waste."

"Mine *is* a little worn," he admitted. "If you're sure, I would be honored to wear it."

I smiled. "Thank you."

His eyes widened as two ravens – one black as midnight and the other bone white –circled us from the low-hanging clouds, twisting downward until they flew around us. "Odin?" he breathed, eyes darting all around us.

"Hodor?" I cried.

The birds flew back into the air and disappeared into the clouds.

Armund looked to me. "I didn't feel the Alfather, but those were his ravens. Why did you speak your brother's name?"

"He is with Odin. I've seen him in a dream. Huginn and Muninn were with him then, too. We were talking about his shield and I was thinking about him..."

"Thor favors you. It seems Odin does, too."

Their favor was nice to have, but it wouldn't save me from the future Skuld intended to hold me to, the future for which I'd bargained in a moment of agony and desperation, not knowing what the future could hold.

"My grandmother was völva," I told him. "She tried to smother me when I was an infant." Armund inhaled sharply. "She told my mother I would be a scourge upon the earth."

Armund's brows furrowed. "Liv, you are no scourge."

"I'm not sure what will happen to me when this battle begins, but if it starts to appear like she might be right, I want you all to leave. Run. Don't let me catch you if I become something dark and terrible."

He once said he'd dreamt of me, not as I was but as I was going to be. Had he seen me as my grandmother had?

I yawned, unable to fight the wave of exhaustion that crashed over me. I hadn't slept well and was exhausted from trying to stay awake so I wouldn't dream.

"Liv, you must be rested to focus. If you're going to keep us all safe, you have to focus and use all the powers Skuld gave you."

"I'll sleep tonight," I promised him.

"You should sleep now. I can watch over you."

I shook my head. "Not now."

He sighed. "Liv…"

"I promise to rest, but not now." I gave him a small smile that seemed to placate him. He gave up trying to convince me and I walked back to the Jarl's house to get my bag. I had more work to do.

I grabbed my things and walked into the forest alone.

I sat beneath a tall pine and leaned back against its trunk. Removing the shields and my sword from my bag, I began to remove the smaller things: the pot of ash ink, my brush, Gunnar's bone horn, Solvi's comb… and a deep sleep fell over me despite the battle I waged against it.

Solvi sat still as I raked the comb through her hair, wetting the strands and working the teeth through her pile of curls. The hearth was warm and the wind howled outside. Something was cooking over the fire. The scent and sound of sizzling meat filled the air.

Solvi giggled at Ingrid across the room as Mother worked her hair into braids. Mother looked up at me and smiled, and I realized with a start that her face was burnt. Her chest and neck were charred and bloody.

My heart thundered. No…

Ingrid's arm was missing, her side torn open.

"Little bee?" I asked, tears welling.

Solvi turned and looked up at me over her shoulder. The hair I'd just held evaporated until only one tuft remained. Solvi's chest was split open and her eyes were sad. "Why?" she asked.

Gunnar walked into the room from outside, his head wobbling on the neck that barely held it, his bone flute in one hand and a wooden sword in the other. "It's almost time," he said.

Father's ragged form came shuffling in behind him. He paused inside the door to stomp caked mud from his boots. I clung to Solvi's comb and covered my mouth, carefully easing past them and just making it outside where I retched until my stomach was hollow.

A hand clamped onto my shoulder. I looked over it to find Hodor there, his throat split open and dark, sticky blood covering his clothes. "Liv, he's coming."

"I know," I croaked.

"You have to prepare."

"I have been."

He crouched down beside me. "You have to prepare. Not the Jarls. Not the army. You."

I cried as I looked at his wounds. "I will make sure Fenris Wolf never does this to anyone again."

He nodded once, finitely. As if he believed me.

Then he slowly faded away. Everything did.

I blinked to find Skuld sitting across from me, holding Gunnar's bone flute. I was clutching Solvi's comb so tightly the teeth bit into my skin. "Why did you send that vision?"

I could still taste bile burning the back of my throat.

She stared at me. "So that you don't forget."

Anguish laced my voice as I responded, "I remember them every minute of every day. I breathe because of them. I would never forget them."

Skuld sat Gunnar's flute down and I quickly took it in my free hand, clutching it and the comb to my chest protectively.

Her hair was sloppily pulled back at the nape of her neck, like mine, strands escaping wildly, drifting in the wind that gently swayed the pine boughs.

Composing myself, I calmly told her, "I would never forget them; it just hurts to remember. But as soon as I see Fenris's sails, as soon as I see his face, the rage bubbling inside me will emerge and he won't be strong enough to stand against the monster he created."

Skuld watched me with my eyes. "I was wrong," she admitted.

"About me forgetting?"

"No, I know you've pushed the pain away. I wasn't wrong about that. I was wrong in thinking *I* made you into a warrior. Your mother and father did that. Then I was wrong in thinking I molded you into something Fenris would fear, but he did that when he killed your family. I've only added my favor and power to what was already made."

My hands shook uncontrollably.

"Your heart dies for them daily…" she said of my family, "but it lives for *him*."

Calder.

"Yes."

"Humans lose themselves to hatred piece by piece, but it is also how love restores them, Liv."

I wasn't sure if I was imagining the pity shining in her eyes – in my eyes – or if it was there under the surface.

"I want to live," I told her sharply.

"Yes, I know," she answered with my voice.

"But you don't care."

Her eyes snapped to mine. "Do not presume to know my feelings," she warned. "Or to know what is best for the whole. One life can affect many."

"I know that better than anyone, Skuld."

In that moment, I realized what Armund and Calder meant when they said I was nothing like her, felt nothing like her. She was merciful, but her mercy came with a heavy price. To Fenris, I wouldn't be merciful at all. I'd never been more grateful to have been born to Hella and Erik, to have been honed and sharpened and made deadly.

"The bargain we struck… I made it as I lay dying. The only thing I had to look forward to was killing Fenris. I only had revenge. But then Calder came and found me and showed me that there were things worth living for. Why did you bring us together just to tear us apart? It's cruel."

She shook her head. "Humans understand nothing."

"Then help me! Help me understand how it makes sense! You have the power to let me live, to build a life with Calder. Why won't you let me?"

She shook her head again.

"You do not need him, Liv."

"I know!" I shouted, leaping to my feet. She rose, too. "I know I don't need him, but damn it, I want him! I. Want. Him! I want to live!"

Skuld shot me a sharp look before lunging at me.

308

THIRTY

Skuld had overtaken my body. My mind was trapped within, unable to even blink an eye.

She sat in the trees, enjoying the feel of being confined in something so simple, but wonderful, as a human's body. She marveled at Odin's creation. Midgard was lush and fresh and cool. A place she wanted to visit more often.

I could feel her emotions, sense her thoughts.

Sharing my body with the norn gave me insight no one else on earth had. Even as I wanted to shove her out.

Voices came from further in the wood.

"She probably just needed some time alone," Armund offered reassuringly.

He was with Calder. "I feel like she's slowly slipping away from me and I'm not sure how to stop it."

"You can't," Armund said as the two walked closer. "Is it her pulling away?"

"No, it's life tearing us apart."

I could hear Armund's vertebrae move as he nodded. "It will. It'll do that again and again, pull you both until the fabric that knits you is threadbare and weak. But you must not let it tear, even in the slightest. If a tear starts, it's hard to stop it from spreading."

The pair stopped. Skuld went completely still, listening to them as intently as I did.

"Son, how... how do you feel about Hilda?"

"Grateful. She makes you happy," Calder told him.

"I feel the same about Liv when it comes to you," Armund admitted as they trudged uphill among the thin trees.

Skuld plucked hair from my head, threading it through the eye of her needle, and began to hum. She craved their attention and inwardly, I thrashed. I was afraid of what she'd do to them if they gave it to her.

"Don't hurt them!" I roared from inside our head.

Skuld shushed me and pushed the needle through the center of a bone she'd warmed and flattened.

Armund went still. "Listen. Liv?" he called out.

Skuld moved my eyes to his, but Calder recognized her right away. "Skuld."

"Why do you keep overshadowing her?" Armund asked.

Skuld answered raspily, "Through her, I can breathe."

Armund eased closer, careful not to make any sudden movements. He extended his hands outward, palms up. "But can she?" he dared ask the norn.

Skuld's anger flared and she left my body. I slumped sideways, but Calder was there to catch me, diving onto his knees, reaching out for me before I could hit the ground.

I clung to him for a moment before righting myself. "I fell asleep," I admitted. "I was so tired, and then..."

"Is that why you've been avoiding sleep?" Armund asked. "Because she's there?"

I shook my head and smiled at Calder. "There might be another reason."

I looked in my lap, at the ground around me, and took in the armor. There were two bony greaves to match a pair of vambraces, thicker plates for my thighs, and a crown fashioned from the bones of fingers and toes. With trembling fingers, I picked up Gunnar's small bone flute and Solvi's comb and held them out for Armund and Calder to see.

"This flute belonged to my younger brother, Gunnar," I began in a rusty voice. "This comb was my little sister Solvi's. I called her my little bee. Her hair was so curly, it would form a nest on her head. Mother didn't have the patience to comb it, so I would."

The insects all around us went quiet. The earth began to tremble. The sun set and darkness flooded the shadowed forest.

I looked at Calder, emotions roiling through me. Tomorrow night, he would know I'd lied to him and he'd spend the rest of his life hating me for it.

"One more sunset," I said gravely. I held Calder's stare, wishing I could stop time, or somehow convince Skuld to listen to reason.

I sat outside near the cliffs with Calder, Fell, and Tyr. The afternoon sun was hidden away by ever-thickening clouds. The men oiled the leather armor they would wear so it would be pliable and move with them instead of being a stiff impediment. Sig paced. He could sense the tension in the air. The tone of the town had completely shifted overnight. Tonight, we would eat an early supper and then hunker down and wait. Tonight, after sunset, Clan Wolf would arrive.

Tyr was quiet as usual, occasionally glancing up from his task. Fell, too, was quiet. Unusually so. "What's the matter?" Calder asked him.

He threw his rag down onto the grass and laid down his leather, the buckles clanking as it fell. He paced back and forth, trampling a section of grass. He raked his hands through his hair, tearing at it. Then he stopped and walked close to us. "You're going to protect us, right, Liv?" he asked me.

"I am." *Where was this doubt coming from?*

"Then who's going to protect you? Hmm? Armund said you want us to turn tail and run home before anyone can attack us, but I don't like the thought of leaving you behind."

Tyr scoffed, but continued to oil his plain, orange-hued leather. "The witch can take care of herself. She'll catch up with us. She's powerful beyond comprehension. She survived a lightning strike sent by Thor himself, followed by a snow slide, for the gods' sakes. If she *wants* to find us, she will."

The witch again? *We were back to that?*

"She's sitting right here. Stop talking like she isn't," Calder growled. His jaw ticked angrily as he fumed, working the oil harder into the leather.

Calder's leather was stained, and thanks to Armund and Hilda, bore a new engraving: a freshly carved serpent in the hide, coiled and ready to strike. *Ivor calls her little serpent. Let's show him that we stand with her*, he said. *And that she, and we, aren't afraid to strike those who draw their blades against us.*

Armund carved his own similarly, as well as Fell's, Brux's, and Hilda's. Tyr didn't want my sigil on his chest, claiming it might anger the gods. Everyone knew it had nothing to do with them.

Fell flicked a gaze from Calder to Tyr, who had finished oiling his armor and began sharpening his knives again. He'd sharpened them all week. I couldn't imagine they needed it, but Tyr seemed as anxious and unsettled as everyone else, whether he would admit it or not.

Fell nodded to his whetstone. "What are you planning?"

Tyr's hand went still. "To kill wolves, of course."

312

"Anything else?"

"Is there someone you want dead, brother?" he challenged, looking at Fell expectantly.

Calder knew what he was planning. "Make sure no one sees it," he told him softly.

Tyr's eyes narrowed at him.

Comprehension dawned on Fell as he figured it out, eliciting a string of curses. "You're going to get us all killed before we can slip away, Tyr."

"I can throw from a distance."

"Through a battlefield with people constantly moving and shifting? It would be like throwing a blade just above the water's surface and trying to avoid its waves!" Fell sputtered.

Tyr shrugged. "It's not your concern, Fell."

"It is when we fight as one," Calder reminded him.

Tyr shook his head. "I'll be careful. No one will see it."

I knew he could be. He threw knives so often, it would only take a flick of his wrist for the blade to soar. And I couldn't fault him for craving the man's death any more than I could fault myself for seeking vengeance against Fenris Wolf.

"I hope you go for his heart," I told Tyr.

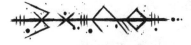

After our early, heavy dinner, I dressed in black trousers and pulled the matching tunic over my head. I emerged from Ivor's longhouse with my bag on my back and my bone-drenched wand in hand. My sunlight hair whipped back and forth in a wind that grew more unsettled by the moment as I walked to Calder, who was with his family and kinsmen on the beach.

"Calder?" I said, unfurling my palm to reveal Solvi's comb. "Will you braid my hair?"

His brows kissed. "Of course." He looked around at the houses and tents nearby, then ran to one. Hefting a heavy stump, he plodded toward the water.

"I can just sit on it there," I told him.

"No. You used to sit in front of the sea on a boulder. There's not one here, so we'll make our own."

The gesture meant everything. He plunked the stump down and motioned for me to take a seat, then handed him Solvi's comb.

I stared at the sea as he combed my long hair. As he separated and braided, tying the ends with dark leather I'd cut from the top edge of my bag, I stared at the foaming, churning, frothing sea and watched the sun sink closer to the western horizon. This was it. Hours were all we had left.

"The clouds look strange," he murmured.

The sky was green. The clouds raced across like they couldn't bear to witness what was about to unfold, eager to get away.

"It's going to storm, but it won't rain," I told him. At dinner, Skuld had sent a vision.

"Will Thor watch the battle?" he asked.

I nodded. The gods always watched.

In a normal battle, Odin of the Aesir and Freyja of the Vanir gods would watch us fight and pluck up any of the fallen who fought bravely, who they felt earned a spot at their tables. The Valkyrie would carry them to their rightful places, where they would spend eternity. I could almost see the swipe of golden wings in the clouds above as if they hovered, even now.

But this was not a normal battle, and Skuld showed me how she would ban them from plucking souls from any of the Wolf warriors.

In my vision, the sky had lit up with lightning, striking over the sea as their ships approached. Fenris and his warriors were ready, screaming into the raging wind and sea. He stood on the prow of the lead ship, pointing his axe at something on the shore...

Pointing his axe at me.

I was there waiting for him. Dressed in black and bone, cloaked in rage and pain, vengeance embodied. But something more powerful would make me draw my sword instead of my wand. Something I'd felt deep inside all along.

I had earned my shield before Skuld made me hers. I'd faced my notoriously fierce and terrifying warrior mother and won.

I was a shield maiden.

And that was how I would face Fenris Wolf. Not as Skuld's völva. As *me*.

This battle, I realized, had been planned for a very long time, maybe from the start. I was born to Clan Urðr for a reason. The clan was named for the norn who had woven our past, even as Verdandi wove our present, with Skuld providing strands with which to weave it and deciding when one strand should be clipped like the roots at the base of Ygdrassil. Skuld, who was even now sharpening her axe blade. I could almost hear it, the slick, raking sound of the metal head echoing across the heavens.

Calder finished my braids. I looked up at him over my shoulder. "Can I braid yours?"

He nodded once and sat on the stump when I stood. I took Solvi's comb from his hand. He pulled three leather straps from his pocket. I made a larger braid down the center of his head and bound it, then braided two on each side, meeting them beneath the large braid and tying their ends together.

I removed my sword and cut two long strips of leather from my bag. One, I tied to Solvi's comb. The other, I threaded through the holes of Gunnar's bone flute. I tied them to my wand, hanging them from the ribs that spun and swirled from the base.

315

The wind rustled them and the bones clacked together as they touched, were pulled apart, then pushed together again.

Calder carefully removed my bone armor from my bag and laid it out for me. "How does it tie on?" he rasped.

"I have to be the one to tie it on," I told him, unsure why, but knowing I did. "Where's your leather?"

"Still inside Ivor's house."

"You should put it on."

He hesitated for a moment before jogging up the path to the Jarl's house and disappearing inside. He emerged a moment later, the leather tugged over his head but not laced.

I sliced long strands from the underside of my hair and pushed them through the armor, tying the plates onto my body over my dark tunic. The hair should've been too weak to support the weight, but Skuld insisted if I used it, she would strengthen it. And she did.

As I tied the greaves onto my shins, fitting the thigh armor, securing the vest of bones over my torso and the vambraces on my forearms… I felt my family with me. Their spirits were close.

They were watching.

I could almost hear Ingrid's and Solvi's laughter, the raucous timbre of Gunnar's cheers, and feel Hodor's quiet support. He wasn't the sort to yell except in the heat of battle, but I sensed him telling me I was ready for this.

I felt Father's cool gaze, heard the grit of his teeth that always clenched before battle.

Oskar's comforting presence filled me. Even though I didn't wear his bones, I kept his memory firmly entrenched in my heart.

And then I felt Mother. I could almost see her tying her leather armor on as Calder tightened the threads on his, cinching it to his taut chest and waist. I could hear her axe blade split the air as she limbered her muscles.

Seven ravens, black as kohl, flew toward me from the trees, swooping toward my head before flying out over the tormented sea.

I wondered if Odin had let me see them just for a second. Father. Mother. Hodor. Oskar. Gunnar. Ingrid. Solvi. All seven watching from above, looking out for the one who threatened me.

All noise faded and Hodor walked in front of me. "You're ready for this. You faced Mother and won. You can win against Fenris. Use Skuld's power if you have to."

I shook my head. "I want to win."

"Don't be stubborn, Liv."

"I don't know how not to be, Hodor."

"I hope she changes her mind," he said, taking the iron serpent coil from my bag and threading it onto one of the braids Calder made. "You deserve to live past this battle."

"How can you say that?" I asked. "Because of me, you died."

He laughed, holding his stomach. "Our suffering ended when Odin came for us, Liv, but that's when your suffering began. It's made you older than you are, harder than you were, but you've grown from it. If you can change her mind, I hope you can finally find peace in your life."

"You sound like you're leaving…" My heart crumbled.

He clapped my shoulder. "And miss the fight? Never."

"What about after?"

He gave the ghost of a smile. "That depends on Skuld. If she frees you from your bargain, I'll watch over you as long as you live. We all will. We are with Odin, Liv. I forgot to tell you that. If Skuld won't release you from your promise and let you live, I'll ask him to come for you, too."

Skuld could prevent him from taking me. I didn't voice it because he already knew.

A raven flew in front of us, soaring on the stiff breeze without flapping its wings. "I have to go," he said. "But I'll be here."

I blinked to see the single raven flying alone, chasing the others who were no longer visible against the dark clouds.

Calder reached me as the sun set behind them, the sky going from pale green to emerald in an instant. I stood on the tips of my toes, dragged his face to mine, and pressed my lips hard to his. "I love you, Calder."

"And I love you." He held my upper arms and leaned in to look me in the eye. "You're going to win this battle. You are going to stop Fenris Wolf. Tonight. For good."

I nodded feverishly. I would win this. For them.

I wanted a life with him filled with more kisses and sunsets than either of us could count. I wanted to live. But if I couldn't, then I wanted to make sure he made it out alive. That he thrived. That he smiled once again the way Armund appreciated.

The hardened faces of our small clan – Armund and Sig, Brux and Hilda, Tyr and Fell – met us on the shore, dressed for battle. Everyone but Tyr wore a serpent on their chest.

Ivor Grandys sauntered over. He noticed the engravings and smirked as he approached. "*Smár ormr*, you look absolutely terrifying," he said appreciatively.

Instead of answering, I waited for him to speak again and tell me what he wanted. If I was a serpent, as he claimed, then he was a circling falcon intent on snatching me up and carrying me away so he could devour me on his terms.

But if I was a serpent, I was venomous, and my bite was deadlier than he could imagine.

"You'll keep your word and protect those with your mark?" he confirmed.

"I will protect those who deserve to keep it. But if anyone attacks me or my kinsmen, my mark will melt away and I will end them."

His eyes narrowed ever so slightly.

"We have a right to the lands our loved ones died for and on, Ivor."

He stood taller, raising his chin. "It isn't me you need to convince. I know you will be an ally to Clan Grandys when this is all over. The other chieftains, however, believe you want all the lands. They are convinced you plan to claim them as yours and rule over us all."

"That's the last thing I want," I told him honestly.

He searched my eyes, then turned to Armund. "And you?"

"I only want what's rightfully Clan Bjern's. Nothing more and nothing *less*," he told Ivor.

Hilda and Brux stood together behind Armund, Fell and Tyr watching the exchange closely.

"I came to ask what you needed from us," the chieftain finally said. "Tell us what to do, and it will be done. Do you want us on the shore?"

"I want Fenris to think the town is asleep. I want the warriors ready, but hidden. Archers on the hill. Some poised along the shore side, hidden and ready to pour the casks of oil into the sea at my command. I want everyone else in and behind the houses in the town. Let them hide in the boats in your harbor. I'll keep the flame from their hulls. I can direct it.

"I want Fenris to be shocked when we appear just before the hull of his ship rakes the bottom and it's too late for him to turn the ship about and run away, and I want every warrior who came to fight ready to slaughter any who stand with him. But remember... Fenris Wolf is mine."

Jarl Grandys nodded. "Very well, völva. I'll relay your orders."

"Ivor?" I stopped him. "Tell them what I said about my mark and protection. If any of our allies betray us, the death I deal Fenris will look like child's play compared to what I'll do to them."

He inclined his head, spun on his heel, and retraced his steps where the other chieftains were waiting for his word, staring hungrily at our small party like bugs they needed to trample.

Behind me, the sky grew dark and lightning forked ravenously across the sea. Sig grew nervous when the first rolls of thunder peeled across the sky, pacing near Calder's legs.

THIRTY-ONE

The Jarls gave their orders and the warriors divided, hiding in the shadows, inside homes, along the shores and cliffs and everywhere they could, armed to the teeth. Shields were buckled on and spears, axes, swords, and knives were sharpened and ready.

Some wore leather armor, others didn't bother. Men and women of all shapes and ages wore my mark on their foreheads. But even if I had no bind rune to offer, they would be willing to die to protect the lands to which they belonged, and the loved ones holed up at the Grandys stronghold waiting for word about the battle's outcome.

Thunder rolled overhead, not deafening like it had sounded on the peak, but a dull rumble that spread over land and sea, as if it were announcing the battle to come. I didn't want to stand on the shore and wait for him, like I'd seen in the vision. I wanted to be like the spider who wove silken, sticky strands where the Wolf couldn't see them. Only when he was too close would he realize he was stuck. The more he fought, the more tangled he would become, my web keeping him for me until I devoured him.

Was this me changing Skuld's plan, or did she add a different thread to her loom at the last minute?

My small clan waited with me beyond the town, opposite the cliffs where Jarl Grandys lay in wait with the archers just inside the tree line. "Fight as one," Armund warned us all. "Live as one," his kinsmen echoed.

No sooner than we'd said the words…

On the horizon, dark beneath the clouded sky, Fenris Wolf's ship materialized. It looked so small from where we stood. Calder tensed, catching a glimpse when lightning split the sky.

Armund let out a single sharp, shrill whistle and everyone went still. Sig let out a low growl, his eyes finding the anomaly. He barked once, then walked to Calder's side and waited as the wolves approached.

"Liv," Armund said, handing me a flask.

"I don't want mead," I replied, confused.

"No, but you need this. It's blood. And it's fresh." His cool eyes reflected the lightning forking over sea and sky. "I asked Ivor to have whomever prepared the meal to save it for you."

Calder grasped my wand while I held my hands out. As Armund drenched them, time seemed to stand still.

A bolt of lightning slowly inched from the clouds, splitting the air with a sizzling hiss as it landed in the water, eliciting a rising plume of steam as it pulled itself back into the sky. Fenris's ship sailed through the vapor, its wolfish prow head charging toward us. They were much closer now. As they approached, I saw many ships, some trailing just behind Fenris's while others were still tiny on the horizon.

"How many?" Tyr asked.

Fell's eyes ticked at each one. "Twenty-nine that I can see, but not all are as large as the first few."

"Because they sail on stolen ships. Some of them ours," Calder growled.

"And ours, and Nyerk's..." I added. The bones I wore began to shift, tightening to my body, a perfect cage. Calder watched them cinch, listening as they raked over one another, fitting to my clothes and form.

"Even in death, they protect you," he whispered, brushing a hand over my shoulder where plates guarded my skin. He leaned in and put his lips near my temple, kissing me tenderly. "I'm not leaving you," he said.

My own bones cinched. "You have to, Calder. I'll catch up to you, but you have to get Armund out of here," I whispered urgently. His eyes stubbornly fought mine. The muscle in his jaw ticked. "You have to save him."

"Do you know something? Is he...?"

"Yes," I lied. "You have to take him and run."

He searched me and I wondered if my lie would show through.

The moment was broken when Brux struck his shield with his axe once on the wood, where only a dull thump would echo.

"They are the ones who took our friends and families. They slew children. They stole our way of life and crushed it in their hands," Brux said between gritted teeth. His breathing became shallow hisses as he worked himself into a rage.

His mother looked just as angry as she stood rigidly beside him. She rolled her shoulders, testing the weight of Mother's axe. Armund wore Hodor's shield proudly, nodding at me to tell me he was ready. Fell met my eyes. He trusted me to keep them from harm. I could feel the power pulsing in every stroke of the bind runes on every forehead around me.

There was power in ash. Power in words. Power in blood and bone.

My sword hung on my back. I loosened the straps of my shield and tightened them another notch, then took up my wand from where it lay beside me.

Tyr stared at our foes, his eyes combing over every ship.

"You have to stay together," I warned my new family and friends. "The second the battle sways in our favor, you must run. Fight your way out. Get horses and go," I told them. "I'll come as soon as I'm able."

I got nods from all but Calder. I melted into him when he wrapped his hands around my waist. He raked his thumb along the rib bones I wore over mine and I felt his tender touch down to my marrow. "Do you *promise* you'll come?" he asked.

I looked at him. "As long as I draw breath, nothing in this world could keep me from you, Calder."

He swallowed, kissing my temple. "Obliterate them. Then, leave this place and come home with me."

"My heart is yours," I told him. "There's no other place for her. I'll find you."

"Swear it?" It was a challenge and question in one.

"I swear," I told him, fighting the tears that burned my eyes.

"Good," he said, "because when we part during this battle, it will be the last time. Understood?" My breath hitched. I managed a nod. His eyes locked with mine. "And when we make it home, we'll solidify that promise, if you're willing."

My gods, Verdandi, why are you giving me this man only to take him away?

"Of course I'm willing," I choked, hugging him tight.

The others looked away. All but Tyr, whose green eyes were as sharp as his knives and burned a thousand times hotter than the lightning surrounding us.

He stabbed his sword at the sea and murmured, *Höggva úlf.* Slaughter the wolves.

Fenris was near. His ship sailed into the shallows and its long hull raked over the pebbles as it swept onto the shore. His warriors snarled like animals as they leapt over the rail. Their faces were painted in varying shades, each looking like a wolf had scratched its claws over their foreheads. Except for Fenris. His marks were drawn in scarred flesh. He'd survived something terrible but had learned nothing about mercy.

His warriors marked themselves to match him, in support of his vision and plan.

I thought of the serpents on my friends' armor. They'd done the same, backing me when Ivor called me a serpent.

Fenris's eyes searched the village as he stepped from the choppy waves. He tugged his armor down at the waist and wheeled his arms, stretching the tendons, keeping himself loose. He drew his sword, the same one he used to chop me almost in two.

More boats ran aground. Wolf warriors jumped out, congregating on the shore.

Then more boats, and more. Fenris, when he was happy with his numbers, motioned for them to go into the town.

It was time.

Our best swimmers had already slipped into the waters, emptying small casks of oil as they went, slipping in and out between the ships, slickening the water and waves with grease. They moved fast, working until all the casks were empty. Only then did they drag themselves out of the water at the cliff base. One let out a whistle and Fenris's head jerked up at the sound. He gestured for his warriors to stop.

But it was too late. The last of his ships ran ashore into the oily water.

The Chieftain of Gertn led those hiding in the long-houses outside to meet our enemy, my bind rune emblazoned on their foreheads. Together, they worked themselves into a berserker rage, slamming axes against their shields, stomping, growling, shouting and shrilling to the skies.

In response, Fenris's people howled and raced forward, their weapons raised. They were ready for battle and hungry for blood.

I raised my wand and pointed it at Ivor. Fires ignited along the high cliff, a trail of beacons in the dark. The archers lit their fabric-wrapped arrows, notched them, and let them fly. They streaked across the darkness like a tribe of shooting stars.

Some embedded into the wood of the ships themselves. Others were over or undershot, but it didn't matter. Fire found the oil along the sea's surface and spread across it to the ships. I gathered the oil around the boats and bolstered the flame, commanding it to consume and devour. To leave no plank untouched.

Every one of Fenris's ships, his enormous vessels and those he'd stolen, turned to ash almost instantly. Their proud sails burnt away and charred remains sat in drunken, skeletal angles in the water.

Now, they had no way out. No way home by sea. They would have to try to take the land.

It ends here.

The archers shot into the Wolf pack as they could, careful to avoid hitting our allies, but Fenris caught on and led the attack. Soon, swords clashed, axes bit into axes, and grunts and growls filled the air.

I walked toward him, the blood on my hands feeding me with energy, the bones that embraced me humming, the crackling lightning overhead turning frenzied. Slowly, their people began to fall. But none of ours was harmed.

I whispered to Skuld to keep them safe, drawing the bind rune again and again in my mind and pouring my intent into it. *Damn the wolves. Save those who fight with me.*

Skuld was with me. In my skin and in my mind. Her laughter was in my ear and on the wind. Thor was here. Odin came. His ravens Huginn, coal black, and Muninn, pale as clouds, circled like vultures scenting carrion. Or was Hodor watching over me instead? I knew he was here, just wasn't sure how close.

My small clan joined the melee. There was no need to block the ships now that I'd destroyed them, but there were so many of them, and despite our numbers, we were evenly met.

Solvi's comb and Gunnar's flute rattled as my wand's long handle began to writhe.

I saw Fenris through the crowd.

His wheat-colored hair, his cruel expression, even his build... I would never forget him; his every feature was branded into my memory like a curse. I could find him in a sea of ten thousand.

His eyes caught on me and his lips parted. I walked through the fight, no axe slicing me, no sword swiping at my skin. Time slowed again. The shouts of men and women were drowned out, the flames of the ships illuminating the scene with golden firelight as his warriors fell to the swords and weapons of mine.

I watched his brows draw together. My footsteps were slow, purposeful, endless. I thought I'd never reach him, that time would forever feel sluggish. Until he shoved one of Ivor's men away and stalked toward me. As if his willingness to fight me was the catalyst, time sped up again.

He pointed his sword at my heart at the same time I pointed my wand at his.

Skuld had given me her power, but I didn't want it in this moment. I had begged her on my shores – *I refuse this fate. Weave a new thread. Stop Fenris Wolf. Let me be your hands. Let me be your shield, your blade. I will live as your vengeance. Then I will be content to die.*

"Skuld, I fight as your hands, your shield, and your blade. I fight as your vengeance... and I fight as *mine*."

I planted my wand's staff in the pebbled soil and drew my sword.

Fenris smiled when he approached. "I knew I'd find you here, *smár ormr*," he said.

My stomach dropped when I heard the phrase fall from his lips, the same one Ivor Grandys uttered each time he greeted me.

Ivor Grandys will pay for his treachery.

I sensed the mark I'd given the jarl and yanked on the power binding it from him to me, satisfied when I felt it fade away.

Fenris wore a satisfied smile, delighted in the knowledge that he'd caught me off guard. "Grandys and Wolf have always had respect for one another. We've been allies since before you and I were born. He told me where I'd find you and warned me to come prepared. He claimed you were powerful, but I wonder how strong you really are? You were easy enough to cut down on the shore."

I gritted my teeth, disgusted. I looked around to find Ivor and his people, but saw none of the faces I'd come to know. Ivor had played both sides, hoping to align himself with the victor, knowing only one of us would win. In doing so, he lost. He just didn't know it yet.

A wicked gleam entered Fenris's eye. "Are you ready to fight cleanly? Fairly? Without your wand, or eels and fishes, or fire? I cleaved you once. I will do it again."

My answer was given when my sword bit into his.

"You killed my father!" he roared.

"*I* didn't kill him," I gritted, parrying a blow he brought down hard and fast. "I didn't even know your father. But you took *everything* from me. *My* father. *My* mother. *Two* brothers. *Two* sisters. Three were small, innocent children, you cowardly monster. And don't forget that you tried to kill me. Tried, and weren't strong enough," I taunted.

His upper lip twitched. He chopped at my side, like he had on the shore in front of my home, but this time, I easily blocked the blow.

I blocked every swing and every chop, jumping out of reach of every thrust and jab.

He was aware of everything happening around us. How his warriors were falling, but none of mine were. "It's the mark, isn't it?" he growled.

I launched an attack, keeping my movements swift and unpredictable. I stabbed toward his middle, toward his ribs, and sliced across his throat, my blade just missing as he leapt back at the last second. His sword hit the metal rim of my shield and I used to momentum to quickly slash his leg behind the knee, severing the tendons. He struggled to move into a defensive crouch with one leg, but in his eyes swam fear.

I reveled in it, in the painful hiss he let out when he tried to walk.

He limped, trying to recover, but I stalked his movements. I wouldn't allow him to run away to lick his wounds. There was no place I wouldn't hunt him now that Skuld had unleashed me.

The battle had swayed in our favor, and many of his kinsmen lay dead on the ground or discarded on the shore. Some bobbed in the sea water. I searched for Calder.

He was fighting with Fell and Tyr, his back to us. Brux and Hilda were close, but I didn't see Armund.

A bark came from further into town. Sig must be with Armund.

Fenris cursed and pointed at my side. His eyes were wide and hopeful. "That is proof that you *do* bleed, serpent."

Blood leaked from the mortal wound he'd made the time he left me dying on my own shores. The hair had broken, and the skin was open and weeping. My side hadn't been ripped open all the way, but every flood began with a trickle of water.

I had to finish him before I couldn't. I had to protect them. My eyes darted over to Calder just as he planted his axe in the stomach of the man he faced.

Fenris was slowly retreating, stumbling and clumsily stepping over the body of one of his men, painting a lush carpet of blood over the beach. I rushed him, furiously raining down blow after blow until he could no longer keep up, sweat beading on his brow. "Please," he pleaded.

I laughed in disbelief.

"Please? Are you *begging* me now, Fenris? What about when I pled with you? What about my little brother and sisters? Did they cry and scream for their lives when you cut them down? Did my parents yell 'please' as you and your men slaughtered them because they tried to protect their home and children?"

I cut the back of his other knee and watched him teeter and then fall. Still he fought, slicing at me until one sharp sweep took his hand off at the wrist. He screamed and rolled on the ground, holding tightly to the wound as it spurted, spraying crimson droplets in the air. The fine mist settled over me and I suddenly felt Skuld again.

Finish this, she seemed to say through the droplets.

I stomped to his side and gripped the handle of my sword in both hands as Fenris begged me to stop, one trembling hand clamped over the stump where the other hand used to reside. Unflinching, I thrust the blade of my sword through his heart, pinning him to the earth. His arms drifted apart and his blood slickened the earth as he gurgled. Fenris twitched uncontrollably as the light dimmed in his eyes, and then, he stared into the heavens.

Muninn and Huginn were there, circling me. My side throbbed.

"Odin!" I cried out. "Fenris Wolf does not deserve Valhalla! Freyja, he does not deserve your great home."

Calder heard my cry and left the others to run to me.

"No, Calder!" I screamed. "You have to *go*." He looked at my side and though I wore black, he could see I was covered in slick blood from the waist down. "It's his," I lied, pointing at Fenris. "You have to get the others and ride for home. Now."

"I can't leave you like this," he argued, carefully lifting the edge of my tunic. The one place the bones didn't cover was the wound that had never truly healed. "Liv," he breathed.

Tears sprang to my eyes. "I was saved once, Calder. She won't save me again."

He shook his head in disbelief. All around us were sounds of the dying, followed by the stillness of the dead meeting the clashing of swords and shields, axes and fists. But even those were going quiet. The army we'd amassed had almost won.

"You have to get Armund to safety."

"Sig went with him. He's safe."

I could feel the hair that laced my side start to pull as if Skuld was curling her finger around it and yanking, loosening her stitches one by one. Inhaling loudly, my step faltered. "Then you need to run, before they turn on you," I breathed, stumbling.

Calder's eyes were wide. "Liv!" He caught me as I fell to my side.

A cold sweat spread over my skin. My ears were muffled, like water had filled them. "You have to go, Calder," I begged.

"You said you'd go with me," he said pitifully as he eased me to the ground. "You can't do this to her!" he roared into the heavens.

The sky was magnificent. The storm had dissipated, and the once erratic bolts of lightning faded away as the dark clouds were pushed from the inky, black sky, revealing a glittering tapestry woven across the heavens.

"The stars," I managed to say. My lips were dry. I could feel the wet, sticky blood on my clothes, but this time, there was no pain. Skuld granted me that small mercy.

"Liv, stay with me."

I heard Calder's voice, but he sounded so far away. My teeth began to chatter. *When did it get so cold?* I turned my head toward the sea, dimly noticing the blistering fires that blazed earlier had burned out. *That must be why.*

"Liv?" Calder kneeled in front of me, his strong hands holding my ruptured side together.

"I borrowed time from the gods to kill Fenris, but I'm glad I found you, Calder. You made every second worth it."

"No!" he bellowed. "Don't you *dare* give up."

"I'm not," I promised. My lips were so, so dry. My tongue and mouth, too.

My body relaxed, blissfully falling numb and far removed from any lingering pain.

I was bone tired.

It was hard to keep my eyes open.

But then I heard the rolling waves of the sea as they ebbed on the shore, accented by the sounds of victory being celebrated. Overhead, Muninn and Huginn wheeled across the sparkling sky.

Is Hodor here? Is Odin?

I licked my cracked, dry lips and repeated the prayer I'd uttered what felt like a lifetime ago. "Odin, save me," I mouthed. The birds came no closer.

"Freyja," I tried. She did not answer. A tear leaked from my eye, trickling into my braids.

My breath rattled in my chest.

"Frigg?" Nothing, just as before.

"Thor, save me. I bear your mark. You gave me your favor." My heartbeat slowed and grief threatened to swallow me whole. "I deserve better than this." My voice was rusty, barely there. Not from disuse, but drained, like my body of its blood.

A colder wind cut across me.

Calder screamed for his kinsmen, for anyone who could help. I heard Sig bark, followed by Armund's calming words.

The Aesir would not cross Skuld to save me. Not even Thor, who'd branded Ygdrassil on my skin with his lightning.

My lips would not move anymore, so I pleaded for the norn who'd already saved me once. I had nothing to lose from begging now.

Skuld – I ended him. I won. Fenris will never hurt anyone again. But I'm still not ready to die, not when everything I've ever wanted is trying his best to save me.

Weave a new destiny for me. Weave a future where I can live out my days with him.

I refuse this fate. Weave a new thread. Let me live out my days with Calder, then *I will be content to die.*

I blinked and the tapestry of stars faded. I could see Calder's face, but couldn't hear his voice. My bind rune faded from his head.

No, they need to escape safely…

Protect them, Skuld. Even if I can't. Protect them.

Please.

Calder cried and raged at the heavens, begging the gods like I was. Sig raced to Calder's side and whimpered, sensing something was wrong but uncomprehending the magnitude.

Over his shoulder, Armund shouted to Odin, then cried out to Skuld, telling her that if she saved me, perhaps she could use me to breathe.

Armund was supposed to be on his way home. He was supposed to be safe.

Death was here for me, just like Armund sensed.

And like Skuld, death felt like frost.

THIRTY-TWO

"Liv Eriksson," a thousand voices hissed over me. Skuld hovered over me, once again wearing a tattered cloak. "I'll accept your bargain and let you live, *if* you accept mine. Once a moon cycle, for one night, you must let me overtake you so I can breathe and experience things as you do."

"Breathe?" I tried to mouth, confused by what she was asking.

"Do you accept?"

Yes, I thought desperately. *I accept.*

"You're lucky my sister is such a romantic and that she gave Calder to you. You are also fortunate his father is such a quick thinker, and quite a good negotiator."

I tried to raise my head, but it felt as if the weight of a thousand ships rested on my brow.

Skuld grumped, "Verdandi threatened to weave you back to life every day if I didn't spare you. She's stubborn enough to do it, too, though after a time, I wonder if Calder would grow weary of watching you die and return to him."

Skuld looked to Calder beside her. He hadn't left my side even as my breathing stuttered and slowed to an imperceptible rhythm. He glanced to her, then back to me, his clear eyes steady and sure as he faced the norn. I felt him squeeze my hand.

More tears streaked into my hair, the only proof that I still lived. She pushed back the hood of her cloak, still wearing my face, then pulled a needle from behind her ear. Skuld held a thread up so I could see it. The strand was so dark it siphoned the light from all around us, like maybe it was there with the norns in the darkness, back in the time before fire met frost.

"This will not break, Liv. It is a strand from our loom, one that will hold you together until your natural life is over. Even when you lay rotting in the earth, the strand will remain."

She smiled at me and then set to work mending me. The stitches didn't hurt this time and instead of weakening me, the thread strengthened me, little by little, stitch by stitch. Before, I could always feel how fragile the hair was despite the strength of the scarred skin, but the thread she used this time was stronger than iron and infused with dark magic only the norns were strong enough to wield.

"Thank you," I managed to rasp, feeling life ebb back into my veins. "And your sisters."

I searched for Armund and mouthed the words *thank you* to him. He inclined his head. Feeling returned to my extremities and I felt Calder's warmth, the pressure of his palm against mine, his fingers enclosing my smaller ones.

I closed my eyes while she finished sewing, too weak to say anything else, my mind thanking her repetitively.

Skuld tied the strand and pulled the axe from her waist, swiftly cutting the end of the thread she'd given me. Then she placed a hand over my heart. "I cannot let you live with all my powers in your skin. I'll leave enough to keep us connected and so you can protect yourself and those you love, but I take back my fire. Not that you needed it, shield maiden."

I nodded and felt the frost I didn't realize had been welled within me fade into her hand.

Fell and Tyr stood with their backs to us on one side while Brux and Hilda guarded the other, weapons poised and ready, anticipating the attack they knew would come now that the battle with Fenris was won.

"Skuld?" I croaked, and she looked at me with eyes that mirrored my own. "Don't let them kill us."

She smiled. "It has been quite a long time since I've battled anyone."

"My sword is lodged in Fenris's heart," I offered, "if you want a blade."

It appeared in her hand in a blink, the blade coated in blood. She tested its weight as she stood and ordered Calder to help me up. He helped me sit and held me until my head stopped swimming, then hugged me so tightly, the bones encasing me popped.

"Sorry," he breathed against my temple, kissing me there.

"I need to stand, but I need your help."

He nodded and closed his eyes for a moment, then hooked his arms under mine and hoisted me like I weighed nothing. He steadied me as I took in what was happening around us.

To my eyes, Skuld still looked like me, but did she look like that to everyone?

Ivor Grandys watched her carefully, then his eyes found mine and his lips parted as his eyes widened in disbelief. I gritted a deadly smile at him, a promise that we had *much* to discuss.

"You dare threaten those I favor?" Skuld asked in a thousand voices that hissed from her lips but seemed to echo from every direction in the air around us.

A crowd of men parted to reveal Jarl Varsyk dead, a sharp knife embedded in his eye socket.

Tyr smirked proudly, staring at his accusers.

"Are you angry about his death?" she asked.

No one dared murmur, let alone reply.

When Skuld's venomous laugh rang out their ire evaporated, replaced by fearful expressions. "Liv is *my own*. She does as I instruct, as do her kinsmen. Those who survived the battle only breathe because I will it. Those who died are dead because I demanded it."

Skuld winked at me before turning to Ivor. "Jarl Grandys, *my own* knows of your treachery. If I were you, I would plead for her mercy and beg for your life. I leave the decision of your future in *her* hands."

Ivor's face grew paler in the moonlight and his kinsmen shrank away. Murmurs rolled through the crowd of dirty, sweaty, bloody survivors.

Skuld spotted my wand planted in the soil. She walked to it, plucked it up, and brought it to me, then leaned in and spoke in a voice only I could hear. "Lay them to rest so your heart can heal, Liv." She looked at Calder. "I told you the thread of her life was entwined with yours. Now I'll knit the thread of your futures together. Don't for one second take her for granted, or I'll tear the threads apart."

He nodded and his hand tightened on my shoulder. He held me up now, but soon it would be me holding him up just as staunchly. It would allow us to fight and survive together, loving one another through the harshness this land and life had to offer. Back to back.

Fell carried my bag. He must have grabbed it from where I stashed it in the trees before the battle began. The leather was flat now that I wore the bones it had held, the bag mostly empty except for the small pot of ash ink. I would bury it along with what was left of my family. I knew the perfect resting place – on the near mountain, beneath the tree where Tor lay.

Skuld walked us to our horses where she returned my sword and gave me a secret proud smile.

I climbed onto Mordi's back with my wand and sword. Calder swung on behind me. Instead of steadying himself, he steadied me as I swayed in front of him, still weak.

The rest of my small clan mounted their horses, and after Skuld chanted softly on the wind, we rode into the night on fleet feet, Sig running alongside us with his tongue lolling, eager to be on the way home.

Mordi raced through the night. He carried us away from the blood-soaked shore, away from death. He carried us home.

I leaned my head back onto Calder's shoulder and thanked Skuld again.

For showing me mercy when she could've held me to my bargain.

For believing I was strong when I felt I was crumbling.

And for giving me a chance at a future with Calder and the family I'd come to cherish.

340

THIRTY-THREE

My body still held a finite amount of power. I could feel it flicker deep within like a faraway star. Skuld said it would flare when I needed it and I trusted her. Now more than ever.

I scrubbed a hand down my face and wondered what she would do with my body on the night of the next full moon… and all those that came after. I had no choice but to endure it, trapped inside myself with no escape until sunrise.

It left me to ponder what a norn would do if she were human, and if she, being in human form, would be forced to shed her immortality and become vulnerable.

We'd ridden through the night, pushing the horses and Sig to the brink of exhaustion. All of us were tired to the bone and starving, but when the first familiar path emerged and we made it to the outskirts of Skögar Village, our spirits and weariness lifted.

Was this how Mother and Father felt when their ship ran aground after they'd sailed across the sea, survived the task they'd been sent to do, and returned home?

Calder urged Mordi faster. Fell challenged us to a race, and of course, Calder and I accepted. Mordi charged through the trees, his hoofs pounding the wet earth. Fell's horse was just as fast. I closed my eyes and laughed, my heart light for the first time since… I couldn't remember.

Fell beat us to the first longhouse – barely – but when Brux's longhouse came into view, he groaned. "I can almost smell the fresh bread."

Brux smiled proudly. "If you want to stop, I'm sure Elga has some bread or stew or something. That woman is always cooking."

"And she's a better cook than I am," Hilda added, riding up to us beside Armund. She gave Brux a pleased smile as he swung off his horse's back and called out for his wife. Elga threw the door open and rushed outside. Brux caught her, spun her around, and soundly kissed her.

When they parted, he asked if she would cook a little something for us. She gave him another loud, smacking kiss. "A little something?" she flirted. "I think I can handle that." She looked around our group, her eyes ticking on each face. Counting us. Then breathed a sigh of relief.

She gave me a nod, which was more than I would've been capable of if I were her.

Elga pulled Brux into the house. Fell followed, no doubt planning to sneak a morsel before the rest of us had a chance.

Hilda shooed him in. "Move along. I want to see my granddaughter." The baby whimpered and began to cry, but she settled as Hilda's coos filtered through the open door.

Tyr promised he'd be back and rode off toward his house without a backwards glance.

Sig, who'd somehow kept up with us the entire way without complaint, fell over and let out a sigh just outside Brux and Hilda's door.

Armund chuckled and petted the poor guy. "I'll see to the horses, Calder."

Calder thanked him and swung down from Mordi's back. He gripped my waist gingerly and I slid down the length of him, my body heating.

Armund chuckled and shook his head. "Do you want me to take your things to my house, Liv?" he asked.

"Yes, please," I offered graciously as I handed my wand to him. Fell still had my bag, and I'd lost my shield somewhere on the Grandys shore. Part of me wished we could go back for it.

Calder's eyes locked with mine. "How are you feeling?"

"Happy."

He snaked an arm around my waist and kissed my lips. I became drunk on the feel of him. We were safe. We'd survived... Together.

A fire burned in his clear blue eyes to match the one igniting in my belly. Wordlessly, he took my hand and pulled me toward him as we walked away from Brux's home and down the wending trails that led down into the decimated valley, toward the sea.

The tide was low. Pale moonlight danced off the calm, rolling waves as Calder stepped into the water and lured me in. Water filled my leather boots and I felt the lurch of every pebble beneath my feet.

Instead of tugging me in deeper, Calder knelt in the gentle waves. With a quick jerk, he broke the strand of hair tying the greaves to my left shin and sat the bones of my loved ones on the shore, then he took off its match. He hands roved upward, caressing behind my knees, higher, up the backs of my thighs... and he deftly removed my thigh armor, igniting a fire under my skin.

He rose, finding the plates on my shoulders and freed me of them. Then he peeled away the vambraces on my forearms and clamped his hands on my waist, brushing his thumbs over the cage of ribs.

I swallowed thickly and eased the cage open for him, then stepped out of the water to place it with the other bones on the shore.

Calder watched as I peeled my bloody tunic off, then stepped out of my trousers. His eyes were hungry as I waded back in.

He let out the leather bindings at his sides, slipped off his leather armor, and laid it with mine. Then he stalked toward me, bending to splay his hands on the backs of my thighs. When he lifted me, I wrapped my legs around his waist, and we kissed as gentle waves swelled over us. He walked us deeper into the water, where it caressed our waists, then our chests.

I peeled his shirt off, not even bothering to make sure where it landed as I tossed it toward the shore. He sat me down to remove his trousers. My serkr was next.

Nothing lay between us when he lifted me again.

When my skin met his heated flesh and my chest pressed against his, our bodies meeting so tightly not even a grain of sand could fit between us, he paused, his eyes searching mine.

There was power in words, yes.

But sometimes there was more power in things left unsaid.

In action.

I joined him in every way and made sure he knew I meant what I said; that we would fight at one another's backs for as long as we both drew breath. That he was mine and I was his from this point forward.

That I didn't want to be parted from him again.

His icy eyes met mine and I couldn't help but get lost in them.

"I'm yours," he breathed as he moved against me with the swelling sea.

I clung to him desperately and whispered in his ear, "You're mine, and I... am yours, Calder."

THIRTY-FOUR

In the days that followed we rested, but sitting made me restless. There was still one more thing I needed to do to truly begin healing. To leave the tragedy that befell us in the past where it belonged, in a section of the weaver's tapestry Urd would preserve and admire. I vowed to remember the good parts that came before… To never forget the family that molded the girl who avenged them.

Calder and I spent our days helping finish the cattle fence, felling trees to start the long process of rebuilding the longhouses in the valley, and took time to enjoy one another. Mostly at night when we snuck to the beach to be alone.

Three large wagons filled with goods pulled into town one afternoon, a peace offering from none other than Jarl Ivor Grandys. An apology, per those who brought the goods. In the wagons were supplies: iron nails, tools, barrels of food stores, seeds, wool… I wasn't sure what else. Ivor's men unhitched the wagons and left almost immediately, anxiously watching us over their shoulders as they rode away.

The Bjern survivors who hadn't gone to battle with us looked to their new Jarl for an explanation, to which Armund replied by rocking back on his heels and telling them, "You can thank Liv for the provisions."

His eyes met mine and sparkled knowingly.

Once the cattle were free to roam within their new pen and Mordi had recovered, he carried Calder and I to Amrok Village, where we arrived late in the afternoon. As Mordi trotted past Leif's house, I told Calder how our chieftain was slain, how Hodor and I had fought with the only things we could find.

We dismounted and let Mordi wander as we walked together into the valley. I showed Calder where Arne had lived and where Jarl Wolf had washed up, and told him how when Gunnar found him, Solvi had shrieked at the sight while Ingrid watched quietly as the adults examined him, she and Solvi clinging to my legs.

I showed him the near mountain and took him up the paths to the hidden lake, whose water was as clear and pure as Calder's eyes, and told him stories from when I was small. I smiled wistfully as I recalled the many hours Hodor and I spent on the shores, talking and dreaming of our futures.

I showed him all my favorite places until the only place left was my home. My feet carried me there where I saw the bind rune still emblazoned on what was left of the structure, black as the thread binding me, on the boards that hadn't burned. Even the rain hadn't washed it away. Stepping among the cinders, I shared stories of happy times inside the walls, then showed Calder where I found them. He squeezed my hand comfortingly when emotions arose that were hard to choke down.

We spent hours in the ruins of my childhood, talking. Exchanging stories. Learning even more about one another.

We watched the sun set together and I admitted counting them down in the days that led up to the battle, though I didn't tell him I knew they would be my last. I told him how I remembered him explaining how precious time was by holding the water and letting it dribble away, but imagining it being a melting sun and our time together running out.

Calder held me and his strong hands ran up and down my back. "Thank you for showing me your home and the life you had before." He took my bag from his shoulders. In it were the bones of my family, shaped into the form of my armor and wand.

"I want to bury them next to Tor."

He nodded. "Then that's what we'll do."

And we did.

That night, under clouded skies and a warm wind off the fjord, with wildflowers swaying all around us on the hill, we dug a hole around strong, gnarled roots that reminded me of Skuld and her sisters and the tree of life they tended.

My heart was at peace when I lay my family's bones inside with the small pot of ash ink. Calder and I covered them with earth and placed heavy stones on top of the grave. Tor's grave beside them was still fresh, but it had already begun settling. Soon, theirs would settle, too.

Time had a way of wandering on, whether we wished it to or not.

Calder was quiet for a long moment, staring at the graves with his brows pinched. "Are you sure you want to leave them?" he asked carefully. "We could build a life here."

I'd considered it. We *could* build a life here alone. It would be serene, peaceful. But we needed to be surrounded by people we loved and could trust. We needed family and friends. I shook my head. "We can always come back to visit them."

Calder sucked in a breath, staring toward the fjord. "Look."

In the fjord, ripples spread over the water from the spot where Oskar sunk. More spread from the place where Arne and Olav had settled beneath the surface. And when I looked at the earthen grave, I could've sworn ripples formed over the disturbed soil.

That night, Calder pitched a tent for us. I built a fire and we speared fish to cook, eating them with some bread Hilda brought over. Then, we sat on the boulder I loved and stared at the stars.

"I want us to marry as soon as we get home," he said out of the blue. "It won't be a traditional wedding, but ours isn't a traditional story."

I smiled. "No, it isn't." Calder was not a man who wasted time. I remembered the water sliding through his parted fingers and my heart swelled.

"I don't have rings, but I'll get them somehow. I'm not sure when."

I draped my legs over his as he balanced us both on the boulder. "I'm not worried about rings."

"A ring on your finger will tell other men you're mine," he said, bringing my hand to his lips and kissing said finger.

"The gods help any woman who questions who *you* belong to," I half-teased.

His eyes searched mine as he hugged me closer. "I love you. I thought I did before, but when you collapsed on the shore... when the gods didn't help you and I thought Skuld would let you die, I knew. It thundered through me. I love you, Liv."

I swallowed around the knot in my throat. "I love you, Calder. The thought of dying and leaving you..."

He looked at me knowingly. "Did you know you were going to die? You kept telling us to run and leave you, that you'd catch up, but something about it never rang true."

I sighed. "Yes, I knew. I hated keeping it from you, but I couldn't tell you. You wouldn't have left me."

He pinched his lips together. "If our roles were reversed, I wouldn't have told you, either."

A small knot in my chest loosened with his words, and the guilt I'd felt by lying to him eased. "I was worried what would happen when I fell and could no longer protect you; about 'our allies' turning on you all. They would have."

"In a heartbeat," he added. "Speaking of allies, I'm surprised you let Ivor go after what he did."

I smiled and leaned back, pleased with myself. "I didn't."

His brows kissed.

I leaned into him and whispered, "I sent him a parting gift."

Calder's head tilted to the side, his smile appearing. "What did you do?"

We rode back to Skögar Village, our hearts lighter after our excursion. We hadn't even gotten off Mordi's back before Calder began talking to his father about his plans. Armund just laughed. "I figured the two of you would insist on marrying sooner rather than later. As your Jarl, I give you my blessing." Calder jumped from Mordi's back, hugged his father, and smiled up at me. "Tomorrow?"

Armund and I laughed. *He can't be serious.*

He stared us both down.

He was serious.

"That isn't much time, son," he said.

Calder glanced at me and held my gaze. "I don't want to wait another minute. Tomorrow's a lifetime away."

350

THIRTY-FIVE

Calder was gone when I woke, but he'd given Fell a message for me: to bathe, dress, and meet him on the shore. I rushed to the water with a bit of soap and a dress Elga had given me to replace the one I'd left behind in Sten Town, somewhere in Ivor's house. His servants had taken the dress Hilda had given me to wash, and I never saw it again.

I washed my hair and body and quickly dressed, eager to see Calder before the ceremony later that evening, which he'd planned for sunset.

He didn't keep me waiting for long. The sounds of hooves plodding the ground came from the far side of the village as Mordi and a dappled mare dragged something behind them, Calder guiding them across the pebbled beach. I walked toward him, wondering what he was doing, and covered my mouth when I realized…

The horses dragged an enormous boulder behind them.

Calder smiled when he saw me. And though I fought it, a tear escaped and slid down my cheek.

He positioned it in the middle of the beach, untied the tangle of ropes he'd used to secure it, and whistled loudly. Fell jogged out from the trees and took the horses, smiling at me.

"Thank you, Fell."

"It was all Calder," he shouted over his shoulder as he guided the horses up the hill again.

I knew it was, but I appreciated him helping Calder pull it off. I turned to find Calder waiting by the boulder, a bone comb in his hand. Walking to him, another tear fell. He'd carved a comb to match Solvi's – down to the last design Father had made in it.

"I have nothing of substance to offer you, Liv. Just what little I have. But I promise to always pay attention, to show you that you'll always matter to me, and strive for the rest of my days to make you happy."

I cried in earnest, and he held me until I calmed down.

"Liv…" he said tentatively, kissing my temple. "Can I braid your hair? And then, will you braid mine?"

Elga loaned me a vibrant red dress, the wool so thin and finely spun, it felt like silk. I ran my hands down my stomach. She and Hilda had worked all afternoon to weave a circlet, which they wouldn't let me see until now. Hilda scampered away to pull it from wherever they'd stashed it. Elga waited outside the longhouse, waiting for word from Armund.

The door opened and I turned, expecting Hilda and finding Tyr closing the door behind him. His near-white hair was washed and freshly braided. His clothes were clean, and he'd left his blades at home – at least the ones I could usually see.

A nervous feeling settled into my stomach.

"You're probably wondering why I'm here."

"I am."

He stood completely still and stared at the floor for a long moment, motionless as a statue. Then he turned his piercing green eyes toward me. "I wanted you to know I'm happy for you and came to beg for a fresh start between us. You know what Calder means to me, and I know what you mean to him. If he wants you to be his wife, I want that, too." He nervously plucked his shirt away from his body. "I just want him to be happy. And… thank you for not telling him." He cleared his throat, embarrassed.

"Thank you, Tyr."

Pressing his lips into a thin line, he nodded and left, leaving me alone again and wondering what had just happened. My heart broke a little for him in that moment.

Though I'd always respected Tyr despite his feelings toward me, my respect for him grew tenfold. He was a good man. Calder's brother, if not by blood, then by life. Someone who put the wants of those he loved above his own. That proved the sort of man he was.

The door opened, spilling sunlight in again. Hilda beamed as she brought the circlet inside. When she placed it in my hands, tears stung my eyes. "It's beautiful," I told her. "Thank you."

Weaved from yellow, red, and purple wildflowers and dried wheat sheaves, it was substantial and intricate, fitting my head perfectly when she placed it. "You're a stunning bride, Liv. Calder is lucky."

"I'm the lucky one."

She smiled and leaned in to whisper in my ear. "The house where the animals were penned? It's been cleaned completely out, and all those who've been staying at Calder's house moved into it today. You'll have your house to begin your lives together."

I gasped, "How did anyone have time?"

"Overnight," she said with a wink. "Even the children helped."

353

My heart felt like it might burst – in the best way. "Thank you."

"I'm glad Skuld saved you, glad she released you from being her own," she said with a maternal tilt to her brow.

"Me too."

She used a comb to straighten my hair now that the circlet was in place. "Are you afraid for the next full moon?"

"I'm terrified."

She nodded sympathetically.

Not wanting to spend my wedding day thinking about the norn taking over my body at the next full moon, I changed the subject. "I expect you'll dance with your favorite Jarl tonight…" I led.

Hilda playfully swatted my shoulder. "Only if he asks."

"Oh, he'll ask," I laughed. Armund needed little encouragement now that he knew Hilda returned his feelings. He chased her incessantly. In fact, I thought the two might be planning a ceremony of their own soon.

Elga peeked inside the house. "It's time. Your groom is waiting for you on the shore."

I stood and hugged Hilda, and as I exited the longhouse, Elga handed me a bouquet of wildflowers and wheat, arranged to match my circlet, tied with a fine red ribbon to match my dress. "With how pretty you look, he'll not even notice the hard work we put into the flowers," she teased.

"Thank you, Elga," I said, stopping in front of her.

She smiled kindly. "I know I didn't trust you and wasn't exactly… kind, at first. But you did what you said you'd do. You killed Fenris and brought my husband and his mother back to me and my daughter. I trust you now, Liv."

I found Calder as soon as I reached the hill that emptied into the valley. He stood on the shore in dark trousers and a white linen shirt that flapped in the warm wind, his sword at his side. His wet bark hair was neatly braided, his jaw cleanly shaven. His icy eyes never left me as I walked down the hill and onto the pebbled shore.

Armund, Tyr, and Fell stood with Calder. Around him, his kinsmen gathered, made up of older men and women, Brux and Elga and their mother, Hilda –who watched Armund, and the children who would grow to be the future of our people, who would allow the merged Clan Bjurɗr to grow and thrive – I hoped into something even stronger than the two had been separately.

Calder's calloused, warm hands found mine as the sun set in the west, but he abandoned them to wrap his arms around me and kiss me so tenderly, so deeply, I forgot people surrounded us for a moment. Armund laughed. As we pulled apart, smiling, he gave us sage advice: to not let anyone come between us, to know that family and kin would always have our backs and we should have theirs, to talk to one another often and about everything, and never take one another for granted – something Skuld had even mentioned.

We didn't have rings, and I had no dowry to offer him. We only had each other.

But Armund told us, "Most marry for security, for help with life's demands and to survive it. Few are fortunate enough to marry for love. But I think it's clear that you two are fortunate in this regard. I hope you always remember that if you have love, you have everything."

I couldn't agree more. And when he announced we were married, a husband and his wife, Calder smiled and pulled me to him. "I now have everything," he whispered before kissing my ear and making me shiver.

As he pulled away, his eyes caught on something in the sky. Seven ravens soared from the trees, flying over our heads and out to sea.

"They are with you still," Calder said, voicing what I knew in my heart.

When I woke the following morning, Calder lay beside me, his head propped on his hand. "Good morning, husband." I grinned, running my hand over his muscled stomach, side, and back.

He leaned in for a kiss. "Good morning, wife. Someone left us a gift."

My brows kissed. "Who... and what?"

He nodded toward the hearth. Propped against it was my shield, and tied to it with a fathomlessly deep black thread were two iron rings.

I barked a laugh.

"It's a little unsettling to know she was in here while we slept," he said, his icy eyes studying mine.

"Not as unsettling as it is to think about the night of the next full moon."

EPILOGUE

When the men he'd sent to Bjern Town returned to his stronghold and entered his hall, Jarl Ivor Grandys stood from his ornately carved chair, a deer skin slipping to the floor. He didn't deign to pick it up.

"How were the gifts received?" his voice boomed across the empty space.

"They received them well. We had no trouble," one of the six spoke for them all.

"You didn't stay long."

"No, the völva was there, and to be honest," the man cleared his throat, "we didn't want to linger."

Cowards. They dropped his wagons and scurried home, most likely before the *smár ormr* could see what he'd sent for them.

The speaker was holding a rectangular, wooden box. "What's that?" he barked. Without waiting for an answer, he strode forward and took the box from the man's hand, tilting it to examine it. There were no markings. The wood was smooth and wore a dark stain. A small brass hinge held it closed, but there was no lock on it. "What's inside?" he asked the men.

Their speaker pursed his lips and shifted his weight. "We don't know. It isn't ours. No one in Bjern gave us anything to take back, but when we were unhitching the horses outside, it was in my satchel."

Ivor shook the box and dismissed his men. They left the room, closing the door behind them. He wondered for several long moments whether he should throw it away or open it, but his curiosity won the battle of wills and he lifted the brass hinge. Raising the lid slowly, he wondered if it might be empty, just something the men had forgotten they had brought along. And then... movement.

And pain. A small orange serpent striped with black and white had bitten him, and still clung to the web of skin between his thumb and forefinger.

Wincing, his mouth opened in a wide gasp, he removed the beast and carried it across the room, tossing it in the fire where it writhed. He almost expected it to scream or laugh.

He examined his hand. Twin beads of blood pooled, but he felt fine. He told himself it was just a message, letting him know the witch hadn't forgotten, and wouldn't.

He calmed himself with those thoughts as the snake died, then tossed the box into the flames and watched the fire dance around it. It didn't catch.

His brows furrowed just before his knees buckled and his heart seized.

His temple hit the stone floor, his heart racing fast, far too fast, then slowing.... Slowing.....................

361

362

BONUS SCENES

SKULD

Liv and I spoke the language of sunsets, and as the orange glow evaporated in the fjord water, I rose above the sea's surface, slogging from the water. It sluiced from my skin and lay an aqueous trail behind me... not that anything in the worlds would dare follow it.

She did not tuck herself inside her dwelling and try to plead with me to void our bargain. No, my shield maiden met me in the rubble. There were signs of rebuilding, of reclamation all around her. Her face was stern and her unflinching eyes met mine. "Skuld."

"The moon is full," I drawled.

Her husband stood at her side, such a loyal warrior.

"What will you do with her?" he asked, crossing his arms.

"Whatever I wish."

And before either could speak another word, I sprang forward and entered her body. She was loud, voicing her discomfort, but I laughed and laughed. In Liv's body, I smelled the briny air, tasted the fish she'd eaten for dinner, and felt the beach rocks shift underfoot as I walked away from Calder. Her muscles were sore from work. Her head slightly ached.

I'd never felt anything like it. Pain, apprehension, flavor, love... All the things a human could experience but a norn could not.

"How will I find her?" he shouted as I ran toward the sea, charging into the shallows.

I turned to him and smiled, raking Liv's waist-long golden hair back from her face. "She will find you, Calder. Not even I could keep her away."

I swam into the ocean and floated on the waves with the moon far above me and the sea floor far below... and I breathed.

CALDER ARMUNDSSON

Pounding on the door. "Calder!"

I opened my bleary eyes and tried to look over the room. It was dark, save for the orange-red embers glowing in the hearth, their glow sliding over the roughhewn walls. Nothing was amiss. My heavy lids drifted back down.

"Calder!" my father shouted from outside. He pounded again. Louder this time. More urgently. "Wake up."

I threw off the blanket and crossed the floor, scrubbing a hand down my face before unlatching the door. The sky was dark as pitch behind him. A large flock of sheep wound through the pines with their newborn lambs, bleating as they ran around to the back of my house, seeking shelter further into the woods. *Why did Father drive them up here?*

"Get dressed and get your weapons!" he barked, walking inside and raking anxious hands through his long, graying beard. "*Now*, boy."

I fully woke at the urgency of his tone and ran to tug on a kyrtill and boots. "What's happening?"

"Raiders from Clan Wolf," he answered gruffly, his broad back to me. Over his shoulder, I could see one of the houses at the base of the mountain near the bay burning, the tall blaze silhouetted brightly against the black night. "We need to rouse the others." He bounced anxiously on the balls of his feet, the sword that never left his side swaying with the movement.

I took up my shield and a second one I'd just had made, handing it to my father. He deftly strapped it to his forearm, buckling it tightly. I strapped mine on, the familiar soft leather hugging my skin, then grabbed my axe and called for my dog.

"Sig."

Sig eased around Father and came to stand beside me, his eyes immediately zeroing in on my shield. He barked once, signaling he was ready for whatever came.

Standing on all fours, Sig's back came to my waist. His thick, grey fur and silver eyes looked between me, Father, and the sheep, unsure of his duty. The elkhound could herd them or protect us, depending on my order. Tonight, I needed him with us. "Come." I strode out of my door without bothering to shut it. If we didn't stop the raiders, they'd burn it anyway. "Go get Tyr. I'll wake Fell. We'll meet on the pass and descend together."

Father nodded, limping into the night. He was in no shape to fight. We both knew his knee wouldn't allow him the movement and agility he'd once had. He'd taken a sword to the joint a few years back, the blade lodging solidly in the cap. While I did everything the healer told me to do, his bone was never the same. Though, to her credit, the wound hadn't festered.

Fell's house sat in a clearing much like mine, quiet and dark in the deepness of night. I swung my arms to loosen my muscles as I jogged toward Fell's with Sig at my side, my leather soles slapping the packed, dry dirt with a rhythmic cadence.

I shoved his door open. "Fell!"

A loud thud came from further in the room. He scrambled up from the floor, having rolled off his cot, living up to his name. "What?" he shouted, raking a hand through coarse red hair. He took in my shield. "What's happened?"

"The village is under attack. Clan Wolf." I strode inside, finding his boots drying near the hearth.

Fell let out a string of curses as he tugged on a linen shirt and a pair of trousers. I threw his boot. He caught it against his chest and tugged it on moments before I launched the other to him. While he laced them, I grabbed his gear, tossing his belt to him as we ran outside. He buckled it around his thin waist and held out a hand for his shield, swiftly buckling it to his arm as we raced.

"Axe or sword?" I asked.

"Both."

I figured as much and had them both ready for him.

He slid his sword into a thick leather strip on the belt and took up his axe. If I hadn't woken him from a dead sleep, he'd have tucked knives into his boots, too. But there was no time. We had to move. If we tarried, they would torch more houses and kill more of our clansmen.

Fell gave Sig a pat as he bounded alongside us. "You're ready for battle, aren't you, Sig?" he cooed. His eyes hardened when sounds of slashing steel and the scent of smoke poured from the valley into the hills, fogging the air. "Armund?"

"He and Tyr will meet us on the pass."

Fell nodded to the burning longhouse. "Did they make it out?"

"I don't know." I hoped they had. A family lived there. Five young boys, all under the age of ten.

We ran to the worn, serpentine trail that led down the steep slope and emptied into the valley below, beating Father and Tyr there. I wanted to ask Father to stay and guard our homes, but knew he wanted to be part of the fight as much as I wanted to keep him from it.

I was thankful he'd survived the last battle he fought, but he would have rather died. Now, he considered himself a burden. He hated his knee; the constant pain and limitations it put on his life. He'd be thrilled to die bravely in battle tonight and leave me behind, but I would do everything in my power to keep him alive.

I loved my father. And luckily, so did my friends.

Tyr and Father jogged toward us as fast as Father's knee would allow. Tyr, more than a head taller, stayed at his side. I knew he would protect him with his life. Tyr lost his parents early. His mother died birthing a girl child two years after he was born, and his father died when he was only eight, cut down during a raid.

We were friends before his father died. After, we became brothers.

Tyr's almost white hair was raked into a knot on the back of his head, but it shone in the light cast by the silvery moon. Also glinting were his many blades. He was armed to the teeth. He'd always slept that way, as if waiting for trouble to find him at night. Tonight, I was thankful for his unease.

"Sig," he greeted first, then nodded to me and Fell. "Let's head down."

The path narrowed, only wide enough for one man at a time. Tyr set the pace, his nimble feet avoiding rocks and tree roots he knew by heart. Father followed second and I ran behind him with Fell trailing the rest of us.

Tyr was agile and strong. He never used a shield, preferring the heft of a weapon in each hand so he could remain on the offensive and end his fights quickly. Fell, on the other hand, needed his shield more than any of us. He enjoyed toying with those he battled, teasing and taunting until they were driven mad and made a mistake they wouldn't live to forget.

I wasn't sure I had a battle style, other than to come out alive and protect Father if the stubborn fool would stay close enough to allow it.

The four of us kept our steps quiet but quick. Sig ignored the trail altogether and cut down the grassy slope, quieter than a deer. The moonlight seeped into his gray fur as he raced toward the house being devoured by fire.

Our village wasn't large by any means, but it didn't have to be for another clan to attack us. There had to be a reason, some wrong to right, or some desperation pushing Wolf to our shores. I had heard of no dealings with Clan Wolf, hadn't even heard the name since I was a boy.

Not that it mattered what brought them here; they came to destroy us.

"You boys stay together," Father warned as we rushed toward Sig, who waited below, his eyes carefully watching the shadows for any threat to us. "Fight as one, live as one."

"Fight as one, live as one," the three of us echoed.

It was the first and best piece of advice Father gave us, and one he reinforced often. We'd fought in one battle for our king when Clan Tralt tried to steal some of our land, but we fought as one unit, as one family, as brothers. The strategy kept us alive, and Clan Tralt was no more. Clans Grandys and Urdr joined us and we avenged their attack. There weren't enough warriors left to harm us, or anyone else, again.

"Stay with us," Tyr urged, looking down at Father with a pointed look. "Fight *with* us, Armund."

Father wanted us to stay together, but never wanted to be with us. He fought alone. Always had. And Tyr's words would do nothing more than mine.

Father snorted in response. "You can give me orders when your ghostly white beard grows longer than your goat's, Tyr."

We chuckled, but kept our eyes trained on the village below. Father had always told me to live separate from the village's heart, because the heart was the first target of every enemy's blade. Unfortunately, his wisdom was playing out before my eyes.

When we reached the bottom of the pass, we went quiet, assessing what was happening, trying to plan the best way to win this battle rather than just jumping in, axes raised and mouths roaring.

There were thirteen homes in the valley, but the closest to us was an unsalvageable inferno. As we approached, the roof collapsed with a loud rumble. Further into the cluster of homes, our clansmen fought behemoths hailing from the northernmost lands.

"I'll find any children and send them up into the hills," Father instructed calmly, gripping his sword tightly and bringing up his shield. I glanced at the design I'd asked for overlaying the wood. Strips of hammered metal formed a protection rune. I hoped tonight it served its purpose, and that the Aesir were watching and favored us in this battle, I prayed we would arise the victors. "The three of you go fight with our kinsmen. You go with them, Sig."

Odin, god of battle, guide us.

Frigg, preserve our lands and keep them safe from those who would harm it. Preserve our lives.

Thor, may our blades be as sure and heavy as Mjölnir.

Frejya, help us cut down our enemies.

One of our kinsmen, Brux, defended his house, wrestling with a wiry fool whose double-headed axe was too dull. It caught in a piece of wood and he couldn't yank it free. Tyr strode toward him, grabbed his shoulder almost as if he were a friend, and with his free hand, thrust a knife into his back. I could almost hear his lung deflate.

If only they would all be so easy to kill.

Brux thanked us as Tyr jerked his weapon free with a quick squelch. Three more men rounded one of the houses to see why their kinsman hadn't lit the roofs. They found Tyr, Fell, and Brux, who lashed out at them without hesitation.

I ducked into the home where Brux's wife, Elga, held her newborn daughter in one hand, a sword in the other. She was young and fit, but had just given birth two days ago. Her body wasn't ready for battle. Dark circles rimmed her eyes as she eased the weapon down when she saw it was me. "Brux?" she asked of her husband, her whole body shaking with rage.

I waved her outside where she could see him with Tyr and Fell, already battling more of Clan Wolf's men. "He's alive and will fight with us. I know you're strong and can fight too, but you're in no shape to fight right now, Elga. You need to get someplace safe. Sig will go with you up the pass to our house and guard you and the baby."

She looked down at the swaddled child, torn. But her brow set with her decision. "You need Sig's help. I can make it on my own. I'll skirt the shore."

"Sig will come back as soon as he knows you're safe."

She hesitated.

"Brux can't worry for the two of you *and* fight them off. You know that." If a man's attention was divided, it weakened him.

She held the baby against her heart, finally assenting. "I'll go."

"Sig," I said, crouching to see him better. "Go with her." I patted his back.

My dog obeyed, the gray wolfhound attaching himself to Elga's side.

"Thank you, Calder."

I nodded before she slipped into the night. I watched her for a long moment, until her feet hit the rocky shore. Sig would know if there was a threat nearby. He ran with her, steady and strong. She sprinted, clutching the crying infant to her chest, and Sig positioned himself between her and the village, keeping closest to the threat like I'd taught him. I lost sight of them behind a house, then a few minutes later, Sig was back at my side. Elga and the newborn were safe.

Brux and Fell battled two men, neither gaining ground nor losing it, matching every blow with equal ferocity. I slinked along the edge of the house and struck the Wolf bastards from behind. I quickly hacked into one's kidney, then flayed the ribs of another, biting into his heart, judging by the amount of blood that spurted after I pulled my axe free.

They fell like trees.

"Elga?" Brux asked, worried.

"She and the baby are safe."

371

He pursed his lips and beat on his shield once in response. I mimicked the motion, my axe head clanging off my shield's metal.

Tyr appeared behind me like a specter, his face set like stone. "I lost sight of Armund."

Good gods. Where had my father gone?

Sig whimpered beside me, his nose pointed to the hills beyond the village where moonlight caught on pale articles of clothing. People were fleeing from the village. Children. Some of the women.

"It looks like Armund found most of the children," Fell noted, nodding toward the hill we'd descended.

I saw my father limping at the base of the hill, waving them away from danger and rushing them onto the dirt paths that wended into the hills.

Several of the Wolf men took notice and were circling around some of the houses to attack him together. Sig ran toward them as fast as his flanks would push him.

"Follow me," Tyr said, leading us up the hillside to where Father stood, the children far above us now.

Sig was at Father's side by the time we reached him, his gums pulled back as he snarled, his teeth gleaming in the firelight.

Tyr deftly slid a small knife from his leather bracer, pulled his hand back over his shoulder, and launched the blade through the night. It hit its target, lodging in a stranger's throat and severing his voice before he could alert his brethren that we were there, and before the bastard could throw the fiery torch he carried onto another thatched roof. The man fell back, choking on blood and iron, his body jerking with the spasms of death. The flame of the torch flickered just above his head.

Tyr threw three more knives, the slick blades flying with deadly accuracy.

372

We ran from the hill, clashing with the bastards that would die on this soil.

Suddenly, a roar came from my left side and I barely had time to raise my shield before a broad sword bit into the metal edge. My teeth ground together from the blow and my arms shook from the force of keeping the man from slicing me in two.

A man with stringy, ashen, sweat-soaked hair puffed his cheeks and tried to cut me in half. I raised my sword and met him blow for blow, unwilling to die, but more than willing to make him pay for what he and his kinsmen did to mine.

Fell and Tyr fought at my back, each holding his own while the Wolf I fought snarled, spittle flying from his meaty lips as he rained blows down on my shield. I blocked each one, keeping my back to my brothers, gritting my teeth against every clash of his sword against my axe and every dent he made in my shield's iron.

Finally, he left his middle vulnerable. I thrust my sword up through his stomach, the tip visible from his back. His blood drenched my hand, but I held him while twisting my blade and ripping it from his body, pushing him so he fell on the ground. His head made a sickening thump, but it didn't kill him.

His eyes locked with mine. "Kill me."

I crouched beside him for the briefest second so he could see my face and his blood on my hands. "You've shown us no mercy, and mercy is the last thing you'll receive."

His puffing cheeks and angry, gritted teeth were satisfaction enough. Let the fool bleed out. Let him take his own life, if he craved death so feverishly.

I called Sig.

Fell and Tyr were still fighting, though Fell had managed to wound the wrist of his opponent. The man clutched it to his chest and fought stubbornly with sloppy sword strokes, though with the hand he never fought with. Father had always made us practice with both so that if we were in his position, we could fight well.

Sig appeared at my side.

"Sig, protect Father," I instructed. "There's something I need to do."

Sig bounded into the darkness to reach my father's side. I ran around the melee as Fell split the heel of the man fighting him. When his opponent fell to his knees, my friend delivered a sharp stab to his spine. The man collapsed, his breath escaping him with a loud exhale.

The two of us circled the man attacking Tyr and made quick work with our axes and swords. He fell alongside his bloody friends and the three of us ran to help Father, who had gone back down into the village to see if he could usher anyone else to safety high up in the hills. Sig's frantic barks rang out in the night and my stomach coiled with dread.

The further we ran into the village, the more men we saw fighting, growling and roaring and hacking at one another. Unfortunately, the invaders were being pushed into the wood. If those who'd managed to flee were going to stay hidden, if our homes were to survive this, we had to drive them back to their ship.

We needed to circle around and come at them from the wood so we could send them scurrying back to their boats. As it was, there weren't enough of us to guard the village, keep the houses from being torched, *and* drive them out. Several men lay dead, though theirs or ours, I couldn't tell in the darkness. I had a terrible feeling they were ours.

I yelled to Tyr and Fell who rushed to me, keeping eyes all around us. "I'm going to set their ship on fire," I panted, wiping my head with my sleeve. "It'll draw them out. We can't let them reach the houses in the hills. Keep my father alive. Keep the Wolfs in the valley."

Fell raked an angry, blood-soaked hand through his already red hair. "You're insane."

"It'll draw them out," I argued.

He shook his head. "I didn't say it wasn't smart. I just said you were crazy."

Tyr wiped his axe on a tuft of grass. "I can run faster than you."

"But I can blend in better with the shadows, *and* I'm the better swimmer."

Tyr couldn't blend at all. His hair was nearly stark white, and I could see him from half a fjord away in the moonlight. Especially now that it had torn free from the leather strap that held it away from his shoulders.

Tyr snorted. "*I'm* the better swimmer!" he shouted, tightening his grip on the knives he was prepared to throw. "Watch your back, Calder."

Fell grunted his agreement.

I kept to the shadows as much as I could despite the dancing orange light cast from burning houses, staying low and moving quickly. I pulled my shirt over my head and wrapped it around a rake handle I snapped, catching it on fire as we passed the smoldering remnants of the first house they burned down, then sprinted across the rocky bank and waded into the water, pushing deeper until nothing but water was beneath me.

Torch raised, I swam steadily toward the boat drifting on the sea. They hadn't tied it off. Or maybe one of our clansmen managed to sever the rope that bound it to the shore. Either way it was adrift, and in their haste to destroy our clan, they left no one to keep watch over it.

A gust threatened to put out the flame I'd brought. The last of my shirt was quickly burning away. I had to hurry.

I eased the torch into the hull, gripped the rail with strained fingertips, and pulled myself up, hooking an ankle over the side.

A light breeze blew out to sea. I knew that when I unfurled the sail, it would catch the wind. It also might blow the torch out entirely… It was only flickering now. When the sail caught fire, it would slow the ship, but the Wolfs would have to swim out here if they wanted to flee.

I pulled the rope to free the sail and the boat lurched as the wind pushed it. My balance wobbled, but I held the torch steady. The fire guttered out, but the fabric smoked and smoldered. I hoped it was enough. I held it to the sail fabric, but nothing caught. Just as despair started to curl in my gut, a flame appeared on the sail. *How did it catch without me seeing it?*

It went up fast, leaving only stringy, charred remnants waving in the breeze.

I watched the shore to see if our enemy noticed their ship ablaze, and in the firelight, I saw a specter standing on the other side of the sail. The girl's face was fair, but her jaw was set. Her eyes were like blue flame. Her tattered dress was bloodied and torn at her side, exposing a thick scar.

She yelled something, but I couldn't make it out. I shook my head.

Her screams were frantic but silent. I could only hear the breeze in my ears, the drips of water from my clothes onto the planks, and the trickles of fire-eaten sail. She was there, but I saw the fjord through her misty form. She pointed toward the shore. Through her middle, I could see the remaining warriors of Clan Wolf retreating toward their ship. Scrambling over the shore and into the water, cutting through the water toward me… and some of them were fast swimmers.

When I looked back to thank her, she was gone.

I let the torch fall into the hull, then climbed to the rail and dove, breaking the surface first with my hands, then swimming beneath the surface for a time so their best swimmers didn't spot me. I pushed hard to the shore until my boots scraped the bottom of the fjord and my hands felt the scrubby grass along the bank, then pulled myself out in time to watch our people continue the assault.

Sitting on the bank to catch my breath, I searched for her, but the girl wasn't there. Was she a sea spirit, come to help me? Had the gods sent her? Or was she Valkyrie? She was ethereal and beautiful, but there was something sad in her eyes. Something I connected to and felt down to my soul.

Arrows rained down upon the rest of their warriors as they fled. One lodged in the skull of a large man, killing him instantly. His body fell with a splash before bobbing on the choppy waves, while another of his clansman struggled to reach the shaft protruding from his shoulder. A second wave of arrows was unleashed and more of the Wolf Clan fell. Others were wounded but kept swimming.

A leader emerged, shouting a warning to his warriors to use their shields to guard themselves in the water. "Clan Wolf, get to the ship or be left behind!"

His men screamed a warning before arrows landed all around him, cutting into the water with barely a splash. The leader swam deeper and held his shield at the back of his head with one hand, stroking toward the boat with the other. Arrows with bright white fletching soared through the air, catching the moonlight. They pierced the water around him, but never struck true. When he reached the ship, his clansmen hauled him over the side and into the hull.

It didn't take long for them to bring up seawater with their shields, splashing water onto the sail's remnants, extinguishing it along with the wood that had caught when the fire-eaten banner dripped onto the hull.

Their leader stopped near the prow and stared at the sea where the woman had been. Did he see her, too? He backed away, falling over one of his kinsmen, righting himself and shouting for them to hurry.

Those in the ship pulled kinsmen into the hull, grunting and hefting their weight, rescuing them from death by arrow or sea.

When the last of their clansmen climbed aboard, our people fired a slew of flaming arrows that arced across the dark sky, piercing the water with hisses and small puffs of steam. They were too far away to strike now that they'd floated deeper into the fjord, so our warriors stopped shooting. It was a waste of arrows at this point.

The intruders gathered their charred oars and before I could reach the hilltop, slipping between the ashes and elms, they were rowing in sync to their leader's angry shouts, cutting through the water, illuminated by the full moon. Counting their heads, it looked like we'd suffered greater losses than they had.

Father waited at the top of the hill with Sig, Fell, and Tyr. The four silently stared toward the still burning homes that leaked dark gray smoke into an even darker sky. Father's eyes tracked the plume over the water. His head drifted sideways as he stared at the sea. "Something is coming."

Goosebumps spread across my skin as the breeze picked up, dragging more of the smoke away from shore, as if shoving all the bad away with the Wolf ship.

Slowly, he shook his head, his brows furrowed. "Something… far more terrible than the devastation tonight. All I can see in the smoke are bleached-white bones arranged over someone's body – like armor. Who wears bones as armor?" He whispered the question to himself and I could tell he was sifting through memories for any spark of recognition, puzzled when he came away without a clue.

"Could you be sensing Odin?" I said softly. Some said he came immediately after death. Others said he climbed down the Bifrost or smoky pyre pillars to pick and choose which of the dead he might claim after Frejya was finished choosing those who would go with her to *Fólkvangr*, the peaceful meadow upon which the goddess built her eternal home.

He shook his head. "It is not Odin I sense. I *know* the feel of the Alfather."

"A Valkyrie?" I questioned, watching him try to make sense of what he'd seen.

Father brushed me off again. "It was no Valkyrie."

Fell's brown eyes locked with mine meaningfully. Father was rarely wrong about what he intuited. If he sensed something terrible coming this way, and so soon after an attack of this magnitude, something bad was coming.

Fell loosened the straps on his shield and removed it, hooking it over a shoulder. "We have much to do."

Sig brushed against my leg and looked toward the village. I patted his head, giving a quick scratch behind his head. "Let's go, boy," I told him. "We'll need your nose."

Tyr walked beside me, clapping my back and telling me I'd done well, but I couldn't bring myself to tell him about the girl, or the fact that the torch I'd made wasn't strong enough to light the sail.

As Sig and the three of us followed Father out of the wood and into the wrecked village, I wondered if maybe I'd had a brush with a goddess instead of a spirit, after all.

FENRIS WOLF

The sail of a ship finally broke the steady horizon line as I strode along the shore. I'd waited several days for my father to return. When I could spare a moment, I watched the sea for his proud, white sail, its sturdy wool thick enough to weather the salt and resist the tearing gales that came and went out on the water.

He had traveled along the coast, invited by the chieftain of Clan Urðr to celebrate Winternights with his people. In doing so, he missed quite a celebration here. I looked forward to telling him how we fared in the great hunt that followed, of all the game and meat that would sustain our people through the winter. Things had gotten far too lean last year. This year, we would have plenty if we were more careful.

He would be proud at what we'd managed to kill and preserve.

Father had taken one of the newly built ships. It was large and sleek, and its oiled timber glided along the surface swiftly. I walked toward the harbor, eager to meet him.

The wind dragged Father's longship closer, aided by the power of the men who rowed, until they were so close, its sail blocked the sun as I waited impatiently on the harbor dock.

Men on either side of the mast tugged ropes to raise the sail as the others used the oars to maneuver into the slip, careful of the ships bobbing on either side. Someone tossed a rope to me and I tied the vessel off so the sea couldn't carry it out of our reach.

But when the first man disembarked, a man who'd carried me on his shoulder as a boy, he wasn't smiling. He didn't give me a hearty slap on the back or ask me about the hunt. Nor did he tell me how Winternights were celebrated in Urðr the way I had imagined he might. Instead, he held his hand over his chest and bowed.

A sinking feeling filled my gut. My heart thundered like Thor himself beat on it with Mjölnir from within. "What's going on? Where is my father?" I asked sharply, searching the faces of the men still standing on the ship, a gaping hole in the middle of the crowd where they gathered around something inside the hull.

I climbed aboard and pushed my way through them, quickly realizing what their legs had hidden from view. My father lay dead on the ship's damp planks. I fell to my knees at his side, my skin biting into the freshly hewn planks.

His skin was mottled. I reached for his hand, finding it drawn. His fingers were so stiff, I didn't pry them open for fear of breaking them. "What happened?" I asked, though it sounded dull and far away to my ears.

His closest friend Borgt answered, "He died after the celebration." Something was amiss.

"How did he die?" I asked quietly. No one answered. "How?" I shouted, spittle flying from my mouth. I didn't give a damn what Urðr had to say about it. I wanted to hear from those I trusted. My kinsmen.

"We were told it was an accident, but time has revealed bruises on his neck. At first, we thought he drank too much mead and drowned. We were fed lies."

My thumbs slid over the marks.

There, painted purple on his neck, was proof that he'd been killed.

"Who?" I asked.

Borgt knelt beside me. "We aren't sure. A child found him floating face down in the waves."

A tumult of feelings pounded through me with the knowledge that someone in Clan Urðr had betrayed us. Sorrow and rage swirled until there was nothing left to feel. "Prepare his body. At dawn in this very ship, we will send our beloved chieftain, our Jarl, to Valhalla."

"In *this* ship?" Borgt dared ask.

I leveled him with a glare. "Is there another more befitting of your Jarl?"

"How will we learn what happened, Fenris?" my father's most trusted warrior asked. "Will you write to Urðr and demand the Jarl seek out the one who killed him?" someone asked from behind me.

"No. I will go to him myself in the spring. The message I intend to deliver will be written in his own blood, and my quill will be my sword."

Father's men nodded approvingly, banging their chests in solidarity.

The wind rustled my father's dull, graying hair. His stomach was so bloated he looked like he might burst. This was not what a chieftain deserved.

Jarl Urðr was responsible for my father's safety and he failed him. Now, he would pay. And if none of them would tell us who killed him, I would slaughter them all and burn their towns and villages to the ground.

The ship rocked as I climbed onto the dock.

"Fenris!" my father's most trusted friend yelled, quickly jogging to catch up with me. "What will we do now? Who will be Jarl?"

"I will."

He was quiet for a moment. "You'll be challenged."

"Then let them come and challenge me. If my fury doesn't cut them down, I'll fell them with my sword."

"Fenris," Borgt said, catching my elbow. "If you are Jarl, you will be challenged again and again until someone cuts you down, as they did your father. I'm not discouraging you,

I just want you to go in knowing that your days will be numbered."

I snarled and ripped my arm out of his hand. "Then I'll make myself stronger than my father was. I'll wipe away anyone who stands in my way – entire clans, if I have to."

Borgt shook his head. I knew what he would say: that there would always be an enemy. But I was stronger than my foes. They would soon learn that a wolf pack was as strong as its leader was malicious.

I left him behind. He was part of the past. Small-minded. Dedicated, but not a thinker. I needed to surround myself with men who were part beast, as I was. Men unafraid to conquer and destroy all that lay in their path. Starting with Clan Urðr.

384

ACKNOWLEDGMENTS

I'm ever thankful to God for his mercy and blessings in my life. I'm so thankful to my family for their constant love and encouragement, friends for their support, and fans for loving my characters and stories as much as I do.

Thanks to my beta readers on this project: Cristie Alleman, Amber Garcia, Melanie Deem, and Misty Provencher, whose feedback was crucial to bringing this Viking world to life.

A special thanks to Melissa Stevens for designing the perfect book cover, interior, map, tarot card and every other thing related to bringing this book to life visually. And thanks to Stacy Sanford for waving her magic red pen over my manuscript and polishing it beautifully. These ladies are my shield maidens, my Valkyries.

ABOUT THE AUTHOR

Casey Bond lives in West Virginia with her husband and their two beautiful daughters. She likes goats and yoga, but hasn't tried goat yoga because the family goat is so big he might break her back. Seriously, he's the size of a pony. Her favorite books are the ones that contain magical worlds and flawed characters she would want to hang out with. Most days of the week, she writes young adult fantasy books, letting her imaginary friends spill onto the blank page.

Learn more at www.authorcaseybond.com or online @ authorcaseybond.

388

ALSO BY
CASEY L. BOND